A River at my Garden's End

A RIVER AT MY GARDEN'S END

SANDY GORDON

J & J Publishing

Published by J & J Publishing

First published in Scotland in 2010 by
J & J Publishing
Ty Crwn, East Grange, Kinloss, Forres, Moray, IV36 2UD.

Printed in the UK by MPG Biddles Limited, Norfolk, PE30 4LS

Typeset by J & J Publishing
Design by J & J Publishing 01 343 850 123

ISBN: 978-0-9543891-4-7

SERGEANTS MESS

64

CAMBRAI BALL

3RD ROYAL TANK REGIMENT

FEAR NAUGHT

CAMBRAI 1946

"Through MUD, BLOOD, to the GREEN FIELDS BEYOND"
3rd Royal Tank Regiment Motto

ACKNOWLEDGEMENTS

AS I wrote this story quite a number of years ago, I should like to express my thanks to my daughter, Alison, who brought her eighty-five year old father up-to-date with the complexities of the computer system so necessary today in the world of business. I would also like to thank Jacqui, who agreed to publish my novel, and for her expertise in guiding me through the whole process to reach the desired end with patience and understanding.

I often wish that I had clear
For life, six hundred pounds a year
A handsome house to lodge a friend
A river at my garden's end.
A terrace walk and half a rood
Of land, set out to plant a wood.

Imitation of Horace

1937 - 1939

~ 1 ~

NEIL Munro consulted his watch – half past four, and no sign of Sam. He'd been kept in again and it was such a glorious day. If he'd been at his usual time they could have had a dip in the river to cool off. Sam was the limit at times.

Neil stood up and, shading his eyes from the sun, looked back along the path which ran beside the river. He was about to turn away and continue on his own when he saw Sam come in view. He waved both his arms high above his head, then cupping his hands about his mouth shouted, "Come on Sam, get a move on," and repeated it three times before he received an answering wave. Then he saw his friend break into a run. Neil watched Sam draw nearer to where he stood, admiring the easy grace with which the latter covered the distance between them and braced himself for the lunge which he knew Sam would make. They laughed together as they rolled over on the soft grassy bank almost to the water's edge.

They paused, faces close together, Sam's running with perspiration.

"Who was it today, then?" Neil asked.

"Old Snoddie. Didn't do my homework for him at the weekend so he kept me in to do it. Gave me the belt too, of course. That bastard can't half draw it."

"Why don't you just do the homework? It would only take half an hour."

"Never! I hate school! Thank goodness I'm leaving next month."

"Wish I was too."

"No you don't, you like school because you're clever."

"So are you, if you'd only be bothered."

"I've heard that before, lots of times."

"It's true Sam."

"Oh forget it. Here, let's have a swim."

"I haven't time just now. Let's wait till after tea."

"No, there'll be someone out then for their evening stroll. Come on, I'll beat you in." And with that Sam threw off his clothes and splashed his way into the river before diving forward when he reached the deeper water.

Neil looked at the lithe brown body of his friend, hesitated for a moment, then realizing that he had lost out once again, stripped off and followed Sam in his dash across to the little island in the middle of the river.

"I knew you would," Sam crowed as Neil lay back on the sandy soil. "You like doing this as much as I do."

"You're a rebel, Sam, you love going against convention."

"You and your big words, Neil Munro, it's the best way to swim and you know it."

"OK, but one day someone is going to see us and tell on us."

"So what would happen? Who would they tell? The school? Are you frightened you'd get the belt?"

"No, I'm not."

"What then?"

"They might tell our parents."

Sam laughed. "Do you think Dugald Whyte would mind?"

"Why do you always call him Dugald Whyte?"

"Because that's his name and he's not my father. You know fine I don't have a father or a mother."

"But Mr and Mrs Whyte are your foster parents."

"So I've been told, but I'm just boarded out on them."

"They're all right, aren't they?"

Sam shrugged his shoulders. "Could be worse I suppose. I'll say this for Dugald, he treats me just like his own sons – belts me just as hard. Does your dad wallop you?"

"No, not really."

"He's a real dad, that's the difference. Hi, you're not half sprouting hair down below."

The two boys regarded each other's blossoming manhood, laughed, and then wrestled once more.

"You're getting stronger too," Sam gasped, as he finally sat astride Neil and held him down by the shoulders. "I'm going to miss messing about with you when I start real work on the farm."

"We'll still be able to see each other, though."

"I don't know. Depends on Dugald. Never mind, you'll have your toffee-nosed pals from the Academy!"

"They're not all toffee-nosed."

"Bet you none of them would swim starkers like we do."

"Well, maybe not." Neil gave a sudden upward thrust of his hips and sent

Sam sprawling. "Beat you back," he shouted, and did.

"You wait!" Sam gasped on reaching the bank. "I've taught you too many tricks; you're getting as tough and cunning as I am."

Neil grinned, "That was always your intention from the first day we met and you said I was soft."

"So you were, soft as –" but Neil had raced on ahead and Sam's words were lost to him.

Neil had reached the end of the lane leading to The Willows, the red sandstone house where he lived with his father and mother, John and Ella Munro, and his sister Hazel, before Sam caught up with him.

"You can't half shift nowadays, Neil Munro. Bet you'll be the Academy sports champion this year."

Neil laughed. "Flattery will get you nowhere, Sam."

"There you go again. You're a walking dictionary. Come up once you've had your tea."

"OK."

ELLA MUNRO was in the kitchen and called out when she heard her son come in. "Where have you been to this time, Neil? Oh, swimming again, with Sam, I suppose."

"Sam's all right, Mum. Don't you like him?"

"Yes, I like Sam – now. I wasn't too sure when he first started coming round here, but he's quite a fine lad, not had much of a life."

"Sam doesn't want pity, Mum."

"I know, but Neil, he's never had a real home, not like you. Rather sad." Neil looked at his mother who went on, "Never mind, he'll survive. Ready for tea?"

"Dad's not in yet."

"He'll be late, he's down at Rhu."

"Right, I'll give Hazel a shout."

When tea was over Neil hurried upstairs to his bedroom to do his homework. His task over, he tidied up his desk and picked up the framed snapshot his sister Hazel had taken of Sam and him the previous summer. He thought of what his mother had said about Sam. He wasn't quite sure what she had meant by saying it was sad, but as long as she liked Sam, what did it matter?

Neil thought back to the first time he had met Sam. He had gone to the

Whytes' farm with his father and while the latter was busy, Neil had put in the time kicking his football against the rear wall of the byre. He had become conscious of being watched and had turned round eventually and come face to face with a dark haired boy of his own age. The two had looked at each other for some moments before Neil had broken the rather uncomfortable silence.

"Want to have a kick with me?"

There was no reply, just the hard penetrating stare.

Neil tried again. "I'm Neil Munro. My father's the vet and he's come to look at Mr Whyte's cows. Are you staying here at Millside just now?"

"What is it to you if I am?"

"Nothing, I was only asking."

"None of your business."

"Sorry …" Neil began and was quite unprepared for the violent push which sent him sprawling on his back, letting his football slip from his grasp.

"Come on then toffee-nose, see if you can get your ball back."

Neil struggled to his feet and after a moment's hesitation gave chase. With a hard tackle he managed to block the ball, but in doing so fell over, and then found himself pinned to the ground.

"Get off, you're hurting me," he gasped, but he managed no more before he felt his face buried in the long grass.

"Get off, you're hurting me," a voice close to his ear mimicked, then came a roar.

"Sam! What are you doing?"

John Munro and Dugald Whyte had come round the corner of the byre to behold the two boys struggling on the ground.

"The young devil," Dugald Whyte went on, but as he made to move forward he felt a restraining hand on his arm but got no further.

"Leave them be. Neil has to learn to fight his own battles."

"But he'll murder him, he's such a strong lad, and wild with it too. Sam!"

With that Sam rolled off Neil who promptly leapt to his feet and landed a deft blow on Sam's nose causing it to pour with blood. Before the latter could retaliate Dugald had intervened.

"Serves you right, you young varmint. Hold your head back or it'll be all over your shirt."

"I'm sorry, Mr Whyte, I didn't mean to hit him so hard," Neil apologised.

"You did the right thing, Neil, time he was put in his place. That's what he was needing."

"Well now, let's see what I can do for you." John Munro examined Sam. "There, I think I've stopped the flow. Now why don't you two shake hands and be friends. I'm John Munro the vet, and this is my son Neil. What's your name?"

"Sam Cairns." He looked at Neil's outstretched hand and reluctantly shook it.

"Look, I tell you what, if you're agreeable, Dugald, why not let Sam come back with Neil and me and they can have a kick about at our place. You know Neil's got what he calls his own Hampden Park."

"Well, I don't know; he'd better behave or he'll be for it when he comes home."

"He'll be just fine, won't you Sam? Come on, into the car, the pair of you."

IT HAD BEEN the start of the firm friendship which existed now between the two boys. It was Neil's perseverance that had overcome Sam's initial resentment. Although he enjoyed living 'in the country' as he called it, Neil found that the distance between his home and the town meant that he had no one to play with unless some of his school friends were prepared to walk or perhaps cycle out the two miles to The Willows. Despite his rough introduction to Sam, Neil had instantly liked him and was determined to win his friendship. Sam, on the other hand, having spent most of his life in a children's home followed by spells of being boarded out and being rejected because of his unruly behaviour, was wary of Neil and of his father and mother. Neil's football skill, however, won his admiration and although he was stronger and tougher, Sam could never best Neil on his little Hampden Park.

"How come you're so good?" he demanded one evening as they had a breather.

"I suppose I've inherited my skill from my father. He played for Queens Park."

"He what?"

"He played for Queens Park."

"Why didn't you tell me that before?"

"Why should I? Lots of people have played for them."

"Are you in your school team?"

"I've played for the second eleven a few times but my teacher says I'm not tough enough."

Sam looked hard at Neil. "I haven't your skill but I'm tough. I'm going to start to rough you up every time we play."

"What for?"

"So you'll get a regular place in the team. I'll make you tough Neil."

"You know, I think you've already done that."

Sam laughed. "One thing you've made me do is always speak properly when I'm with you."

"You don't need to."

"You wouldn't understand what I was saying if I spoke the way I did before I started being your pal, and besides, your mother wouldn't approve, definitely not."

"Sam, you're a scream when you mimic my mother."

"Better not tell her I do – she doesn't really approve of me."

"She thinks you're all right."

"Does she? I doubt it, but she puts up with me."

The fact that the two boys attended different schools had actually helped to cement their friendship and although Sam often ridiculed what Neil told him about his teachers and fellow pupils at Levenford Academy, it taught Neil to see them in a different light. Sam never pretended to like Hartwell Junior Secondary School, and despite the fact that he was a bright enough lad he was often in trouble. It was something Neil could not understand.

"I'm not saying the Academy is such a wonderful place, but it's all right," he was apt to say when he and Sam had a friendly argument about school.

"I'm not listening any more, I just don't like school and I can hardly wait for the day when I can leave."

And now that day was fast approaching, Neil thought, as he made his way to Millside Farm, and Sam would be starting work there, doing all the jobs Fred and Rob, Mr Whyte's sons didn't like doing. That was according to Sam.

"So why are you so keen on it?" Neil had asked. "It doesn't sound much fun to me. Bad enough having one boss, but you'll have three."

"It's all right for you, Neil. You have everything. I have nothing. I'm going to save every penny I can so that one day I can be off on my own."

"Where to?"

"Anywhere I fancy. To all those countries I've had to learn the capital cities of. You know, France, Belgium, Holland, Italy, Germany."

"You'll have to save a lot of money to do that."

"Not really. I'll get work wherever I go. I just have to put together enough to get away."

"Sam, I believe you're serious."

"Of course I am."

"But what about the different languages in these countries?"

"Trust you to think of that. At least I'm bi-lingual."

"Bi-lingual? What are you talking about?"

Sam laughed. "Beat you that time, Neil. That's one of your big words. I looked it up in old Snoddie's dictionary. I can speak your posh language and the language I use with the boys at Hartwell and at the farm."

It was Neil's turn to laugh. "Sam, I guess you'll manage wherever you go. I wish I was coming with you."

"I'm not away yet."

- 2 -

FRED Whyte had made the long walk into Levenford in a resentful mood. His father had once again refused to allow him to take the old Morris car into town which had led to a heated exchange between the two.

Fred's rage was still simmering when he reached the Railway Tavern in Church Street where he asked for a half and a half pint, which he knocked back in record time. He was about to order again when he felt a hand on his shoulder and he turned to find his friend Angus Fuller close behind him.

"Just in time, eh Fred?"

"Trust you. The usual?"

"Make it pints. It'll save us fighting through this mob for a while."

"You wouldn't say that if you was getting them in."

"I will next time. Come oan, let's grab a couple o' seats and get some privacy."

"Don't make me laugh. They're a' taken by the domino players."

"No, they're no', there's room for us at the end o' the bench against the back wall."

"Oh, aw right."

"What's the matter wi' you the night, Fred? Been fighting wi' the auld man again?"

"What else? He's a mean auld buggar. Just because I have a couple o' drinks when I come into the toon, he won't let me have his car."

"It wid be a' right if you stopped at a couple, Fred, but you know what happens when you get started on a Saturday night."

"You're jist as bad as the auld man. Anyway his rotten car is a heap o' bloody scrap."

Angus roared with laughter. "Then why do you want it so much?"

"It's a' right for you. You don't have that long walk home."

"Serves you right for living on a farm."

"It won't be for much longer if I can help it."

"How come?"

"I'm going to join the army."

"You're what? You must be off your rocker."

8

8

"Listen mate, there's going to be a war, you mark my words."

"Rubbish, you read too many newspapers."

"Well, war or not, I'm going to join up."

"You can't be serious, Fred."

"I am. You don't know what he's like, my auld man. Oh he seems aw right to outsiders but to his family he's a real bastard. Do you know that up tae a couple o' years ago he still took his belt tae me, and he still would if the auld lady hadnae stopped him?"

"I'd have liked my auld man tae try that oan me."

"Your dad's OK."

"Hmm. Sometimes. Here, I'll get them in again."

When Angus had fought his way back he asked, "Fancy going tae Ma Grimstone's the night?"

"What the hell for?"

"You know what for."

"It's a hell hole where she lives," Fred protested.

"How do you know, you've never been there."

"Neither have you. Anyway, I can't stand that snuff she's always sniffing up her nose."

"But the girl's OK, you know, Peggy."

"I wouldn't touch her with a barge pole."

"Maybe you're right, but you never get very far with your Rosie. Have you seen her this week?"

"I said I might see her the night."

"You did, you rotten bastard Fred, and what am I supposed to do?"

"I only said I might. It's time you got a lassie yersel."

"Just because you've taken Rosie tae the pictures a couple o' times you think you're made. I bet you she's been out wi' half a dozen blokes and they've probably had her up against a wall," Angus added.

"I bet you they haven't."

"So you admit she goes out wi' other fellows."

"I never said that."

"You did."

"To hell wi' you Angus Fuller, you can drink on your own. I'm off."

Fred made his way round to the tenement in the Artisan where Rosie lived and climbed to the top floor flat. He knocked at the door and waited impatiently until it was eventually opened by one of Rosie's younger sisters.

"Is Rosie in?"

The small girl stared at Fred but said nothing.

"Is Rosie in?" he repeated.

A shake of the head.

"Where is she?"

A shrug of the shoulders and another member of Rosie's family appeared to join her silent sister.

"She's no' here then, Rosie?"

Two heads indicated a negative.

Fred turned and made his way down the stairs to the street giving a vicious kick to a dog which moved out of the shadows of the close. He slowed his pace when he reached the corner of Church Street. Should he go back to the Tavern again and rejoin Angus? The place would be mobbed by now and Angus probably gone. He stood undecided wondering whether he should just start back home and have an early night and had made up his mind to follow the latter course when he heard Angus call to him.

"Stood you up then, has she?"

"It wasn't a firm date," Fred protested.

"Forget her, mate. Come on, let's try Ma Grimstone's."

"Naw, I don't feel like it."

"Come on Fred, jist fur a laugh. You don't need tae dae anything."

"She'll take your money whether you do or not."

"I'll pay then if you're skint."

"Who says I'm skint?"

"Well, are you game or not?"

"Aw right, let's have a bash at it."

They made their way back along Park Street to the narrow badly lit Vennal, hesitating for a moment at McGroarty's Public House before their resolve strengthened again and some twenty yards further along they entered the darkened Parker's Pend. They groped their way through till they reached the outside stair leading up to Ma Grimstone's.

When there was no answer to their knocking Angus pushed open the door and felt his way along the wall of the narrow passage with Fred close behind him. They leapt back when the inner door suddenly opened and Ma Grimstone appeared.

"What ya wantin'?"

"Hello Ma, Peggy in?"

"What fur?"

"Ye know what fur."

"Who are ye? Polis?"

"Naw, Don't be daft. We're just wantin' a bit o' fun wi' Peggy."

"Who telt ye aboot Peggy?"

"Wan o' ma mates in the yard."

Ma peered at the two young men as they went nearer to where she stood and Fred was repulsed by the smell which reached his nostrils.

"Have ye got the siller?"

"Sure Ma, let's just come inside and we'll square up wi' you."

Ma retreated into the room dimly lit by one gas mantle on the wall above the fireplace. She sat down in an old leather covered armchair and Fred, having adjusted his eyes to the gloom, regarded her. He had seen her often enough in the town, knew the kind of house it was said she kept, but had never paid close attention to her. He took in the long ankle length black dress, badly stained down its entire front, the black boots and the black chimney pot hat perched on top of the small head. The eyes looked unnaturally bright, two pools of fire burning in a circle of dried parchment.

Fred was startled when Ma Grimstone suddenly rose from her chair and crossing to the box bed, drew open the curtain which had concealed its occupants.

"Come oan, yer time's up. There's a queue."

Fred stared open mouthed as two half naked bodies disentangled themselves and a balding middle-aged man rolled off the bed on to the floor. He stood up as the girl he knew as Peggy sat up and asked, "Are you next, son?"

Fred suddenly came to his senses, leapt to the door, wrenched it open and stumbled along the passageway and down the stairs where he leant over the iron railing and emptied the evening's consumption of liquor from his stomach.

"What the hell, Fred, what's the matter wi' you?" Angus pulled Fred upright by the collar of his jacket and continued. "You're a right one, you are, running oot like that."

Fred shook himself free and faced Angus. "You maybe laugh at me for living on a farm, but we're clean folk, mate, spotless. You can have that filthy scum up there if you want, but it's no' fur me."

"Are you sayin' I'm dirty?"

"Suit yersel'. What I'm sayin' is that I'm different from that lot. I maybe hate ma auld man's guts at times, but there's one thing I'm grateful to him fur, and that is hammering in that if we supply half o' this toon wi' milk, everything aboot the farm is to be clean."

"Clean! On a farm! Wi' aw that muck aboot. Don't talk soft."

"It's you that disnae know what you're talking aboot. Anyway, how could ye stand the stench up in that midden. It beats me. And as fur that whore Peggy, she'd hiv tae be the last woman on earth before I touched her."

"Well maybe you're right," Angus conceded, "the place did smell a bit high. And that bloke ..."

Before he could finish, Ma Grimstone had appeared at the top of the stairs and started screeching. "Ah want ma money aff you two scoundrels."

"Ah buggar aff, ye auld witch. Get back inside yer stinkin' sin pit or I'll fetch the polis. Come on Fred, let's get tae hell oot o' here before she sets that big bastard oan us."

The two friends took to their heels and ran, stopping only when they had reached the Common.

"Ahm buggared," gasped Angus.

"Did that fellow really come efter us?"

"He did fur a good bit, but I think we lost him under the station bridge."

"Here, let's have a fag, he'll no' come after us noo."

Fred pulled out his packet of Woodbines and they lit up. After a few moments he asked, "Would you really have had it aff wi' that whore?"

"Naw," was the short reply.

"What did ye want tae go there fur in the first place?"

"Ach, I've heard ma mates oan aboot it and ah jist wanted tae see what it wis like."

"Ah hope ye were satisfied."

Angus gave a grunt but said nothing.

"Well ahm aff hame. Will ah see ye next week?"

"Aye, maybe."

"What dae ye mean by that?"

"Ach, you've got big ideas, Fred. It's only when you're wi' me that ye talk like a' ma mates. You were nae like this when we were at school, you're posh."

"Me! Posh! What are ye oan aboot?"

"Ah suppose you've tae pit on the accent when you're delivering the milk from that spotless farm o' yours tae a' these big hooses oot the back road in case they think it's fu' o' germs."

"You're havering, man. Get lost."

Fred set off across the Common on his long walk home, longing for a drink to help remove the vile taste from his mouth. He knew he would have to wait until he reached the farmhouse where his mother would have a pot of tea brewed. She wouldn't allow him any strong drink at home. Only for the old man, but in two months' time when he was twenty one, then she might relent. She could be hard, but deep down he knew he cared for her and she often took his part against his father.

He thought about what he had said to Angus about joining the army and wondered when he would have the courage to take the decision. It would shake the old man, but with Sam leaving school he'd have him to help. The little bastard couldn't wait to get started; he didn't know what he was in for. Fred couldn't understand why his father and mother had taken him in the first place or why they had kept him. Not that he was much bother now, for they had tamed him, at least the old man had, with numerous applications of his belt. But he had given him a few hidings himself although he had suffered some painful blows in return. For he was a fighter, was young Sam, he'd give him that. Then he'd got friendly with young Munro, the vet's son, that toffee-nosed, upper class little twerp. And he'd contaminated Sam, making him speak properly, and now his own friend Angus was accusing him of doing the same. And somehow he, Fred, resented young Munro's influence on Sam. For although he had initially disliked the kid, he had gradually changed his feelings towards Sam but was loath to admit it. Still, Munro could play football, which was in his favour, for Fred was a football fan, and when he could, attended the local team's matches at Bogside Park. The vet knew his stuff, no doubt about that, and the thing Fred liked about him was that he treated him as a grown-up. He was a toff, of course, what an army officer would be like, he thought. Well, if they were like Mr Munro he could put up with that.

His thoughts turned to Rosie. He wondered if what Angus had said about her was true. But she was a bonnie lass and her name suited her for she had rosy cheeks and a ready smile. She worked in the dairy in Church Street where he delivered milk from the farm and he supposed she did see a lot of fellows who went into the shop. But she had been quite willing to accompany him to the pictures even although it had taken him a while to have the courage to ask her. His visit to her house that night had been his first. He'd left her at the mouth of the close on the two occasions he had taken her out.

She had told Fred she was the oldest of a large family and she was often left to look after her younger sisters. So where had she been tonight, because he was sure neither her father nor her mother had been in the house?

FRED WAS still trying to puzzle it out when he finally turned off from the main road and up the farm track to his home.

"You're early tonight, Fred," his mother observed from the old rocking chair where she always sat. "Are you all right?"

"Of course I am, what way would I not be all right?"

"I was only asking, I'll make the tea."

Fred watched his mother as she busied herself at the range where the kettle on the swey sputtered bubbles of water on the fire which was never out even in the hottest days of summer. He liked when they were alone together in the large farm kitchen; the silence, except for the ticking of the old grandfather clock, filled him with a certain serenity which he would later think back to when he was far from home.

"Rob still out?"

"Oh he shouldn't be long now."

"What about Sam?"

"Sam's moved over to the old bothy."

"He's what?"

"You know fine Fred that that space between our two rooms up the stairs gets very hot and airless during the summer months. Sam asked if he could sleep in the bothy and I said he could if he was prepared to clean it out, which he has. He's made a great job of it and it's what he wanted, a place of his own."

"A place of his own! And what about me? I've to share with Rob."

"Well Fred, you could have moved over to the bothy."

"What? Catch me!"

"What else can we do about it then? We've only the two bedrooms and goodness me they're big enough for two people."

"You're beginning to spoil that brat."

"Fred, you're havering. Besides he's a lot better now than when we first took him."

"Why did you take him? That's what I'd like to know."

"That's none of your business, Fred, but he'll be a grand help on the farm once he starts."

"He'd better be."

- 3 -

LEVENFORD Academy's annual prize-giving ceremony was following its usual pattern and the distribution of awards had begun. Hazel Munro tried to turn her head far enough round to the left to catch sight of her brother who sat at the other side of the centre aisle of the Burgh Hall. She had just glimpsed Neil when she felt rather than saw an admonitory look from her form mistress, Miss Smethwick, and sure enough the light tap on her shoulder was enough to tell her that if you were one of Miss Smethwick's girls you did not look across to the boys. Still she would see Neil when he went up to collect his prizes, for the Rector was about to start on the Third Year winners.

Although Hazel was not receiving any awards she in no way begrudged her brother his academic and sporting successes. She was in fact immensely proud of Neil and she was determined to emulate him to some extent if she could. Like him she had inherited a natural athletic prowess from her father.

Living as they did well away from the town, Neil and Hazel had had to look to each other for companionship and had spent most of their leisure time together until the arrival of Sam Cairns at Millside Farm. Hazel had resented the friendship which had developed between the two and although she was reluctantly beginning to accept that her mother was right when she said that Neil required the companionship of boys his own age, it was hard to lose Neil as a playmate. She had on occasion been invited to join in a game when Sam had come to The Willows, but when Neil and Sam went off somewhere Hazel was always left behind. Yet she was determined to win back her brother and she was hoping that since Sam was leaving school and starting work on the farm he wouldn't have much time to spend with Neil.

Hazel was roused from her reverie by the sight of her brother climbing the steps to the platform to receive his awards, and joined in the applause. As she watched him return to his seat she waited for him to look in her direction and she returned the wink he gave her when their eyes met. The close bond between them was still there, she felt, despite Sam Cairns. She was never at ease with Sam; she always thought he was laughing inwardly at her and it annoyed her when he and Neil seemed to share a private joke.

Hazel continued to let her thoughts wander until it was time for the rendering of the school song at the conclusion of the prize-giving ceremony and then the impatient wait until at last they were all outside in Church Street where her mother and father were standing by the car. In a few minutes Neil joined them laden down with his prize books.

"You've made quite a haul this year, Neil," his father greeted him. "Anything of interest?"

Neil studied the books. "Maybe, but I'm not in the mood to read them right away. All I want is to get out of this suit and up to Millside to see Sam."

Hazel bit her lip as she felt her eyes fill with tears, but her heart leapt when her brother went on, "Mr Whyte is making him start work tomorrow. He's not allowing Sam any holidays at all. I don't think it's very fair, is it Dad?"

"None of my business, Neil. You must remember that the Whytes took Sam in when many wouldn't have looked at him, for he wasn't just the best behaved of boys, was he?"

"But Sam's all right now," Neil protested.

"Yes, I'll grant you that, but he's got to start earning his keep from now on, so really you can't blame Mr Whyte and I'm sure Sam's quite happy about it."

"Well I'm not."

"Now Neil," his mother broke in, "it has nothing to do with you and don't you be going and saying anything to Mr Whyte."

"Don't worry, I won't."

"We'll be going off in a week's time for our fortnight in Aberdeen so you'll get used to not having Sam around."

"I only wish he was coming with us. Sam deserves a real holiday."

"Oh Neil, be reasonable. Sam is not our responsibility. Anyway, you and Hazel have always managed to enjoy each other's company."

Neil didn't say anything as he settled back beside his sister and his father drove off. After a few moments he placed his book prizes in her lap and asked, "Anything there interest you?"

"After looking through them Hazel selected one. "This is written in French, I'll try and read it."

Neil laughed, "I'd better give you my dictionary then. I bet you wouldn't be able to translate the first line."

"Well I'm going to have a try. You can't read all your books at once."

"I've no intention of doing that."

"What are you and Sam doing this afternoon?"

"I don't know. We'll probably go down to the river."

"Can I come with you?"

"No."

Mrs Munro turned round. "I thought, Hazel, that we might go back into town this afternoon and see about something new for you to take to Aberdeen."

"Oh Mummy, you know how I hate going for new clothes."

"Well just this once, let's try and enjoy it."

Hazel was silent, staring out of the window, holding back the tears which seemed to come so easily these days.

When they reached The Willows, John Munro turned round to his two children before getting out of his car. "Listen a minute, Neil, Hazel. This could easily be the last family holiday we'll have together for a while. I don't want to alarm you and I know it's difficult for you to understand, but things are not looking too good in Europe and we could quite easily be drawn into war. But let's forget all about that in the meantime and really enjoy ourselves this summer. What do you say?"

"OK Dad, but do you honestly think there will be a war?"

"I just don't know."

"Oh, I hope not," put in Ella Munro.

"Now Hazel," John Munro went on, "I want you to go shopping with Mum this afternoon for whatever you're needing for Aberdeen and I'm going to give you money to buy a new tennis racquet so that you can give Neil a decent game."

"Oh Daddy, do you mean that?"

"Of course."

"Thank you, Daddy."

"I thought that would bring a smile back to your face."

"Now let's go inside. I must see to the dinner." Ella left the car followed by Hazel.

John turned to his son. "Neil, I know you've reached the age when you can't be bothered very much with your sister, but for this year try to bear with her. You've been good pals up till now."

"But we still are, Dad, it's just that I like doing things with Sam."

"I know Neil, and it would have been grand to have taken Sam along, but it's just not possible. You go off and enjoy your last afternoon with him."

"Hello genius," Sam greeted Neil when they met at their favourite spot by the river.

"What do you mean?"

"I was watching you when you got back home staggering out of the car laden down with prizes."

"Watching?" Neil queried.

"I had nothing to do, so I thought I'd come and see if you were back."

"Why didn't you come to the door?"

Sam was silent for a moment then he said, "I heard your father discussing me and saying this would be your last afternoon with me so I thought …"

"Well, what did you think?"

"Nothing."

"Sam, you're an ass – I'd said that it would have been great if you could have come to Aberdeen with us and Dad agreed, but said it wasn't possible and to go and enjoy my last afternoon with you before we went off because you're starting work."

"Oh, I see."

"Do you?"

"I thought maybe once I became a farm hand your folk wouldn't want you to be friendly with me."

"Don't talk soft, Sam, they're not like that."

"It would suit Hazel though."

"Why don't you like Hazel?"

"I never said I didn't, but she doesn't like me, not that I'm worried."

"Oh forget it, Sam. We'll still be seeing each other at weekends, I hope."

"Well, we'll see. Come on, let's have a wrestling match before we have a swim. Get stripped off."

The two boys struggled with each other for about fifteen minutes before Neil said, "OK Sam, you win, it's too hot for any more. Let's have a race across the island and back."

"OK, then I'll take you to the farm. I've something to show you."

"Is that why you came down here to meet me?"

"Maybe."

NEIL CLIMBED the wooden stair behind Sam to the upper floor of the bothy and stopped short when Sam threw open the door.

"Behold, Neil Munro, Sam Cairn's residence."

"Your residence!" Neil echoed.

"Yes, my first step to freedom."

"What do you mean?"

"It's the first time in my life I've ever had anything that I don't have to share and I was fed up sleeping in that alcove over in the house."

"But Sam, it's not much and what will you do when winter comes?"

"There's a stove here and Mrs Whyte says I can use it if I'm willing to saw up some of the old trees that are lying in the yard. That's where you can help."

"Me?"

"Yes, it takes two on a cross-cut saw."

Neil looked at Sam who went on, "You are my friend still, aren't you?"

"Of course, I'll help you Sam, as much as I can."

"OK. Anyhow if this stove doesn't work, and I don't see why it shouldn't, there's the boiler downstairs which we use to heat the water for our baths."

"Your baths!"

"We don't live in a posh house like yours, you know. There's just a water closet over there. Fred and Rob used to use the big tin bath in front of the kitchen range when they were boys but when they started growing up, as Mrs Whyte put it, they were banished to the bothy."

"And you are too?"

"Oh aye. Once was enough for Ma when she saw me stripped. Still it's better because we can use that big round wooden tub and you can splash as much as you like. I have a dip in it every morning now. I fill it up the night before, leap down the stairs and plunge straight into it."

"It must be jolly cold."

"Not any worse than the river. But Neil, don't you see, you'll be able to come here and we'll be on our own and we can do what we like."

"Yeah, it'll be great Sam, but what do Fred and Rob say about it?"

"Why should they have anything to say about it?" Sam suddenly bridled. "They wouldn't even let me into their room and I know I was supposed to have my bed in there. That's what Dugald Whyte told the folk at the Home, but they were only too glad to get rid of me. They wouldn't have cared if I'd been made to sleep in the byre."

Neil laughed. "Sam, you're priceless."

"What do you mean? It's true, it's always been the same, nobody's ever liked me."

"Sam, that's rubbish. I like you, you're my best friend and all my family

19

think you're OK."

Neil put his arm round Sam. "I'll send you a postcard from Aberdeen and address it to 'Sam Cairns, The Bothy, Millside Farm'. How would that do?"

Sam was forced to smile. "Will you? No one has ever sent me a postcard in my whole life."

"And you can stick it up on the wall," Neil looked at his watch. "I'd better be going or I'll be late for tea."

They made their way downstairs and Neil stopped as he made to open the outside door.

"What's that?"

Sam reached up and took the leather belt which hung from a nail on the back of the door. "That's what Dugald Whyte uses when he gives you a hiding. It was a piece of horse harness once and he cut it just like the belts they have in school."

"It's not as thick though," Neil said as he took it from Sam.

"It stings plenty when you get it across your bare backside."

"You don't mean …" Neil began.

"You see, you won't believe me that Dugald Whyte's a cruel old bastard."

"How often has he used it on you?"

"A couple of times, six of the best. I haven't had it for a while now, but Rob got it the other day."

"Rob! But he's not a boy now!"

"Makes no odds. He got larruped just the same. I saw him get it. I heard the row and I ran in here and then when I realized what was going to happen I flew up the stair. That's when I got the idea of moving over here."

"But what had Rob done?"

"He had a girl in the hay loft."

"You mean …?"

"I don't know just what he had done, but old Dugald was in a right rage about it."

Neil gave himself a crack over the fingers of his left hand with the belt. "I believe it would sting too. I just can't take it all in Sam."

"Well maybe you'll understand now why I want to get away on my own and even if it takes a few years, I'm going to do it."

Sam took the belt and replaced it on the nail. "The next time you give me any cheek, Neil Munro, I'll make you drop your pants."

Neil laughed, "You sound just like Mr Whyte, you really are a good mimic. I'd better behave myself then, and I hope you do too."

"I'll show you the stripes on my backside next time I get walloped."

- 4 -

THAT next time came sooner than Sam had ever expected. Mrs Whyte had always called him to get up when he was still at school, but the following morning it was Fred who clambered up the wooden stair of the bothy, burst open the door, flung back the blanket and before Sam could move had landed two blows with the belt.

When Sam did leap up he lunged at Fred bringing one of his knees forcibly against his crotch. Having the advantage of attacking from the height of the bed, he bore Fred to the ground with both hands round his throat.

"I hate you, Fred Whyte, you're a sadistic bastard. Never do that to me again or I really will throttle you."

Sam released his grip, leapt down the stair and plunged into the tub of water. He had dried himself before Fred appeared to croak, "You little heathen, wait till I tell my old man what you did."

"And wait till I tell him what you did. You know that he says he's the only one who wields the belt. And anyway I'll take you on any day, Fred Whyte."

The two glared at each other before Fred said, "You're just scum, Sam Cairns – a bastard child fathered by a drunkard with a whore. You've five minutes to get on the milk lorry with me to drive the churns into the dairy." And with that he was gone, throwing the belt at Sam as a last measure of his foul temper.

Sam picked it up and hung it on the nail, then was dressed in a flash and out into the yard and was up into the cab before Fred was behind the wheel. All the way into the town he went over what the latter had said. Did Fred really know who his parents had been? He was still pondering the question when Fred brought the lorry to a halt and said, "Move your arse and get those churns unloaded."

Sam was strong but he found the task of lifting the churns from the lorry almost beyond him.

"Bloody weakling we've got here, Rosie," he heard Fred say, then the reply, "Oh Fred, have a heart, he's only a lad. Give him a hand."

"Oh all right, come on!"

"So you're Sam, pleased to meet you. I'm Rosie."

"And you're this fellow's dream girl."

"Cheeky!" Rosie's hand swept across to land lightly on Sam's bottom. "He'd like to think so."

Fred gave Sam a sour look. "Come on, less of your lip, we've to deliver out the Newtown and then to the posh houses on the back road. See you, Rosie."

Sam found it hard to keep up as Fred kept the milk lorry moving while he delivered to individual houses.

"You're a slow coach," the latter taunted, "you should get your friend Munro to show you how to run."

"I can beat him any day." Sam retorted.

"Why weren't you sports champion at your school then?"

"I didn't bother to enter."

"That's you all over, Sam Cairns, you don't bother. Well you'll have to change your tune."

Sam was glad when they returned to Millside and found breakfast waiting.

"Did you manage, Sam?" Mrs Whyte queried.

Before he could answer Fred said, "He's as slow as a snail and he hasn't the strength of a kitten."

"Now Fred, that's not true. You've been up to your tricks again, treating Sam just as you did Rob when he started."

"I'm only doing what the old man did to me."

"Fred, don't speak of your father like that. It's a good job he's not here."
"Where is he?"

"He's away over to McDonald's farm to get tatties."

"In the car?"

"How else?"

"No wonder it's a wreck. Why couldn't he have waited for the lorry?"

"You know fine he's anxious to get started on the hay."

Fred was silent but when Sam accompanied him to the byre he gave vent to his feelings about his father and finished, "The sooner I get away from this place the better."

Sam stopped to lean on the handle of the broom he was wielding.

"Do you really mean that?"

Fred was silent for a moment, staring as if into the distance of some future time. Sam had restarted sweeping again before Fred spoke, "And if you had any sense you'd be of the same mind."

"I am."

Sam's quick answer took Fred by surprise. "I always felt you had some gumption in that head of yours. So you're planning to see the world too? Well as I've told my mate Angus, we'll maybe have our wish granted sooner than expected."

"How do you mean?"

"Do you never read the papers? There's going to be a war and I'm off to the army as soon as it starts. Now I've said it again."

"How old do you need to be to join?"

"I don't know, eighteen maybe. Anyway, I'm all right. Listen though, none o' this gets to the old man, he'd go stark raving mad."

Fred pulled at Sam's arm. "Did you hear what I said?"

"Why should I squeal on you?"

"OK, look, I'm sorry I belted you this morning. I was in a bad mood."

Sam said nothing.

"Do you really hate me like you said?"

Sam shrugged his shoulders.

"We'll be working together all the time, it'd be better if we decided to bury the hatchet."

"You're the one who's been wielding it."

"I said I was sorry. I don't often say that."

"I bet you don't, you're a mean bastard."

"I can be different if you give me a chance."

"What are you after, because whatever it is, it'll cost you?"

"You're a hard one, Sam Cairns."

"Maybe I am, but that's always the way I've had to be."

DURING the next few weeks the tension between Fred and Sam gradually relaxed. It was true that Fred made most of the conversation, but Sam came to realize that despite his desire to leave the farm, Fred knew his job well and was a conscientious worker, and he in his turn saw that Sam was a quick learner.

One wet evening when Sam was resting on his bed he was surprised to hear Fred call from the downstairs room.

"I'm going to have a bath, Sam, come and scrub my back."

"Get lost," Sam shouted back, but after a while he opened his door and looked down at Fred. "The drains will be choked tonight."

"You're a cheeky sod, Sam. The water will be clean enough for you to get in after me."

"I wouldn't contaminate myself."

"Scared of seeing a real grown up man. Is that why you're not coming down?"

"What have you got that I haven't?"

"You're just a boy yet."

Sam retreated into his room and shut the door but in a few minutes it opened and Fred appeared towelling himself vigorously.

Sam kept his head in his book.

"What's that you're reading then?" Fred asked. "Crikey, it's a foreign language. What are you up to?"

"If you must know, I borrowed it from Neil Munro. It's a French book."

"What do you know about French?"

"Plenty."

"Huh, pull the other one. You hated school so you didn't learn it there."

"That's where you're wrong. I did, but I never let on."

"You're a cussed sort of character, right enough, maybe that's why I've begun to like you."

Sam looked up. "It must be a strain for you to like anyone," he began and was unprepared for the sudden lunge Fred made which pinioned him on his back on the bed.

"Now show me how strong you are," and Sam, despite his frantic struggling could not throw off Fred and when the latter did relax his hold with one hand, he started to tickle Sam with the other causing him to burst into uncontrollable laughter.

When Fred stopped his torment he said, "I've found your weak spot, Sam. I didn't think you had one. Do you know it's the first time you've looked at me without a scowl on your face?"

Sam sat up. "OK, you've had your fun, now what is it you want, for you're definitely after something?"

"All right, I'll come clean. I've nowhere to take Rosie to have a bit of privacy, but I could have if I brought her here."

"How do you mean?"

"If you'd make yourself scarce for a couple of hours some evening and we could have the place to ourselves, then … well, you know."

"Know what?"

"Oh don't be awkward, Sam, you know fine what I mean."

"And what if your old man found you here with Rosie. You know what he did to Rob when he had his girl in the hay loft."

"He won't touch me now; he knows I'm too old for getting a hiding. He can shout and swear at me but that doesn't hurt. I can give him as good back. So how about it Sam?"

Sam thought for a moment. "You're sure Rosie would come? It's a long walk out from the town and back."

"I'd run her home in the lorry."

It was a few moments before Sam spoke again. "OK, but it will cost you."

"What do you mean?"

"Five bob a time."

"Five bob!"

"Yeah, if you're so keen to get astride Rosie on my bed, that's the price."

"You're a bloody capitalist, Sam, that's too much."

"Take it or leave it, you can't be all that keen if you're not prepared to pay up."

"How can I afford to pay five bob?"

"Don't drink so much on a Saturday night."

Sam ducked as Fred aimed a blow at his head and caught his wrist in a vice-like grip. "I'm not the weakling you make me out to be, Fred Whyte, and if I bring up my knee, you won't be much use for Rosie."

"You're a cheeky devil, but OK, five bob it'll be."

"Paid in advance."

"You win. Let go, I'm going to get dressed."

THE WEEKS passed and Sam gradually became used to the work on the farm and was less tired in the evenings. He looked forward to the weekends when Neil was free to join him in the bothy or in long walks along the banks of the river. Often on a Saturday night they would head for one of the picture houses in town, and stop at The Willows for supper. That was something Sam had come to enjoy most of all. For the first time in his life he felt he was part of a family, sitting in the comfortable living room by a blazing fire. Some day, he thought, I'm going to have a place like this, a home of my own. He had matured quickly and to Neil's surprise had become an avid reader, always scouring the bookshelves in the Munro home for yet another book. He had caused Mrs Munro some amusement one evening when he suggested they all conversed in French and she had been astonished by his knowledge of the language.

"He really is an unusual boy," she confided to her husband. "On occasion he is still the fierce rebel and at others just a normal interesting and pleasant teenager like Neil."

John Munro tapped out his pipe on the hearth before replying. "Yes, Sam's all right. Just a pity he hadn't come sooner to the Whytes, then he might have taken more interest in school."

"Yet he must have paid some attention, otherwise how could he know so much French? And he's sharp at counting. And he speaks well now, though maybe that's due to Neil."

"He's a bit too bright, I think, to spend his life as a farm hand."

"He doesn't intend to. According to Neil he's planning to go off on his own once he's saved enough money."

"That doesn't surprise me. He'll make out, will Sam, have no fears, if this war we're going to have doesn't put paid to his dreams."

"Oh John, you're always on about this war."

"It's coming, you mark my words."

SAM MANAGED to last out the winter months in the bothy without any difficulty and had grown to like his room where the bare essentials of a bed and a wooden chair had been supplemented by a rug, a table and an easy chair from the Munro's loft.

"They're not being used and you might as well have them Sam, if they're any good to you," Neil's mother had said after he had told her of the lack of furnishings in the bothy.

"Quite a home from home," Fred had commented after he had helped Sam to move the furniture from The Willows.

"It'll make it all the cosier for you when you bring Rosie here."

Fred said nothing, so Sam went on, "When am I likely to start getting my five bob then? It's months since you asked me if you could bring Rosie here. What's wrong? Won't she play?"

"Less of your lip." Fred turned to go.

"Come on Fred, come clean, what's wrong?"

Fred turned his back and his head went down. "Ach, I don't know. All she wants is to go to the pictures and then she's always in a hurry to get back home to look after all her wee sisters. Her old man and old lady are always out at the pub and Rosie's expected to get back and keep house."

"Don't you go in with her then?"

"I did once, but I don't fancy having a go with Rosie with half a dozen of her sisters gawping at us."

"How many are there?"

"There's eight, including Rosie. Seems her old man's a champion jockey. But one of these days I'm going to have Rosie."

- 5 -

N EIL was in the back garden of The Willows playing with Prince, the Munro's cocker spaniel, when Hazel appeared waving a newspaper.

"Neil, look at this."

"What?"

"There's not going to be a war. Look at what it says: 'Peace in our time.'"

"Great. Maybe I'll play for Queens Park after all."

"Oh Neil, do you think so?"

"I'd like to follow in Dad's footsteps. He said if there was a war, football might stop. Anyway there's no need to worry about that now. I bet Sam will be pleased."

"Sam? Why?"

"He's planning to go off round the world."

"He's what?"

"Like I said, he's doing a bunk, just as soon as he's saved a bit of money."

"He's mad, how could he?"

"You don't know Sam. When he makes up his mind to do something he does it. I must go up and see him after tea."

"HEARD THE NEWS, Sam, about the war?" Neil greeted his friend when he had climbed the wooden stair to his room.

"Yeah, Fred told me, he's mad."

"Why?"

"He wants to join the army."

"What's stopping him?"

"His old man; well, he won't admit it, but he's frightened to tell him."

"But his father couldn't stop him."

"Maybe not. You know what I'm beginning to think?"

"What?"

"That it's all big talk. He's been going on about it for ages, from the day I first started going with him on the milk lorry. He's just one great big bag of wind is Fred. When I'm ready for the off, he'll still be rattling into town with the milk churns."

"Sam, are you serious about leaving here?"

"Of course I am. Do you think I want to be a milk roundsman all of my life?"

"But when? Have you made any concrete plans?"

"You and your big words, Neil Munro. I've some ideas, but I'll let you know when I'm going. It won't be just yet, it takes time to save money. I think I'll have to cut down on the visits to the pictures in the winter."

"Crikey Sam, that's the only thing you ever spend money on. You never buy clothes or anything else."

"I'm quite happy with what Ma Whyte provides for me, although they're mostly hand-me-downs, but she's a dab hand with the needle and thread. She's remade some of Dugald's shirts for me and they look like new."

"You really like Mrs Whyte."

Sam shrugged his shoulders. "She's OK. I don't go for the old man though, never will, he's a real bastard especially when he's drunk, but I've learned to keep out of his way when he's had a bucketful. I don't know how Ma Whyte stands for it."

"Fred and Rob drink too, don't they?"

"Not so much, now they're both courting, though Fred doesn't seem to be getting on very fast with Rosie. You know, she works in the dairy in Church Street."

"I think I know the one you mean."

"You got a girl yet, Neil?"

"No."

"Bet you have an eye of some of the fancy pieces at the tennis club."

"How do you know about them? You won't come for a game."

"Me! Don't be daft. I'm not in the same class as the toffs at the tennis club."

"Thanks very much, I'm a toff to you."

"Yeah, you're a toff, but you're different from the others, you're a decent toff."

"I think I'll go home."

"Suit yourself."

Neil was silent, then he said, "Sam, I don't care what you think I am, you're my friend and I'm not going to quarrel with you."

"Frightened I'd give you a hiding."

"You couldn't."

They grappled with each other, rolling over and over on the floor, but neither could gain the upper hand until, perspiring faces close together, Sam said, "Yeah, you're a toff, Neil Munro, but you're OK, thanks to me. I've knocked some sense into you."

"Cheeky devil that you are, Sam Cairns. Come on, let's go along to the river."

THE FOLLOWING Saturday was very wet. When Neil burst into the bothy slamming the door behind him, he found Sam sitting in front of the fire he had lit underneath the boiler.

"What a day, even the football was rained off this morning."

"Lucky old you, Neil Munro. I had to do my usual work. You can't cancel the milk round just because of a few drops of rain."

"OK. OK. Sorry I mentioned it. So now what?"

"So now what what? Can't you see I'm drying out and heating the water for a bath. Then I'm going to bed. I've got a good book about France. Got it from an old dear this morning."

"Oh?"

"Yeah. She lives in a big house along the Stirling Road. It's the last one we deliver to and she sometimes gives Fred and me a cup of tea and gets chatting. Fred laughs at her afterwards but she's all right."

"That'll be old Mrs Burton."

"You know her then?"

"She's Roger Harrison's granny."

"Roger Harrison?"

"He's the head boy at school this year. His parents and mine are friendly. But Sam, you don't really mean you're going to bed to read."

"I am, straight after tea and my bath."

"Well I've got a change of plans for you. Mum's invited you to tea and then we're going to the pictures."

"Oh heck, Neil. Have I to go out again in this weather. What's the big idea?"

"It's my birthday, you chump."

"Why didn't you tell me?"

"I thought you knew. Come on then, get ready. Dad's waiting with the car and he'll run us to the pictures after we've had our tea."

"OK. Seeing it's your birthday."

"Ungrateful wretch, get a move on."

"Anyway, many happy returns, pal, you're getting real old."

"Thanks."

The rain had eased when Neil and Sam came out of the picture house, but Mr Munro was waiting to pick them up in his car.

"Just drop me off here, Mr Munro, I'll manage fine now," Sam said when they reached the end of the farm road.

"Are you sure, Sam? It's no trouble going right up."

"The road's a mess of pot holes – it won't do your car much good."

John Munro turned to look at Sam sitting beside him. "Thoughtful of you, Sam, but what about you and the pot holes?"

"Oh I know where they all are and I can avoid them."

"All right then, as you wish."

AS SAM entered the farm yard he saw the bulky figure of Dugald Whyte lurch from the shadows of the house. He knew he was too late to avoid him, but he went on towards the bothy.

"Here, Sam, you seen that bloody son of mine, Fred?"

The blurred speech confirmed to Sam that old man Whyte was very drunk and he was immediately on his guard, for he knew that the farmer was always liable to lash out with his fists when he was in such a state.

"No, I haven't seen him since this afternoon."

"Well, I saw him in the town in my car with a girl, some hussy he'd picked up. Now the car's back, but I can't find him. He's not in the house, where is he?"

"How should I know?"

"Less of your lip. Where you been?"

"At the pictures with Neil Munro. His father brought us home in the car."

"Oh, he did."

"Yes, it was Neil's birthday, I was down at his place for tea."

"Hmm." Dugald Whyte grunted, "So where are you off to now?"

"I'm going to bed."

"Oh? It doesn't look like it."

"You know fine I sleep in the bothy now. I have been for ages."

Dugald looked confused. "Oh aye, so you do."

He followed Sam over to the bothy and stumbled in behind him. "The boiler fire's still red, wasting coal."

"I was drying my things and heating the water for a bath."

"Well, what's stopping you?"

"Nothing. I'll just get my towel."

"And I'll just have a seat here and have a warm. I'm perished standing out there waiting for that buggar Fred."

Sam climbed slowly up the stair to his room. It had suddenly occurred to him where Fred might be and he opened the door cautiously. Despite what he thought he might find he just managed to stop himself from shouting out when he saw the naked forms of Fred and Rosie lying on his bed. He pushed the door closed and put his finger to his lips as Fred raised himself up.

"Your old man's here," he whispered, making a downward movement with his thumb, "he's looking for you."

"Christ!"

Fred clamped his hand over Rosie's mouth as she opened it to scream. Her eyes dilated with terror as she struggled to free herself from Fred's grip.

The latter hissed at Sam. "Get rid of him!"

"How can I? You're a rotten sod, Fred, you said you'd pay me before you used my room. You'll have to work this one out for yourself."

Rosie twisted herself free. "Fred, I can't stay here all night. My father will kill me if I'm late in."

"Well he won't get the chance if you stay here," was Fred's sour reply. "Now shut your face till I think."

Suddenly they heard a footstep on the stair and Dugald Whyte shouting, "What are you doing up there, Sam? Come down and get your bath. I've filled it for you."

"The old buggar's gone off his head. Since when has he done anything for any one of us?" Fred growled.

"I'm coming," Sam shouted. "I'm just stripping off."

"Hurry up then, water'll be cold."

"Bloody nudist colony this," Sam hissed, as he threw off his clothes and grabbing a towel fled down the stair and plunged straight into the bath. He looked at Dugald as he soaped himself and saw that the heat of the fire combined with the drink was making him drowsy.

"Crikey, what if he falls asleep," he thought to himself, and splashed the water to try to rouse the old man.

The latter brought up his head with a jerk and for a moment gazed unseeingly at Sam, then muttered, "Growing up fast aren't you? Soon be as big a nuisance as that Fred."

"Why do you hate Fred?"

"Because he's …" he hesitated. "Ask his mother. Hell, I'll need to go and have a piss."

When he had gone outside, Sam stepped from the bath and towelled himself vigorously hoping that Dugald would not return, but just as he was about to climb the stair, the door opened and the ungainly figure stumbled inside.

"No sign of him yet. I'll wait here for a while."

"But how will you know Fred's come back if you're in here?"

"I'm not stupid. I've locked the back door and the spare key is kept in here. Didn't you know that?"

"No, I didn't."

"Well it is. You're not as smart as you think, Sam, Fred will have to come for the key and won't he get a surprise then?"

Sam couldn't think what to say. Finally he got out, "Well I'm off to bed. Goodnight."

There was no reply and Sam continued slowly to his room where he found Fred and Rosie fully dressed.

"Did you hear what he said?" he asked when he closed the door.

"Yeah, we did," Fred whispered, "the door was open a crack. Christ, what are we going to do? How are we going to get out of here?"

"My father will kill me!" It was the only thing Rosie seemed capable of saying and Fred again told her to shut up in a menacing hiss.

"Right," Sam said, "I'm going to bed. You two can please yourselves what you do."

"Sam, you've got to help us," pleaded Fred. "Come on, you're the bright spark around here or supposed to be. Look at those books you read, you should be able to come up with something."

Sam thought for a moment. "How much is it worth?"

"What do you mean?"

"There is a way to get out but how much will you pay me to do it?"

"You rotten bastard, Sam, that's all you think of. Money!"

"Fred," Rosie pulled at his arm. "Listen to him."

Fred shook her off. "OK. Give."

"You can shin down the drainpipe from the window. Neil and I have done it."

"You can what?"

"Like I said, we did it to see how we could escape if there was a fire. It was Neil's idea."

"Trust young Munro to think up something like that, but how can we do it?"

"Afraid are you?"

"Of course not, but what about Rosie?"

Sam turned to Rosie. "OK, Rosie. Would you be able to climb down a ladder?"

"Yes, I think I could."

"OK. Now here's what I'll do. I'll go down via the drainpipe, get the ladder from the barn; you two climb down, I climb back up, Fred puts the ladder back and then takes you home."

"Sam, you're a genius! Come on, get your clothes on and get cracking."

Sam didn't move. "Just one thing."

"What's that?" Fred snapped.

"It'll cost you. A quid."

"A quid! You must be out of your mind."

"You owe me for the use of my bed and I don't engineer your escape for nothing."

"Fred, give him it."

"Are you daft? A quid! He's mad!"

"OK, then move off my bed, I want some sleep."

"Fred, please," Rosie pleaded, "I've got some change in my purse which will help."

"I want a quid from you Fred. I know you have money in your wallet, so make up your mind fast."

Fred glowered at Sam. "You're a thieving, rotten bastard," but he pulled his wallet from his jacket pocket and turning his back fumbled about for a few moments. Then facing Sam again he held out a pound note.

"OK. Just one thing. How are you going to get into the farmhouse if he's locked the door and the spare key's in the bothy here?"

"The key hangs on a nail above the door just inside. He'll be so dead asleep by the time I get back I should be able to reach it and put it back without wakening him up." Fred smiled. "That'll shake the old buggar when he finds I've been in bed all night."

"Right, I'm off."

Rosie was shaking with fear as she watched Sam climb on top of a chair, wriggle through the top sash of the window and disappear.

"Oh Fred," she whispered. "I'll never be able to do that."

"You'll have to if you want to get out of here and home."

They waited in silence until after an interval of five minutes which to them seemed an hour, Sam reappeared.

"Go on then, it's not very far down."

"Right, I'll go first Rosie, and help you out. Once you're on the ladder you'll be OK."

"Oh Fred, I can't, I can't!"

"All right. Stay here. I'm getting out."

"Don't leave me Fred. Don't leave me."

"Well come on, you stupid bitch."

"Come on Rosie," Sam encouraged. "I'll help you too."

With a struggle Rosie eventually made it through the window and Sam watched her progress down the ladder, climbed back up to his room, saw Fred remove the ladder and thankfully once again undressed and went to bed.

~ 6 ~

"**A**RE you taking the car?" Rosie asked once Fred had rejoined her from the barn.

"Aye, but we'll have to push it down the road a bit so that the old man won't hear me starting it. Come on, put your shoulder into it."

"I'm never coming here again," Rosie sobbed as she did Fred's bidding.

"Who's going to ask you?" was Fred's sour rejoinder.

They made the journey into town and when they reached Rosie's close, Fred barely stopped the car to let her off. It had suddenly occurred to him that he'd have to stop before he reached the yard and push the heap of junk the rest of the way and no Rosie to help him.

By the time he finally reached the bothy he was in a lather of sweat and paused for a moment before he slowly raised the latch and gently pushed open the door to reach for the key. When he couldn't locate it he moved the door further inwards and was totally unprepared when it suddenly gave entirely, causing him to fall forward and as he did he felt a vicious blow across his shoulders.

Fred struggled to regain his feet as his father continued to rain blows on his back, punctuating each one with foul invective. When Fred was at last able to rise he saw his father had cut off his escape route by kicking shut the door so he had to retreat backwards into the bothy, at the same time trying to ward off the blows from the belt his father was wielding.

"Stop it, you mad bastard," he shouted, "or I'll kill you."

Suddenly he felt the stair to Sam's room behind him and he turned and leapt up it to seek refuge from where he had so recently escaped. He had not reckoned on his father's mobility, for before he could wrench open the door, he found himself belaboured again with the stinging length of leather as the old man climbed after him. Fred turned and almost unseeingly gave his father one almighty punch which sent Dugald Whyte tumbling backwards to the ground where he lay completely still.

"That'll learn you, you heathen," Fred managed to get out as he struggled to draw breath.

"What's going on?" Sam's voice at his side startled Fred.

"Stupid old buggar went for me as I was trying to get the key. Didn't you hear him shouting at me?"

"I must have been fast asleep, I thought I was dreaming at first. Is he all right?"

"Yeah, he's all right, dead stinking drunk."

Sam moved cautiously down the stair. "He looks as if he's unconscious."

"Of course he is. Carries a bottle with him. Probably been supping all the time he was waiting for me."

Sam went nearer and then knelt down beside Dugald. "Hi. Fred, I don't think he's breathing."

"How can you tell in this light?"

"I can tell. Come and have a look."

Fred came warily down the stair towards his father and went down on his knees beside Sam to stare at the inert body.

"What did you do to him?" Sam asked.

"Nothing. He was walloping me with the belt. Look he still has it in his hand and I ran up to get into your room away from him. He followed me and as I turned he tripped and fell backwards."

"You mean you pushed him."

"I didn't bloody well touch him. He was down there when you opened the door. Look, you'd better go and tell Ma. He'll likely have the back door key in his pocket, yeah, here it is."

When Sam returned with Mrs Whyte the latter stood for a moment looking at her husband before she bent over him, feeling for a pulse and a heart beat.

"He's gone," she said simply, "he's away."

"What do you mean, Ma?" Fred spoke in a whisper. "He can't be, he can't be."

"I tell you he's dead."

"No, no, you're mistaken."

Ma Whyte straightened up.

"Tell me what happened Fred," and when her son had gulped out his story she said quietly, "Fred, I want you to go and get into your bed. Sam, you go and phone for Dr Blackwood. Tell him Mr Whyte has had an accident and ask him to come right away."

"But Ma …" Fred began.

"Fred, do as I say. I don't want you here when the doctor comes. You weren't here when your father fell. He was going up to Sam's room when he tripped."

"But why Ma?"

"Because I say so. Go on to your bed. Don't wake Rob. I'll send Sam when I want you." And with that Mrs Whyte pushed her son to the door.

When Fred had gone she turned to Sam. "You'll do as I say now, Sam."

Sam was silent for a moment before he said, "All right, if that's how you want it. It doesn't make any difference to me. I didn't see what happened. But are you sure he's dead?"

Doctor Blackwood confirmed that Dugald Whyte had indeed gone.

"We'll have to have the police along. You say, Sam, that Mr Whyte came in here to wait for Fred."

"Yes, that's right Doctor."

"And where is Fred, Mrs Whyte?"

"He's in his bed, I expect."

"I didn't want to leave my husband and when Sam came back over after phoning for you I felt I needed him here."

"I see. Well Sam, you'd best go and rouse both Fred and Rob, they should be here with their mother."

AFTERWARDS Sam thought about what had taken place. He had at first felt rather awkward when the police inspector had started to question him, but he realized that after all he had not seen what had happened and if Ma Whyte didn't want Fred involved, that was her affair. So he answered everything honestly not volunteering to supply any information that wasn't asked for. If Fred was prepared to tell lies about when he got back to the farm, then he told lies. Lucky for him Rob had had so much to drink that he had been unable to say when Fred had come to bed. The Whytes meant nothing to him; nothing. Well Ma was all right. Sam had to admit he had grown fond of her and he was sorry for her because things had become different. You would have thought now that the old man was gone Fred would have been happy, but he hardly spoke to anyone, did his work mechanically, and didn't even go to the pub.

IT WAS THREE weeks after the funeral and Sam was at a loose end on the Saturday night as Neil was away visiting his grandparents. For once his books held no attraction for him and he decided to go over to the farmhouse and see if Mrs Whyte would let him listen to the radio. He decided to go through the milk house, then hearing voices just as he reached the kitchen door, he hesitated. Fred was with his mother, but as he made to retrace his steps Sam stopped when he heard Fred ask, "But why did you not want to tell the police the truth about what happened? Why did you want me out of the way?"

There was silence for a few minutes and Sam wondered if he should tip-toe away, but he was curious to know the answer to Fred's question. He had to strain his ears to catch what Mrs Whyte said when she began.

"I didn't want you to be blamed for anything Fred. None of it was your fault. You see he never took to you and it seemed to get worse as you got older and when the drink took hold of him."

"But why? What did I do to make him hate me?"

"Because you weren't his."

There was silence until Fred said in a hoarse voice, "What do you mean, I wasn't his?"

"He wasn't your father. Your dad was killed in the war, right at the end. He was one of the last to go out. We were married before he left but he never came back. I found I was carrying you and when Dugald Whyte who had always fancied me, asked me to wed, I just said yes. It seemed the only way out of the situation I was in."

"Did he know about me?"

"Yes, of course he knew, but he said it didn't matter, it wouldn't make any difference, he'd think of you as his own. It was all right for a few years, but I don't know, he changed, and you know the rest."

Fred half opened his mouth but could not find any words.

Mrs Whyte went on, "You're my son and your father was a good man. Blame the war for what happened."

"I can't believe it, I just can't believe it."

Mrs Whyte didn't seem to hear him for she went on, "I thought when I had Rob that was what maybe caused him to turn against you, but he was as coarse with Rob as he was with you. He just seemed to have this rage inside him. Yet he never struck me and although he spent a lot on drink, we never went without. He knew how to run a good farm, but you see, Fred, I wasn't going to let him harm you any more, so that's why I didn't want you to be involved. I don't know what all went on that night and I don't want to know, ever."

Sam was startled when he heard Fred start to sob, and embarrassed, he crept away back to his room.

DURING THE next few days Fred hardly spoke to Sam who felt awkward after his eavesdropping session. In one way he wanted to tell Fred he understood why he was upset, but he knew he couldn't; then he would ask himself why he should be sorry for Fred after the way he had sometimes treated him. Sam wondered if he should tell the whole story to Neil when they met up again on Friday, but the decision was made for him.

Along with Fred he had made the usual milk round, but instead of driving the milk lorry back to the farm Fred turned it round and headed into town.

"Where are we going now?" queried Sam.

"The station."

"The station. What are we going there for?"

"What do you usually go to the station for?"

"I suppose the silly answer is to catch a train."

"It's not a silly answer, it's the right one."

"Where are you going?"

"I'm off to join the army."

Sam looked hard at Fred. "Honest."

"Yeah. I must get away. I can't stay at the farm any longer."

"Have you told Ma?"

"No. I've got a letter I want you to give her."

"You rotten sod, Fred, why didn't you tell her? And who is going to run the farm now? The old man gone and now you."

"Rob and you will manage and Ma will soon get a couple of lads to help you."

"Fred, you're mad, you don't know what you're saying."

"Look, I've always said I was going to join up and now I'm doing it."

"But Fred, you're needed at the farm."

"Hmm. It's too late for my services to be appreciated. I'm off."

"Is it because what happened between you and the old man?"

Fred didn't answer for a moment. "Yeah, you could say that was it."

"Did you push him down the stair?"

"No!" Fred almost shouted. "He fell! He was leathering me with the belt and I just had my arms up to cover my face He was swinging at me all the time and he overbalanced."

"OK. I was only asking."

"I told you before what happened."

By this time they had reached the station and Fred turned the lorry round to face back towards the farm.

"There you are then, it's all yours."

"What do you mean?" Sam cried in alarm.

"You'll have to take it back."

"Me?"

"Yeah, who else? You'll manage, you've driven it before."

"Only along the farm road."

"Well, there you are, if you can do it there, you'll find it a lot easier on the main road."

"Fred, I can't. What if the polis get me?"

"I shouldn't worry. Too cold for them to be out. And Sam, will you tell Rosie?"

"What do you think I am?" demanded Sam as he watched Fred strip off his overalls, noticing that he was wearing his best suit.

"You're just great, Sam, a real friend."

"Get lost, you don't mean that."

Fred reached into the cab for a brown paper parcel, then paused for a moment before turning to Sam. He held out his hand, "I do mean it, Sam. I know I've knocked you about a bit, but I've grown to like you. Wish me luck."

Reluctantly Sam took the outstretched hand and held it for a moment. Then Fred was gone to the ticket office and through the barrier to the stairs up to the platform. Sam watched from the other side of the rail, but Fred did not turn round and there was nothing else for it but to get the lorry back to the farm as best he could.

MRS WHYTE showed little emotion when she read Fred's letter.

"I'm not surprised he's away, Sam," she said finally. "He's never been happy here. I just hope he'll be alright and manage to stick up for himself."

"Oh he'll be OK, but what about us? How are we going to manage?"

"Like he said to you, I'll get a couple of men to help, that'll be no bother. Rob and you will get on fine. I'll keep you right just as I kept Mr Whyte right."

Sam looked up.

"Oh aye, he was maybe the boss, but I always told him what was to be done. Maybe that surprises you but that's the way it's always been."

"I believe you."

NEIL LISTENED intently to Sam's long tale and when the latter had finished asked, "Have you told Rosie yet?"

"No, she was off her work for a few days after the night in question, as the polis would say, and when she came back I could see her old man had knocked her about a bit. She always went through to the back shop when Fred appeared. I don't think he was ever in quick enough to see her bruises."

Neil stood up and imitating Sam said, "So Fred Whyte did not speak to the girl Rosie after the night in question?"

"That is correct, my lord."

The two boys fell about laughing, till Sam said, "I suppose looking back, it was all a bit of a comedy."

"Which turned into a tragedy."

"Yeah. Do you think I need to go and tell Rosie? After all she seemed to go clean off Fred."

"He didn't though, if he asked you to go and see her."

"He didn't have much spunk, Fred. Couldn't go and tell Rosie himself. I suppose I better try and have a word with her."

SAM FOUND it impossible to have a conversation with Rosie in the dairy so eventually he slipped her a note asking her to meet him in town in the evening. Rosie seemed reluctant at first, but she agreed as long as Sam was willing to come to her close. She promised she would be able to leave her sisters on their own for a while because she knew her parents would be at the pub.

It was the first time Sam had arranged to meet a girl and he felt very conspicuous as he waited in the mouth of the close for Rosie. He had almost decided to risk climbing the stairs to her flat when she appeared.

"Sorry Sam, but the wee one wouldn't settle. What was it you wanted to see me about? Is it Fred? Could he not come himself?"

"No, he couldn't."

"Oh, what's wrong with him?"

"Fred's away."

"Away? Away where?"

"He's away to join the army."

"He's never! Well the lousy buggar, and he never came to say cheerio."

"You know what happened when Fred got back to the farm that night?"

"Well, I know the old man fell down the stair and was killed. It was strange how it all turned out. Was Fred there? Did you see it happen?"

"No, I mean I was in my room. I don't know where Fred was."

"I see," Rosie said quietly. "And now Fred's gone off."

Suddenly she burst into tears. Sam was embarrassed and hoped no one would come on the scene in case they got the wrong impression of what was going on.

"Rosie," he said slowly, "Fred asked me to come and see you. He didn't have time to come."

Rosie's sobbing increased and suddenly Sam thought he knew the reason. "Rosie," he stammered, "Fred didn't, you know, what I mean. Fred didn't leave you in the family way?"

Rosie looked up and sniffed. "No, Fred was maybe a novice, but I wasn't. I know how to look after myself. I'm not going to be landed with a load o' weans like my mother has. No wonder she goes out to the pub."

"You mean you've had other men."

Rosie looked at Sam and laughed through her tears. "Sam, you're a funny lad, you're a queer mixture. There's a devil in you, but as Fred said your pal young Munro has tamed it."

"He hasn't," Sam protested. "I'm not a softie if that's what you mean."

"No, I know you're not, you're all right. I've always liked you, for you've got spunk. Aye, I've had a couple of men, but Fred was the best. Oh he was a moody buggar at times, but he's the first man I've really cared for and now he's away."

Rosie's eyes filled with tears again. "I knew I said a lot of things to him that night I shouldn't have, but I was upset. That old man of his was poison." She fumbled for a handkerchief and eventually produced one.

"OK then, I'll be off now Rosie."

"I suppose you'd better. Thanks Sam for coming. See you tomorrow son, when you bring the milk."

1939 - 1945

- 7 -

SAM stood by himself on the platform of Queen Street Station, Glasgow. Around him were hundreds of other young men who had received their call up papers to report to the Seaforth Highlanders' depot at Fort George. Everyone else, as far as he could make out, was being seen off by one or more relatives or friends and scanning the faces he judged that both those going and those staying were not exactly jumping for joy.

Joe Brannigan, who had come to work at Millside when Rob like Fred had left for the army, had offered to run Sam to the station in Levenford, but Sam had preferred to walk in by the river, although it looked rather uninviting in the November mist. He had been glad when the brown envelope from the War Office had finally arrived, for Neil had gone off in September, and Sam had felt his absence keenly. Neil had continued through to his sixth year at school, then on to University and they had remained close friends. He had sometimes wondered if the Munros had approved and he had felt they had become less friendly in their welcome when he visited The Willows. It had been, he supposed, an unusual friendship, but the bond between them had strengthened rather than weakened as they grew into young manhood. Oh, he knew that Neil had other friends, lots of them, but he still counted as number one and Neil looked upon him as his confidant.

At first the war had meant little to Sam. He had listened with Ma Whyte and Rob to the announcement by Neville Chamberlain, the Prime Minister, on the Sunday morning of September 3rd. It had been very quiet in the farm kitchen as they sat round the old wireless set crackling out its never-to-be forgotten message.

"What will it mean, Ma? Will it be like the last war?" Rob had asked.

Mrs Whyte shook her head. "I don't know, I hope not, for it was bad, very bad. I hope Fred will be all right."

AFTER LEAVING the farm Fred had returned to Levenford on only two occasions. He had spent his first leave at home looking smart and proud of his uniform, but when he had visited Sam in the bothy Fred had seemed ill at ease and eventually he had said, "This place gives me the creeps now. It all comes back, what happened that night. It's all right when I'm away but now standing on this stair, I can see him lying down there. I hated him, but that doesn't seem to clear him from out of my mind when I'm here at the farm. I don't think I'll come back again."

He wrote short letters to his mother from time to time but apparently he preferred to spend his leaves in London from where he usually sent a postcard. Sam knew Mrs Whyte had been saddened by Fred's decision, but she regularly sent him parcels containing food and socks which she seemed to Sam to knit by the dozen.

Sam thought back again to that day when war was declared and remembered the thunderstorm that had broken over Levenford in the afternoon. He had been taken aback when Mrs Whyte had declared, "God is angry. He doesn't approve of war." And although Rob had smiled over to Sam, neither had said anything.

SAM LOOKED again at the throng of people milling around; no one seemed to stand in the same spot for long. He saw couples embracing and realized that some of the men departing were quite a bit older than he was, some even had children clasping their hands and then wriggling free to explore some part on the platform before being dragged back by harassed mothers.

His boyhood was all Sam felt he was saying goodbye to and the river. He wondered if he would ever go back to it. You did get leave in the army and he supposed Millside had been the home he had known longest. But there appeared to be no end to this war; it seemed to have taken over; and all the older people were always shaking their heads and worrying about when the next air raid would be.

SAM WELL remembered the night when the Germans had come to devastate Clydebank, just five miles up the River Clyde from Levenford which itself had not escaped unscathed. He had been at The Willows keeping Neil and Hazel company as both their parents were out. John Munro had a meeting in Glasgow, and his wife visiting a sick friend in the Newtown. John had returned just before nine o'clock and Sam had risen to go home to Millside. He had paused to hear the news and as Big Ben struck the hour, the wailing of the sirens had provided an unwelcome accompaniment. Within minutes they had heard the distinctive throb of the engines of the German bombers.

47

"Best get down to the shelter, all of us, you too Sam. Come on!" John Munro said.

They had trooped to the far end of the vegetable garden where the shelter was and once inside lit the candles, sitting close together, straining their ears for the sound of the enemy planes.

"What about Mum?" Hazel asked. "Will she be all right?"

"She should be. The Bowens have an Anderson shelter."

"I hope so," Neil said quietly.

They all stiffened when they heard the sinister whistle of the first bomb as it sped to its target and felt the shelter shake when it exploded.

"Gosh, that was pretty near," Neil's voice was a whisper.

"They'll be following the course of the river," Sam put in.

"Why?" Hazel asked.

"To get to the shipyards."

"Is that right, Dad?"

"Yes," Mr Munro looked at Sam. "They must be a bit off course, unless they've mistaken the Leven for the Clyde. But let's hope they're off target and drop their bombs in the river, whichever one they're over."

They listened as another wave of Junkers passed overhead, tensing themselves for the next explosion. When it came it seemed much nearer and John Munro stood up and moved to the door of the shelter.

"Be careful, Dad," Hazel called in a shaky voice.

"Blow out the candles, boys, I want to have a look."

Neil and Sam followed him cautiously up the steps to ground level, crouching down as they looked up at the starlit sky.

"Look!" Sam said suddenly, "they've lit the decoy fires on the hills."

"How do you know that, Sam?" Mr Munro asked.

"I was speaking to one of the soldiers at the camp, he told me, maybe he wasn't supposed to but he had been up there preparing them."

"I hope they work and draw the Jerries away from the town. Listen! Here they come again. Back inside."

Time passed slowly and the raid continued. Neil and Hazel dozed fitfully, but Mr Munro saw Sam remained alert and then looking at his watch whispered, "It's one o'clock and it's been quiet for almost an hour although the 'All Clear' hasn't gone. Let's have a look out."

As soon as they emerged from the shelter Mr Munro gasped, "My God, Sam, look at the glow in the sky, there are fires everywhere and not just on the hills. The town must have got it, and what about their mother? I wonder if I should go and look for her. Listen! Someone's coming." And with that he ran round to the front of the house to the track from the main road.

"John, it's me," a voice called.

"Oh, thank goodness you're safe. I was worried sick about you, but you took a risk coming out."

"I know, but I couldn't bear to wait any longer. When it seemed as if they'd gone, I decided to make a dash for it."

"You must be all in. Look, you go down to the shelter – it's quite warm there, and I'll make some tea."

"Can we not have it in the house?"

"If the 'All Clear' goes, we will, but I've a feeling they're not finished with us yet. Go on, Sam will help me."

Mr Munro and Sam had just returned to the shelter when the sound of enemy aircraft was heard again.

"I guess we're in for a long night," John Munro said as he dispensed the tea. "I didn't ask you, Mother, if there were any bombs dropped near where you were."

"There must have been, they sounded very close. It was terrifying. That's why I wanted to get back home. At least we're that bit away from the town."

It was a long anxious wait in the shelter before the 'All Clear' finally sounded and they all crept wearily out.

Sam went off immediately to the farm and found Mrs Whyte in the kitchen.

"What did you do?" he asked her.

"I sat under the stairs and prayed. I was all right. Are you able to take in the milk?"

"Of course."

AT LAST they were on the train, four on each side of the carriage, strangers, united in a common bond – they were all in the army now. Sam, at a window seat, looked round at his companions. After the noisy and tearful farewells and the drawn-out waving as the train slowly lurched its way out of the station, a silence had fallen which wasn't broken until the young man opposite him leaned forward and asked, "Where are you from then?"

"Levenford. What about you?"

"Glasgow. Jordanhill. Looking forward to this lark?"

"I don't know. I'll tell you in a couple of months."

"All my friends are away now, so I'm quite glad. Folk begin to look at you and you know they're wondering why you're still a civilian."

"I guess that's right."

"I'm Ross Clark by the way, student, single, only son – but I've got two sisters."

"Sam Cairns. No family."

Ross opened his mouth to ask for further information when he saw that Sam had sat back and was gazing out of the window. Sam had been surprised that he had suddenly experienced the feeling of being entirely on his own, something that had not happened for a considerable number of years. He realized that despite his longing to be away from Millside he had come to regard it as his home and grudgingly admitted to himself that he would miss Mrs Whyte, not to mention Neil and his family. And Rosie. Poor Rosie.

SAM HAD set off with Joe Brannigan at the usual time on the morning after the raid to take the milk into town. Their first call at the dairy had found the owner, old Mrs Worth on her own and worried because Rosie had not turned up.

"I hope she's all right, Sam. I've heard the bombs were dropped out the Glasgow Road where Rosie stays now."

THE TRAIN slowed to a halt seemingly in the middle of nowhere and Sam found his thoughts interrupted by the general discussion which sprang up about where they were, how far they had travelled, when they would reach Fort George, and where the hell was that bloody place anyway?

Sam surprised his fellow travellers by telling them exactly where Fort George was and how many miles from Glasgow.

"How do you know all that? Have you been there?" queried a stocky fair-haired man who was sitting diagonally across from Sam.

"No, I've never been there but I looked for it on the atlas and worked out how far it was."

"Brainy lad, are you. University?"

Sam burst out laughing. "Not me, mate," he said, but didn't offer any further information, and when the train restarted its slow progress north, Sam turned again to gaze out of the window, and to think once more of Rosie.

– 8 –

FRED had returned a second time to Millside a year after Dunkirk, a more mature man having briefly tasted some rearguard action before experiencing the trauma of being pulled out of the sea into a weekend pleasure craft and transported safely back to Britain. It was to Sam that he gradually unfolded his story, seeming to feel more at ease with him than with his mother, and having done so, it appeared to release some of the tension within him and he was ready to ask what had been happening in Levenford. He listened without comment as Sam brought him up-to-date and then said, "Is Rosie still at the dairy?"

"Yeah, where else would she be?"

"Oh I thought she might have gone off with one of the Commandoes I see knocking around here."

"No, not Rosie. You know what, Fred, for some reason I can't understand, she's still sweet on you."

"Pull the other one mate."

"No, honest, she's always asking if there's any news of you."

"If you're having me on, Sam Cairns, I'll do you."

"Straight up, Fred, and listen, it's made for you."

"How do you mean?"

"Well, Rosie doesn't live at home any more. She's moved in with her cousin out the Glasgow Road."

"How did she manage that?"

"Her cousin's man was called up and she didn't fancy staying on her own."

"And Rosie's folk let her go! Who looks after the tribe when they're out at the pub?"

"Linda. That's Rosie's sister, who's next eldest."

"That's very interesting, Sam. Thanks. I'll maybe give Rosie a call."

Fred reckoned that Rosie would be on her own in the early afternoon when Mrs Worth went to her house above the dairy to have a rest. The shop was empty when he entered quietly so he stood listening for a moment. Then seeing the door into the back room was slightly ajar, he knocked on it and ducked behind the counter. He heard Rosie's hurried footsteps and he watched her in the mirror advertising Gold Flake cigarettes which hung above the door, seeing her puzzled look as she found the shop empty. He waited until she moved outside to look, and when she retraced her steps to the back room, he leapt out from his hiding place, seizing her round the waist and clamping his hand over her mouth, whispered, "A good soldier always covers his rear."

Fred looked into Rosie's startled eyes, then withdrawing his hand, kissed her firmly on the lips. When he released her, Rosie, finding her breath, managed to say, "Fred, you're a devil, you nearly gave me heart failure."

"And I thought you'd be pleased to see me."

"Of course I am, Fred. You've taken your time to come back."

"Well, you know how it was. It took me a while to get over the old man's death. I felt I wanted to forget Millside."

"And me?"

"No Rosie, I didn't forget you."

"Hmm. I can hardly believe that. I bet you've had half a dozen girls since you joined up."

"That's where you're wrong. I've never bothered with them."

"There must be something wrong with you then."

"What do you mean by that?"

"It's not natural. Look at you, a big, brawny soldier, bursting with health."

As Fred's face took on a sulky look, Rosie went on, "Unless you were saving yourself for me."

Fred was silent for a moment. "Maybe I was. Was Sam right when he told me you weren't going steady with anyone?"

"So, you've been discussing me with Sam?"

"I was only asking."

"Fred, I was only teasing you. It's great seeing you again. Are you going to take me out tonight?"

"Do you want me to?"

"You great goat, of course I do. Anyway why did you come here if you weren't going to ask me out? Listen, I hear Mrs Worth coming down. Meet me outside the picture house at seven o'clock."

"I'll be there."

WHEN THEY came out of the pictures Rosie linked her arm in Fred's and said, "Come on home for some supper and meet my cousin, Isa. I've told her all about you."

"What have you told her?"

"You'd like to know. You're still the same old Fred, questions, questions, questions."

The verbal sparring continued until they reached the tenement off the Glasgow Road and entered the ground floor flat where Isa awaited them.

"So you're Fred. My, Rosie, he's a handsome soldier, all right."

"Your man's away too?"

"Aye, stationed in Yorkshire in the Royal Signals. He's not due on leave again for another two months. Thank goodness for Rosie. I'd go mad on my own here."

When supper was over, Isa cleared away and announced she was off to bed.

"I'll be seeing you again, Fred."

"Oh aye, I expect so."

Left alone Fred and Rosie sat in silence for a few moments before Rosie said, "Come and see my bedroom."

She closed the door behind Fred and turning to him asked, "What are you waiting for?"

"You mean?"

"I mean you can stay the night – but only if you want to."

"Only if I want to! Oh Rosie! I love you, I've been a fool to stay away for so long."

"Well, let's make up for lost time."

Fred woke to find that Rosie had gone, but when he padded across to her dressing table he found a note propped up against the mirror.

"Lover boy," he read, "make yourself some breakfast. You'll find eggs in the pantry, and anything else you want. Come and see me in the dairy before you go out to the farm to collect your things for I want you to stay with me for the rest of your leave. I love you. Rosie."

"Bossy bitch," but Fred was smiling and remembered the peace he had felt as he lay with Rosie in his arms after their lovemaking.

WHEN HE returned to Millside Fred found his mother in the kitchen.

"Angry with me?" he asked, putting his arm round her shoulder.

"No, son, why should I be? You're a man now, and can please yourself when you come and go."

"Listen Ma, what would you say if I told you I was thinking of getting wed?"

"I'd be happy for you, Fred, if the girl is right for you."

"Of course she's right for me. It's Rosie in Mrs Worth's dairy, you know her."

"Oh aye, she's a bonnie lass. Have you fixed a date?"

"On my next leave, I hope. And Ma, I'll be staying with Rosie while I'm here. Oh I'll come out and see you every day and give you a hand if you want me to."

"No need to do that, Fred, you're on leave, you need a rest, you enjoy yourself."

"Ach, there's not much to do during the day. I'll do the odd job for you, keep me out of mischief."

"I'm glad to see you look so happy, Fred, you've looked so sad since the old man died."

Fred turned away, then looking back at his mother, asked, "Did you love him Ma?"

"I loved your father, Fred, but Dugald Whyte was good to me. No, I never really loved him, but we got on fine together. The drink spoiled him though."

"Aye, he was hard enough without it."

"Never mind, Fred, it's all in the past."

"Maybe, but it's hard to forget."

BEFORE HE left to return to his unit, Fred told Sam he was going to marry Rosie on his next leave and asked him to be his best man.

"That's a laugh, Fred. It's not so long since you were belting the daylight out of me at every opportunity."

"That's not true, Sam. Maybe we didn't start off on the right foot, but you must admit you were a right little bastard when you first came here."

"OK. Let's say we've both improved and all right, I'll hold you up on your big day."

"Thanks, Sam, and would you look after Rosie while I'm away? You know, have a chat with her now and then. Give her a bit of your company."

And Sam had done just that, for he found Rosie easy to get along with and once a week he walked out to the Glasgow Road and spent the evening playing cards with her and her cousin Isa, listening to Rosie reading bits from letters she was receiving regularly from Fred.

"You've certainly hooked him, Rosie. I wouldn't ever have believed Fred would have written so often to anyone."

"He's great, I just can't wait till he comes home again."

SAM CLOSED his eyes and saw again the tenement reduced to a heap of rubble, felt again in his nostrils the stench of burning timbers, heard again the laboured breathing of the rescue workers as they toiled in their frantic and futile search to find any survivors.

He had waited with Joe Brannigan for four hours until finally Rosie and Isa were found huddled together and watched in silence as their lifeless forms were carried away. He recalled how he had felt completely numb and unable to show any real emotion and could remember nothing of the journey back to the farm.

Sam had not understood at first when Mrs Whyte had said that he would need to write to tell Fred because she had only met Rosie once. When she handed him some notepaper and an envelope he had looked at her in wonderment, till she said, "Get Neil to help you, Sam, he's good with words."

And together they had managed finally to put something down, but it had seemed pitifully inadequate.

UNKNOWN TO Sam, Fred had returned a third time to Levenford. Walking slowly after leaving the station, he paused on the pavement in Church Street and looked across to the dairy, and for a brief moment seemed to see her behind the counter. His heart gave a jolt and he made to cross the street when suddenly the image was gone. He continued on his way, turning left at the parish church and on out the Glasgow Road, past the offices of the shipyard.

Part of the tenement still stood, the windows gaping voids, the chimneys on the gable end pointing silent fingers to the sky. He went nearer to where the mouth of the close had been and could pick out the room where Rosie and he had found contentment in each other's arms.

"They never had a chance," a voice at his side said, and Fred turned to see an old bent, grey haired lady, leaning on a walking stick, seemingly looking into the past, re-living the night of the horror.

"You were Rosie's young man, I recognised you. I lived upstairs from Isa. I was away visiting my sister the night it happened, so I was one of the lucky ones. Or was I?" she added. "War's a terrible thing."

Fred could not find his voice and when the old lady took one of his hands in hers, he felt his eyes fill with tears.

"She didn't suffer, son, that's one thing you can be thankful for. She was a bonnie girl, always with a smile and a word to cheer you up. God rest her." And with that she was gone.

FRED RETURNED to the station but found he would have some time to wait for the next train to Glasgow. He wondered about going to see his mother, but felt he wanted to be alone in his grief. His footsteps took him along to the river and to the path leading round to the golf course. It was warm and sunny, and he lay down on the grassy bank and looked up to the cloudless sky. He felt light-headed and it seemed as if he was about to float up into the air. He closed his eyes and sat up before he opened them again, shading them with his hand as he looked into the shimmering heat of the summer afternoon.

"It was my punishment, Rosie, for killing the old man, for I suppose I did finish him off by pushing him down the stair. I didn't mean to do it – it was an accident. The old lady got me off the hook at the time, but you never really get away with that sort of thing. I thought I had managed to put it out of my mind when I came back to you again and we were so happy together. But I knew it was too good to be true. But why you, Rosie, why had you to be the one to go? Why wasn't it me? Why am I left to live on with my guilt?"

Fred suddenly realized he had been speaking his thoughts aloud and he looked about him anxiously to see if anyone was around to overhear him. But there wasn't a soul in sight, even the golf course was deserted. Fred rolled over and burying his face in the grass shouted, "Why? Why? Why?" at the same time beating his fists on the ground.

IT WAS DARK when the train finally reached its destination and Sam and his companions wearily tumbled out on to the platform to be immediately greeted by the raucous commands of NCOs urging them to get a move on and into trucks lined up on the road outside.

The kitting out; the meal of sausages and mash; the barking voice of the pint-sized Sergeant McAllister as he tried to form the men allocated to his squad into three lines before marching them off to their billet, brought the realisation to Sam that finally he was in the army.

He found that Ross Clark was in the same room with four other men and they were herded along the corridor on the ground floor of the barracks by the poker-faced Corporal Donaldson, who flung open the door and said, "Put your kit in and come with me to the store and draw a paliasse."

"A what?" queried a small dark weasel-faced lad called Hughie Brice, who spoke with a pronounced Glasgow accent.

"A mattress," Ross Clark answered.

"Straw's next door," the corporal announced once they had received their paliasse covers.

"Crikey, this is roughing it," Ross remarked to Sam as they tried to achieve a reasonably level surface without too many lumps.

They trooped back to their room with Hughie bringing up the rear and when he entered he said, "Where's the beds?"

"You kip on the floor," the enigmatic corporal replied. "Reveille at 7.30; breakfast 8 o'clock; on parade half past eight." And with that he was gone.

"Bloody hell!" Hughie exploded, "we've to sleep on the effing floor. I'm reporting sick first thing in the morning."

"Why, what's wrong with you?" inquired Martin Crammond, a tall balding man who had laid his paliasse down opposite to Sam's."

"I'll find something wrong with me. I'll say it's my back. My mate worked his ticket that way. I'm not staying in this bleeding set-up one moment longer than I can help."

"Good luck to you, friend," called Dougie Brown, who appeared to be the oldest occupant of the room, and turning to Eddie Christie who completed the half dozen muttered, "We've got a right one there."

They busied themselves with their blankets, the emptying of their kit-bags to examine the various items which they had drawn from the Quarter-Master's store, trying on their ill-fitting battle tunics.

"Made to measure," quipped Dougie Brown. "Aye, for a hulking great elephant. I'm for some shut-eye."

When Martin Crammond produced a pair of pyjamas, Hughie fell about laughing.

"Jesus," he roared, "what have we here? A real toff. Pyjamas! You'll get drummed out the regiment."

"Since you're so keen to get back to civvy street perhaps you should wear them," was Martin's apt reply, and finally silence fell in the room which as to be home for their first six weeks in the army.

~ 9 ~

AS the train carried Sam to Yorkshire at the end of his initial training, he thought back to his time at Fort George, to the memory of the day after their arrival, the long queue snaking out from the hut where the Medical Officer was giving them their first jag and Hughie in front of him suddenly lying prostrate at his feet. That had taken a bit of living down. At least in Yorkshire there wouldn't be the bagpipes to get you out of bed at reveille. Not that Sam had any real objection to the skirl of the pipes after the bugle call. It was the howling of the dogs which followed. There was no chance of snatching a few extra minutes under the blankets – you just had to get up. And when it was physical training on the ramparts with only a pair of shorts to protect you from the snell winds, it really had brought the best – or worst – out of Hughie.

"If it was brass monkeys running around up here they would need to have a squad of welders standing by. Look at me," he would moan as he dropped his shorts, "I'm having a sex change – what will the wife say?"

They had grown used to Hughie who had so far failed to work his ticket and Sam thought in a way he would miss his unconscious humour, for along with Ross Clark, Sam was one of the few members of their platoon who had been selected for training with an armoured regiment. Hughie was destined to be an infantryman.

Sam had struck up a friendship with Ross Clark, who in some ways reminded him of Neil Munro. He had been more prepared for army life than Ross and he had been able to help him on occasion when the going was tough.

Ross leaned across to Sam and said, "A penny for them."

Sam smiled, "I was thinking about the past six weeks."

"It seems a life time. Thank goodness we've said goodbye to these bloody rifles. If there was anything I hated, it was rifle drill, and I couldn't shoot for toffee."

"I wasn't so hot either."

"Modest man. Remember the carry on we had on Christmas Day with our gas masks on, all steamed up, not able to see a thing, and charging these

58

wretched dummies with our bayonets. What a carry on!"

Sam laughed. "Yeah, it was a bit of a lark at times, Hughie and all. Just as well we're not going to Glasgow or he'd be off the train and away."

"I wouldn't be surprised if he doesn't try to get himself lost when we change trains at Edinburgh. Hi, we're nearly there. Time to say goodbye to our dear Sergeant McAllister and Corporal Donaldson. I wonder what the next lot will be like."

"AT LEAST WE have a bed of sorts," Ross observed, when along with Sam he staggered into one of the huts at the camp near Barnard Castle and surveyed the rows of double bunks. "Let's bag an end one and we'll have neighbours on one side only; I'm all for a bit of privacy."

"Not much chance of that. Toss you for the bottom bunk."

So they began the second phase of their training, and soon grew accustomed to the idiosyncrasies of their new NCOs and their hut mates. They came to enjoy their free time better, looking forward to their weekend trips to the YMCA in Barnard Castle as a change from the NAAFI.

When leave came, Sam returned to Levenford, but missed Neil's company and although he did the odd job about the farm he did not show any real enthusiasm for his old life. He found he was quite glad to get back to camp which Ross found difficult to understand.

"It's like this, Ross," he explained, "I've never told you very much about myself, but you see I have no family, no real home. I was fostered with various folk, but I was a bit of a rebel and didn't stay very long at one place. To be truthful I was thrown out every time."

"But you're not a rebel now, Sam, are you? I know you're pretty tough, I mean physically so, but you conform, just like the rest of us."

"You've got to in the army or else you land in the glass house. OK when I was thirteen or so I went to live on a farm and met a boy of my own age – his father is a vet – we became friends and I suppose he knocked some sense into me – just as I taught him a thing or two."

"So what about the folk at the farm?"

"The old man died – I didn't like him. The old lady's all right, but she's not my mother. You know, it never used to bother me, but since I've got older I've had this longing to find out who my father and mother were."

"And can't you?"

"No. I've no idea how to go about it and when there's a war on I guess it's

59

impossible to find out anything."

"Sorry, Sam," Ross said quietly.

"No need to be. I'm OK."

"Maybe. Even though I missed my old friends when I was on leave, I did enjoy my home comforts including my mother's cooking and drinking tea that wasn't doctored to prevent you from getting randy."

"Do you think they really do that?"

"I'm sure they do."

"So, did you mange to work off your randiness when you were home?"

"No such luck. How about you?"

Sam laughed. "Not likely."

"Say Sam, do you not fancy one of the ATS girls in the cookhouse?"

"Wouldn't touch them with a barge pole. Most of them are a pretty rough lot. Anyway if you're right, unless you stop drinking the char, it won't bother you a lot."

"More's the pity. Seriously though Sam, do you not fancy having a bash at it?"

"At what?"

"Sex, you numbskull. After all you might get killed in this bloody racket – it can happen you know, when you're fighting a war. Do you want to die a virgin?"

"Who says I'm going to die? I've got too much lined up to do with my life to let the matter of a war interfere with my plans."

"Sam, that's ridiculous. How can anyone look forward to the future? How can you be sure of anything?"

"I can."

"Sam, you're crazy. Sometimes we'll be going to meet the Jerries face to face – unless you're going to opt out from the fighting."

"Why should I do that? I'm not a coward."

"I didn't say that you were, Sam, but you can't deny there's a terrific risk."

"Listen Ross, I bet if you asked the other lads in our hut you'd find they think as I do. At the moment we're simply playing at soldiers, none of us can imagine what it will be like for real and that's how it should be. If you don't feel you're going to survive this war, then, Ross, you might as well pack it in now."

Ross sat in silence for a while before he said, "You're an amazing fellow, Sam. I sometimes think you're having me on the way you talk about never doing anything at school, being a farm worker, not knowing anything about anything; in fact, you're a fraud, a bloody fraud. I don't believe half of what you've told me."

"Suit yourself, mate."

Ross was in full flow. "You make out you're the country yokel, but you're smarter than anyone else in our troop; you can pick up everything first time; you're the NCOs' blue-eyed boy."

"That I am not, and if you've finished, I'm going to get some fresh air."

When Ross caught up with Sam he said, "Sorry Sam, if I offended you, I didn't mean you to take it so personally."

"That's rich. Who else were you talking about then if it wasn't me?"

"Well, OK. I went a bit far, but it's because, Sam, I don't have your courage. One day, as I said, we'll be going into action, and frankly I'm not looking forward to that. It's me who's the coward."

"Rubbish. The trouble with you Ross, is you think about things too much. Take each day as it comes, and go out and get yourself a girl. You're the one who needs to lose his virginity. Not me. You see, Ross, I was born a bastard, and I've no intention of committing any product of my loins to the life I've had."

"You should have joined a monastery."

"Why? Some day I intend to get married and have a family – oh yes, I learned from the Munros what a family means, and I'm going to have one some day. You think I'm hard, well I suppose in a way I am, but when all the lads talk about their homes, their parents, their wives and sweethearts, brothers and sisters, get parcels and letters, don't you think that I might be a bit envious? The only person I correspond with is my pal Neil – and all I can write about is what I'm doing here."

"But Sam, you never seem to care, you always appear to ride above all that sort of thing. I don't know, I can't understand you."

"Look Ross, my upbringing has been different to yours, so my thinking's different, but I want to be just an ordinary lad with a home and family. Oh let's forget it. What started all this anyway?"

"I guess it was the main topic in the army – sex."

"You're right, but maybe that's what keeps us all sane, keeps us all going on, striving towards that goal – having a regular bit of nookie."

"You're quite a philosopher, Sam."

"Maybe, but in the meantime I'm going on drinking the char – you can please yourself."

THE TRAINING over, there was a scramble round the notice board to see to which units they had been posted.

"We're in luck again, Sam," Ross called, as he stood on tiptoe to scan the list for their names. "We're both going to the Westminster Dragoons. What a relief! I was certain we were going to be split up."

"Sorry about that, Ross, you're not getting rid of your philosophising pal yet."

"There's one thing, Sam, join the army and see the world."

"Well, see England, but I daresay we'll maybe go a bit further afield in due course."

"I wish I could look on it all like you with a calm detachment."

"Hi, you remind me of my pal Neil Munro with your big words."

"Look who's talking."

"I tell you what Ross, it's that girl you met on your last leave, she's got you on a string boy. You asked me to come and see you in Glasgow and what happened? You stood me up."

"I didn't Sam. We just had the one meeting instead of the several we had planned."

"Yeah, and I was left on my tod. You've got it bad, Ross."

"She's great, really great, and to think she's lived in the same street for years. OK. I've fallen for Stella, and I can't wait till my next leave."

- 10 -

FRED rolled in bed and opened his eyes and for a moment wondered where he was. The bedroom door opened and a dark haired girl entered carrying a tray.

"Surfaced at last have you? Know what time it is?"

"No, let me guess, Val. Eight o'clock."

"Half past eleven."

"Christ!" Fred leapt from the bed and looked around for his clothes.

"Where's my shirt and pants?"

"I washed them."

"You washed them!" Fred's voice rose to a scream. "You washed them! What the hell for? How am I going to get back to my unit?"

"Are you worried? You said last night you couldn't care less whether you ever saw your so and so regiment again. You're scared, Fred, dead scared you land in trouble."

"I'm not, it's just that I couldn't stand being locked up."

"Relax Fred. You won't be."

"But I will, I will."

"Get back into bed, you're getting all shrivelled up standing there in your birthday suit."

Fred tried to push past Val but she barred his way and then stood on his foot.

"You bitch!" he roared hopping about. "What are you playing at?"

"Fred, I'll put you out of your misery, it's tomorrow you go back, not today. You were so damn drunk last night that you didn't know what day it was."

"Are you sure?"

"Of course I'm sure. I looked at your pass. Go on, into bed, get some food down you and maybe you'll be some use to me. I might as well have been lying with a stone statue."

"Sorry."

"Sorry! I should say you should be, Fred. You spend your leave hanging around me, keeping me dangling, then when you've just a couple of days left you finally pluck up courage and ask if you can come home with me. Then what happens, you get pissed up to the eyeballs and you're useless, can't get it up. And who the hell is Rosie?"

"Rosie?"

"Yes, Rosie, that's all you could say when you were making feeble attempts to get your leg across. Come on, give."

"Can I have breakfast first?"

"Oh go on. The tea will be stone cold now." Val ungraciously thrust the tray at Fred who had climbed back into bed. He looked at her as he ate, seeing her for the first time in daylight, noticing the hard lines on her face, and then wondered how many soldiers she had entertained in the room.

He thought back to how he had met her on a previous leave in London, visiting a pub near the YMCA where he was staying, in the early evening before it was crowded with servicemen, many of them Americans. Val had been on her own behind the bar and had engaged him in conversation. He had been glad of someone to talk to, for he had long realized that his idea of having a rip roaring time in London on his own just didn't work out. Fred was still mourning for Rosie and had of late grown to prefer his own company. He had not, however, been allowed to become a loner, for surprisingly enough he was popular with his fellow soldiers who knew him to be straight as a die and always ready to lend a helping hand. Despite his faults, Fred had never been afraid of hard work and had become a competent soldier. He had, however, refused promotion, being reluctant to take on any form of responsibility. His mates knew about Rosie and had tended to make a point of always including him in any off-duty activities. Fred, however, had no inclination to return to Levenford again but spending his leave in London had not helped to relieve his depression until he had met Val. Strangely enough he had not told her about Rosie, despite spending every evening in the pub sitting at the corner of the bar chatting to her whenever she had some free moments and on occasion sharing supper with her in the back room. He had decided when he was due again for leave to return to London and seek out Val. Bringing his thoughts back to the present, he looked up again.

"Rosie was my girl at home; we were getting married, but she was killed in an air-raid. I can't get over it." Fred's voice sank to a whisper.

"Oh Fred, why didn't you tell me before, you poor lad? I knew from the first time I saw you, there was something bothering you. I could tell by your eyes, they had such a sad look. I'm sorry I was sharp with you."

"It's all right, I deserved it, you must have thought me a right waste of time, but to tell you the truth, I've never managed it with any girl since Rosie. I wanted to, but I could never get her out of my mind. I'm sure they all thought there was something wrong with me."

"You must have loved her very much."

"I did."

"I know how you feel. You see, I've never told you much about myself, maybe we've got a bit in common there."

"Go on."

"My man didn't come back from Dunkirk – he's a prisoner of war. It's hard waiting for him, very hard. We weren't married for very long before he went away and I guess it was the same between him and me as it was with Rosie and you."

"He'll come back, you wait and see."

"I hope so, but it's not easy. It's lonely without him. Oh, I know in the pub there's always a stir and I've plenty of offers, but you're the first fellow I've ever allowed into my home, you've got to believe that."

"I do, Val, I do, and I've been a dead loss in giving you some comfort, but if you're willing, I think it's time I did just that. Come on, my lovely, let's just forget for a while."

FRED RETURNED to his unit in a happier frame of mind, but he realised that while the last hours of his leave shared with Val had been enjoyable he had no feelings of real love for her. It had helped being able for the first time to unburden himself about Rosie and about what had happened to old man Whyte. Val had been understanding and comforting, but the guilt which lay at the back of his mind could not be erased. The stepping up of training activities and exercises, then the moving of the unit to the south coast, all signaled that something big was on the way. And Fred was glad. He wanted to go back into real action again, seemingly having no fear of whatever the outcome might be.

IN MARCH 1944 Sam and Ross had also joined the thousands of servicemen who had moved to the south of England after being stationed at Thorpeness in Suffolk since the New Year.

Sam stood in the upstairs bedroom of the house in Bournemouth where they were billeted.

"I wonder," he said to Ross, "whose house this was, and where the people are now who used to live in it. It's funny what war can do. I would never have imagined that one day I would be sleeping in a semi-detached in a residential district in an English south coast resort."

"If you had, I bet you wouldn't have chosen to share this place with me and Kent and Ernie."

Sam laughed. "Maybe not. Never mind, if you like you can always bring Stella here for your honeymoon, once this lot's all over."

Ross crossed to look out of the window before he said, "That seems a long way off."

"Come on, cheer up, let's go out tonight and see what this place is like. I don't suppose we'll be allowed on any of the beaches to have a swim in the sea."

"You'll need a pair of wire cutters and one of our flail tanks to blow up the mines if you want to do that."

"Guess you're right."

SAM AND Ross found Bournemouth interesting but expensive. Their days were spent working on their tanks parked in the street beside their billets, their evenings found them visiting the numerous cinemas in the seaside town. They were intrigued when they boarded their LCT and set off on their first big scheme, sailing to within six miles of France. For both it was a new experience and while Ross soon found his sea legs, Sam, to his dismay, discovered that the rolling motion of the boat made him feel distinctly queasy. He was not alone, however, and the offer of a large plate of bacon and eggs after a night spent lying awake on his bunk feeling like death warmed up did not appeal to Sam or his fellow sufferers.

"It's simply to get you used to crossing the Channel," Sam's tank commander, Corporal Mike Burden explained. "You'll be OK after a while."

"How long are we going to be on this wretched boat?"

"Three days."

"Three days! Crikey, I won't survive that long."

"You will, Sam, come on up and get some fresh air, that'll put you on your feet again."

"More likely on my back, Corp …"

But Sam gradually managed to come to terms with the ship's movements and began to enjoy the variation in their training. When the time came to make a landing on a beach on the English coast, he was his old resolute self again.

Later when they returned to their billet, the four crew members, Sam the gunner, Ross the wireless operator, Ernie the driver, and Kent the co-driver discussed the whole operation.

"What amazes me," Ross began, "was how we were able to sail across the Channel almost to France and not be disturbed once by Jerry."

"Yeah," Ernie went on, "makes you wonder just what the hell he's playing at."

"If it's like that when we do go over it'll be a piece of cake. What do you say, Sam?"

"Maybe, but if my bloody machine gun jams like it did, when it's the real thing, we'll be up the creek."

"What do you reckon to Mike as a tank commander?" Ross looked at the others who seemed non-committal.

Then Ernie said, "One thing, being on the Corporal's tank, we're the junior crew, so we don't spearhead any attack."

"Not unless the others are knocked out or bogged down," Sam put in. "For a Cockney Mike's not bad, but he's not brilliant."

"The trouble with you Scots bastards is that you're so modest," Kent made a playful swipe at Sam's head. "Now, if we had a Yorkshire lad in charge, we'd be all the way."

The friendly banter continued for a time until it was time for bed, but before he fell asleep, Sam felt a sense of belonging. They had come together from very different stations in life to form a tank crew. They had learned to work with each other, they were beginning to work for each other, and they were mates. Sam recalled what he had said about Mike Burden and smiled. Mike was all right, and he was always ready to muck in with the rest of them. He'd likely be as good as anyone when the real action started was Sam's last thought before he fell asleep.

WHEN THE second scheme, similar to the first, was undertaken, Sam and his mates felt that, as a crew, they had performed better, having experienced no major hitches and planned a little celebration when they returned to Bournemouth.

They were surprised, however, when instead they headed for a new destination, Camp B4, where they were billeted under canvas.

"I wonder where we are," Ross mused as Sam and he strolled round the camp which they discovered was an American one. The tents, being of American design, were very comfortable. The cookhouse was staffed by Yanks, who they decided, after their first meal, knew how to serve up some first class grub.

"According to Mike, we're about fifteen miles along the coast from Southampton."

"Just about as far away from home as we could be without actually leaving England."

"You're right, Ross."

"I wonder if we'll get another leave before we go overseas, because that's where we're going."

"We won't. When we were mobilized in March for overseas service all leave stopped. You know that, Ross."

"Even so, I keep hoping. It's OK for you, Sam, you don't have a girlfriend back home, but I have Stella."

"You'll just have to dream about her then, my friend, because here we're cut off from civvy street – we've had it."

"You're so bloody matter of fact about everything, Sam, so damned definite. Couldn't you give me a glimmer of hope that I'll see Stella again before we go into action?"

FOR THE middle of April the weather was exceedingly fine and life under canvas was ideal. Work on the tanks continued with occasional visits to the camp cinema in the evenings. The presence of the Americans in the camp was an added interest and the boys found themselves imitating their drawl and using some of their expressions.

They were quite disappointed when, early in May, they moved to Camp B9 which they did not find as attractive either in type or situation.

"Beggars can't be choosers," quipped Kent, "but at least the weather's still glorious. You know, it's hard to believe that we're getting ready for the big push."

But bit by bit they were being equipped for what they now knew was to be the Second Front; their spirits were high and there was laughter aplenty as they continued their preparations. None of them realised just how near their initiation into battle was, although they had given up all hope of seeing home again before they went across the Channel.

Suddenly on Friday 19th May it was announced they could have a 24 hour pass.

"A lot of bloody good that is!" Ross stormed. "How can I get home to Glasgow and back in that time. We Scots are being discriminated against. What do you say, Sam?"

Sam shrugged his shoulders. "I suppose you're right, Ross, but I'm not bothered."

"Oh, it's alright for you, you don't have a girl at home, you don't have anyone, I do!"

Sam looked at his friend and said nothing.

Kent who had heard the outburst from Ross said, "What about you two coming home to York with me? I reckon we can make it there all right and have a bit of time to enjoy ourselves. What do you say?"

"Thanks, Kent, but it's Glasgow or nothing for me."

"Sam?"

"I'd like to, Kent, if your folks won't mind, but I'd prefer if you came too, Ross."

"No, I'd only be miserable."

"And what are you going to be here on your own?"

"Oh there'll be others left behind. I'll be all right."

"No you won't, all our mates will be away, come on, Ross, it'll do you good and you can always phone your girl from York."

"Yes, Ross, come with us," urged Sam, "you'll be in the depths if you stay here."

Ross remained silent, then he said, "OK, I'll come. Thanks Kent."

"On one condition though, Ross, you've to enjoy yourself, no wet blankets allowed on this trip."

THE JOURNEY to and from York was uncomfortable and tedious but the three young lads enjoyed themselves to the full in the relatively short time in between.

As they travelled south again Sam said, "It's been like a dream, I can hardly believe it happened, but it was great, thanks to you, Kent. What do you say Ross? Glad you came?"

"Yeah, of course, and managing to speak to Stella, even if it was only on the phone made it worthwhile. You didn't let on you had so many girlfriends, Kent."

"Safety in numbers, mate."

"And you were doing all right, Sam, with that blonde. I didn't think you had it in you."

"What do you mean by that? Just because you're the great Romeo from Glasgow you think no one else can attract the female sex."

Kent laughed as Sam and Ross continued their derogatory exchanges, till he finally said, "Let's get some shut-eye, I'm shagged out."

"I'm not surprised, the time you took to say goodbye to your dark-eyed beauty."

"Well, I might not be seeing her for a while. I had to give her something to remember me by."

- 11 -

BY the end of May it seemed that it was simply the time for waiting. Preparations appeared to be almost complete and with the camp now sealed, enclosed by barbed wire, sentries patrolling its entire perimeter, permission to enter or leave only by signed permit, everyone knew that the big day could not be far off. Yet there was no real tension among the soldiers who were able to relax in the continuing fine weather and even manage some bathing in the Solent. This Sam in particular enjoyed.

"You should have volunteered for the Commandos," Kent told him, after watching Sam's display of powerful swimming. "You're so fit and so dashed good at every physical sport."

"And hopeless at sport in the bed," quipped Ross. "But I'm glad you didn't Sam, we'd have missed you if you had gone when they asked for volunteers."

"Did you really consider it, Sam?"

"No, my motto is never to volunteer for anything. Besides, I reckon we'll have a tough enough job in our set-up and at least we have a couple of inches of armour between us and the enemy."

"Yeah. A couple of inches, it's not much."

ON THE first day of June they received their initial briefing and studied aerial photographs of the part of the French coast where they were to land. It seemed so easy working it out in their tent and all around there was an air of suppressed excitement, with everyone raring to go, brimful of confidence.

"You know," Ross remarked, "the briefing we've had this morning and again this afternoon, it's like the last lesson the teacher gives before you sit an exam and then you do just what we're about to do – go and have a game of football to try and forget what's going to happen tomorrow."

"And tomorrow," Mike broke in as they made their way to where the inter-troop game was to be played, "we are moving the tanks to the marshalling area."

"So we've had it," Ross said quietly.

"I guess so."

LATER AS they made up their beds for what they knew would be the last time in the camp, Ross remarked, "Do you realise that not one of our tank crew has ever been in action before. In fact, have any of our troop been at the receiving end of real bullets?"

"Some of the officers and NCOs have when they were in North Africa."

"Not many, though. Most of them are as green as we are. But maybe a lot of the Jerries will be in the same boat."

"Look Ross," Sam put in, "just make up your mind that everything's going to be all right and it will be. Come on, let's go for a stroll around the camp and see if there's anything going on."

ON SATURDAY 3rd June, Sam and Ross stood and watched their tank being driven on to the LCT, then slowly followed it.

"I guess that's the last time we'll be on British soil for a while, what do you think, Sam?"

"Yeah, it's goodbye to dear old Blighty for the present. Pity the weather's broken. The sea looks quite rough; it'll be pretty choppy out in the Channel."

The weather had not improved when they set sail at eight o'clock on the following morning, but when conditions worsened all the ships returned to harbour. And, as there was nothing else to do, Sam, Ross and Kent stretched out on the back of their tank and slept for most of the day. The ship was packed with tanks and infantrymen and there was little space to move about.

On Sunday morning 5th June, they set sail again and this time there was no turning back even although the sea was even rougher than on the previous day. Sam suffered a recurrence of the sea sickness which he had experienced on his very first exercise, but he was persuaded by Kent to take some tablets which had been issued.

"I know, Sam, you say you've never taken a pill in your life before, but come on, try a couple of these. They'll maybe sort you out."

And much to Sam's relief they eventually did, but they all experienced a very uncomfortable crossing. The waves were continually breaking over the side of the ship and swamping them. During the night one or two of the smaller craft had to be abandoned and some of the men from these boats were picked up by their LCT.

"This is getting a bit serious," Ross whispered to Sam, as they watched the survivors trying to dry out.

"Yeah, it is. You know, I'll be glad when we get to wherever we're going.

Life on the ocean wave is not really my idea of fun."

"It'll literally be out of the frying pan into the fire."

"That's exactly what my friend Neil would have said. I wonder if he's got caught up in this lot. Maybe though, since he's training to be an officer he won't be ready yet for action."

Ross snorted. "We swaddies are just canon fodder."

"You can't say that, we've got officers with us and they'll be right in the thick of it – at least they should be."

"I know, what I meant is that they can train us quicker than officers."

"Stands to reason, Ross, they've to lead and make decisions."

"And we bloody well follow and get blown up if they make the wrong ones."

"Oh, come off it. That attitude won't get you anywhere."

"Sam, I wish I was as brave as you."

"Rubbish! I just don't think too much about it. Be on the alert, Ross, and we'll be OK."

AT FOUR O'CLOCK on the morning of 6th June, Sam and the rest of his crew started preparing the final details for the landing. After stowing all their personal kit they undid the chains which had held the tanks to the side of the ship, before Ernie started up the tank engine. Sam climbed up and then down into the turret and had a final look over his guns, making sure they were properly loaded, checking the ammunition, firing gear and traversing system. He polished his periscope as he had never polished it before. When he was satisfied everything was in order, he climbed out and sat on top of the turret.

What a sight met his eyes!

The outline of the Normandy coast was just coming into view and it presented a rather uninviting picture in the grey of the morning, but after having had the experience of the 'Ancient Mariner', Sam was glad to see land.

Around were ships of every size and description. The sky was ablaze and resembled the coloured robe Joseph wore. The noise was deafening, but Sam reckoned the British forces were making the most of it and he felt an unusual thrill at the magnificent sight of the armada sailing on, nearer and nearer to the coast.

Sam watched the small boats carrying the infantrymen being launched from the LSTs before it was time to climb down into the turret as his LCT bearing the Flotilla Commander sailed on, the tip of the arrow-head formation. He gulped down the tot of rum which Mike handed to him, then made himself comfortable on his seat, rested his foot near the firing buttons, placed one hand on the elevating wheel, the other on the traversing wheel, and glued his eyes to the periscope. He was ready!

Then he relaxed for a moment looking across to Ross and Mike, but they were giving nothing away, so he called Kent on the intercom and asked if he and Ernie were OK. Kent replied that they were and then Sam realised that they were there!

The ramp of the LCT was down and the first tank lumbered forward across it and disappeared completely into the water. For a moment consternation, but then relief as the crew managed to scramble back on board. The ramp was hurriedly raised and the captain prepared to manoeuvre for another position.

Suddenly the boat rocked as shells tore through the engine room and Sam was thrown against the side of the turret.

"Christ!" Mike yelled. "What the hell!! Is everyone all right? Ernie? Kent? We're OK in the turret."

When Ernie and Kent responded in the affirmative, Mike said, "We're starting to drift and we're going to be a sitting target. Bloody hell!"

They all held on to anything they could as the boat was hit again and then again.

"All we can do is sit tight and hope," Mike went on.

After a while Sam risked a look out of the turret but hurriedly withdrew when a sniper's bullet whined dangerously close.

"There's a number of lads who have had it and some wounded," he announced. "Can we do anything, Mike?"

"No, too risky at the moment."

Gradually they seemed to drift out of range of the guns and they could see the landing had been successful and men were pouring inland. There appeared still to be fierce resistance at the part of the beach where they should have landed but they realised that they were powerless to do anything to change the situation.

A tenseness grew amongst them as the LCT moved slowly towards dry land and then suddenly stuck on a row of wooden stakes on top of which were tied what looked like two beer bottles.

"These are certainly not beer bottles," Ross announced after the boat had been rocked violently several times. "They are explosives and we're setting them off."

"At least we're practically on the beach," Sam countered, "we should surely be able to get off soon."

"But we're awash now and taking on water all the time."

"Come on, Mike," Sam suggested, "let's get out and see what's what."

Mike and Sam climbed hurriedly out of the turret and were relieved to see all the wounded had been attended to, and at that moment someone was able to lower the ramp. Mike and Sam leapt back on to their tank till Ernie had it on the beach, then jumped down on to French soil and looked round at the LCT.

"My God! Look at that boat, Sam, it's full of holes; how on earth did it stay afloat?"

"But it did, Mike, maybe it's a good omen."

"I hope so, Sam."

They turned and looked ahead of them. "God, what a carnage, these poor lads. Come on, Sam, we'll have to move some so we can get the tank through. We can't go over them."

Sam stood motionless. It was the first time he had experienced violent death. In his mind he suddenly saw Dugald Whyte lying at the foot of the stair in the bothy. He hadn't looked dead, only asleep, but as he was able to focus again on the scene which he now beheld, Sam had to take a grip on himself as he saw the terrible wounds which had been inflicted on the infantrymen as, storming up the beaches, they had been cut down by the enemy fire.

Without being aware of what he was really doing, he helped Mike to move several bodies out of the path of their tank.

"Maybe just one more, Sam," Mike said as he bent down to another inert body.

"Christ!" he suddenly yelled, "he's still alive, but how I don't know. He's holding in his guts. Sam, what the hell, what are we going to do with him?"

Sam knelt down beside the stricken soldier and then recoiled. "My God, it's Fred!"

"Fred? What are you talking about?"

"He's Fred Whyte, I worked with him, lived with his folk. Dear God, will he ..." he stopped as Fred opened his eyes and stared up at Sam.

"Fred, it's me, Sam. Sam Cairns. Remember. At Millside."

"Sam – hello Sam." Fred's eyes closed again, then he spoke slowly and with great effort.

"Sam – finish me off. I'm done for. Put me out of this pain – tell Ma – I –" His voice faded again.

Sam looked across at Mike kneeling on the other side of Fred. "What are we going to do? Does he have a chance?"

Mike shook his head slowly. "How he's still alive beats me, and able to talk. I can't bring myself to look below his waist again."

"Fred," Sam spoke close to his ear. "Fred, can you hold on till we get help? You're badly hurt, but you'll pull through, don't give up."

"Listen Sam, we've got to get the tank off this beach before the tide comes in, there's nothing we can do for him."

"But we can't just leave him to die in agony."

Fred's eyes opened and the request was repeated in a whisper. "Please, Sam, finish me off, use your revolver, I want to go."

Sam looked around desperately, "Look Mike there's an officer over there. Ask him."

Mike and Sam stood up as the officer approached.

"What's the trouble, Corporal?"

"Sir, we were moving the bodies so we wouldn't go over them with our tank and we discovered this lad was still alive."

The Lieutenant knelt beside Fred. "Just. Look, you'd best get moving with your tank or else you'll be like me, and not have one. I'll attend to this chap."

"Very good, sir, but –" Mike hesitated for a moment.

"Yes Corporal?"

"It's just that Cairns here knows him. Worked with him."

"Oh, I see. Well, Cairns, I'll look after your friend, now get a move on."

THREE TIMES the tank was bogged down before finally they reached firmer ground and they were ready to move forward.

As they prepared to climb into the turret Sam turned to Mike and said, "Could I go back and see how Fred is; it wouldn't take more than a couple of minutes? We're only about thirty yards from where he was lying."

Mike hesitated for a moment. "Come on then, before the tide takes him if he's still there, and we'll have to watch how we go, there are mines everywhere. Keep behind me."

Mike went ahead with Sam following, then he turned and said, "Wait here, the officer's gone. I'll see if your friend's still there."

Sam started to protest. "It's an order, Sam, don't come any further unless I say so."

He watched as Mike in a crouching run reached the line of bodies, saw him hesitate for a moment, then turn and joining Sam again, took his arm and said, "Back to the tank."

When they were aboard, Mike said over the intercom, "Get moving, Ernie," and they all had to be on the alert until they finally reached their harbour for the night. They found theirs was the only tank out of their troop of five to have made it, and being the junior crew, they had a feeling of satisfaction.

"Maybe we didn't manage to do a proper job on the beach, but we've lived to fight another day," was how Kent summed it up. "By the way, Mike, what took you and Sam back to the beach?"

"Oh, we had to report to an officer that we were clear and able to go forward." Mike looked at Sam as he spoke and gave a slight shake of his head before going on, "Now, Ernie, you get a meal going, Ross and Kent start digging a slit trench; Sam, you come with me to see what the orders are for tomorrow."

When they were out of earshot of the others, Mike said, "Your friend's gone, Sam, there was nothing anyone could have done for him."

"Did that officer do anything?"

Mike hesitated. "He didn't let him suffer any longer, Sam. He must have been going through hell."

"The inhuman bastard, put down like a dog. He could at least have tried to get an MO to him."

"Were you close, that fellow and you?"

"No, but Fred was all right in some ways, he didn't deserve to die like that."

"I think, Sam, he did it himself."

"Did it himself?"

"That officer chap put his revolver in Fred's hand and he pulled the trigger himself."

"How do you know? You're making it up."

"No, I watched while you were digging out the tank when we got bogged down the second time. I saw what he was doing."

"Fred wouldn't have had the strength."

"You'd be surprised, Sam. One last great effort, and then curtains."

"Poor Fred."

"Best forget it, Sam. You go back and give them a hand, I'll report to the OC."

SOME TIME round midnight Sam stretched out in the slit trench and looked up to the sky lit by tracers. He tried to think that he was in France, but his thoughts kept returning to Fred, then to Millside and Ma Whyte. Fred had been her favourite, and now he was gone. He remembered the day Fred had told him he was going to marry Rosie. Maybe, he said almost half aloud, as he stared up into the sky again, maybe they're together once more. Then, mercifully, out of sheer tiredness, Sam fell asleep.

- 12 -

THE following morning saw Mike and his crew move on to Brecy, having some exciting moments on the way. The deafening noise of gunfire which seemed to go on without a lull brought to them the realisation that they had well and truly joined battle. They remained in the harbour at Brecy during which time Sam was able to procure milk and eggs from a nearby farm, finding he was able to converse in French sufficiently well to be understood.

Kent, who had accompanied him said, "Sam, did you really leave school when you were fourteen and work on a farm, or are you having us on?"

"Yes and no."

"How come the French patter then?"

"I don't know, I was interested in it somehow and taught myself after I left school, but my friends, the Munros, helped. I always wanted to come to Europe."

Kent laughed. "This is one way of doing that, but not the way I'd have chosen."

FOR A FEW days the conflict raged some miles ahead of them and as they wandered about in the vicinity of their harbour, they found time to explore a chateau, skirting round fields scattered with the hugely bloated bodies of dead cows.

Then they were called upon to move out to support an infantry platoon as they took a small village, and had to maintain their position till well after dark. Sam was called upon by Mike to fire a few rounds at something that suddenly moved ahead of them.

"What was it?" Kent asked over the intercom when Sam had stopped firing.

"You better ask Mike."

"OK. It was only a bloody cow, but you can't take any chances."

"Crikey, that'll be another one lying on its back with its legs in the air."

This pattern of moving out of a harbour in short forays to stand sentry was repeated several times, and while the weather remained fine the crew felt they were having a relatively easy time.

SOME WEEKS later Mike returned from a briefing meeting with the news that the crew, with the exception of himself, was being transferred to the 3rd Royal Tank Regiment.

"Our role as an assault force with our flail tanks is over, so you're moving on to a fighting regiment."

"A fighting regiment?" queried Ross. "We maybe haven't been very warlike so far, but I never thought we were non-combatants."

"It's the difference in the role. Anyhow the four of you are going to replace some casualties after the attack on Caen."

"What about you, Mike?" Sam asked.

"I'm to remain here in the meantime, maybe I'll join up with you later."

"Will we be staying together?" Ross asked.

"I don't know, you'll find out when you get there, I mean to your new mob. Best get packed up, you've to be ready in an hour."

Ross was very disappointed, when they arrived to join their new regiment, that while Ernie, Kent and Sam were all joining Sergeant Guy Buxton's crew, he was allocated to Corporal Frank Medway's tank.

"Why can't we be kept together?" he asked.

"Simple, I suppose," Kent answered, "Sergeant Buxton still has his wireless operator and wants to keep him."

"Never mind, Ross, we're still in the same troop, so we'll see a lot of each other."

"I doubt it, and it won't be the same. I always thought we'd see this thing through together, Sam."

"So we shall, Ross, don't be downhearted."

THEY WERE soon moving forward in the sweep through France, into Belgium, and then Holland, where hostilities came to a halt temporarily when neither side was able to move because of the state of the ground.

Sam and Kent had managed to purloin their officer's binoculars and took it in turn to observe the Germans from the lee of the farmhouse wall where they had been stationed for two weeks. They had nicknamed their billet 'The House of Fear', since only a hundred yards separated the opposing armies, and night raids had come to be an accepted fact of life. Trip wire flares had so far prevented either side from making any real inroad in the other's defences, but it meant that neither could drop its guard.

"Blow this for a lark, Sam, I'll be glad when the weather hardens up sufficiently to allow us to get out of this hellhole."

"You're right. I don't like this static warfare, it gives you too much time to think."

"And what are you thinking about, Sam?"

Sam smiled. "Funnily enough, I was remembering our trip to York."

"Yeah, that is worth remembering – the last time I had my ashes drawn."

"You had your what?"

"Caught you out there, Sam – in other words, the last time I had a woman."

"Hmm, so you did have it off with your dark-eyed beauty as Ross suggested. What was her name again, Marlene?"

Kent grinned. "Well, Marlene was the dark-eyed beauty, but I'm afraid I pulled a fast one on Ross and you. Sure, Marlene and I have been going together for a while, but I've never had it off with her."

Sam looked puzzled. "But you went off with her from the pub and we didn't see you for a couple of hours."

"That's right. I saw Marlene home, which didn't take more than fifteen minutes. I made the excuse that I had to get back to you and Ross."

"So?"

"It's a long story, Sam."

"Well, it so happens I haven't a date tonight, so I've plenty of time to listen."

Kent grinned again. "OK. I worked in a factory in York alongside quite a number of females – we made chocolate mainly – and I daresay I was quite popular with them, being a good looking lad."

"Modest as ever, but go on."

"When the time came for me to leave to join up, the girls threw a bit of a party for me – well, it was the usual thing when one of the lads was called up and I was one of the last, I reckon. Anyway, after it, I walked one of the girls home – I'll come clean, she must be thirty if she's a day, but a good-looker, a widow, Dolly by name. When we got to her place she invited me in for a farewell drink, as she put it, and then when I said I'd better be off she asked if I was going to give her something to remember me by. So I thought, well, here goes and landed her a nice juicy kiss on her cheek. You know what she said?"

"No, go on, it promises to be an interesting reply, I take it."

"Sarcastic bastard, you are Sam."

Kent relived the scene.

"Is that the best you can do, Kent? And I always thought you were a real Romeo. Come on, try again, on the lips this time."

Kent laughed. "If that's how you want it, Dolly, OK."

"That's better," Dolly said, when Kent finally released her, "but come on lad, you've to prove yourself a man before you go off to fight for your country."

"What do you mean?"

"This," and Dolly proceeded to unbutton the flies of his trousers. Kent gave a gasp. "Come on, have you lost the power of your hands? It's best without clothes."

"You mean …" Kent stopped.

"I mean I'm going to make a man of you tonight," Dolly went on, as she drew Kent's shirt over his head and then made him step out of his trousers.

"Now let's see how expert you are at undressing me. Come on, don't be shy."

When she was as naked as Kent, Dolly said "It's your first time, isn't it?"

Kent was able to whisper hoarsely, "Yes."

"Well, you're ready for it all right," Dolly went on, "and you've certainly got the equipment, now's your chance to put it to proper use."

"I'll never forget that first time," Kent said to Sam. "It was all so unexpected, that's what made it so terrific, I suppose."

"She practically raped you, then."

"Maybe, but I didn't object. The first time I went home on leave I wondered whether I should go and see Dolly. Maybe, I thought, it was just a one off. Maybe she had, as she put it, set out to make a man of all the young lads in the factory who had been called up. And then I was going with Marlene, so I left it for a couple of days, by which time I was feeling pretty randy. But, I thought, she can only turn me away."

"And obviously she didn't."

Kent stretched himself. "No, she didn't. She said, 'You've taken your time to come for another lesson'. And every leave I've had it off with Dolly."

"Lucky you, Kent, but how is it all going to work out?"

"I haven't thought of that. I feel Marlene is the girl I'll end up being married to, but I'm not rushing into anything."

"You wouldn't think of marrying Dolly?"

"Crikey, no, and she would never herself think of that. She told me she always had a crush on me and often wondered what I would be like in bed."

"And has she given you a pass mark?"

"I reckon so, and by the way she knows about Marlene."

"Does she entertain any of the other lads from the factory?"

"Not that I am aware of. In fact, I'm certain she doesn't. So, come on, Sam, what's your story of how you lost your virginity?"

"I haven't."

"You haven't! I don't believe you."

Sam laughed. "No, Kent, honest, I haven't."

"Haven't you wanted to?"

"Of course I have."

"What about the girl you saw home when you were up at my place?"

"What about her?"

"Didn't you try anything there?"

"No, not really, I just don't seem to be cut out for casual sex. I'm not very good with girls and as I told Ross once, being born a bastard makes me wary of fathering one."

"Sam, you're quite some fellow," Kent said after thinking over Sam's last remark for a few minutes, "but I reckon you're one of the finest I've known."

"Whatever you're after, Kent, with your flattery, you're not getting it. Come on, let's get back inside and see if there's any buckshee grub on the go."

During this period of static warfare all the A Squadron tanks and crews had come together to share not only the shelter of the farm buildings which were still intact but also the duties such as guard watch and night patrol. This meant that Ross had been able to see Sam and Kent on a daily basis.

They moved cautiously back into the farmhouse where they met Ross.

"Hi Ross, how goes it?"

"Fine."

"Fancy a game of cards tonight to pass the time?"

"I would, but I have a prior engagement – I'm on bloody guard."

"Crikey, it doesn't half come round quick – if you're on tonight, it'll be our turn tomorrow. What do you think Sam?"

"I suppose so. Well let's hope it's a quiet night for you Ross."

"It'll be cold, bloody cold, you can bet on that."

"It'll give you plenty of time to think of Stella."

"Yeah, sure Kent, but thinking doesn't bring her any nearer."

"Ah, you never know, this war can't last forever."

"With the progress we're making in this damn place, it's going to go on for a long time yet."

Kent and Sam made their way back to their dug-out beside their tank.

"Poor Ross, he doesn't half miss his Stella."

"Yeah, he's certainly stuck on her."

"Think he's had her in bed yet?"

"Kent, you have sex on the brain just now."

"It's this place, I keep telling you, there's nothing else to think about. But go on, what do you reckon?"

"About Ross and Stella, I don't know, I doubt it, and anyway it's none of our business."

"You're right, I guess where they're concerned it really is love. With me, it's only trying to satisfy my sexual appetite."

- 13 -

S AM woke early, stiff with cold and decided it would be warmer to be up and about. As he pulled on his boots, Kent stirred and asked sleepily, "What time is it?"

"Half past six."

"Gosh, it's still the middle of the night. What's the panic?"

"I'm frozen to the marrow, I'm going over to see if there's any tea going at the cookhouse – the night patrol will just be coming off."

"OK. Bring me back some."

"Will do."

Sam walked through the early morning haze and was about to enter the cookhouse when he heard his name called. He turned and saw Sergeant Guy Buxton approaching.

"Sam, I'm glad you're up. Come into the barn. I've some bad news for you."

"Bad news? What's happened? Am I being posted somewhere?"

"No, nothing like that. During the night the patrol ran into a bit of bother and your mate Ross copped it."

"Ross! You don't mean he's ..." Sam's voice trailed off in disbelief.

"No, it's not as bad as that. As far as I could gather, Ross, who was on guard duty, heard a noise and went forward to investigate. One of the Jerries trod on a mine apparently. He was blown to pieces and unfortunately Ross was close enough to collect quite a bit of the shrapnel."

"Is he badly hurt?"

"According to the MO his right leg is in a pretty bad way and he's peppered with shrapnel in various places, but not too serious. He was damned lucky. Another few yards and he would have been a goner."

"Where is he now?"

"Oh, he's been whipped off in the blood wagon to the nearest field hospital, but I guess he's got a Blighty one."

"You mean he'll be shipped back home?"

"Yeah, if he survives."

"If he survives! What do you mean? Is his life in danger then?"

"He lost a lot of blood, Sam, and it was fortunate really we got to him so quickly and that the Jerries decided they'd had enough for the night and withdrew. It's a wonder you didn't hear the mine going off even although it was only a small one - a killer all the same."

"I did waken at one point, but you get used to noises in the night, so I guess I must have dropped off again when nothing seemed to be happening."

"No matter, but why Ross had gone so far forward, I don't know. The infantrymen were so shaken up that none of them could say exactly what had happened. I never thought Ross was the type to seek a bit of glory."

"He wasn't, but he had guts, despite his talk of always being shit-scared and if he thought anyone was in trouble he would have gone to help without considering the consequences."

"Look Sam, don't get me wrong, I didn't mean to criticise Ross. I like him, he's a good lad, but our fellows on guard duty stay to our own perimeter. Where we found Ross he was way out from it and where he knew there could be hidden mines."

"Do you think he'll be OK? Is there any way of finding out?"

"Our MO is a super chap, I'll have a word with him."

When Sam returned to the bivouac and handed Kent his mug of tea, the latter said, "That took you long enough. Did you have to make it yourself?"

Sam looked hard at Kent. "It's got a lot of rum in it and you'll need it for I've got something to tell you."

"What goes, Sam? Who's the kind fairy who supplies the rum?"

"Guy. Now listen."

Kent shook his head in disbelief when Sam had finished. "Ross of all people. Do you really think he'll be all right?"

"I hope so. I know we've lost other lads before, but Ross – well – he was something special. We've been together right from the start."

"Sod this fucking war!" Kent spat out the words.

"Yeah. My feelings exactly. But at least there's always hope for Ross."

"There better be. Just one thing Sam. Don't you go catching a packet or I'll never forgive you."

"Likewise you, friend."

IT WASN'T until the regiment had returned to Poperinge to be fitted out with new tanks for the assault into Germany over the Rhine, that Sam received a letter from Ross. He sought out Kent and said, "Let's find a quiet spot and read what he says."

Dear Sam and Kent

I always wanted to get back home but I didn't ever think I'd do it this way. Sad to say my army days are over, sad in that I'm away from two of the best friends I've ever had. Despite my pessimism I did think we'd see it through to the end together, but it was not to be.

I really don't remember much of what happened that night – maybe just as well. Probably my own fault for being so nosey. Still I'm a lot better now, but will be here in hospital for some time yet. Stella's been down to see me, and guess what, we're engaged. What a girl! Imagine being brave enough to take on a fellow with only one leg! They had to amputate the right one just below the knee. But I'm having an artificial limb, so I shouldn't be too bad. They had to dig out bits of shrapnel from most parts of my anatomy, but fortunately my balls were intact. That was what worried me most.

Write soon. Regards to all the lads.

Ross

"Well, he's a cool one; lost a leg and passes it off as if it was a front tooth. Crikey, he's amazing. What do you think Sam?"

"Yeah, he's a brave fellow. It's bad enough being left with one leg but I suppose it could have been worse. I'll write this time, you can the next. OK?"

"Fine," said Kent, as he finished reading the letter a second time. He smiled as he handed it back to Sam. "I like the bit about his balls – shows you he's got his priorities right."

Sam started his letter that evening.

Dear Ross

Great to hear from you. Kent and I have wondered how you were and where you were. We are both gutted to hear about your leg – but knowing you we're sure in time you'll cope. So you're engaged – be sure to keep the wedding on ice until we can come home – that's if you'll invite us!

We've come back to Poperinge to get new tanks – that'll be censored, I bet, but first we're looking forward to having a slap-up Christmas dinner. We're billeted in an old house, three storeys high, a funny sort of building. The only water is down in the basement so we've to troop down there in the morning to wash, and as we're on the top floor it's a bit of a bind. What is worse is that there is an old man who seems to own the place – where he sleeps is a mystery – but he's there every morning no matter how early you go down and hands you a cup of black coffee which is absolutely vile. He's not pleased if you don't drink it and gabbles away, waving his hands, calling on the Almighty, until you feel you've to knock it back. I usually manage to pour most of it down the drain while he's attending to someone else.

Some of the locals are telling us the Jerries have broken through the American lines and are counter-attacking, but we're not listening to them.

I'll write some more tomorrow night for Kent and I are off to one of the cafés for a beer. It's as weak as a new born babe, but it's a little bit of civilization.

BUT SAM did not manage to continue his letter until much later, for on the following day the orders were to pack up all their kit and after lunch they were aboard a fleet of three ton trucks heading for Brussels where they were to pick up their old Sherman tanks to which they so recently had said goodbye.

"So the locals were right about the reports on their radios," Sam mused as he tried to make himself comfortable. He sat wedged tight against the side of the lorry crammed to capacity with tankmen all bemoaning the fact that they had missed their Christmas dinner.

"We've to get it when we come back."

"You're a sucker if you believe that."

"Trust the bloody Yanks to let the Jerries through."

"Who the fuck is this bloke Von Runsted anyway?"

So the disgruntled conversations went on until finally they reached Brussels.

"We won't even get our own tank back," Kent lamented. "Look at this lot, scabby, that's what they are, only fit for the shit heap."

"Here we go then, lads," Sergeant Guy Buxton tried to sound enthusiastic as they started their slow journey into the Ardennes. "Good old Brits," he went on as they got a wave from an American tank crew going the opposite way. "Well, I suppose they don't really know much about tank warfare. Bloody Yanks!"

The beauty and grandeur of the mountain scenery was lost on Sam and the members of his tank crew. They could only concentrate on keeping warm while deciding whether or not they were facing friend or foe, for some American tanks had been captured by the Germans who had also clad themselves in Yankee uniforms.

"At least we've some decent air cover this time," Guy remarked, as he watched the RAF's show of strength in the sky.

It was a relief when the short campaign was over and they started on their journey back down from the Ardennes which Sam, when he continued his letter to Ross described as hair-raising.

He wrote.

You'll remember that these Sherman tanks were originally built for desert warfare with air being blown back into the turret. It was so cold that apart from Ernie and Guy, the rest of us dismounted and trotted along behind the tank to try to keep warm, and also because of the icy road, it was waltzing all over the place. You know, Ross, the tears were running down my cheeks and turning to ice. I had to chip them off. How about that! It made me think back to Fort George and Hughie Brown and his famous remark about brass monkeys looking for a welder after doing PT on the ramparts. I wonder what he would have said if he'd been in the Ardennes. Yes, it was bloody freezing. But at least we all survived and now at last we have our new Centurian tanks, a big improvement on the Shermans in every way, I'd say. I'm getting used to the new guns and have done not too badly on the firing range.

You'll think I'm a fine pal having taken so long to write, but having read this, you'll understand, and Kent has promised to write soon. How's it going with you, I wonder? It's hard to visualize you as you must be now, but keep your spirits up, Ross. Knowing you, you'll manage with Stella to help you, you'll be fine. I'll come and see you whenever I can, but can't give you a definite date! Ha! Ha! I wish this bloody war was over. I feel we're winning, if only someone would blow the full-time whistle.

All the best,

Your old pal, Sam.

THE NURSE bent over Ross. "Something wrong?" she asked. "Are you in pain?"

Ross shook his head and his eyes filled with tears. "Sorry, it's just that I feel so far away from everyone. I miss my mates terribly, just as much as I miss Stella, my girl. I'm sorry, you must think I'm soft."

"No I don't. It's a normal reaction. You've had a pretty rough time and you've been wonderful, you really have taken it very well. You've shown tremendous spirit."

"Maybe, but I'm feeling down today and I shouldn't after getting a letter from Sam. He's a real friend."

"Well, I have news for you. Your artificial limb is ready now, it's had several modifications and it should be just right and tomorrow you start learning to wear it and to use it. Oh it'll take time, but the sooner you master it, the sooner they'll move you up to Glasgow."

"Will they?"

"Of course. And you'll probably be allowed home in no time."

Ross felt the tears roll down his cheeks. "I just can't stop them."

"It's you who's worried about them, I'm not. You're still weak, Ross. All these little ops to remove the shrapnel have taken their toll, and the skin graft you had on your forehead some weeks ago. And you know, the surgeon made a really great job of it. He's a marvel."

"Yes, he is. I'm almost like new again up there."

"That's better! Come on, let's get you sitting up and what about telling me what your friend Sam's been up to?"

"Would you really like to know?"

"Of course. You've told me quite a lot about him already. Let me hear if he writes a good letter."

"He does, does Sam. I'll never believe he was only a farm hand. I'm sure he was having me on."

- 14 -

SERGEANT Guy Buxton and his crew of Ernie, Kent, Sam and Blair Rooke, the wireless operator, had survived the initial drive into Germany, having had the exciting experience of leading the advance over the Rhine. Now the most experienced crew in the squadron, they often found themselves spearheading an attack.

"Not another wretched wooded area," Kent groaned as they all studied the map when Guy returned from the morning briefing.

"'Fraid so, and it appears there's only this one road straight up to it and through it," Guy pointed to the line he had drawn with his marker.

"And I suppose the Jerries are dug in there with their guns all primed, ready to fire," Ernie made his comment in a matter of fact voice.

"Yeah, as far as we can make out, they are. It's these pockets of resistance that are causing the bother and holding up our advance no end."

"Some of the soldiers we took yesterday were just boys of twelve."

"Yeah, but they were fanatical."

So the crew's discussion went on until Blair, who was keeping wireless watch, called to Guy that it was time to get ready to move off.

The early morning progress was uneventful and they reached the road leading to the wood without drawing enemy fire.

"Here goes then," Guy called over the intercom. "Keep a reasonable distance between us and the leading tank, Ernie, till we see whether or not the Jerries are still there or if they've gone further back."

The words were no sooner spoken than a barrage of shells erupted from the dense mass of trees ahead of them, falling just short of the front tank, which immediately started to reverse, and in turn caused the entire line of tanks on the road behind it, to do likewise. The noise set up was ear splitting as the engines bellowed their protest at being driven so fast in reverse gear.

"Come on, Ernie, give it all you've got. The bastards haven't got the range yet, but they're liable to any moment."

Then the command came to deploy on the scrub land on either side of the road and to re-group at a safe distance. This done, Guy was ordered to move forward and try a diagonal attack.

He listened to his instructions, and having acknowledged them, said, "Here we go again, lads, everyone on the alert."

They moved over the rough ground for some fifty yards till Guy suddenly called, "Stop, Ernie! There's a ruddy great ditch ahead. The sides look pretty steep, I doubt if we'll manage to cross it. I'll call up the OC."

They waited in silence while Guy's message was in turn sent by their Squadron Leader to the Commanding Officer, then they heard Guy say, 'Wilco, out.'

"OK. Ernie, deposit this fucking tank in that fucking ditch," which Ernie did.

"Of all the stupid sods!" Kent was livid. "It's all right for that bastard sitting on his arse some miles behind us issuing orders. He wants to come up and see for himself."

"Or believe what his tank commanders tell him," added Sam.

"OK. Let's get out and see what's what," Guy called. "Keep your heads well down."

They surveyed their tank with dismay, tilted as it was at a crazy angle with no hope of moving it from the ditch.

Ernie's pride was hurt. "It's the first time I haven't been able to move it and we've been in a few difficult places before." He swung his boot at the tank track. "I wish that was the bloody CO."

"At least we seem to be out of sight of the Jerries," Blair said, as he hung his headset over the side of the turret so that he could listen for any orders, but everything seemed to have gone quiet.

Suddenly as of one man they turned and came face to face with a German soldier.

For a moment they were all too stunned to move until Sam said, "Where the hell did you come from?"

His words spoken in English had the effect of making the German raise his arms above his head and call, "Me Kamerad."

Sam stepped forward and disarmed him and then searched him for any other weapons, but he only found a sheath knife in a pocket along with his army identification card.

"Me Polski."

"A fucking Pole, is he? A likely story," Ernie glowered at the prisoner who by this time was shaking like a leaf.

"Wait a minute," Sam interrupted, "till I muster up some German."

The others stood in silence while Sam asked a few questions in his halting German.

Then he explained. "It seems, yes, he is a Pole, conscripted into the German army. He's only 18 and he hates it. Like you see, he's scared stiff. Says there's quite a number of guns in the wood but the soldiers there don't know how to operate them very well."

"Sam, you're a genius," Guy clapped him on the back, "but what are we going to do with him? I'd best ask the OC."

Ten minutes later the headset crackled into life and the orders came. The squadron was moving back two miles, abandoning the attack on the wood. Guy and his crew were to remain where they were. They'd be pulled out at first light.

"You mean we've to stay out here on our tod for the whole night?" Kent demanded.

"That's what the man said," Guy's tone was resigned. "Wait till I ask him again about this fellow."

After another ten minutes the order came direct from the CO. "Shoot him!" Then wireless silence was enforced.

"Bloody hell!" Guy looked at each member of his crew in turn, then said, "Sam, you're the gunner. You heard what the CO said, you'd better get on with it."

"Get lost Guy," Sam's voice was tense but steady. "You can shoot me first if you like, but this fellow has surrendered, and as far as I am aware, there's such a thing as the Geneva Convention, which says you don't shoot prisoners."

Everyone had gone quiet. Polski, as they had started to call their captive, with a puzzled look, surveyed each member of the tank crew in turn. Something was badly wrong he felt. What had been the message over the radio?

Ernie broke the silence. "As usual this is where the buck stops. We're always the ones left to do the dirty work. Bastards!"

"OK. Agreed lads, but back there I dare say they're all under pressure, which doesn't help us I know, but what the hell are we going to do with this bloke?"

"I'm going to brew up," Ernie turned away, "it's nowt to do with me, anyway. I'm just the driver of this heap," and he scowled again at his tank, nose in the ditch, tail in the air.

Guy looked at Sam again. "I knew you couldn't shoot the poor fellow any more than I could, Sam. This is what shows the futility of war; there's no sense in it at all. It's different when you're in the thick of it, but you don't have time to think about it. You're really fighting for your life, for survival, that's the name of the game. When it comes down to situations like this, well …" Guy raised his hands in a gesture of despair.

"Mind if I solve the problem my way?" Sam asked.

"You can try anything. You're second in command here, you know that."

"Right." And without saying another word to Guy, he took Polski by the arm and drew him away.

Guy and the rest of the crew watched wonderingly as they set off across the scrubland in the direction of the road. They saw the two figures suddenly fall to the ground and then disappear in the hazy twilight.

Kent took a step forward. "God, Sam, you haven't killed him," he gasped as he felt Guy's restraining hand on his shoulder.

"Wait, Kent, there's been no shot."

"But he took Polski's knife. Sam's so strong, he would have him down on the ground and one thrust would finish him."

"Sam wouldn't do that after what he said earlier," Blair's voice was no more than a whisper. "He may be tough, but he's not a cold bloodied killer."

"This is bloody war, though," Ernie growled. "I hope Sam comes back soon, brew's ready."

His words went unheeded as they waited, straining their ears for any sound which might alert them of Sam's return.

"Crikey," Kent burst out at last, "I hope the bastard didn't do for Sam. Maybe he wasn't such a fucking innocent after all. Guy, let me go and look for him."

"No, you'd get lost – Listen! Here he comes."

Sam regarded his fellow crew members then turned to Ernie, "Char ready then? I could do with a mug."

"Sam, what happened out there?" Kent demanded fiercely. "You had us all worried sick."

"Sorry to disappoint you, but there were no heroics. I simply crawled over with Polski to the road, gave him my one and only white handkerchief, explained to him as best I could that if he went to the right, he'd be going back to the Jerries, if he went the other way he'd be heading towards our mob, and I left him to decide. I didn't wait until he'd made up his mind, but I think he was going to try his luck with the 'Tommies' as he kept on about."

"Well done, Sam," Guy said quietly, "now let's get some grub going and then we'll have to take it in pairs to mount guard."

Later as Sam and Kent sat back to back keeping watch while the others dozed in the ditch by the side of the tank, Kent said, "You know, I had some good mates back home before this lot started, but I don't suppose I had any real deep feeling for any of them. But this ruddy war has changed a lot of things. When five blokes are thrown together, eating, sleeping, fighting for their lives, day in day out, knowing each one has to pull his weight or else, it forges a sort of bond among them."

Sam gave a quiet laugh, "Kent you've gone all lyrical, big words and all."

"OK. I'll shut up."

"No, don't. I'm interested in what else you have to say."

"You're a cheeky sod at times, Sam, but OK, I never thought I'd ever have any special feelings towards another bloke, but if you hadn't come back tonight, I don't think I could have carried on."

"Kent, I'm no hero. I had every intention of coming back. I wasn't out to do anything that you or Guy or Ernie, or Blair wouldn't have done. But you're right, war does bring this sense of comradeship, of working together. Before, I had one real friend who was special, Neil Munro. Now I've had Ross and you and the others. It's made me see a lot of things in a different light. I bore a grudge against the world in general before, because I thought I had nothing, and it owed me everything. Well, maybe I still haven't very much material wise, but I have my life and oh Kent, how I want to get through this lot and begin to really live."

"Yeah, me too. What do you aim to do Sam, when we do get back to civvy street?"

For a moment or two Sam didn't answer, then Kent heard him whisper softly, "What's that clicking noise. Do you hear it?"

"Yes, I do now. It's weird. Get your revolver ready."

"Yes, but …. Wait!" and then Sam called, "Halt! Who goes there?"

Two figures loomed up out of the darkness. "Friends! We're from the Royal Signals. We've brought you a field telephone so you can be in touch with us if you need help."

"Big deal!" But Kent's voice held relief in it.

The two signalmen didn't waste any time in starting their return journey after they had given a brief explanation as how to operate the telephone.

"At least they've not forgotten about us entirely. That clicking noise was them letting out the cable. Could have been anything. Certainly put the wind up me."

"And me," Kent added. "I won't forget this night in a hurry."

"You can say that again."

They settled down to continue their vigil.

"I was asking, Sam, what your plans were when you retire from the army?"

"At the moment, I have none, but I've no desire to go back to the farm. On the other hand I'd like to work outside. I don't think I could bear to be cooped up in a factory or an office, not that I'd ever aspire to that. What about yourself?"

"I suppose I'm being big-headed in thinking I'm too good now to go back to working in the chocolate factory, but I'd like to do something better. Maybe I could train as a motor mechanic, I've picked up quite a lot from the courses I was on and from all the practical experience you get in this lark."

"Nothing to stop you aiming a bit higher, Kent, that's exactly what I want to do, I only wish I hadn't been so stupid at school, I mean the way I carried on. Oh I did learn quite a lot, but I never worked at it. I liked being a rebel, idiot that I was. I used to laugh at Neil Munro, but he had sense."

"But you're pretty good at the language racket. How come, Sam?"

"I don't know, it was the one thing I liked at school, although I never let on, but I wanted to travel, and after I left school, I took to learning French. It seemed to come quite easily to me and then Neil was doing it at school right up to his sixth year, and his mother was pretty good at it too. So I got quite a lot of opportunity to practise it."

"And your German's not bad either."

"I can manage a little. I hadn't spent much time on it before I was called up."

"I'll say it again, Sam, you're a bit of a genius."

"No, I'm a bit of a fraud really – crikey –" Sam broke off in mid sentence.

"What's up?" Kent demanded.

"Turn your head slowly to the left and tell me what you see."

Sam felt Kent stiffen when he did his bidding.

"Christ! There's a bloke pointing a rifle at us!" Kent's voice was hoarse with fright.

"That's what I see too. Don't move or speak."

They sat motionless, fully alert, hearts pounding, eyes glued to the apparition.

They were both still watching, bodies tensed, when they heard Guy call.

"Sam! Kent! Come over here, I've brewed up, I thought you'd be glad of something warm before you kip down."

"Don't say anything," Sam whispered. "We were maybe seeing things."

"Both of us?" queried Kent.

"It's a mystery, if it is a bloke, why hasn't he done something. He hasn't moved at all."

They crawled down into the ditch and gratefully took their mugs of hot tea.

"I'll take over now, Blair and Ernie can do the last stint. Anything to report?"

Sam explained the field telephone.

"Gosh, I must have dropped off. I didn't hear them bring it. Good of you not to wake me."

"There was no point, Guy. Anyway, the blokes were only too glad to dump it and get back to their base as fast as they could."

"They were shit scared, I reckon," Kent put in, "even more so than we were, when we heard them coming."

"Well, OK. You two try and get some shut-eye. I'm just going to sit at the top of the ditch, so I'll be able to call you if I need to, seeing I'm keeping watch on my own."

When the dawn eventually came Sam and Kent returned to where they had sat when on guard and discovered their rifleman had been a small tree broken in half, probably by the shelling.

"Funny how both of us thought exactly the same," mused Kent.

"Yeah, your mind can play tricks on you when you're in a situation that we were during the night."

LATER WHEN they had thankfully rejoined their squadron in time for breakfast, they learned it had been decided to by-pass the woods. Another route had been found.

"And we're being held in reserve today," Guy announced.

"Thank goodness for that," Sam said to Kent. "I'll maybe be able to close my eyes for a while and catch up on some sleep."

"Good idea. Roll on a long time!"

1945 - 1956

- 15 -

THEY had raced the Russians to the Baltic ports and now unbelievably the war in Europe was over. It came almost as an anti-climax – the sudden release from the strain of being on a continual alert had filled them with a feeling of lethargy. They were divorced from the celebrations going on throughout Britain, and Sam especially could not relate to anyone at home who would be experiencing a sense of relief that their loved ones were safe.

He watched Kent busy writing letters, first to his mother and then to Marlene, and he thought of Millside and Mrs Whyte. There would be no letters from her sons, for Rob had also been killed in action. Perhaps he should write to her, but maybe hearing from him would make her sorrow all the harder to bear.

"I'm just about finished, Sam," Kent said, looking up at his friend. "I'm just going to write a few cheeky lines to Dolly. I bet you she's living it up tonight."

"Decision time is approaching for one Kent Mollison."

"Plenty of time for that, Sam, old friend. We'll be in the army for some time yet."

And when they found 'Far East' written into their pay books, they realised that there was some way to go before they would be back in civvy street. Then the 'Bomb', as it was called, changed all that, and they got down eventually to working out when they would be demobbed.

"We'll have a few leaves before we're out, Sam, so remember, if we can work it so we have them at the same time, you're welcome to my place."

"Thanks, Kent, I'll be glad to take you up on that, if it's all right with your folk."

"They'll be only too pleased to have you. My mum thinks you have a good influence on me."

"How does she make that out?"

"Ah, you'd be surprised what I've told her about you in my letters."

"Have you ever thought of signing on, Kent?" Sam asked suddenly.

"Signing on!" Kent looked at his friend in amazement. "Signing on!" he repeated. "You must be joking. I can't wait till I'm a free man again."

"You have a home and a job to go back to, even though you've said you want to try something else."

"And you have too. Of course, like me, you want a change, but it's something to start off again with."

"In a way I've quite liked the army – you know, it's an open-air life."

"Maybe, but Sam, you're far too intelligent to spend your life being ordered around all the time. You're not allowed to think for yourself. There's always someone above you to tell you what to do, no matter how high you rise, you're never your own boss."

"It's the same in civvy street."

"No, it's not, you can tell your boss in civvy street to get stuffed and walk away and no one is going to sling you on a fizzer."

"Hmm." Sam looked thoughtful. "I suppose you could say that, but there's always the chance of travel in the army."

"Believe me, Sam, you'll travel all right, but only to where there's danger. No, we've done our bit for our country and some. My opinion is that it was us civilians who won the war. How many regulars have we ever had in our mob? Oh, I know they're coming in now, some of them have been prisoners of war, poor sods. But the army of 1939 was out of date; their weapons were ancient, as were their ideas of warfare."

"But the generals have all been regulars."

"That was only to be expected, but they had to learn to think quite differently, and some of them got the chop because they were no damned good. Another thing, Sam, these lads who have been in the army for years think they're old if they're thirty five or so. Crikey, my dad's nearly fifty and you know what he's like. But you're not really serious, Sam, are you?"

"I've given it some thought, but there's plenty of time before I have to decide."

"Sam, I'd be very disappointed if you stayed on in the army. I'd thought that perhaps you would maybe come and live in York and we could work together – or I could come to Scotland."

Sam looked at this friend and then gripped his shoulder. "That's the nicest thing you've ever said to me."

"Cheeky sod! But what do you think?"

"Well, it's an idea."

They moved around Germany until finally they settled in the barracks at Flensberg where they went off occasionally on exercises, mounted guard from time to time, played football for the regiment, did some cross-country running, attended some rehabilitation courses, drank beer in the sergeants' club in town, did some fraternising with the Germans, and more often than not, usually managed to wangle their leaves together.

In June 1946, however, they had not succeeded and Sam went off on his own.

AFTER HIS long train journey from Hull, Sam decided to walk from Levenford Central Station to the farm, taking the route along by the river. He found the path overgrown in parts, but he noticed the golf course which had been rather neglected during the years of war, was now in reasonable shape. When he reached the spot where he and Neil had swum as boys, he stopped and clambered down to the edge of the water and then made his way to their secret hide-out and was amazed when he found it was still intact. He crawled into the dome formed by the tangle of bushes and knelt down, reliving for a few moments the happy times Neil and he had spent there. They had never managed to be on leave at the same time with the result that Sam had rarely spent more than a few days at the farm before going off to meet up with Kent. He had always felt at a loss when he returned to Millside and while he was willing enough to lend a hand on the farm, he found the lack of someone to share his leisure frustrating, realising that Neil had been his only friend in Levenford.

Sam retrieved his haversack and continued on his way to the farm. Before he reached the yard, Bess, the collie, came bounding to meet him and her excited barking brought Mrs Whyte to the door of the dairy.

"Oh Sam, this is a surprise, why didn't you let me know you were coming?"

Sam had never been able to bring himself to address Mrs Whyte as 'Mother' or even as 'Ma', like Fred and Rob, but now he was an adult he realised she had afforded him real kindness and that her welcome was sincere when she went on, "You're a sight for sore eyes, Sam, and my, you're looking well. Come away in and we'll have a cup of tea."

Sam put his arm round Mrs Whyte and thought how small and frail she had become.

"It's nice to come back here. I would have let you know, but I got this leave a week early, for I'm going on a course when I get back."

"A course, Sam? Does that mean you're going to sign on as a regular?"

"No. I haven't made up my mind yet about that."

"I hope you're going to stay for a while this time."

"I might. My mate didn't get away with me so I won't be going to his place. I'll see what's doing here before I decide. I don't suppose there's any chance of Neil being home?"

"I haven't heard, but you can go down to The Willows yourself and see."

When Sam finished his tea he rose from his chair. "The bothy's still available for me?" he asked.

"Yes Sam, but you can have a room upstairs."

"Thanks, but I'll have my old hide-out, then I can come and go as I please."

"As you wish, Sam. There's a place at the table for you whenever you want a meal."

"Thanks. I'll go and have a wash and then maybe go along and see if any of the Munros are home."

THERE DIDN'T seem to be any sign of life as Sam approached The Willows, but he felt that wasn't unusual. John Munro was seldom at home in the afternoon and if Neil was by some chance on leave, he would probably be with his father on his rounds.

He lifted the latch to open the gate and paused for a moment. It was unusual for it to be closed at this time of day; in fact, on reflection, Sam could not remember when he had ever seen the gate closed, for John Munro was liable to be called any hour of the day and night. He continued on his way up the short drive, hesitating for a moment at the front door, before continuing round to the back of the house. Everything seemed very quiet, but Sam thought he'd just make sure that there was indeed no one at home. He lifted the knocker and let it fall three times before stepping back to look down the large vegetable garden which the Munros assiduously cultivated. When there was no response to his knocking he wandered down the path to look at the strawberry beds and he was in the act of bending down to pluck a large red berry when the sudden knock on a window made him almost fall forward. Regaining his balance, he turned and looked up at the house and another knock drew his attention to the bedroom window above the living room. He saw the figure of a girl disappear from sight and then the back door was pulled open and she stood looking at Sam.

Slowly he retraced his steps up the path.

"Goodness, it's you, Hazel. I hardly recognize you. You gave me quite a fright."

"Me give you a fright, Sam Cairns. You, a big brave soldier."

Sam smiled and stood looking at Hazel, who went on, "So, what do you see, soldier?"

Sam smiled again. "A very pretty young girl."

Hazel opened her mouth, but for a moment no sound came out, then recovering she said, "Well, if you hardly recognized me, the same applies in your case, for the Sam Cairns of old certainly didn't pay anyone any compliments, especially one Hazel Munro."

"Maybe I have changed, maybe I've learned some sense, but you are different too. Let me see, it's over three years since I set eyes on you."

"And whose fault has that been?"

"Mine I suppose."

"Exactly. Just because Neil wasn't here you didn't bother coming near us."

"Now that's not quite true. I always called down and last leave I did spend some time with your father, but then you weren't at home. Where is everyone by the way?"

"Mum and Dad are off on holiday up north. Dad was needing a break and he finally found someone to stand in for him."

"And why didn't you go with them?"

"Someone has to look after the hens and the pigs, not to mention the dogs and the cat, so I volunteered to stay. As I say, Dad was worn out and Mum too, for that matter."

"Maybe I can give you a hand while I'm here."

"Oh, you're going to stay at Millside then? I believed you always went off to spend your leave with some of your army friends in England."

"Yes, I do, but not this time."

"Don't deny yourself their company just for me."

"Hazel, can't we shake and make it up. Oh I know I treated you pretty rotten in the past, but well, things were a lot different then."

"Sam Cairns, you have changed. OK. Let's shake and be friends and I'll appreciate your help. You won't be needed at Millside?"

"No, I'm afraid I've opted out of there, and anyway Ma Whyte always says I've to enjoy myself when I'm on leave. She seems to think I've had a hard time of it in the army."

"And have you?"

"It's not so bad now the fighting has finished. I daresay it was pretty bad for a lot of folks at home."

"Yes, the air raids were ghastly."

"Well, it's all over now." Then changing the subject, Sam asked, "So what would you like me to do?"

"Nothing at the moment, so let's have a seat in the sun and you can tell me all about life in the army."

A couple of hours later Hazel said, "Gosh, look at the time. The animals will be ravenous and you too, I expect. Would you like to stay for tea?"

"I would if it's no bother."

"Of course not. Look, if you attend to the hens and pigs, I'll get busy in the kitchen."

"Fine."

After they had eaten, Sam asked, "Have you to keep guard on this place all the time or are you allowed to go out?"

Hazel laughed. "It's not the military barracks, Sam. Where are you suggesting we go?"

"Well, I don't know, what do you think?"

"Sam Cairns, you're the limit. Asking a girl out and then not knowing where to take her."

"Well, the truth is, I've never taken out a girl before."

"That I do not believe. Look, can you ride a bike?"

"Of course I can."

"Right, if you pump up the tyres on Neil's old faithful we'll go along to Balloch."

Despite the fine evening they found the path along by the river at Balloch almost deserted and Sam marvelled how much he was enjoying Hazel's company. Seeing him smile, she asked, "What are you looking so pleased about?"

"I was just thinking again about us and how we used to be in the past."

"I'm doing my best to make up for Neil not being here."

"And I thought you were just enjoying my company."

It was Hazel's turn to smile. "I didn't say I wasn't. Let's sit down here for a while and talk."

"What about?"

"You."

"Me! There's not much you don't know about me."

"Sam, there's lots, you're so different."

Sam thought for a moment. "I suppose really it all started with Neil. Looking back it all stemmed from his standing up to me and being better than I was at lots of things and yet never letting me feel he was. And then he accepted me as a person, there was no side with him. Oh I know I didn't fully realise all that at the time, but it's only now as an adult I can put it into words. Then when I started working on the farm, funnily enough Fred helped me along in the growing up process, even though he gave me a rough passage on occasion. When I was called up I was more prepared for it than most. I was used to being ordered around from my days in the children's home, so it was nothing new and I was able to shrug off all the inconveniences which most of the other lads found irksome. From Neil I suppose I had learned the art of being friendly and I found I was able to help those who weren't making out so well, and of course I had always enjoyed the outdoor life."

"You saw plenty of action?"

"Yes, but so did lots of others."

"How did you feel when you were in the fighting?"

"I don't suppose I ever thought much about it. It was just a job to be done and we got on with it. But that's enough about me, what about you?"

"Oh I finished school, went to the PE College and now I teach at the place you liked so much."

"You mean at Hartwell?"

"Yes."

"Gosh, they didn't have teachers like you when I was there. They were all ancient birds."

"Oh Sam, they couldn't have been. Some of them are still there. Come on, it's time we headed for home."

When they reached The Willows, Sam said, as he wheeled the bicycles into the shed, "I'll come tomorrow then and give you a hand."

"That'll be fine."

"I don't suppose you'd like to have another cycle run?"

Hazel thought for a moment. "I tell you what I'd like to do."

"What's that?"

"Go for a swim." Hazel looked at Sam and smiled.

"You mean in the river?"

"Yes, just like you and Neil used to do. Daddy would never allow me to swim there."

"So, when the cat's away."

"Will you take me?"

"You're a big girl now, so why not? I dare say you're a pretty strong swimmer."

"I think I'll pass."

"OK. See you tomorrow."

- 16 -

THE weather continued fine and Sam went every day to The Willows to help Hazel. Then it was off to the river for a swim in the afternoon and a cycle run in the evening.

"I've certainly learned more of the geography of this place in one week than I did during all the years I lived at the farm," Sam said as they sat at the front in Helensburgh on the last evening of his leave.

"You say that as if you weren't coming back once you're demobbed."

Sam shrugged his shoulders. "I just don't know what I'm going to do. I could sign on."

"You mean, stay in the army?"

"Yes, I like the life and I'm not trained for anything."

Hazel went quiet and after a few moments Sam said, "You don't seem to think much of that idea."

"It's nothing to do with me, it's your life."

"Well, I'm tempted, but I'll wait a while yet before deciding."

The sun went behind a cloud and suddenly Sam felt all the joy he had experienced with Hazel had evaporated. "Thanks, Hazel, for giving me a wonderful time. I don't know when I've enjoyed myself so much."

Hazel stood up. "We best make a start back, it looks as if it might rain."

They were only half way home when the heavens opened and in no time they were both soaked to the skin.

"Do you want to stop and shelter?" Sam shouted to make himself heard as he cycled alongside Hazel.

"What's the point, we might as well go on."

By the time they reached The Willows they were both exhausted after battling against the driving rain.

"Lucky I lit the stove this afternoon, at least there's hot water for a bath."

"Well, that's fine, I'll get away up to Millside and get out of these wet clothes."

"Oh Sam, you're not going to leave now. You can have your bath here and put on something of Neil's. Please stay for a while. Look you can have first go."

"I would like to strip off, so OK, but ladies first. No, I insist. Just you go get a towel for me and I'll have a rub down while you're in the tub."

"I won't be too long."

Some fifteen minutes later Sam heard Hazel call, "Come up, Sam, it's all ready for you," and when he reached the bathroom Hazel went on, "I've put in Neil's dressing gown, you can put it on when you're finished. Take your time and I'll have something hot for you when you come back down."

When Sam returned to the kitchen, Hazel had supper ready. As they ate he looked at Hazel but said nothing. He couldn't understand what was happening to him and gave a start when Hazel broke the silence by asking, "Everything all right Sam?"

"Yes, just great, as I said in Helensburgh, I can only say thanks very much, and that seems pretty lame."

"Oh Sam …" Hazel began, and Sam saw a tear roll slowly down her cheek.

Without thinking what he was about, Sam was out of his chair and kneeling in front of Hazel asking, "What's wrong?"

"Oh Sam," Hazel said again, "I'm going to miss you."

Sam stood up, pulling Hazel to her feet, drew her into his arms, "And I'm going to miss you too, for I've fallen in love with you, Hazel. I don't know how to say it, but I want you for my own, if you'll have me."

"Sam, I love you too. And I want you, oh, how I want you."

When Sam released Hazel after a long passionate kiss, he looked at her and laughed. "Who would have believed it that we'd come together like this? Thank goodness it rained."

"And it's still raining. Sam you can't get soaked again."

"I've no intention of doing that." He lifted Hazel in his arms and carried her upstairs.

"I'll sleep in Neil's room if you like," he said when he reached the landing.

"If you do, I'll come in with you."

"Then we'll just use your room."

WHEN THE alarm clock woke Sam at six o'clock he discovered he was in bed alone. He sat up hurriedly and saw Hazel standing looking out of the window. He rose and crossed to her and putting his arm around her, kissed her gently on the cheek.

"All right, my darling?"

"Yes."

"Sure?" He turned her to him. "Hazel, I'm asking you to marry me. I know I have very little to offer you, but I'll work my fingers to the bone for you."

"I know you will Sam, and I want to marry you, but we'll have to wait a while till I sort things out."

"Oh I know your mum and dad will be surprised, but I hope they'll take it all right."

"It's not Mum and Dad, Sam, it's Roger."

"Roger. Who's Roger?"

"Roger Harrison. I'm engaged to him."

Sam staggered back and sat on the bed.

"What are you saying?"

"Oh Sam, don't be angry, please let me explain. It's you I love and it's you I want to marry. You see, Roger is on holiday just now, but we've been engaged since last Christmas."

"I don't believe it."

"Sam, please. Roger and I have been friends since school. He teaches at Hartwell and his parents have always been very friendly with mine."

"What's that got to do with it?"

"Well, we seemed to see a lot of each other and as Roger didn't pass his medical for the services, he's never been away. Oh, I'm not explaining this well at all."

"He didn't pass his medical? What's wrong with him?"

"He had polio as a child which affected one of his legs and he walks with a limp."

"But Hazel, if you're engaged to this fellow you must love him, you intended to marry him, how can I be sure that you love me?"

"I do, Sam, I do. I didn't realise what real love meant until this week, please, please, Sam, try to understand."

Sam turned away. "Just for the first time in my life I felt I had someone who belonged to me, really belonged, someone whom I could live the rest of my life working for, loving and being loved."

"But you do, Sam, you have me."

"How can I be sure? Once I'm away, will this Roger fellow take over again? Will your parents allow you to cast him aside for me, Sam Cairns, born a bastard, an unwanted child, tossed from one place to another, a farm labourer? How can I stand comparison with the son of life-long family friends, a teacher, a university graduate? Tell me that!"

Hazel went to Sam and pulled him round towards her. "Do you still love me, Sam?"

"Yes, I do, with all my heart, I love you. But do you?"

"Yes."

"But you still love Roger?"

"Not in the same way as I love you, Sam. You're a real man."

"Are you saying that just because I took you to bed and made love to you?"

"No, of course not. It's you I want, Sam, not Roger."

"Well, you'll have to prove it."

Hazel stepped away from Sam. "I'll do that, but you must give me time."

Sam nodded. "All right. I will. Now I must get off to Millside to collect my things."

"What about breakfast?"

"I'd better have something there and say goodbye to Ma."

"Can I come to the station with you?"

"If you want to."

Hazel's eyes filled with tears and Sam said softly, "All right, I didn't mean to upset you, it's just that last night everything was so wonderful and now this morning, it's like the weather, everything's grey."

"Sam, please, trust me."

They kissed briefly and Sam set off for Millside returning in just over an hour to find Hazel waiting at the end of the drive up to The Willows.

"I'm taking my bike so I can ride back."

"Fine. Do you mind if we go by the river? I always like to say my farewells to it."

"Oh Sam, you will come back," Hazel pleaded.

"I hope so."

They walked in silence till they reached the station. "Don't come up, Hazel, I don't want to see you upset. Goodbye, my love, take care." And Sam was off up the stairs to the platform.

"What's got into me?" he asked himself as he waited for the train to arrive. "I don't remember when I last cried and here I am feeling like doing just that."

As the train moved slowly away over the station bridge he lowered the carriage window and saw the lonely figure of Hazel standing at the entrance to the Common. He waved and shouted, 'I love you', not caring who heard him and saw Hazel wave back, knowing full well that the tears were rolling down her cheeks.

"WELCOME BACK, Sam," Kent said as he entered the room they shared and found his friend lying stretched out on his bed. "Good leave?"

When Sam didn't answer Kent paused from stripping off his denims to look across to the bed. "Hey, what's the matter with you?"

"I've fallen in love, Kent."

"You've what? Sam, you old devil. But why are you looking so cheesed off? Oh, I see, you're missing her more than somewhat. Well, I'll be damned. Who'd have thought? My good friend Sam has fallen – and how – it seems. What's she like? Have you …"

"Don't, Kent. I know what you're going to ask. Let me tell you the whole story. I must or I'll go mad."

"I'm all ears."

When Sam had finished, Kent said, "But you should be jumping for joy. Hazel would appear to have fallen for you as hard as you've fallen for her."

"How can I be sure? She's engaged to this fellow Roger. Won't she just turn back to him now I'm away?"

"Sam, how can you have any doubts? From what you've told me, you've made a conquest."

"I felt as if I'd made the first real break through in my life and then she told me about him."

"Sam, let's be practical. You went to bed, you made love, you took no precautions – get my drift. Come on, you're not that ignorant of the facts of life."

"I wouldn't want Hazel to marry me just because she was pregnant. I want her to marry me because she loves me."

"And she's said she does. Look, we're going out to have a quiet celebration tonight."

"Kent, I couldn't. I'd rather not."

"And stay here feeling miserable? Sam, this is the first time I've ever seen you not in command of the situation. Come on, get your finger out, go and have a shower, freshen up and then we'll go out. Don't argue – we'll drown your sorrows."

- 17 -

NEIL had arrived home on leave and had wandered into Hazel's room. "So, how's it feel to be a teacher, then?"

"I like it."

"How many pupils did you belt today?"

"Neil, you are an idiot at times, I don't use the belt."

"Ah, you just fix them with a stare and they fall into line immediately. You must be a real battleaxe. I always thought the pupils at Hartwell were real demons, at least Sam gave me that impression."

"Well, Sam was wrong."

Neil wandered around the room, then stopped suddenly, "Here, where did you get this photograph of Sam? Gosh, he's a handsome devil now. I wish our leaves would coincide, I'm longing to see him again. But come clean, how did you get hold of it?"

"I saw him when he was home on leave and he was showing me some snapshots and he left me that one."

"And you just happened to have a photo frame that fitted it. Better not let Roger see it. How was Sam?"

"Great."

"Gosh, that's a change for you. You're friends now I take it."

"You could say that."

"I'm glad. I always felt rotten about the way Sam and you never seemed to hit it off. Now are we going to have a game of tennis tonight?"

"Yes, of course we are."

They cycled to the tennis club where normality was gradually returning and were soon engaged in a hectic doubles game, which they eventually won. As Neil turned to congratulate Hazel she stumbled and would have fallen if Neil hadn't caught her.

"What's wrong?" he gasped.

"Oh, I'm suddenly quite dizzy."

"Here, come and sit down in the pavilion."

Neil looked anxiously at his sister. "I'm going to phone Dad and ask him to come for you."

"No, Neil, I'll be all right. Just give me a few minutes."

But Neil was not convinced and Mr Munro arrived in ten minutes looking very anxious.

By the time they had returned to The Willows Hazel had recovered slightly but was still very pale.

"I'm going to ring Dr Blackwood and ask him to come along and see you," Mrs Munro announced when she had settled Hazel in bed.

"No, Mummy, please don't do that, I'll be all right."

"Now Hazel, I'm taking no chances, you look dreadful. It's so unlike you to be taken ill, you're always so fit."

Hazel turned her face to the wall and her mother left the room, then reaching back she lifted the photograph of Sam from her bedside table and looked at it through her tears.

"Oh Sam," she whispered.

DR BLACKWOOD was an old friend of the Munros and was soon at The Willows.

"Now what's my best girl friend been up to," he quipped as he entered the living room.

"You've put her to bed. Fine, I'll pop up and see her."

It was a good half hour before he reappeared and the Munros looked up anxiously.

"Nothing to worry about, Hazel will be as right as rain after a good night's rest. I think she would like to see you, Neil."

"Right." And Neil went off upstairs.

"Now, Bill, just what is the matter with Hazel? You haven't sent Neil away just for nothing."

Dr Blackwood pursed his lips, removed his spectacles and started to polish them.

"Are Hazel and Roger planning to marry soon?"

"Hazel and Roger planning to marry soon?" Mrs Munro repeated. "No, they haven't set a date yet. Why do you ask?"

Dr Blackwood replaced his spectacles and looked first at John Munro and then at his wife. "I don't know how to say this, but if you don't want your first grandchild to be born out of wedlock, they'd better start planning now."

"What do you mean?" John Munro's voice was a mere whisper.

"I mean that Hazel is pregnant."

"Oh no, not Hazel, she wouldn't do a thing like that." Mrs Munro had risen to her feet. "How can you be so sure?"

"I've been a doctor too long, Ella, not to be sure. I'm sorry to have been so blunt about it, but there's no point beating about the bush."

"I can't believe it," John Munro shook his head. "And Roger, I'm going to have something to say to that young man."

"John, it can happen in the best of families. Wait till tomorrow at least. I've given Hazel something which will give her a good night's sleep. Don't go for her tonight."

"Does she know?"

"She knew without my having to tell her."

"Hazel, how could you …" Mrs Munro's voice trailed off as she searched for her handkerchief.

Dr Blackwood crossed the room and putting his arm round her said, "Ella, it's not the end of the world. At least Hazel and Roger were intending marrying, so they'll just have to tie the knot as soon as possible."

"It's a disgrace."

"Ella, don't think of it like that. We all make mistakes in our life. This is a time when Hazel needs your help and love, not your anger."

"It's easy for you to say that."

"Perhaps, but I am right."

"Maybe you are," put in John Munro, "but it's very hard not to be angry."

"I'll say no more. Don't hesitate to call me if you need me."

When Dr Blackwood had taken his leave, Ella Munro went through to the kitchen and when her husband joined her he put his hand over hers and said, "We'll get over it, but it'll take time. Look, here's Neil, try not to show him you are upset."

"Hazel's asleep now, I think I'll go and rescue her bike from the tennis club."

"It'll be locked up by this time."

"Yes, I know, but I left the bike at the back of the clubhouse, so I'll get it all right."

"I'll run you in then."

"No need, I'll enjoy the walk. I'm needing some fresh air after all the excitement, if that's what you would call it," and with that Neil was off.

John Munro watched his son disappear down the drive and looked thoughtful as he returned to the kitchen. He stood at the door, and then said, "I think Neil knows."

His wife looked up quickly. "Oh, I hope not."

"My dear, Neil's a grown man, he's seen active service and a bit of life I expect."

"What do you mean?"

"What I say. He's not the young innocent boy who went away to the army in 1942."

"How I've hated this war and all it's done to us."

"I daresay we should count ourselves lucky to have survived as we have."

"It's only a few moments ago that you were saying how angry you were about what's happened and now you seem to be putting forward excuses."

"I was angry and I'm still angry, but maybe Bill Blackwood's right. Hazel needs us now as she's never needed us before."

"I feel hurt, terribly hurt. I don't know what the Harrisons are going to say."

"We shouldn't have gone off on holiday and left Hazel on her own."

"Wait a minute. Roger was away on holiday at the same time as we were. It must have happened before that, so we can't blame ourselves."

"Let's go to bed. I'm worn out, I know I'll never sleep."

IN THE MORNING Mrs Munro took a tray up to Hazel's room. "I'll phone the school today and say you won't be in today."

"Oh Mummy, I'm fine now. I'd rather go."

"Dr Blackwood said you were to rest."

"Mummy, I'm not ill. I've still time to get to school."

"No, Hazel, you know we've got to talk and the sooner the better. Besides your father is waiting to see you once you've had your breakfast."

Hazel looked at her mother. "All right, I'll come down," she whispered. "Just leave me on my own for a few minutes."

"Eat your breakfast first."

Hazel was fully dressed when she appeared in the living room some twenty minutes later followed by Neil.

"Neil…" his mother began.

"I want Neil here."

"All right, Hazel," John Munro said, "it's a family matter so Neil can stay. Now you must know how disappointed your mother and I are that this has happened. More than disappointed, angry, very angry, and I'm going to have some strong words to say to Roger."

"To Roger! Oh, you mustn't say anything to Roger."

"He is equally to blame, Hazel, and you can't expect me just to let him off scot-free for his part in it."

"You mustn't! You mustn't!" Hazel almost shouted the words.

"I just don't understand. What do you mean, I mustn't speak to Roger."

"Because Roger is not the father."

John and Ella Munro were stunned to silence.

Eventually Neil said, "Hazel, you'd best get it over with."

Hazel rose from her chair and walking across to the window stood looking out. After a few moments she turned and in a quiet voice said, "I'm not going to marry Roger, I don't think I ever really wanted to. I'm going to marry Sam Cairns for it's Sam's child I'm going to have and I love Sam."

"What are you saying girl?" John Munro rose from his chair and shouted the words across the room.

"I said, I'm going to marry Sam Cairns."

"You must have taken leave of your senses. How can you marry Sam Cairns, he's a farm hand?"

"Mother," Neil broke in, "please don't speak like that."

"You keep out of this," his father interrupted.

"Look, Dad, this is a family matter and I have a right to speak my mind. I won't have Mother saying that about Sam. He's one of the best and I'm glad he and Hazel are going to be married."

"I don't know who you think you are, Neil, just because you're an officer in the army you seem to have some very big ideas about your importance. Let me remind you that in this house I'm the master."

"In that case I'm leaving. I can spend my leave where I'll be treated as a grown up, not as a child. Hazel, I'll keep in touch with you and if I can help in any way, let me know. I'm sure things will turn out all right in the end." Neil embraced his sister and left the room. In a moment his mother had risen from her chair and followed him upstairs.

"Neil, my dear," she said amidst her tears, "please don't go, please, please, we need you here. Your father didn't mean what he said, he's upset, we all are. Come downstairs again and help us sort this out."

"No, Mum, I think it's best I go. This has been coming to a head between Dad and me the last couple of leaves. Things aren't the same between us any more. He's changed, just as I have changed, but he still treats me like a little boy."

"Oh, Neil, he doesn't, not really; he's so proud of you and he worried so much about you when the fighting was still on. Please, I couldn't bear to see you go away in anger, not on top of Hazel's trouble."

"Apart from Dad's remarks, Mum, I find it difficult to forgive what you said about Sam. I thought you liked him. He's always come to see you when he's been on leave and you've said in your letters what a fine young man he was now, how he'd matured, how well he spoke, how polite he was, and then you dismiss him as a mere farm hand. I've made lots of friends in the army, but I've never found anyone quite like Sam. I haven't seen him for some years but we've written to each other regularly and he still means as much to me as he always did."

"All right, I'm sorry I made that remark, but it still doesn't change anything. I was angry enough when I thought it was Roger but now that Hazel tells me Sam is the father, I think it's outrageous. What will everyone say?"

"Who cares what anyone else says? Hazel and Sam fell in love and well, maybe it was unfortunate he got her pregnant, but it happened."

"How can you speak like that, Neil?"

"Oh Mum, I know Dad still lives in the Victorian age sometimes, but I thought you at least were a bit broad-minded. There is such a thing as love."

"What do you know about love? What are you saying?"

"I'm saying I'm a man, someone who's had a bit of experience of life. I've a lot to learn yet, but I'm not the innocent schoolboy I was when I left home."

"Neil, you're talking as if you were a stranger to me."

"In that case, all the more reason for me to leave."

"Neil," his mother pleaded, "please stay, if only for another couple of days till we sort things out."

"Hazel is willing to do it all herself. She told me so last night."

"You knew all about this last night?"

"Yes. Dr Blackwood wasn't quite as smart as he thought."

The bedroom door opened and John Munro stood looking at his wife and then at his son.

"How long are you two going to stay up here? Can't you come down, Mother, and talk some sense into your daughter."

Ella Munro rose from the bed where she had been sitting. "I don't think there's much point. Hazel has got herself into this mess; let her sort it out on her own. I'm washing my hands of it."

"But you can't, you have to do something."

117

"Such as? If Sam Cairns is the father of the child, she'll have to marry him, and it'll be up to him to look after her from then on."

"For goodness sake you can't do that. You can't just cast her aside."

"Why not? She's brought disgrace on us so she must pay," Ella Munro looked steadily at her husband, then burst into tears.

It was Neil who consoled her. "Look Mum, as you said earlier, we're all upset. Let's go downstairs and have some coffee before we do or say anything else."

"I thought you were leaving," John Munro looked at his son.

"I'll go tomorrow, but sooner if you want me to."

"Don't be ridiculous, Neil, there's no need for you to go at all."

"I'll see," Neil said quietly. "Come on, Mum, go and make some coffee."

When the three of them returned to the living room they found Hazel about to go out.

"I'm going for a walk."

"I'll come with you," Neil said.

"All right."

"Have some coffee first," pleaded Mrs Munro.

"We'll have some when we get back, we won't go too far."

"How long will you be?"

"Half an hour."

Neil and Hazel walked in silence until they reached the river, slowing their pace until they stopped at one of the few remaining wooden benches still standing by the side of the path, now almost completely over grown.

"Let's have a seat here for a while before going back," Hazel said.

"OK. Want to talk some more?"

"No really. I just wish Sam could be here."

"Have you written to Sam to tell him about the child?"

"Not yet."

"You must do so right away so that he can get leave. He must be due home again soon."

"I wonder what he'll say."

"Look Hazel, I'm sure Sam is not innocent. He must have known there was a pretty good chance he'd get you pregnant. I don't mean to be rude or unfeeling." Neil waved his hands in the air.

"The number of times I've come and sat here since Sam left. It's so peaceful; I know why you loved coming here when you were boys and why you didn't want me along. There's something magical about this spot; so few people seem to come this way. Maybe though now the war's over it'll become a popular walk."

"I doubt it. Folk won't much be interested in walking, they'll want to get on with enjoying themselves after all these grim years."

"I hope Sam doesn't feel like that. I'll want to come here with him often."

"You've really fallen for him, Sis."

"Yes, I have."

"You're very lucky."

"I know. What about yourself?"

"Oh, me? No, I haven't been so lucky."

Hazel pulled her brother round to face her. "There's someone then?"

"Was. Come on, I don't want to talk about it. It's time we were getting back."

- 18 -

IT was another six weeks before Sam came home on leave and as he started the long walk from the station, he felt for the first time in his adult life something akin to panic. He had thought of delaying the time of his arrival until Hazel could have met him and now he had regretted not doing so. If Hazel had been at the station to meet him they could have talked on the way to The Willows and that would have settled him.

He had read her letters so many times that he knew them all by heart. He had felt his replies had been inadequate when he had tried to comfort her over all the unpleasant experiences she had been through; of her confrontation with her parents; with Roger Harrison, and then with his folks, of the talk at school and in the town. Sam had thought she should have gone away somewhere, anywhere, but Hazel had said that was not possible, and even if it had been, she was determined to stick it out. She wasn't ashamed because she loved him.

Sam repeated these words over and over again as he took to the river path, slowing his pace slightly as he reached the golf course where he saw some distant figures walking up one of the fairways. Then on over the stile, the wood of the step rotten now, and the posts leaning at a drunken angle, to where the path veered away from the river bank and he could see the little island. He closed his eyes and he saw Neil in the water alongside him as they struggled to be first over to that little sandy haven. Would that he could find such a one today.

Sam shook himself out of his reverie and quickened his pace again. He glanced at his watch as he turned into the track which led along to The Willows. Half past eleven. Most likely Mrs Munro would be on her own; he could of course go on to the farm and make his appearance at lunchtime when Hazel would be home. But no! Best get it over with.

Sam's knock on the back door was light and he was poised to repeat it when the door was opened by Mrs Munro. He held out his hand, but Hazel's mother turned away, so after a moment he followed her through the kitchen to the living room where he stood facing her as she sat in her old rocking chair. He licked is dry lips and tried to begin, but no sound came out, but when he saw two tears start to roll slowly down Mrs Munro's cheeks, he knelt down in front of her and taking her hands in his, said, "I'm sorry it's happened this way, but Hazel and I would have married anyway. The baby coming just makes it sooner than planned. We love each other and I'll work hard to give Hazel a happy marriage. You don't need to worry about that. I know I've hurt you, but if you could only try to forgive us, it would make such a difference."

Ella Munro looked at the handsome young man on his knees in front of her. Was this the ruffian who had come as a foster child to the Whyte's farm? Was this the rude, sometimes surly boy, who had never seen eye to eye with her daughter Hazel? And now he wanted to marry her! Of course over the years he had changed. Long before he went off to the army. And somehow the war had turned him into a man, a real man. But he had nothing. No job. No training. How could he support and wife – and a child?

At last she found words. "You've given me a very sore heart. I don't know when I'll be able to forgive you, if ever."

Sam stood up. "I've said I'm sorry, Mrs Munro, I can't say any more. I've promised you I'll look after Hazel and make her happy, and I meant that. I know that in your eyes I'm a nobody, but I'm going to prove to you and a lot more people that I can be a somebody. I don't want to fall out with you because you're Hazel's mum and you've been good to me in the past, very good, and I appreciated it, even although I maybe didn't show it sometimes. But I've grown up and things have changed, we're going to be living in a different world and I intend to be a success in that world, someone you'll be proud of, someone you'll consider one of your family. But if you don't want to accept me, I'll just have to go along with that."

Sam turned away, then added. "I'd like to wait, if I may, and see Hazel, and then I'll go up to the farm and I'll stay clear of you until the wedding."

"There's no need to be like that," a voice from the doorway said, and Sam turned to face John Munro. "You certainly have created this mess, but the least we can do is to try to make some sort of show for Hazel's sake. I heard all you said to my wife so there's no need to repeat it. I only hope your deeds will match your words, young man."

Sam looked at John Munro straight in the eye. "I have every intention that they will. You once said I had a very stubborn streak in me. You were right. I still have and I'm going to succeed."

"Time will tell. But what are your plans? You're not going to stay in the army, are you?"

"I did think about that, but no, I want to be with Hazel all the time."

"So?"

"I haven't decided yet what I'll do, I have a number of ideas."

"Well, I'm not going to play the heavy handed father. Despite what she's done, I still love my daughter very much and I have no intention of turning her out. Her mother and I have arranged for you to have the two attic rooms until you are demobbed and can find a place of your own."

"That's good of you. I appreciate it. Thank you both. Now if you don't mind I'll take a walk along and meet Hazel."

When Sam went out John Munro sat down opposite his wife. "Well?" he began. "What do you think now he's here?"

"It's hard not to like him," Ella said after a while.

"Yes. Even when he was a young tearaway, I never disliked him; now he's the man he is, well, I'm not surprised he swept Hazel off her feet. If he'd just had a bit more sense and waited, but then, what could you expect?"

"What do you mean?"

"I'll say no more."

"John …"

"No, I've said enough. Here they come."

THE WEDDING took place in the front room of The Willows. Kent Mollison had travelled up to Levenford to be Sam's best man, and Hazel had as her bridesmaid a teaching colleague, Joan Traynor. The only other people present were John and Ella Munro, Dr and Mrs Blackwood, old Mrs Whyte from the farm, and the minister.

It had been decided there were to be no speeches so after the simple ceremony, Dr Blackwood proposed a toast to the bride and groom and Sam simply replied, "Thank you on behalf of my wife and myself."

Mrs Munro had decided that despite all her regrets she would provide as grand a meal as possible and that she did. When it was over, and Sam and Hazel had gone off to Helensburgh to spend the remaining days of his leave there and the other guests had departed, she turned to her husband and said, "I had always pictured my daughter being a lovely radiant bride in white, walking down the aisle in the church, drawing admiration from all the guests and then a big reception in an hotel, but it was not to be."

"There's always Neil."

"A son's wedding isn't the same, but yes, Neil will do it the right way, I'm sure."

"I hope so. I don't know about you, my dear, but this has really worn me out. I'm dog tired."

"I am too, but I'm glad it's over. Maybe the talk will die down now – at least till the baby comes and then they'll all know."

"As Bill Blackwood says it's happened before, but when your own children are involved, it's bitter pill to swallow."

"Sam was very quiet. Despite myself I felt sorry for him, not having a family."

"He's got Hazel now. I suppose we'll have to accept him as our son-in-law. There's nothing else for it."

"No, we can't undo what's been done."

"What a pair of miseries we are. Here, I'm having another drink. What about you?"

"All right, just a small one."

SAM CLOSED the bedroom door of the hotel in Helensburgh and turned to face Hazel. His heart was beating wildly and he swallowed hard several times before he finally spoke.

"Hazel, I want you to know that I still love you, and I love you even more now, and I'll do everything I can to make you happy."

"I know, Sam," Hazel said quietly.

"The point is, Hazel, do you still love me?"

Hazel moved over to where Sam still stood leaning against the door as if he needed its support to keep him upright. He could see Hazel's eyes fill with tears.

"Oh Sam," she whispered, "how can you doubt me? I love you. I want you to put your arms round me and hold me tight. I need you, Sam. Love me, oh, love me now!"

- 19 -

KENT stepped off the train at Glasgow Queen Street, made his way up the stairs from the low level to the main station hall and looked around for a telephone kiosk. When he eventually found one which was free he took the slip of paper from his wallet, asked for the number, waited for his call to be answered, then inserted his money.

"Hello," he said, when a female voice spoke, "is that Stella Clark?"

"Yes, it is," the reply was given in a questioning tone.

"I'm Kent Mollison. Your husband Ross was one of my mates before he was wounded."

"Goodness, yes. Ross has spoken a lot about you. Where are you phoning from?"

"I'm in Glasgow, at Queen Street Station. I've been up for Sam's wedding. You've met Sam. I was wondering if I could come and see Ross tomorrow before I go back to York."

"Of course, but why not come tonight?"

"Well, I don't know my way about Glasgow and I'll have to find somewhere to stay and by the time I do that it would be too late."

"But what I mean is, you can stay with us tonight. You must."

"Is Ross at home just now?"

"No, he still goes for physiotherapy in the evening. It saves him missing classes at the University. Look, I'll give you directions how to get here, it's quite easy. You've just to go out of the station to George Square and you'll get a bus. And Kent, I won't let on to Ross you're coming; it'll be a wonderful surprise for him."

"If you're sure it's OK, I'd love to come tonight. Thanks very much."

"Right, listen carefully."

WHEN KENT reached Jordanhill and walked down the avenue of imposing looking houses, his thoughts went back to his own very modest home. He paused as he finally reached the gate of number forty three and wondered to himself what Ross must have thought on his visit to York. For a moment he wished he had not come, feeling he would be out of place in this setting, which despite the war years, still retained the aura of grandeur. But Ross had been a good friend so he'd do it for him. Funny that Sam had not mentioned that Ross came from a wealthy family – but then if he remembered correctly Sam had never visited here, even before they had gone over on D-Day. The arrival on the scene of Stella had put paid to that and Ross had still been in hospital in the south of England when Sam had gone to see him – was it on his last leave? Ross had taken longer to get over his injuries than had first been expected, having suffered from depression which had led to a breakdown in communications between him and his former army friends.

Kent pushed open the gate and walked up the drive, but before he could ring the bell or knock, the door was opened and a very attractive girl with long blonde hair reached out to draw him inside, putting a finger to his lips as she whispered, "I've been watching for you. His mum and dad have gone upstairs so Ross is on his own."

Kent followed Stella through the hall to a room at the back of the house. She opened the door quietly and said, "Ross, there's someone to see you."

Kent entered the room and looked across at the figure lying back in the armchair, eyes tightly closed, as if in pain.

"Is it someone I must see? I'm tired, Stella."

Kent turned to Stella, but she indicated to him to move over to where Ross sat. He did so, knelt down beside the chair and took hold of Ross's hands.

"I thought that now I am a sergeant, you might have leapt to attention."

Ross opened his eyes side. "Good God! Kent!" Ross choked on the words.

Kent turned back to look at Stella but found she was no longer in the room and the door was closed. He stood up, ruffled Ross's hair and said, "Come on, I feel just like you, but let's see that famous smile of yours."

With an effort Ross composed himself. "Sorry, Kent, I've been going through a bad patch recently. Can't seem to snap out of it. I'm sorry."

"Just take your time, I understand. You're looking fine, and it's great seeing you again."

Ross sat back and closed his eyes again. "I've just been for physiotherapy and it always tires me out. Oh, it does me good, I know, and tomorrow I'll feel the benefit of it. I must keep at it, I must stop complaining. Come on, just seeing you has made me feel better, tell me, are you up to see Sam, and why isn't he here with you?"

"Now this is going to shake you, Ross. This afternoon I was best man at his wedding."

"You were what? And didn't he invite me. The lousy sod."

"Now hold on, let me tell you the whole story."

Ross listened quietly and when Kent had finished said, "Well, that's different, I'll forgive him, and I'm sorry for him."

"Don't be, he's as much in love with Hazel as you are with Stella."

"Stella! I'm sure she wishes she never married me."

"Hey, I don't believe that."

"I hope you're right, Kent, she's a gem. I couldn't do without her. I know I'm difficult and altogether a bit of a wash-out as a husband and I hate myself for being so."

At that moment Stella re-entered the room. "Wasn't that a nice surprise for you Ross?"

"Yes, it was."

"I've made up a bed for Kent."

"Oh good. How long are you staying for?"

"Just for the night."

"Oh, can't you stay over the weekend? When are you due back?"

"Wednesday."

"Then you can stay."

"But Ross, it'll be bother for you and Stella, and your folks. Besides I know how difficult this rationing business is."

"Oh do stay, Kent, please, it would be lovely for Ross and we'll easily manage," Stella looked pleadingly at Kent.

He thought for a moment. "It's really very good of you both; all right, I'll stay till Sunday night. I must have a couple of days at home before I go off again."

THE FOLLOWING day being Saturday, Kent went with Ross, his father and mother, and Stella first on a tour of Glasgow and then in the afternoon to the shores of Loch Lomond where they left the car and had a stroll in the late autumn sunshine.

Kent noticed that Ross alternately had spells of non-stop chat followed by periods of silence, and he did his best to respond to the openings which Mr and Mrs Clark seemed to make for him to keep the conversation going. And despite being somewhat puzzled by the way Ross was acting, Kent was enjoying the company. He felt that while the Clarks might definitely be upper class, it certainly made no difference to their attitude to him and he appreciated it. Thinking back to how Ross had been when in the army and how he had mucked in with the rest of them, Kent gave him a large plus mark. The thing that was puzzling was why Ross had chosen not to become an officer, but looking at him, as yet again he had lapsed into one of his long silences, Kent felt that perhaps he had always been a bit unsure of himself.

When they returned home, Ross announced that as soon as they had had a meal, he was going to bed. This did not seem to surprise his parents or Stella, but afterwards when the latter was left alone with Kent, she asked,

"What do you think of Ross?"

Kent pursed his lips and shook his head slightly. "He's not the Ross that I knew before."

Stella looked down at her feet. "No," she said softly.

"Physically he's really in good shape now – apart from his leg, but as you've seen he manages very well with the artificial limb. He won't admit that though. At first he was great about it and he persevered until he conquered it, but then somehow he took a dislike to –" Stella stopped. "I shouldn't bother you with all this. Ross might be angry with me, but I feel I can't go on much longer." Then the tears flowed and Kent was off his chair and beside Stella on the settee, holding her while she sobbed her heart out.

When she had quietened, Kent said, "I'm a good listener, and after all, the members of a tank crew who are together for some time get to know each other rather well, and Sam, Ross and I were pretty close and very good friends. So if I can help in any way, I'm ready to try."

"Thanks, Kent. The truth is that Ross has become ashamed of his body – you'll have noticed he keeps himself well covered up. It is a bit of a mess, but the scars will fade, he's been told that. He hates his leg, curses it, ridicules himself; seems to blame himself for being so stupid; his back took a lot of shrapnel and of course he had a skin graft on his forehead, but you hardly notice it the way his hair is styled now. Then he gets frustrated because he can't play football any more."

"But there are other sports he could manage. What about swimming?"

"Oh, you're right, Kent, but you see he would never show himself in a swimming pool."

"I see."

"The doctors said the depression wasn't unusual and I thought once we were married everything would be fine."

"And it hasn't been."

"No," Stella's voice dropped to a whisper, "and we haven't ever made love."

Kent's mouth fell open. "You haven't – you can't be serious. But you are. Oh gosh, Stella, that's hard to believe. I don't know what to say. Aren't there doctors who deal with this sort of thing, what are they called – psychiatrists – that's it."

"Ross wouldn't go near one. I daren't suggest it. In fact, you're the first person I've told."

"Oh help. I'm out of my depth here, Stella. But last night Ross told me how much he loved you, how he was ashamed of being difficult, but I didn't realize just all that was meant by that." Kent shook his head.

"I'm sorry, Kent, to have poured out all my troubles to you, but you seem, I don't know – whenever I saw you – you seem such a strong person, just like Sam. I only met him once but he made a big impression just as you have. I can see now why Ross was so friendly with you both. He relied on you to bolster him up. He's maybe always had a bit of an inferiority complex."

"Listen, Stella, Ross was a good soldier and as brave a one as any of us. He never shirked anything and he was popular with all his mates. I'm sure he'll get over this. I know it's easy saying that, but deep down he's got what it takes."

"I only wish I could believe you were right."

Kent took Stella's hand. "Look, you're a very lovely girl. I could fall for you myself. There, I knew that would bring a smile to your face. I'm going to have a word with Ross, man to man."

"OK Kent, not tonight, he'll be asleep now."

"OK, but I'm determined to do it before I leave."

"Tomorrow morning I usually go to church with his mum and dad, so he'll be alone then."

"Fine, just the job."

"WE'LL LEAVE you to enjoy the Sunday papers then, Kent." Mrs Clark said as she and her husband left with Stella.

Kent climbed the stair and opened the bedroom door quietly.

"Well, you are a lazybones, nowadays, Ross, and you used always to be the one who was up with the lark. Come on, remember what the little fat corporal used to yell at us. 'Hands off cocks, hands on socks.'"

"OK. You go and read the papers and I'll get up."

"Getting modest in your old age, are we?" Kent gave a tug at the blankets and Ross immediately pulled them back under his chin.

"I said, go away, Kent, and I meant it."

"Well I'm not going away until you get out of that bed," and before Ross could make a move to stop him, Kent had whipped all the blankets from the bed and thrown them on the floor.

"You bastard! Get out!" Ross screamed.

But Kent only moved closer to Ross roughly removed his pyjamas, then lifted him naked from the bed. He carried him across the room to a full length mirror and held him up in front of it.

"Now, what are we looking at, a man or a mouse? For goodness sake, Ross, what have you to be ashamed of? You're still a man, damn you, and a very lucky one. I know you'll say it's easy for me to speak. OK. I was one of the very fortunate ones. But at least you're still alive. Yes, you've lost part of a leg, but you've mastered your artificial limb. Admit that! Sure, you've got a pattern of dents all over where the shrapnel caught you, but you got all that fighting for your country, for your home, your family and for Stella. Yes, Stella, you lucky bastard. There's a girl for you! And you've got brains! I wish I had some of yours. You've fitted in again at your studies without too much bother. What more do you want?" Kent slapped Ross hard across the buttocks. "You're behaving like a spoilt child. Stop being so sorry for yourself. That mine could have killed you."

Kent stopped exhausted from his outburst.

"I hate you, Kent. I thought you were my friend, but you're not."

Kent slapped again. "I am your friend, that's why I'm telling you all this, you dumb bastard. Who were you kidding when you were always getting the hots for Stella, and what have you done? Nothing. Bloody nothing! You, you …! Wait till Sam hears about this."

Ross almost slipped from Kent's hold. "What the –" Kent pulled him upright, then lifted him back on the bed. "Come on Ross, be your old self again, be a man."

There was no response and Kent rose to go, but as he was half way through the door Ross called, "Kent, please!"

"Kent," Ross began, "I'm sorry –"

"Stop using that word sorry. I meant everything I said. I don't take anything back."

"I suppose Stella told you all about me."

"Yes, she did. You've almost succeeded in breaking that girl's spirit, you fool. You told me when I came here that you loved her. You've a funny way of showing it."

"Kent," Ross tried again. I deserved all you said. I know I'm being stupid, but –"

"No buts – just get on with your life – as a married man."

"All right, I will, believe me, I will. Kent – you won't tell Sam, will you?"

Kent sat down on the bed. "Sam means a lot to you, Ross, a lot more than I do, no, don't protest, it's true, after all you started off with him, and anyway it doesn't matter. OK, I won't tell Sam on one condition."

"What's that?"

"You should know, but I'll spell it out to you – get your wife pregnant tonight."

"But Kent –"

"There you go again with your buts. I know you've still a long way to go at University, that you're not earning while you're a student, but I'm sure you're well enough off. You seem to need something more than your lovely wife to live for – start a family, and then you'll soon stop thinking about yourself all the time."

Kent went to pack his haversack and then went downstairs. He was starting to write a note on the pad beside the telephone when Ross appeared.

"You're not going now, are you?"

"Yes, it's best I get away before Stella and your folk get back."

"But why? Stay till evening. Dad will run us in to the station. Kent, we're still friends, I hope. It means a lot to me."

Kent crumpled the note. "OK, I'll wait. It would be rude to go without thanking Stella and your folks. As to our still being friends, well, that's entirely up to you."

"Write your address on the pad. I'll send you word as soon as I've – well, you know."

Kent smiled. "Hit the bull's eye."

"Yes, hit the bull's eye. Anyway, I've got to keep upsides with Sam."

"That's the spirit."

"And I'm the odd man out", Kent said to himself.

- 20 -

NEIL lay stretched out, face down on his bed and listened to the sounds of doors opening and closing, marking the departure of his fellow officers leaving for a night on the town. He waited until there had been a period of silence before he sat up and reached out to read again his mother's letter.

> *The Willows,*
> *Levenford.*

23rd February 1947

My Dear Neil

I was pleased to have your letter on Saturday morning saying you had received your parcel. It did not take long to reach you after all.

I really thought your demob would have been earlier than May, but the time will soon pass. Dad and I are so looking forward to having you at home again. We'll have a full house, but it will be just great after all these worrying years.

The arctic weather continues; the frost was very severe this morning. The electricity was off last Sunday forenoon, though not today, but it is cold in the house. I am sitting writing this with the travelling rug round my legs. They have been curling on the pond behind the cemetery and skating on it too. Only five weeks till Easter, surely the weather will have improved by then.

Neil folded the letter. He had read it over several times and knew the rest of the contents almost by heart. He could picture his mother sitting at the table by the window writing in her scholarly hand, and for a moment he experienced a twinge of homesickness.

He rose quickly and pulling on his greatcoat made his way downstairs, out of the officers' block and across to the mess. It was deserted, as it often was on a Saturday evening, but for Georges, the young German who kept the bar.

"Good evening, sir," he greeted Neil.

"Hello Georges. I'll have a beer please, and take one for yourself."

"Thank you, sir."

"'Neil', Georges, when there's no one about."

"OK, Neil, what is wrong tonight?"

"What makes you think there's something wrong?"

"Isn't there? You look sad, or maybe I should say worried."

"Georges, you're too clever by half. Yes, I suppose I am worried, worried about going home."

"How can you say such a thing, Neil? You should be happy to be going back to your own country and your family."

"I know, but –" Neil's voice tailed off.

They drank in silence for a moment or two before Georges said, "But there's Anna Maria."

"Yes, there's Anna Maria."

"You love her very much?"

"Yes, and I can't take her with me when I go on demob."

"Are you sure, Neil, that you do really love her, or is she just very good in bed for you?"

"Georges, if I hadn't come to regard you as one of my best friends, I'd hit you for saying that, but you're so perceptive. Yes, we're made for each other – completely. I'm absolutely sure of that."

"So, what are you going to do about it?"

"I don't know. I suppose I could sign on, but what my folks would say to that I daren't think. I'm not all that enamoured with army life in peacetime and I would really like to get back to University."

"So, there's no problem. Go home, and if Anna Maria loves you as much as you love her, she'll be prepared to wait until she can be with you in Scotland, no matter how long it takes."

"Georges, you make it sound so easy."

"I only wish I had a home and family to go to."

"Sorry, Georges, I know you've lost all your folks, you have virtually nothing. To you, I have everything, which is right in a way, but I can't have the one person I want, Anna Maria. Oh, it's selfish, maybe it's wrong, but I know she is the one for me."

"You haven't mentioned Anna Maria in your letters to your parents?"

"Gosh no. How could I? She's a Ger...?" Neil suddenly stopped and looked in horror at Georges. "Oh no, no, I don't mean – Georges, you must understand."

"Yes Neil, I understand," Georges said quietly. "It is only natural that your parents would be horrified at the idea of your marrying a German, one of the enemy. Please don't apologise, it's only natural. But if you get the chance, tell your parents that we are not all bad. There were many Germans who did not want the war, who detested Hitler and his Gestapo."

"I will, Georges, I will. You make me feel very humble at times. You so seldom feel any self pity, you just accept your lot and never complain."

"I am one of the lucky ones, to have this job and have a room here to call my own."

"I'm sure you could land a job as an interpreter, your English is so good."

"Ah Neil, you have helped me a lot with it, but if I was an interpreter I wouldn't have my room. Then they seem to prefer girls for that job, girls like your Anna Maria. I take it she has gone off to Hamburg again for the weekend?"

"Yes, to see her aunt who was the only one of her family to survive the bombing. How about a game of snooker, since you don't seem to be having any other customers tonight?"

"Is it all right?"

"Of course it is, if anyone were to object it's me they'd have to deal with, not you."

"OK."

They played at a leisurely pace until ten o'clock when Neil said, "Right, one more drink and then I'm off. I must try to write home and tell them about Anna Maria."

"Good luck, then. I'll see you tomorrow."

"Yes," Neil said as he finished his drink, "I'll be in at lunchtime. Goodnight, Georges."

"Goodnight, Neil."

HE COULD start with the weather. It was even colder in Kiel than in Levenford – he was sure of that. He could write about Georges – he had mentioned him before – and that would lead on to Anna Maria. Yes, it seemed so easy, but when he sat down with his pen poised over the paper, Neil found he just could not write what he wanted to say. Finally after numerous attempts he gave up, undressed and got into bed. But sleep was slow to come.

He thought of his father and mother; then of Hazel and Sam and their baby due next month. He wondered just how it would work out; whether, when the baby arrived, his father and mother's attitude to Sam would change.

"Oh Sam," he spoke the words half aloud, "we're certainly causing a few problems. How I wish I could talk this over with you. You would understand. Funny the friends I make. Take Georges, a young German, one of the enemy as he would say, yet we're on the same wavelength; I feel just as I did with you, when we're together, at ease. I wonder what you'd think of Anna Maria. You must have changed, for you were never interested in girls, but now with Hazel, well – and that's how it is with me. I love Anna Maria."

THE FOLLOWING afternoon Neil tramped his way through the snow to the room which Anna Maria had in a house in Kiel. He let himself in and immediately set to building a fire in the stove which stood in one corner of the room. The old man who owned the house somehow managed to give Anna Maria a small but regular supply of wood which allowed her to keep the room at a reasonable temperature. Neil consulted his watch as he waited, still clad in his greatcoat, for the stove to really get going, and wondered if he should start preparing a meal. Anna Maria was returning with Jake Robson, who had been Neil's troop sergeant during the fighting. He had gone to Hamburg to collect supplies of spare parts and had worked in a forty eight hour pass as well. Although he no longer came under Neil's direct command, his admiration and respect for Neil remained and he was always willing to do any service for him.

Neil stood indecisive, thinking about the long journey and the state of the roads. He knew Jake was an excellent driver, but he'd take no risks, so perhaps they might be later than they had anticipated.

Neil stretched out on the bed and thought of Anna Maria. He knew his mother would be appalled if he told her he wanted to marry a German. Her idea was that he should marry a Scots girl, preferably one who lived in Levenford. Neil smiled to himself. Yes, he'd had several school romances, but they had been the fanciful forays of adolescence. Those days seemed so far off. And he never managed to make even the beginnings of real romance on any of his leaves. In fact, the only time he had experienced real feelings of love had been his affair with Susan. But it hadn't been the love he had for Anna Maria.

Neil buttoned up his greatcoat and went to look out at the front door. The light was fading fast and snow was beginning to fall. They'd probably be another hour at least before they were back, he thought, and returned to the room which was beginning to throw off its mantle of cold air. He lay down on the bed again, since neither of the two chairs Anna Maria had managed to procure were particularly comfortable. Neil's thoughts went back to Susan.

HE HAD MET her when he was stationed in Little Burton, a village about five miles from Banbury. At a loose end one Saturday afternoon, he had wandered with some of his fellow officers into a garden fete where Susan had been in charge of the tea tent. He had been immediately attracted to her, but had noticed as she handed him his cup of tea that she wore a wedding ring. Nevertheless Neil found himself joining in the 'chatting-up' of Susan which followed, and when his companions decided it was time to get back to camp, somehow or other he had remained behind and helped Susan with the clearing up.

"You're quite domesticated, well trained by your mother, I suppose," Susan said as Neil folded the dish towel.

Neil laughed. "Mum may have tried but she didn't succeed. I'm afraid my sister Hazel was landed with the kitchen chores."

"Typical of the modern male."

"That's not quite fair. You see, Dad's a vet and we have a number of animals at home and I had to help him to look after them."

"All right, I'll let you off. Are you going to follow in your father's footsteps?"

"He'd like me to, but no. I think I'll end up teaching."

"Oh, I wouldn't have the patience for that, even if I had the brains for it."

"Ha, ha, pull the other one. You look clever enough to me."

"Flattery will get you nowhere, young man. By the way, I'm Susan Britton."

"And I'm Neil Munro."

"Have you to get back to the camp now?"

"Not really, tea's never very exciting on a Saturday and the mess dance doesn't start till eight o'clock."

"I've heard of these from some of my friends."

"Oh, would you, I mean – no, I can't ask you."

"To come with you to your mess dance?"

"Yes."

"Because I'm married?"

"Well, it wouldn't be right, would it?"

"Look Neil, may I call you Neil? Tom, my husband is in the Royal Navy. He's a doctor. He's my father's assistant, or was, until he volunteered to serve. The last time he was home on leave we both agreed that it wouldn't be natural if we tried to live like saints, that to keep our sanity we had to have some sort of social life, that we should accept reasonable invitations, provided we always remembered we were married and that we both loved each other very much."

"So, have I made you a reasonable invitation?"

"Yes, you have, so when will you call for me?"

"Shall we say eight o'clock?"

"Fine, that gives me time to have a bath, wash my hair, and generally titivate myself."

Neil smiled. "All for me?"

"Yes, why not? Now I live in the cottage at the end of this lane, which runs alongside the Rectory garden where we are now. It's the only one, so you can't miss it – Rose Cottage a very aptly named little dwelling, I may say, thanks to the previous owner."

When later they walked the half mile which distanced the camp from the village, Neil asked, "In a place this size, won't there be a bit of gossip going when they see you out with me?"

"Sure to be, but there's a war on, as you well know, Neil. No, I'm not worried. I'm a trained nurse and as my father hasn't been able to get anyone in Tom's place, I do my best to assist him in the surgery and with confinements, and even delivering prescriptions, so I'm well known to most folks. Dad has a scattered practice and is kept pretty busy."

"I said you looked a clever sort of person and yet you scoffed at me."

"Well, I'm the practical sort, not so hot on the theory side, but I usually manage to cope. Now that's enough about me. You tell me something about yourself."

SO THEIR friendship started and Neil came to spend most of his off duty hours with Susan, dropping into the cottage as if it was his home, listening to her records on an old gramophone, helping her in the garden, or just relaxing in a deck chair.

"I've told Tom about you," Susan announced one day as they enjoyed a walk through the woods which lay to the north of the village.

"You have?" Neil sounded slightly put out.

"Yes, why not? We don't have secrets from each other."

"And he doesn't mind?"

"Why should he? I told you what we had agreed. Anyway, he's been out with at least three young ladies."

"Safety in numbers."

"I hope so."

"Did he say anything about me?"

Susan laughed. "I better not tell you."

"Go on, I want to know."

"You won't feel hurt?"

"Do you think I might?"

"I told him how old you were and he said I'd get taken up for cradle snatching."

"How old is he then?"

"He's twenty nine and I'm twenty five."

"A couple of ancient birds."

"Touché, Neil. But Tom went on to say that despite your tender years you sounded quite nice."

"I should be thankful for small mercies."

"You are hurt then?"

Neil shrugged his shoulders. "No, it's OK. It's just that I don't like being patronized."

Susan stopped and taking both Neil's hands in hers said, "Look, Neil, to me your age doesn't matter, you're now a very good friend and you've saved me from becoming very fed up with this war."

"Well, you've certainly been terrific for me, Susan, I'm glad I've given you a little in return for all you've given me."

They walked in silence until they reached the cottage. "Come on in, you've time for a cuppa."

As she busied herself in the kitchen Susan said, "We had planned everything so differently, you see. I've lived here all my life and I wanted a change. Of course it would be cosy for Tom to eventually take over from Daddy and do a rerun of what he and Mum have had. But Tom was keen to go abroad and so was I. Then this wretched war came. I'm happy enough in my work here and there's plenty to do and I shouldn't complain. There are a lot of folk much worse off than I am. In fact, I'm on a good wicket here, as Tom would say."

"He's a cricketer then?"

"Yes, a good all-rounder, just like you."

"How did you know that?"

"Ah, one of your friends told me when I was dancing with him last week. Said you were quite an athlete."

"I try."

"Modest fellow. Here, tea's ready."

As he left for the camp that evening Susan reached up and kissed Neil on the cheek. "You'll forgive Tom for his stupid remark. If he met you, I know he'd become as fond of you as I have. Good night, Neil, and take care."

Neil returned the kiss and said softly, "I like you a lot, Susan, good night."

- 21 -

A WEEK later when Neil arrived at Rose Cottage, Susan's first words were, "Is it true?"

Neil gave a sad smile and nodded his head, "I'm afraid it is, we're moving in a couple of days. At least I am, for I'm going on the advance party to our new quarters."

"Oh Neil, I'm going to miss you."

"I dare say there'll be another unit coming here to take our place and who knows what dashing young officer you'll sweep off his feet."

"No, Neil, there won't be another, you've been special. I don't know why, but right from the time you spoke to me at the fete, we've had this togetherness."

Neil put his arms round Susan and held her close, his lips gently caressing her hair. "Yes, you're right. I've never experienced such a wonderful relationship with a girl before. To me, you're a super person, and I shan't forget the times we've been together and the happiness we've shared."

"Do you know where you're going?"

"Yes, I do. I can't tell you where and actually it's not very far from here."

"But far enough to make it impossible for you to pop in and see me whenever you're off duty."

"'Fraid so, but I could perhaps come at a weekend. That's if you thought it would be all right."

"Oh Neil, could you? At least that would be something. And of course it would be all right."

"It'll depend, of course, what we're to be doing in our next phase of training."

"How I wish this war was over. Tom, far away for months on end on convoy duty, now you quite near, but really just as far."

"Would you like me to write?"

"Of course. I'd be hurt if you didn't, but phone me if you can, especially when you know you can get away so I can arrange to be absolutely free to entertain you."

NEIL SOON realised the training had become more intense; lectures, briefings, then a succession of schemes which left little time for relaxing. The weekend freedom which he had anticipated had not materialised, for under a new commanding officer, the junior subalterns were expected to be at his beck and call twenty four hours a day, seven days a week.

"Frustration is the name of the game at the moment," he told Susan when he managed to phone her. "When I'm going to manage to come and see you, I just don't know."

But even commanding officers went on leave and immediately the pressure was off. Neil found himself free of all duties for a twenty four hour period and despite being unable to contact Susan by telephone, he decided to risk going to see her. The train journey to Banbury was accomplished successfully, but having arrived there Neil found that the bus service to Little Burton was, to put it mildly, limited, and the next bus would not be for another four hours.

Neil said to himself, "Perhaps it's undignified for officers to hitch a lift, but on the other hand, you're encouraged to use your initiative, so here goes."

He started walking and he was in luck, for he had only gone about half a mile when an old Rover car slowed to a halt.

"Where are you heading, soldier?" an even older man enquired of Neil when he had wound down the window of the car.

"To Little Burton."

"Well, I can take you within a mile. I turn off then up to my farm."

"Thank you very much, sir, a mile will be no problem. I'm very grateful."

"What brings you here?"

"I was stationed here some time ago."

"So you're back to see the girl friend."

"You could say that."

"War – it's all a matter of loving on the one hand and of hating on the other, but it's not quite the same this time."

"Sorry?"

"This war. It's different. Fought in the 14-18 myself, in the trenches. Terrible it was, but maybe this is worse. The air raids. I suppose we've been lucky round here, but any camp will be a target. Where are you from?"

The old man's abrupt questioning amused Neil, but he managed to give answers which seemed to satisfy him and when the car came to a halt at the end of the farm road, the old man said, "I'd take you all the way, lad, but it's the petrol, you know."

"Thanks again, sir."

"Goodbye, and good luck with your girl friend, soldier."

THERE WAS no answer to Neil's knock when he eventually arrived at the front door of Rose Cottage and everything seemed very quiet and the place had a deserted look about it. He wondered if he should call on Susan's parents, but he was rather reluctant to do so for he had felt that they had not altogether approved of his friendship with his daughter.

He peered into the garage through the tiny cobwebbed window and saw that Susan's car was there, but there was no sign of her bicycle, and his hopes rose. He knew she often went on her bicycle to visit patients who didn't live too far away, but then wondered if she would be doing that on a Saturday afternoon. He wandered round to the back of the house, tried the door there, but it was securely locked.

He recalled Susan's words. "There was a time when we never locked our doors here, but now, well, who wants to find a German paratrooper in the sitting room? Not that I always remember."

But she had remembered this time and Neil turned and walked disconsolately down the garden to the summerhouse, almost hidden under the arch of rambler roses, still blooming in the late autumn. The door was unlocked. Neil stood undecided as to what to do. Idly he picked up the newspaper lying on the table beside the divan which took up the whole of the back wall of the summerhouse. His heart leapt when he saw it was that day's edition. So Susan had been at home, at least in the morning, and she was probably not far away. Neil walked up the garden to the back of the house, took off his black beret and hung it on the door handle, then returned to the summerhouse, stretched out on the divan and fell fast asleep.

Half awake he brushed his hand across his face to waft away some insect which was annoying him, but it persisted, so he made a more decisive movement with his hand. It seemed to do the trick, but as he settled to sleep again, he felt the slight pressure of two lips on his, and opening his eyes, found Susan bending over him.

"Some soldier you are, Lieutenant Neil Munro, no defence at all. I could have done anything to you."

"Such as?"

"That would be telling. Have you been here long?"

Neil looked at his watch. "I must have been asleep for more than an hour."

"Why didn't you let me know you were coming?"

"I did phone, but there was no reply."

"Never mind, let's go in and have something to eat. I bet you're starving. How long have you?"

"I'll have to go back tonight."

"Oh, must you?"

"I have an overnight pass, but I'll have to get the last train from Banbury, and I've to get there first."

"I can run you there, I've just filled up with petrol."

"But –"

"Oh, I'll use my bike when I run short. Come on – food calls."

THEY FOUND the easy, friendly relationship which they had previously enjoyed had not suffered from their separation. Susan was eager to hear all about what Neil had been doing, and in turn she filled him in with all the village happenings.

"The new lot at the camp don't seem to be as friendly as your unit was, no Saturday night hops. The Bull, though is doing a roaring trade, and the church canteen is always pretty busy too. I sometimes lend a hand there, but Dad and I seem to have been on call non-stop recently."

They chatted on till suddenly Susan stopped in mid-sentence. "Goodness, that's the siren, it must be a raid."

"That's what it usually means, so what's the drill here?"

"I go down into the cellar beneath the kitchen, the hatch is under the table. I don't think I've ever shown it to you."

"We'd better go down then."

They had just opened the hatch when they heard the first bombs fall.

"Gosh, that was close. I wonder what they're after round here."

"You'd be surprised, Neil, what the targets are in this area."

"Oh, how come you're so knowledgeable?"

"Well, you know I get around quite a bit and I see lots of things on my travels. There's a big ammo dump been set up about five miles on the other side of the village – at least that's what I think."

"Crikey, if you're right and they're on target with their bombs, there's going to be one hell of a bang."

"How would they know, though?"

Neil shook his head. "I can't say, but they must have their agents working here, just as we have ours over there. On the other hand, it may be sheer luck, and of course, there's quite a concentration of military forces in this area, so really they've a fifty fifty chance of hitting something, no matter where they drop their bombs."

The drone of enemy planes overhead continued, interspersed with ack-ack fire, but no more sounds of explosions.

"They seem to be heading further south," Neil said after listening intently. "I think I'll have a look out and see what's happening."

"I'm coming too."

Neil took a ladder and propping it against the side of the cottage climbed on to the roof to gain a high vantage point.

"No sign of any fires as far as I can see, and it's all quiet in the village, no sound of anyone moving about."

"I'm afraid you won't get your train now, Neil."

Neil looked at his watch and gave a resigned sigh. "You're right. Even if it was held up it'll have gone by now. I'll just have to hope I can get some form of transport in the morning to get me back to camp by nine o'clock."

"Will you be in trouble?"

"If I'm later than that I could be, but as tomorrow's Sunday I might be OK, provided the CO doesn't suddenly arrive back from his leave and start from where he left off."

As they stood at the cottage door the silence was broken by the 'All Clear' sounding.

"Best try and get some sleep and I'll run you to Banbury. I think there may be an early morning local train which carries the milk even on a Sunday. We can try."

"Thanks, Susan."

"Come on then."

She led Neil into the bedroom. "But where are you going to sleep?" he asked.

They looked at each other for a moment without speaking, before Neil drew Susan into his arms. "If I'm to have the bed, I'd like you to share it with me," he whispered. "I want to make love to you, Susan, but if I'm out of order, please say so, and I'll leave now."

Susan slowly unbuttoned his tunic, then unknotted his tie. When she had pulled his shirt over his head and he was bare to the waist, she said softly,

"Now you help me, Neil."

Her breasts were firm and when he brushed his lips lightly across them, her hands went to his waist belt and his trousers slid to the floor.

"Oh Neil," Susan murmured, "I'm needing to be loved so much."

His hands worked neatly to reveal her entire nakedness and their bodies moulded together as one. Then gently he lifted her on to the bed and she reached out to him as he knelt above her, and guided him to feel his strength within her, giving a little cry which caused him to pause and ask, "Am I hurting you?"

"No, my darling Neil, love me, slowly, don't be afraid. I want all of you. I want to have all the power of your body in mine."

They climaxed together and slowly their heartbeats regained their rhythm.

"I do love you, Susan." Neil managed to say as he drifted into sleep.

HE STIRRED drowsily, then reality came, and he sat up quickly. Susan, standing beside the bed, smiled and said, "I thought I'd let you sleep as long as possible. I've brought you hot water and what you need to shave. While you're doing that, I'll rustle up some tea and toast, then we'll get off for Banbury."

"Susan –" Neil started, but she put her fingers on his lips, then leaned forward and kissed him gently on the cheek.

"Don't say anything, Neil. What we had last night between us was special, something I won't ever forget. Now, best get moving if we want to catch that train."

The hurried breakfast, eaten in silence in the kitchen; the car journey through the semi-darkness; the quick embrace before his dash to the platform; and the final wave from Susan as she stood at the barrier, all seemed to recede quickly into the past for Neil as he sank back in the empty compartment and closed his eyes.

His mind was in turmoil. Had it really happened? Had he made love for the very first time with a girl with whom he had formed a very special relationship, but was another man's wife? Had Susan meant what she said? He felt guilty. He would write and apologise, but no sooner had he decided this, than he remembered the ecstasy of their union. And he remembered too, the only conversation they'd had in the car.

"Phone me when you can, and let me know if you made it back in time."

So she hadn't dismissed him altogether, but would she want to see him again?

THE TRAIN slowed to a halt seemingly in the middle of nowhere and Neil looked disconsolately at his watch. No way was he going to make the camp by nine o'clock at this rate. He lowered the window and looked out, but it seemed as if he was the only person on the train. It seemed as if the engine driver and his mate had decided to abandon their train such was the unreal stillness which pervaded the scene. Neil considered getting out to investigate, when he found, crossing to the other window, that there was the same eerie silence. He thought again of Susan and tried to picture her driving back to Rose Cottage, tidying the kitchen, making the bed where they had lain in each other's arms. And would she pick up the photograph of Tom, her husband, which stood on her dressing table? And would she feel any remorse? Had she done it because of what Tom had said about cradle snatching? To prove he was a man? No! Although the remark still rankled, he had experienced a new emotion, but it had been all too brief.

Suddenly the train gave a jolt and Neil fell back on to the seat and as he stood up again to look out, another erratic movement sent him sprawling almost on to the floor. When he managed to right himself the train had gained a steadier rhythm and was gradually picking up speed.

When he alighted at Banbury the first person he saw was his troop sergeant, Jake Robson, who saluted smartly when Neil reached him.

"Morning, sir," he called, "I was hoping you'd be on this train."

Neil returned the salute. "How on earth, Sergeant Robson, did you know?"

Sergeant Robson grinned, "You'd be surprised how I get my information, sir. Best keep it a secret"

"All right then. I am certainly pleased to see you, but what goes?"

"I've got transport outside, I'll fill you in on the way to camp."

"Sounds ominous."

As soon as Jake Robson set the Jeep in motion he said, "We're off this afternoon on a special course, hush-hush, you know."

"You mean you and me?"

"Yes, sir, just the two of us – hand picked by the old man. By the way, he's back. First thing this morning."

"He's back! Goodness, he didn't take much of a leave."

"That's him all over, sir. Apparently lives for the army. Seems though that the adjutant should have told us before we'd been selected, but there was a slip up."

"Selected, you say. I bet you it's because he thinks I'm not up to scratch."

"No, I don't think so, sir, quite the reverse."

"Sergeant, that's big of you to say so, but I can hardly believe it."

"No matter. All hell was let loose when he discovered we hadn't been told, and then when I got the message from the RSM to pass on to you, well, I didn't know what to do, knowing you were out of camp."

"I did have a twenty four hour pass."

Sergeant Robson was silent so Neil went on.

"I had it from Major Arthur."

"Sir, if you don't mind me saying so, Major Arthur would sign anything put in front of him. No offence meant, but anyhow, I knew I had to find you and I did. End of story."

"Well Sergeant, I won't press you to fill in the details, all I can say is, thank you for saving my bacon, I appreciate it very much."

"Any time, sir."

"Thanks again, Sergeant."

SO NEIL had no time to contact Susan and when he returned to his base after a period of three weeks, he was due for leave. He wondered if he should try to visit Susan on his return journey from Levenford, and decided to put his proposition to her. He listened to the telephone ringing and was about to hang up when a male voice answered, "Hello, who's calling?"

For a moment Neil was thrown, but recovering, asked, "Could I speak to Susan, please?"

"Who is it?"

"Neil Munro."

"Neil Munro." The voice at the other end of the line repeated the name, then after a moment's silence said, "Hold on, I'll fetch her."

Susan sounded breathless when she answered, "Hello Neil, how are you?"

"I'm fine, thank you, how are you?"

"Great. Tom's home, as you'll have gathered. It's marvellous having him here."

"That's tremendous for you." Neil somehow tumbled out the words.

"Did you phone for anything in particular?"

"No, not really. I'm off home on leave myself tomorrow for ten days."

"That'll be nice for you and your mum and dad. Enjoy yourself. Now I must dash, we're just on our way out to meet friends. Thanks for phoning. Goodbye."

"Goodbye, Susan."

Neil replaced the receiver feeling he had been kicked where it hurt most. On his way back to his billet he met Sergeant Robson, who after saluting him, stopped and said, "Have a good leave, sir."

"Thanks Sergeant."

"Something wrong, sir? You don't look so good."

"I'll be all right."

"Anything I can do, sir?"

"No, thank you Sergeant. You're off on leave too, so likewise have a good time."

"You bet. I will, sir, but remember if there is anything I can help you with, you've only to ask."

Neil looked at Jake Robson. "Sergeant Robson, I know you're at least six years older than I am, but I'm not a child altogether." Neil gave a snort of disgust. "Oh, I didn't mean to sound as if I was putting you in your place, its just – well, it's a personal affair. I can't discuss it with you. I appreciate your interest in my welfare. Maybe I'm not cut out to be an officer."

"Why do you say that? Of course you are, one of the best. May I, with respect sir, say you're also a human being just like the rest of us, and like us, you have your problems too." Sergeant Robson laughed. "That sounds a bit crazy, but maybe you get my meaning."

"Yes, I do. Maybe I'll be able to sort myself out during my leave. If not, I'll just have to use you as my father confessor."

"I'm not that old, sir."

DURING HIS leave Neil reluctantly came to the conclusion that it would be best to try to forget Susan. Obviously she loved her husband and wanted to ignore what had happened between them and it would only be embarrassing for them both if he visited her again. In the event, on his return from leave, Neil found his regiment on the move yet again, and gradually Susan and their moments of ecstasy became but a bitter sweet memory.

NEIL WOKE with a start as Anna Maria opened the door and hurriedly rose from the bed.

"Sweetheart," he said, gathering her in his arms, "how I've missed you."

"But I haven't been away for a long time, Neil."

"It seemed so to me, come beside the stove, you look frozen. I'll prepare supper while you thaw out. I had intended to have something ready, but I knew you'd be delayed and I waited, and then I must have fallen asleep."

"It's all right, Neil, my darling."

Later, as they lay close together in bed, Neil said, "I do love you Anna Maria, with all my heart, you must know that, and I intend marrying you when it is permitted and to take you to Scotland."

"And I love you too, Neil, with all my heart."

"I've decided, though, to take my demob and go home and start on my University course again. The sooner I qualify the better, for then I'll be able to make a home for you, though I hope you'll be with me before I do finish my course. You understand?"

"Of course I do, Neil, it is for the best. I shall be ready to come to you as soon as it is permitted."

"I shall hate leaving you here, but if I sign on, I could easily be posted away."

"You've made the correct decision, Neil, and besides, I have talked it over with my aunt. I can go and live with her in Hamburg. There is a good job there waiting for me and we will be better off together. I wouldn't like to stay here on my own when you have gone."

Neil was silent for some time, then he asked, "Are you sure you'll be all right?"

"Of course, I have survived so far and now things can only get better, but I shall look forward to coming to your country."

Neil drew her close to him again. "You are the most wonderful girl I've ever met. I know my family will love you."

- 22 -

IT was the end of September and Neil was beginning to realize that his days of idleness were numbered and that soon he'd have to face up to adjusting to life at the University again. He had enjoyed the long hot summer which had followed the arctic conditions of the winter months both in Germany and Britain, occasionally going with his father on his rounds, helping with innumerable jobs which were requiring to be done in and around the house, but most of all enjoying again the company of Sam and Hazel, and not least their baby daughter Sara.

And it was Sara he was looking at as she lay asleep in her pram under the shade of the willow tree which stood at the bottom of the garden.

"She's lovely." Neil's mother had crossed the grass to join him.

"Yes, she's a little beauty."

His mother's words gave Neil hope, for since Sara's birth, Ella Munro's attitude to Sam and Hazel's marriage had softened. Neil knew that she had not fully forgiven them and deep down the hurt remained, but the presence of her first grandchild in her house had made a difference. And it was this change which encouraged Neil to think that when eventually he was able to bring Anna Maria over from Germany to be his wife, his parents might come to accept her.

Neil was aware that at the moment both his father and mother were still horrified by the idea and he knew full well that they were hoping that he would forget her. The shock and disgust they had expressed when Neil had told them of his plans was etched clearly on his mind.

"A German!" his father had thundered, "You'd think to bring a Hun into my house. Never!"

Neil tried to keep his temper, "Yes Dad, a German, but like many others she was not a Nazi, her father lost his business and eventually everything he possessed, because he refused to join the Nazi party. And then all Anna Maria's family were killed in the bombing, and apart from an aunt, she is now on her own."

"And she latched on to you, an easy option."

"It wasn't like that at all. We love each other very much and I intend to marry her. It was Anna Maria who persuaded me to take my demob and not sign on in the army for a further period."

"Is she a Catholic?" his mother suddenly asked, "or did they give up all religion in Germany when Hitler took over?"

"She's not a Catholic."

Then Sam had intervened and Neil could well remember the cold anger which his father had directed towards him. Neil would not forget his words for a long time, even though an apology had later been given.

Sam had spoken in a quiet voice. "As Neil has said, not all Germans are bad. In fact the ones I got to know well after the fighting was over I liked better than any French or Belgians I met. I don't think you should judge Neil's girl till you meet her."

And his father's cruel retort. "When I want your opinion in this house, I'll ask for it. In the meantime you have nothing to say on the matter. It doesn't concern you."

Hazel had begun to protest, but Sam had said softly, "No, don't say anything, we'll go upstairs." Then turning to his father-in-law, "Hazel and I are obliged to you for giving us a roof over our heads and we're grateful, but we'll be moving out as soon as we possibly can."

Little Sara, however, had caused John Munro to think again, and he had taken Sam aside and said, "You've got to realise just how much my wife and I have been hurt by you and Neil. My words to you were hasty and I'm sorry. It's very difficult to accept the three of you as adults now, I suppose we still think of you as children."

"That's all right, but I still intend to get a place of our own just as soon as I am able," Sam had replied, but Neil knew that was a pretty forlorn hope at the moment, for Sam's earnings from his job as assistant gardener in the local nursery were meagre indeed.

Neil felt that on the surface The Willows was a happy enough household but there was always the possibility that he was sitting on the proverbial time-bomb. It was on the days when letters arrived from Anna Maria that the tension surfaced, but as neither of his parents ever enquired about her, Neil had decided that for the moment it was wiser to say no more about the matter. If there was to be another eruption of passionate feelings later on, then he would deal with it somehow. He wondered if he had erred in not seeking some temporary employment to make some money while he waited to resume his studies at the University. But he'd felt he needed a period of relaxation. It was something he could do during future vacations; he'd have a wife to support.

"I'll go and make some tea; we won't likely have many more days like this to have it outside." And Ella Munro retreated back up the garden into the house.

When she returned with a tray some twenty minutes later, she handed Neil a letter and he knew by the look on his mother's face that it was from Germany. He was disappointed to discover, when he looked at the handwriting, that it wasn't from Anna Maria as he had expected, but from Georges, who had worked in the mess bar. He put it aside and chatted to his mother as they enjoyed their tea and it was only some time after she had returned to the house that he opened the envelope and started to read.

Dear Neil,

You will see from the address that I am writing this from the home of Anna Maria's aunt, Brigitte, who sent for me to come here last week and has asked me to write this letter as she has little English.

It is with great sadness that I do so, and I am having the difficulty to know how to set down what I have to inform you. Anna Maria did not tell you that she was with your child when you left on your demob. She thought you might try to stay on and she felt it not right to keep you here because of that. Anna Maria's new job in Hamburg as an interpreter with the civil government was good and she was happy about the baby as it would be a join with you until you could take her to Scotland. Brigitte says everything was fine, but two weeks ago Anna Maria was knocked down by a car and bad hurt. They took the baby away in hospital but Anna Maria died. Brigitte says she looks after your little girl always. I am sad for you, Neil.

Your friend, Georges

"SARA STILL outside?" Hazel asked her mother when she returned with her shopping.

"Yes, Neil's with her."

"I'll bring her in now."

When Hazel returned carrying Sara, she called to her mother. "No sign of Neil in the garden."

"Are you sure? I haven't heard him come into the house."

"I'll have a look when I go upstairs with Sara."

When, some time later, Hazel returned to the kitchen where her mother was busy preparing the evening meal, the latter asked, "Is Neil in his room then?"

"Neil? Oh, yes, I mean, I did look into his room but he wasn't there."

"I wonder where he went off to. It isn't like him to leave Sara on her own. Are you sure he wasn't in one of the outhouses?"

"I'll have another look."

Hazel came slowly back into the kitchen holding Georges' letter in her hand. "Mum, this letter, when did it come?"

"With the afternoon post. It was later than usual. I took it out with the tea, but Neil just put it aside."

"I know I shouldn't have read it, but when I picked it up off the grass, my eye caught on the words, 'but Anna Maria died.'"

Ella Munro sat down, her face pale. "Have you read it all?"

"Yes, I have."

"Read it to me."

When Hazel finished her mother covered her face with her hands and wept.

"Mum, what are we going to do?" Hazel asked after a few moments. "Where has Neil gone? Will he be all right?"

Ella Munro raised her head. "Poor Neil," was all she said.

Hazel went slowly out to the garden again, then round to the front of the house and down the drive to the lane which led to the main road. She thought of calling her brother's name but she felt within herself that Neil was not within earshot. She moved on until she was within sight of the traffic which now and then disturbed the peace of the early evening. Glancing at her watch, Hazel reckoned that Sam should appear on his bicycle within the next few minutes and sure enough he did.

"Hello, sweetheart," he called as he braked hard and dismounted and kissed his wife. "This is a nice surprise." Then noticing Hazel's serious face, "Here, what's wrong? Is it Sara?"

"No, she's all right, Sam, it's Neil. You'd better read this," and Hazel handed him Georges' letter.

"Good grief! What a thing to happen and there's a child! Neil will be pretty cut up, is he?"

"He's disappeared."

"Disappeared!"

"Yes. Mum took the letter out to him in the garden in the early afternoon and he hasn't been seen since. He's vanished."

"Leaving the letter, I take it?"

"Yes. Sam, where will he be?"

Sam put his arm round Hazel. "Come on, let's get home. Neil will want to be on his own for a while."

"But Sam. Where has he gone?"

"Think Hazel. There's only one place."

"Oh! The river!"

"That's where he'll be."

"We'll have to go to him."

"No, not yet. I'll go and look for him after we've had our meal."

"But will he be all right, Sam?" Ella Munro asked anxiously, when they went into the kitchen and told her what they thought. "I mean, he wouldn't do anything ..." and her voice trailed off.

"Neil? No. He'll be upset, but he'll not do anything silly, I'm sure of that."

"We won't wait for Dad, so you can get off to look for him. Everything's ready."

They ate in silence and when John Munro arrived he looked at the clock, then pulled out his watch. "You're smart tonight," he said in a slightly disapproving tone.

"Listen, Dad, to what Hazel has to say and I'll bring through your soup."

"What's going on? It's not Sara, is it? And where's Neil?"

"Sit down, Dad, and listen."

When Hazel had explained what had happened, John Munro said, "Are you sure he'll be at the river, Sam?"

"Yes, I'm certain that's where he'll be. I'll pop up and see Sara and then I'll be off."

"Sam," John Munro put out a detaining hand, "Sam, tell him we want him to come home."

Sam nodded.

THE SUN had gone and a cool breeze was stirring the trees into shedding more of their leaves as he made his way along the familiar path to the river, thinking back to how Neil and he had always raced to see who could reach their hide-out first. Now he moved with stealth, unwilling almost to disturb his dearest friend in his grief. He saw the lone figure kneeling at the water's edge, motionless, unseeing, and with footsteps, slow and heavy, joined in the silent vigil.

After a while Sam was constrained to put his arm round Neil's shoulder and felt the tenseness, the emotion seeking release, the blank despair.

The water lapped almost to their knees and then Neil spoke.

"If only I'd the courage to end it all, but the river's always been our friend. Sam, she wouldn't let me do it. It must be true or I wouldn't be here. I didn't want to believe it. That's why I threw down the letter and ran. Anna Maria couldn't be dead, there had to be a mistake, but when I reached here I knew. I knew my dream had vanished. I was alone, quite alone. She's been at my side ever since I left Germany, but suddenly she was gone."

"But you're not alone, Neil, you have a little girl."

"My little girl! She'll never be mine."

Sam was silent.

"You'd better go back now. Thanks for coming, I knew you would."

"I'll wait until you're ready, Neil, I'm not going to leave you here on your own."

It was Neil's turn to be silent until he said, "All right, but I want you to go in first and tell my mother and father I don't want to speak about it. I don't want their sympathy."

"I'll do that for you, Neil, but I want you to know that they are both very upset for you, especially your mother."

"Just do as I want, Sam."

"I will, but I am going to say one thing to you, Neil. It may not be the right time, but if I say it now perhaps you'll remember it later on."

"What are you on about, Sam?"

"Just remember me and how I have felt all these years not knowing my father."

Sam turned away abruptly before Neil could reply.

- 23 -

*M*Y *dear son, Sam,*

It is with sadness that I write this letter as I know that if you have to read it, I shall be gone. My one plea is that you will find it in your heart to forgive.

Your mother was a very beautiful lady whom I loved with all my heart. She had many talents which made her perhaps a little headstrong. We met in Glasgow when I was on shore leave for a spell while studying at college and we fell deeply in love. When my course was finished I was due to go off on a trip to the Far East which meant I was to be abroad for two years at least. We decided to marry, against, I must admit, the advice of both sets of parents, but we were very, very happy. Parting with Alanna was very painful for me as it was for her. Being at sea for long periods I did not receive letters very often but I accepted that it was something I had to live with, and even when they stopped altogether I wasn't unduly worried, disappointed yes, but I was certain that Alanna would still be waiting for me when I returned home to Glasgow.

It still pains me to record what had happened so I shall be brief. We had agreed that we should not start a family for a few years to give us time to establish a settled home, but without Alanna knowing it she was already pregnant before I had set sail. It is trite to say that these things happen despite thinking you take care that they should not. And in fact Alanna was not aware that she was going to have a child until she was in her seventh month of pregnancy. I was told by a doctor that, although it is unusual, it can happen. Alanna was the type of person who would not have given the possibility a second thought. When she did discover that she was going to have a baby she was very, very angry. You see, your mother wanted to pursue her career as a teacher of modern languages unhindered by any family commitments. Although I'm sure she loved me as much as I loved her, in a way my absence abroad suited her. I only discovered all that had happened years later.

When you were born, I'm sorry to say, you were rejected by your mother, and for a while you were cared for by Alanna's parents. Then she took up with a teacher in her school and ran away with him to America, never to return to Scotland. Her parents were elderly and unable to look after you so you landed in a home and they both died before I returned from that trip. My parents had no contact with Alanna or her folk, so they knew nothing of this, and I myself did not know of your existence until you were about ten years old, and it took me several years to track you down. It was not an easy task. Of course I had been heartbroken when I discovered Alanna had gone off to America, where she died in 1936, and I could only find solace in the sea, as it were, but when I knew I had a son, I was devastated; yet what could I offer him? Would he want to know me? I learned you were a difficult child and had been unsuccessfully fostered a number of times. I wanted to have you for my own, but with my being at sea most of the time, how could I have given you a home? I should have found a way, but sadly, I didn't.

You will be surprised to know that my grandfather was the vet who lived at The Willows before John Munro, and I used to love going there on holiday, and often went with him to Millside Farm where there had been Whytes for several generations. I knew I could not ask the Munros to foster you, but I felt if I could get you to a place which I had loved as a boy, I could perhaps give you something. I suppose it was a crazy idea, but I pulled it off. I persuaded the Whytes to take you to Millside. I wasn't terribly keen on Dugald Whyte. I thought the money I was prepared to pay him was the attraction rather than you, but I liked Mrs Whyte and felt she would be sympathetic to you.

I did see you briefly at the Home, just before you went to Millside, but it was decided that it was best I should not be introduced to you then. It was agreed that Mrs Whyte should write to me from time to time to tell me of your progress, which she did, but her letters were rather brief.

I had many plans for you when you left school, but unfortunately in 1938 I had an accident which landed me in hospital for a year, and then of course the war came, but when it is over I am determined to meet you. If that happens I shall tell you all this face to face, but in case I should not survive the war I have written this letter. How I pray that you will not have to read it.

You may have thought, Sam, that you were born illegitimate, but that is not so. If I had been at home I'm sure it would have turned out differently. I'm certain your mother would have given you all the love you deserved.

I am writing this before I rejoin my ship. Perhaps when I return to this country again the war will be over and I can tear up this letter and meet you face to face at long last.

Mike Cairns.

SAM SAT in silence for a few moments before he looked up at the lawyer seated behind the broad expanse of his desk. He had read the letter a second time after handing it to Mr Simpkins to read.

"This letter is dated March 1945. Why didn't he contact me when the war was over as he says?"

"Your father did not mention that on two occasions the ship he was on had been torpedoed and while he was fortunate to be rescued almost immediately the first time, when it happened again, he drifted about in the open sea in a rubber dinghy for several days before he was picked up. He wasn't in fact able to join his ship as he indicates in his letter for he had suffered greatly from his ordeal and became seriously ill and was hospitalized from then until he died two months ago."

"But why didn't he send for me?"

"Mr Cairns, I can only tell you what I learned from the doctors who attended him and I'm afraid it's only what I've already said, that your father was terminally ill. I would surmise that he was simply unable to make the effort to try to contact you. You were his only relative; he had no one else, and apparently had only infrequent visits from the one member of his crew who had survived. All the others were killed outright; your father and his Number One were thrown into the water and miraculously found in a dinghy which had come from another ship which had also been struck. That is all I was able to glean from the doctors."

Sam held his head in his hands. "My God, he died alone, he had only to say the word and I'd have gone to him. Can't you realise that all my life I've wanted to know my father. Oh, I can't believe it, how it could all have been so different!"

"You could always visit the hospital and speak to the doctors."

"Where is it? Where did my father die?"

"In a military hospital in Portsmouth and he's buried there. He was respected by all who knew him and well looked after."

"I wish he had tried to get in touch with me when he wrote this letter. Why did he want to wait till the end of the war?"

"I suppose that was the natural thing to do. You were still engaged in the fighting in Germany, whether he knew where exactly you were I don't know – and he hoped to go back to sea again. He left your letter together with his will and covering note to me with instructions as to what was to be done on his death. Oh, and by the way," Mr Simpkins rose from his chair and opening a large cupboard behind him continued, "this case contains your father's personal effects which he asked you should have. You will, of course, wish to open it in the privacy of your own home. Now, may I read you the will?"

Sam barely took in what Mr Simpkins read in his precise, clipped tone, and then realizing he had finished, took a copy of the will, folded it and placed it in his pocket.

"I know, Mr Cairns," Mr Simpkins continued, "that you have had a severe shock and that you will require time to absorb all you have learned. I suggest that you may like now to go home and come back and see me in a week or two, when I shall be pleased to advise you as to how you should use the money your father has left you and make arrangements for you to visit Portsmouth if you so wish. Now, does that suit you?"

"Yes, yes, fine. Sorry. I'm pretty confused, yes, I need time to think. I'll be pleased to see you again and take your advice. Thank you, and my apologies if I've seemed ungrateful."

"Mr Cairns, my sympathies are with you, what more can I say?"

Sam walked slowly back to Queen Street Station and stood looking at the indicator board without being able to take in when the next train left for Levenford. He moved away to stand along from the bookstall holding tightly to his father's case, almost oblivious to the home going workers who crossed and re-crossed in front of him after they had thrown down their coppers for one of the evening papers. He felt absolutely alone, then suddenly choked with grief, and had a sudden burning desire to hold Hazel and Sara in his arms. He started forward and ran towards the gate at the top of the steps leading to the low level platform, demanding brusquely of the ticket collector when the next train was to Levenford.

"It's in, you'll just make it, if you look smart."

Sam tore down the steps and flung himself into the nearest carriage just as the train started to move away. The other occupants of the compartment looked up at Sam as he almost fell across their feet and then reluctantly made room for him to sit down.

"You'll get your case up on the rack, son," a man with a cloth cap and smoking full strength Capstan advised.

"Oh, I'll manage it fine on my knee."

"What's in it, like?" enquired the man. "Been robbing a bank?"

Sam said nothing.

"Must be important if you can't put it up on the rack."

"Maybe it is. Now do you mind if we finish this conversation?"

"You young folk are all the same nowadays. Can't say a word to any of you."

Sam's patience suddenly snapped. "If it hadn't been for the young folk of this country, people like you wouldn't be sitting in this carriage enjoying a smoke on your way home to your evening meal and then down the pub for a pint. So will you now leave me be."

"Yes, leave the lad alone," a rather stout lady put in. "Never mind him, son, he's just an old nosey parker."

Sam turned away as the man started on the interfering old besom, as he called Sam's champion, and he knew within himself that he was terribly upset and wanted to be on his own to think. Yes, he had to sort himself out before he saw Hazel.

WHEN JOHN MUNRO returned from a visit to a farm near Cardross, he was surprised when Hazel ran out to his car.

"Sam's not home yet, surely he can't be kept as long as this by the lawyer."

"Not home yet, but I saw him crossing from the station into the Common just before six o'clock when I was on my way to Upper Erndale."

"Where can he be? Did he see you?"

"Yes, I sounded my horn and he waved."

"Did you really see him go into the Common?"

"Not really, but he was heading that way."

Hazel stood for a moment thinking, then she said, "I know where he'll be," and with that she was off before her father could say another word. She saw the lonely figure sitting on the river bank and recognised her husband immediately. When she reached him and sat down on the grass beside him, Sam put his arm round her and said quietly, "I thought you might come looking for me."

"I was worried, Sam."

"I needed time to think. Sorry, I didn't mean to upset you."

"Was it bad news?"

"Yes, and no. Shall I tell you about it now?"

"If you want to."

"I want to, but first I have something to say to you."

"Go on."

Sam turned to look in his wife's eyes. "I love you very much, my darling, and I'll always love you."

"And I love you too, Sam."

"This spot is special to me. I just felt I had to say how much you mean to me while we're here together."

When Sam had finished relating what he had learned from the lawyer, Hazel held him tight and whispered, "You have a family now Sam, that's all that matters."

"Yes I know; it will take me a while to get over the fact that I might so easily have met my father. I shall always regret that I didn't."

"What's in the case, Sam?"

"My father's personal belongings. I haven't opened it yet. I will, when I feel more composed."

"And the money?"

"Yes, the money. Of course it's wonderful, and it gives me a really good feeling inside to know that my father, yes my father, saved it for me, his son. But you know, Hazel, I'd have given every penny of it just to have known him."

"And your mother?"

"My mother? Strange, I have no feelings about her at all, she just doesn't figure, but at least I suppose I owe some of my intelligence to her. When I think about it, if she'd accepted me, my early life would have been quite different. I'm not surprised I had all that resentment inside me. But then, I wouldn't have met you, my darling."

"Ready to go home?"

"Yes, they'll be getting anxious."

WHEN SAM had finished relating the happenings of the afternoon to John and Ella Munro, he turned to the former and asked, "Did you have any idea of who I was, or who my parents were?"

"No, Sam. I often thought the Whytes knew something, as indeed we know now they did, but neither of them ever broke their trust. On the other hand, how much had they been told? I should imagine they were well rewarded for having you."

"And they hardly spent a penny on you, Sam, when you were with them," Ella put in. "That was mean. No wonder Dugald Whyte was never short of money for a dram. I think we all owe you a lot, Sam."

"No, don't say that. You always made me welcome here."

"You deserved better, Sam, you were far too good to be a farm hand."

"It didn't do me too much harm, toughened me up, I reckon."

"You were always tough, Sam," Hazel said, putting her hand on her husband's.

"Maybe, as long as I wasn't too objectionable."

"I used to hate you because you'd never let me join in when you went off with Neil."

"I've told you before, I wasn't used to girls when I was in my teens – and no use with them."

"I'm glad you changed then, Sam," and Hazel kissed him lightly on the forehead. "Come, let's have an early night, you must be tired."

"Yes, I am."

- 24 -

"I'VE decided, Hazel, what I'm going to do, at least what I'd like to do, for I want your approval."

"You mean with the money your father left you?"

"Yes."

"Go on then, I'm all ears."

"I've been working now at old Porter's nursery for two years and I feel I've learned a lot from him. And I enjoy the work, even although it's hard graft and sometimes not too pleasant when the weather's foul. Porter is thinking of retiring in a couple of years."

"So you're going to buy him out," Hazel broke in.

"No, not exactly."

"What then?"

"He owns all his land and he's going to sell it to a builder so they can build a new house on it."

"Well I never. So you'll be out of a job?"

"I could be if I didn't strike out on my own."

"Strike out on your own Sam? But where?"

"You know the big house up the hill on the other side of the road from Millside?"

"You mean Glenleven House?"

"Yes, that's right. It's up for sale."

"But Sam, it must be practically falling down."

"Maybe, but the outer walls are sound. I've had a surveyor look at it very thoroughly. Oh I know it would need a lot of work inside, probably a complete new roof, but it's going for practically nothing."

Hazel remained silent so Sam went on.

"And it has extensive grounds which I could cultivate and in time I'd rebuild the house, make us a real home of our own. What do you say?"

"I don't know, it's all so sudden."

"I'd go on working for Porter meantime and I'm sure by the time he gives up I'd have the ground ready for growing the vegetables he supplies to the shops."

Hazel protested, "How would you manage to do that? Where would you get the time?"

"Porter's willing to give me time off."

"So you've discussed it with him?"

"Hazel, I had to. Oh I know I should have told you before this, but I wanted to work things out first, to be sure of my facts."

Hazel sat silent, so Sam went across and knelt on the floor beside her chair. "I want to do it for you, I want to be a success for you, to prove that I am worthy of you. Want us to be independent, to have a place of our own. It's not that I'm not grateful for what your parents have done for us, but I want to be free to please myself in my own home. And in a way, I owe it to my father."

Hazel looked down into the earnest face of her husband and smiled. "Sam, you're so different from the wild boy you were when you came to the farm."

"Would you rather I was still like him?"

"No, Sam, I prefer you as you are now, although you've still got that boy's spirit and I hope you'll never lose it."

"Will you come and see Glenleven House then?"

"All right, if that's what you want, Sam, I'll go along with you."

"But I want you to want it too."

"I will, Sam, I will."

HAZEL'S HEART sank when she saw the dilapidated state of the house, but as she listened to Sam outlining his plans with such enthusiasm, she gradually, if reluctantly, warmed to them.

"You see, Hazel, folk are beginning to think about their gardens again and with all these new houses being built, there'll be a demand for plants and that's what I intend to do, grow flowers and vegetables and sell them from here as well as in the shops."

"But the house, Sam, can you afford to make it habitable?"

"Yes, it'll take money and time, but we'll do it in stages."

"Oh Sam, I wish I had your confidence."

"Hazel, if you don't, then you cannot believe in me, it's as simple as that."

Hazel moved close to Sam and laid her head against his chest. "Oh I do, I do. I believe in you, Sam. I shouldn't have said that, it's just –"

"Just what?"

"We're going to have another mouth to feed."

Sam was taken aback, but he recovered to say, "Why didn't you tell me before?"

"The doctor only confirmed it yesterday. Oh Sam, I'm sorry."

"Sorry! But it's wonderful, and all the more need for us to get a place of our own."

"I suppose you're right, but I won't be able to help you much."

"You'll help by being behind me. It's going to work, Hazel, this is going to be our place."

THE LETTER arrived a week later. Hazel looked at the postmark when she picked it up from the hall table.

"It looks like 'York," she said to her mother who was standing with her. "Who does Sam know in York?"

"York?" her mother repeated. "Wasn't that where the lad who was Sam's best man came from?"

"Fancy you remembering that. You know, I can't even recall what he looks like."

"I was taken with him. Strange as it may seem to you, I do remember him quite well. I had quite a conversation with him, at least he talked and I listened. He must have known how I was feeling at the time, but he chatted away friendly as you like."

"You surprise me at times, Mother."

"Maybe I do, but Kent, now that's his name, helped a lot that day."

When Sam came home and read the letter he turned to Hazel and said, "Yes, it's from Kent, and he's coming up here."

"Goodness, what for?"

"Says he's on holiday."

"On his own?"

"Yes. I thought he'd be married by now. He didn't answer my last letter, but that's months ago and I just thought that most army friendships – well, they just fade out. But it will be great seeing him again. The problem is, where is he going to stay?"

But when Mrs Munro heard Kent was coming she immediately said, "He can easily stay here; there's Hazel's old room, where could he stay otherwise?"

"Well, thanks, I appreciate that." Sam sounded rather surprised.

KENT HAD been demobbed a few weeks ahead of Sam and had returned to York intent on enjoying his long leave before looking for employment. He knew his job at the factory was guaranteed, but like many other returning servicemen, he was undecided as to what he really wanted to do, and this indecision soon turned into restlessness as he drifted in and out from his house to the pub; to the cinema, sometimes with Marlene, sometimes on his own, and then back home to laze about, missing the comradeship of his former army mates.

In his preoccupation with his own problems, Kent had not noticed that his mother did not appear to be her usual self, and it came as a shock one afternoon when he returned from a session in the pub to find a message left by a neighbour that his mother had been taken to hospital. When he joined his father at his mother's bedside, Kent could not take in what was happening. He could not believe that his mother was dying; that she would never again greet him with a smile, and in her unhurried fashion, fetch his dinner which she had kept hot for him in the oven, with never a word of reproach for his late homecoming.

He felt anger more than grief and later when he managed to speak to his father he asked if he had known that his mother was ill.

"Yes, Kent, I did, but your mother didn't want you to know."

"But why? Why for God's sake? I had a right to know. How do you think I feel about how I messed her about, always out boozing, coming in at any time I liked, never doing anything for her?"

"She wanted you to enjoy your leave, she said you deserved to. She didn't want to bother you with her illness. I suppose, like me, she hoped it would get better."

"You should have told me."

"I often thought about it, but you were our only one, Kent. You see she lost a baby before you were born and she had several miscarriages. You were very precious to her."

"I wasn't even there when she had to be taken away. I didn't even get the chance to say goodbye to her."

"Oh, but she knew you were with her at the end. She gripped your hand, just as she did mine; yes, that was her goodbye."

"I can't take it, Dad, I just can't take it. If I'd known, I would have been prepared for it."

"I know, it's hard, son, terribly hard."

KENT RETURNED to his old job at the factory, having lost interest in seeking something else. The house seemed an alien place without his mother, and he spent as little time in it as possible. After a short time the pub held no attraction for him and he took to going on long hikes on his own. His conversations with his father were brief and without realising it, he was leaving most of the household chores to him.

It came as a shock to Kent when his father announced that he was employing a part-time housekeeper.

"You're doing what? How could you allow another woman to come here and take my mother's place?"

"Look, Kent, I don't want to fall out with you, but I can't go on working all day and coming home here every night to start cooking a meal, cleaning the house, seeing to the washing. I must say you've done precious little to help."

Kent flew out of the house in a rage, resenting his father's remarks, but knowing they were true. His steps unwittingly took him to Dolly's house, and when she opened her door, she ushered him in without a word. She said nothing when Kent sat in silence for some time before suddenly breaking down. Quietly Dolly tiptoed from the room and waited some fifteen minutes before returning.

"Here, love, drink this," handing Kent a glass of whisky, "It'll help."

Kent looked up at Dolly. "You must think I'm soft."

"Rubbish! You've been bottling up your grief for months now, the dam had to burst sometime; now it has, you'll be able to face up to life again, because you've been trying to run away from the facts too long."

Kent said nothing, then, "This stuff certainly has a kick, where did you get it?"

"Never mind that, it's time to talk, Kent."

"Yeah, maybe it is."

"I know your mother's death was a shock to you, but have you ever thought about your dad, how it was to him?"

"Maybe not."

"What you mean is that you haven't, you've just thought about yourself."

"OK. You're right. It's a strange thing. During the war you just accepted death. When one of your mates copped it, you were shaken up for a while, but then you just carried on. I guess you had to. But when my mum died – well, I just couldn't take it. She was special to me."

"And you were to her. Sons are more special than daughters. There seems to be a closer bond between a mother and her sons. I should know, I was one daughter with four brothers."

Kent smiled. "I guess there's something in what you say."

"And you can't blame your dad for wanting some help in the house."

"No, it was stupid of me to act like I did."

"You see, Kent, maybe your dad thought that you would get married and stay with him with your wife. Not the best way to start off, but it would have been the solution, at least for a time."

Kent looked at Dolly in astonishment. "But I never considered that for one moment."

"What about Marlene? You've been going out with her for some time now."

Kent shook his head. "Before I came home, yes, I thought I was heading for marriage with Marlene, but it hasn't worked out like that. Maybe if I'd never been away, if there hadn't been a war, I would have married her, worked in the factory all my days, and led a very uneventful life. But no, Marlene's not for me; she's a nice girl, maybe too nice for the likes of me, so Dad will just have to settle for his housekeeper."

Dolly laughed. "That's more like the real Kent, but I'm sorry about Marlene."

"Don't be, she deserves better, and she'll get it. Meantime, Dolly, thanks a lot. I'd better get back to the old man."

"Any time, Kent, you're always welcome."

"Thanks again, Dolly."

SO KENT resolved his differences with his father, accepted Jane Sillitoe as housekeeper, and soon realised that it was almost as it had been – almost. He continued at the factory, still undecided as to what he would prefer doing instead, and gradually seemed to be slipping into a very comfortable groove with his ambitions slowly but surely fading into dreams of what might have been.

It was his father's announcement that he was going to marry Jane Sillitoe that provided the jolt to lift him out of his lethargy.

At first Kent found nothing to say, being too stunned to find words either of congratulations or condemnation, but after a few days he came to the realization that he could no longer remain at home. His father was disappointed and pleaded with him not to make a hasty decision.

"This is your home, Kent, and you get on well with Jane, and she's very fond of you. Besides where would you go?"

"Dad, it wouldn't be fair to you my being here. I realise it's a good thing for you, but not for me. No one will ever take Mum's place."

"I'm not marrying Jane as someone to take your mother's place. I wouldn't expect you to regard her as such. I'm taking her for what she is herself, for companionship more than anything else and Jane knows that. At my age, a man doesn't have the same feelings of love that he would have when he's in his twenties like you are."

"Meaning?"

"Just what I say."

"OK, Dad, let's drop it, but my mind's made up. As soon as I work things out, I'll be off."

KENT SOUGHT out Dolly again. "I'm not complaining, I'm just being realistic. Dad's not an old man. He's not fifty yet, so he needn't try to tell me that he's lost all his natural desires."

"You're jealous, Kent, that's what's really bugging you. Well, you've only yourself to blame."

"Maybe, so I'd better say goodbye, Dolly. Our fortnight's holiday starts next week, so I'll be off – for good."

"Best of luck, then, Kent. Drop me a line."

"I might."

- 25 -

KENT sat on the river bank and lit a fresh cigarette.
"That's my story, Sam, and here I am, looking to you for help. But first, tell me what you've been up to. Let me hear your success story."

Sam gave a wry smile and looked for a while at the river as it flowed on its relentless way.

"It's been a struggle, Kent, but I'm very happy. I've a wonderful wife, a beautiful daughter, another child on the way."

"Congratulations, Sam, you deserve it all, but come on, fill in the details."

So Sam brought Kent up to date, including his intention of buying Glenleven House and starting his own nursery.

"You mean a market garden?"

"Yes, that's maybe what you call it in your part of the world. Do you think I'm being too ambitious, Kent?"

"Ambitious? I only wish it were me who had all these plans, Sam. You make me feel a useless clot."

"Nonsense, if my father hadn't left me money I'd just be struggling on trying to make a decent living. Come on, let's get back."

They had almost reached The Willows when Kent stopped and said, "Sam, this market garden place, it's going to take a lot of hard work to get it into shape."

"Yes, it will."

"OK. How about taking me on? You know I'm a hard worker, that I can put my hand to most things."

"You can, Kent, and I'd have you before anyone else, but how could I afford to pay you a reasonable wage?"

"I'd settle for what you could manage."

"But Kent, you'd have to find somewhere to stay and pay for it."

"How long do you reckon it'll take before you start producing stuff for selling?"

"Two years at least."

"Well, I have a bit of money. My mother, God bless her, never spent a penny of what I allocated her from my army pay. She banked it and supplemented it from what she made working part-time during the war. I only knew about it when my dad handed me the bank book when I left home. I felt a right heel, because he had kept putting something in every week after Mum died. I couldn't have had better parents if I'd chosen them myself, and what have I done in return? Nothing!"

"Don't feel like that, Kent. When I visited your home I saw for myself just how highly your mum and dad regarded you."

"OK, Sam, but what do you say about taking me on?"

"Let's sleep on it and then I'll take you to see Glenleven House tomorrow."

"PRETTY GRIM, but I feel within myself that it has great possibilities, that I can make a success of it. I've got to, Kent."

"Then let me help you."

Sam was silent as they wandered round behind the mansion block to what had once been a paved courtyard, now hugely overgrown with a variety of weeds sprouting from all the cracks and crevices which had developed over the years.

"What were all these then?" Kent asked, indicating a row of outbuildings.

"Stables for one, where they kept the ponies and traps, I reckon. Someone said the folk who lived here never had a car. And, I believe, above them was the living quarters for the – well, I don't know what he'd have been. Mr Munro said the coachman, gardener, and handyman."

"Can we have a look?"

"Sure."

They climbed a wooden stair and looked into what seemed to have been a living room, a bedroom, a kitchen and a bathroom.

"You know," Sam said when they had completed their tour of inspection, "this place is in far better condition than the actual house, although that's not saying much. I think Hazel's dad said one of the servants had stayed on for a couple of years after the folk who owned it had died, then left when the war started."

"And the place has been empty since?"

"So it seems."

Kent sat down on an old chair in the kitchen. "Sam, I want to make a fresh start. Won't you let me make it here with you? I could live in this place and besides working the land for you, I'd be here as a watchman while you rebuild the house."

"But Kent, this is an absolute dump."

"It won't be so bad once it's cleaned up. It'll be every bit as good as the bothy you slept in over at the farm."

"But I was a boy then."

"Sam, we roughed it plenty in the army, I'm not afraid of hard work, you know that, I'll soon have it shipshape."

Sam was hesitant. "It's an idea Kent, but I'd only be able to pay you a small wage each week. It would just be enough to live on. I'm against the idea of you eating into your own money till we see if it's going to work out. I'd like you to keep that in reserve."

"Then it's a deal. You fix the wage and let me have this place rent free. I'll use some of my cash to furnish it with the bare essentials, but I'll try to keep the bulk of it, just in case, or to buy a share in the business when it's flourishing. How's that for optimism?"

"No flies on my old friend Kent," Sam smiled. "OK, there's no one better I'd like to have as a partner. But you've a lot to think about if you're going to do for yourself."

"Who was the best cook on the tank crew then?"

"If I remember rightly, it might just have been you."

"It was, so don't worry on that score. I'll soon get the range in the kitchen going and I think I saw a huge pile of logs in the place next to the stable."

"You're right. Fancy no one thinking to take them when supplies of coal must have been short during the war."

"Must be honest folk around here."

THE PURCHASE of Glenleven House and grounds went through without a hitch and within a week Kent had taken up residence in the coach-house as he laughingly termed it, despite Mrs Munro's protestations that the place was not fit to live in. John Munro simply shook his head, half in disbelief at Sam's recklessness, half in admiration.

When he talked it over with Dr Blackwood he said,

"The war changed everything and we're an outdated generation in many ways. We've never been prepared to take real risks, we've always been too canny. Now these lads, who were away for five years or so, and who saw real action, and survived, they seem to realise that there must be a new beginning, a better way, and that there is a chance to change things. It's just like how we used to muffle ourselves up in all our clothes – shutting our skins off from the air and sun, and all the goodness around us. Now these lads are casting aside long drawers and waistcoats, ties and collars and being free, free to breathe and to live. And that's how they look at life now. Throw aside the restrictions and let's get on with it."

Dr Blackwood smiled at his friend. "You'll be an MP one of these days, John, if you're not careful, making speeches like that."

"Catch me!"

"But you approve of what Sam's doing then?"

"Despite everything, I've always liked Sam, and I'm proud of my grandchild as any grandparent is, and looking forward to the next arrival. So, yes, on balance, I support Sam's venture."

"Then, tell him that, and be willing to give advice."

"Only if he asks for it."

"He will. You have had your differences but Sam has always looked up to you."

SO IT WAS that John Munro started to sit at Sam's planning meetings with Kent and Neil, who had taken on the job of looking after the money side, and his local knowledge and relationships with many of the tradesmen in the town and farmers in the surrounding area were of immense value in the buying of materials and cutting costs.

Progress at first was slow and there was little to show for all the hard graft Sam and Kent put in on the old house as they stripped down each room in turn, but when eventually the extensive repairs to the roof were completed and new windows installed throughout, they felt they had turned the first corner.

Sam had hired a contractor to clear the grounds of Glenleven and plough all the land before levelling off an area where he had erected his first greenhouse. Once planting could begin, the work on the house had to be curtailed much to Hazel's disappointment, as seeing her new home beginning to take shape, she was longing to move in. Sam had insisted in installing central heating despite the cost.

"It's a large house and it's the sensible thing to do," he argued, "and we need only heat the rooms we require. As soon as we have the sitting room, two bedrooms, the kitchen and a bathroom ready, we'll move in, but you'll have to be patient, and besides, everything has to be right, not only for us, but also for Sara and Karen."

For Hazel, rather to her disappointment, had produced another daughter.

"I'm sorry, Sam," she had whispered to him when he visited her after the birth. "I know you were hoping for a son."

"Don't worry, my darling. I'm just happy that you're both all right. I'll love this little girl just as much as I love Sara."

KENT REVELLED in the work both outdoors and in. His living quarters were still rather spartan, but as he explained, they were easily kept and comfortable enough for him. At Sam's insistence no work was done on Saturday afternoons or Sundays, when Kent divided his time between visits to The Willows, visiting a pub in Levenford with Sam and Neil if he was home, and to exploring the local area on foot.

"Don't you ever miss your mates in York?" Sam queried one Saturday night as they enjoyed a drink together in the Castle Arms.

"Never have time to miss them," Kent replied. "Besides, although I went boozing with quite a crowd of lads, most of whom were ex-service, I wasn't close to anyone."

"What about your girl friend then?"

"Marlene? Finished. Completely."

"Dolly?"

"Good old Dolly," Kent laughed. "I'm surviving without her. I've lost the urge. You work me too hard."

"Now Kent, you know, you just won't stop when you're told."

"But I'm happy here, Sam. I'm enjoying every minute. I feel I'm doing something worthwhile."

The months passed and the steady progress continued, till the day arrived when Sam announced to Hazel that it was time to buy some furniture for their new home.

"I've kept money aside for it and you'll know best what we need. I'm going to leave it all to you."

"But Sam, I'd like you to help me choose."

"No, I decided on the layout of the house when we reconstructed the rooms, your job is to furnish it. You have an eye for that sort of thing. Now make sure you buy good stuff."

It was an exciting period as the rooms were filled with furniture, carpets laid and curtains hung. Hazel was surprised but delighted when numerous friends said, "We didn't get a chance to give you a wedding gift, so here's something for your new house."

Neil had written an article for the local paper about Sam's enterprise and had also placed adverts advising readers to watch out for the opening of The Glenleven Nursery and these had certainly alerted the wide circle of friends and acquaintances. The article had also raised such interest that quite a number of townspeople had taken a walk out to see the restored Glenleven House. Among them was Dr Blackwood.

"You've really transformed the place," he told Sam and Kent. "I remember visiting the folk who lived here years ago, but they kept themselves very much to themselves. It was quite a grand place in a way, but very old fashioned and as they grew old they just allowed it to become run down. They had no family and the only relatives you say, Sam, are in Australia and very elderly now."

"Yes, lucky for me in a way. They just wanted rid of the place so I got it for a song."

"You've worked hard, both of you."

"Still a lot to do though."

"I don't doubt that. Are you going to manage to run the place on your own?"

"We could be doing with some help at times, but I'm not thinking of employing anyone full-time just yet. Kent and I will have to manage somehow."

"You could always take on students during their holiday periods. My daughter's often at a loose end during the long summer vacation. I'm sure she'd jump at the chance of a job with you."

Sam looked at Kent. "How does that strike you?"

Kent grinned. "I'm all for some female company, but it can be pretty messy work sometimes. What's your daughter studying?"

"Medicine, but Jo wouldn't mind getting her hands dirty and she is an outdoor type."

"Best thing is for her to come along and see me when her holidays start and we'll give her a try. She can always look after the shop we're going to have to start with and if she wants to work in the gardens, then she'll get her chance."

"Fine, Sam, I'll tell her."

ON HIS KNEES thinning out some annuals, Kent raised his head slightly and became aware of a pair of very shapely legs.

"Don't tell me. You can only be Jo Blackwood."

"How did you know?"

"Ah, that would be telling." Kent stood up and smiled at the neat girl with golden hair. "I won't shake hands, as you can see I'm rather grubby, but you've just arrived in time for a cup of char. Tea."

"Oh, But –"

"No buts. Come on, follow me young lady."

Jo was left standing as Kent strode off, so after a moment's hesitation she ran to catch up with him.

That night Jo sat down and wrote to her grandmother.

Dear Gran,

I started a holiday job at Glenleven Nursery – although to be honest I didn't do very much as I was shown round and had various things explained to me.

The assistant gardener is called Kent Mollison and he comes from York. He was in the army with Sam Cairns who owns the place – that's why he came to be there. He's nice, not tall, just average height with dark hair and a moustache, very suntanned from working outside mostly with his shirt off. He's very friendly, smiles a lot and I suppose he pulled my leg most of the time, but he did it in a nice way.

I think you met Sam once, so I don't need to tell you about him except that he and his wife Hazel and their two little girls are moving to Glenleven House very soon. You should see what they have done to it. It was in a dreadful state but it's really lovely now. It's not completely finished, but downstairs the lounge, dining room and kitchen are all ready, and upstairs two of the bedrooms. And would you believe it, there are three bathrooms, one in what is called the master bedroom. I could hardly take it all in. Sam was left quite a lot of money by the father whom he never knew – but I think you've been told all that story.

And Kent has a place of his own. He and Sam are really very good with their hands for they've done a lot of work themselves. Well. Kent has what he calls the coach-house. He is very amusing. It was where the handyman lived when the house used to be occupied. The rooms are above what were the stables, and Kent has done them up to look like new, and he says that one day he's going to convert what were the stables into rooms when he can find the time.

You should see the furniture he has. Apparently the stables were full of old chairs, tables, chests of drawers, which at first were going to be thrown out, but as Kent had no furniture for his place, he decided to see if he could resurrect anything from the junk, as he called it. The father of one of the joiners who was working on the house was a retired carpenter and he helped Kent to restore the furniture so it looks almost like new. They spend the winter evenings working on it. Sam has some pieces for his house too.

Then they are each making their own private garden. Sam's is to the side of the big house away from the entrance for the public, so it's quite secluded and will be lovely in time. Kent has his at the back of his place and it's screened off. He's making it so the front of the house will look into the garden and the door from the courtyard will be his back door. That seems very complicated, but on your next visit I intend taking you to see it all.

I haven't said much about the actual gardens where they grow fruit, vegetables and plants for sale, and of course the greenhouses. They've put a lot of work into them as well but I couldn't take in everything, I was so fascinated with their houses, but I'll have to pay attention tomorrow to what I've to do. I'm sure Kent will help. I really liked him.

I hope you are well and that you'll be able to visit us soon.

Love from Joanna.

AS HE HAD hoped, Sam had taken over from Porter the supplying of produce to the shops in Levenford and he was encouraged by the number of customers who came to Glenleven to make their purchases. Jo's time was divided between attending to the shop and working with Kent in the gardens.

"How do you know so much about growing all the different plants?" she queried one afternoon when they were both on their knees planting bulbs.

Kent grinned. "I don't really know all that much. Sam's taught me a lot and of course old man Porter has been here frequently giving us advice. Then I've studied numerous gardening books – they've been my bed-time reading."

"And you enjoy doing this?"

"Of course." Kent sat back on his heels. "For the first time in my life, Jo, I'm doing something worthwhile. I was a lazy blighter at school, couldn't be bothered, then I went into the chocolate factory. Now I know somebody has to do that kind of job, but I ask you, what is there in making bars of chocolate for folk to guzzle. Now here, I plant seeds or bulbs, I watch them grow, I tend them and I am creating something wonderful. Tell me, how does that compare with your bars of chocolate?"

Jo regarded Kent with a serious look on her face, then she said, "But I like chocolate."

Kent looked at her for a moment, then burst out laughing, "Just when I thought I was putting over a bit of philosophy, you go and spoil it."

"Oh, Kent, I'm sorry. I didn't mean to."

"I'll forgive you." Kent tried to look serious. "Jo, you're priceless," he went on, "but I love you for it. Come on, time to brew up."

So the friendly relationship grew throughout the long summer vacation interrupted only by Jo's going off on holiday for a fortnight with her parents, and as October grew near, the time for re-starting her studies at St Andrews University was fast approaching.

"Why St Andrews?" Kent asked her on her last day. "I don't know much about the geography of Scotland, but I reckon Glasgow is nearer."

"Daddy went to St Andrews University and I always fancied going there and I did. I wanted to be a real student, I mean living away from home."

"So you're not a real student if you travel from home every day?"

"Well, maybe it's a daft idea but –"

"But what?"

"If I had been at Glasgow University I would have been able to see you during term time."

"Jo, I'm flattered, but I'm sure once you're back at St Andrews you'll soon get together with all your boy friends there and forget all about me."

"Do you think so?"

"Yes, I'm sure of it."

"And will you forget all about me?"

Kent put his arms around Jo. "I shan't forget you, Jo, how could I? It's been great having you here, you've been a great help. No one to make my cups of char now. Yes, I'll miss you, but you've your studies to attend to. You stick in. I want you to be a success. Promise you will."

"I promise."

Kent kissed Jo lightly on the forehead, then releasing her said, "Here, I've a little parcel for you."

"Oh Kent, thank you. What is it? May I open it?"

"Of course."

"Chocolates!"

"You did say you liked chocolate. Now off you go and say cheerio to Sam and Hazel and the girls."

"Goodbye, Kent." And Jo was gone.

- 26 -

NEIL cycled into town, skirting the Common, under the railway bridge, into Leven Place and dismounted at the library. Propping his bicycle against the outside wall, he ran up the steps and into the dignified, early morning quiet of the Reading Room. He went straight to the stand where the newspapers were displayed and opened the Glasgow Herald at the page showing the latest University pass lists. He scanned the long columns of names until he found, Neil A Munro, 2nd Class Honours in English Literature, and stood for a moment, his eyes glued to his name, before he managed to read those of his friends who also had completed the degree course successfully.

Leaving the library, he cycled to the newsagent in Church Street and purchased a Glasgow Herald. Thus armed he cycled in a leisurely fashion back to The Willows, experiencing a sense of euphoria which was entirely new to him.

He dismounted halfway along the Bonhill Road to savour the splendour of the June morning, throwing back his head to gaze up to the pure blue sky. The long, hard slog was over; he had achieved a success at last, something nobody could take away from him.

Suddenly he wanted to share his news and he mounted his bicycle and pedalled briskly for home. His mother was alone in the kitchen and he went up behind her, put his arm round her waist and whispered, "This is your son, Neil Alexander Munro, Master of Arts with second class honours."

His mother literally whirled round to face him. "Oh, Neil, the results are out!"

"Yes, and I went to great expense of actually buying a Glasgow Herald to make sure you'd believe me."

"Oh, Neil, wait till I get my glasses." Then as she read aloud his name she turned again to her son. "Neil, I am so proud of you, you deserve your success, you've worked so hard all these years and after having such a sad time. Dad will be delighted, and Sam and Hazel. Are you going to give them a ring?"

"No, I'd rather go along and tell them. Mum, I'd just like to say thanks for everything. You've been wonderful to me all along and I wasn't very nice to you or Dad for a while."

"It's all in the past, Neil. We could have been more understanding, but it was difficult for all of us. Will you be going to Germany now?"

"I always said I would once I got my degree, but I'll have to think about it."

"Dad and I will help Neil. You've only to ask."

Neil gave a wry smile but remained silent.

"Neil, he wants to, it's just that he can't find the words."

"All right, but now I'm off to see Sam and Hazel."

As he cycled along to Glenleven House, Neil could not help but think over the four years since he received the letter from Georges telling him about Anna Maria.

For some time he had been too numb with shock to be able to think clearly about what had happened, and then followed a period when he felt it was futile to try to do anything about the situation. Nothing would bring Anna Maria back. He had turned to his university studies, not with enthusiasm, but as something which took his mind away from his own personal tragedy, but even so, he only managed to scrape passes in his first year exams and had been advised by his tutor that unless there was a distinct improvement in his work, an honours degree was out of the question. During the year he had received several letters from Georges which he had read but had not answered. He felt he just did not want to know.

His parents had respected his wish that there be no discussion about the matter which Neil knew within himself was a mistake, and as Sam and Hazel had decided not to broach the subject, he realised by the end of his first year at the University that his inner conflict was slowly but surely bringing him to his knees.

It was when Sara had taken a very bad cold, which had caused Sam and Hazel some anxiety, that Neil had for the first time thought of the child that Anna Maria had borne. His close relationship with his sister and Sam still held, but since during the time he did spend at home he had come to prefer the privacy of his room. He had to a certain extent cut himself off from them as he had with his parents.

When he was faced with the prospect of the long summer vacation, Neil was at a loss as to how to spend the time. He did not have the urge to seek employment, feeling that he had no real need for extra cash and it was while he was mooning about the house one afternoon that Hazel asked him if he would sit with Sara while she went into town with her mother.

"Would you mind, Neil? Sara's asleep, but just in case she wakes, you know she's had this dreadful cold."

Neil looked at his sister, saw the tiredness in her eyes, and felt a pang of guilt that he had not realised how worried she had been about Sara.

"Sure, I'll sit with her. I'll go up right away."

"Thanks, Neil, we won't be long."

"No need to hurry, I'll cope."

Hazel looked rather doubtful but she only smiled.

For a while Neil gazed down at his little niece asleep in her cot, before he moved to the window to read, and absorbed in his book did not at first notice that Sara had wakened. He tip-toed across again to the cot and noticing him, the two small plump arms were stretched out begging to be lifted.

"I don't know if I should, but well, why not? Just a minute. I better have something to wrap around you. I know, I'll take one of your blankets. Come on then, up to your uncle. You do remember me. I daresay I haven't bothered very much about you for some time."

Neil chatted on while Sara answered him in gurgles of delight and this was how Hazel found them on her return.

"Oh, she's awake. My goodness, she looks ever so much better. Neil, it must be you. Look, Mum's making a cup of tea, shall I go and bring it up here?"

"Yes, if you like."

"You don't mind sitting with Sara for a few more minutes?"

"Of course not."

When they had finished their tea, Neil made no move to go. "You've made this a very attractive room even although it's an attic. I hadn't noticed before."

"You haven't been up here for ages, has he, Sara?" Hazel addressed her daughter who still sat on Neil's knee.

After a few moments Hazel went on, "Neil, do you mind if I say something?"

"Why should I?"

"Seeing you with Sara, I couldn't help thinking that you have a little girl of your own."

"So?"

"When are you going to recognise her existence?"

"What do you mean?"

"She is yours, or maybe you have doubts?"

"Of course not. I was the first – you know what I mean. Of course I fathered the child."

"Don't you think then that you should at least answer your friend's letters, or send them something to help with the little girl? Things can't be easy for them in Germany."

Neil's eyes suddenly filled up with tears and he passed Sara over to her mother. He tried to speak but no words came.

"Neil, let go, let it out, you must. You're destroying yourself, you can't go on bottling everything up inside you."

Neil covered his face with his hands. "It's so weak for a man to cry," he managed to say.

"It's not. No one will know, not even Sam," Hazel said quietly, putting one arm round her brother's shoulders.

When he had recovered his composure Neil said, "I've wanted to do something, but what? It's all so hopeless."

"You can at least do as I suggest, write and send something for your little girl. I can help you with that."

"My little girl," Neil repeated the words slowly.

"Yes, she's your little girl, just as Sara is mine."

"You know what they've called her?"

"What?"

"Mari-ella. Somehow Georges knew Mum's name and he linked it with part of Anna Maria's. Don't tell Mum though, she wouldn't approve."

"All right, I won't. So you know quite a bit about her, I mean your daughter."

"I'll really need to read again the letters I've had from Georges. I usually just skim through them and put them away. It hurts so much to think of my little daughter as you call her so far away without a mother or father."

"Oh Neil," Hazel bit her lip to hold back her own tears.

Then Neil went on. "Georges has been marvellous. He stayed on in Hamburg and eventually took over the job Anna Maria had, and has a room in her aunt's house. He seems to be the surrogate father. It makes me feel inadequate, so helpless, so powerless to do anything."

LATER IN the evening as Sam was passing the door of Neil's room he heard music so he paused to listen. He realised Neil was playing the record of Eine

Kleine Nachtmusik he had brought home with him from Germany, and which he often played before he had received the news about Anna Maria. It had been her parting gift to him.

Sam opened the door quietly and saw Neil was standing looking out of the window. Sam closed the door behind him.

"Hazel has told you then?" Neil asked in a choked voice without turning round.

"She only said you were ready for some company. It's a lovely evening, how about going across the river for a swim?"

For a few moments Neil said nothing, then when the music stopped, he crossed to the old gramophone he had resurrected from the attic, took the record from the turntable, and shut down the lid.

"We used to listen to that record together; it was one of the few family possessions Anna Maria had salvaged. I thought it was all I had to remind me of her, but Sam, I have something more precious, my daughter. I'm going to find a way to bring her here, no matter how long it takes."

"That's the Neil I used to know. We'll all do what we can to help you, you can count on that."

"It'll cost a bit of money I expect, and I've wasted a whole year. I'll have to get a job. A holiday job will be relatively easy, but if I could find something where I could earn all year round, that would be the answer. Maybe I should pack in the University."

"No, Neil, you'd regret that. Listen, I've an idea. How about going along to Bogside and asking for a trial. I'm sure you'd stand a good chance of being signed on."

"Sam, I haven't kicked a ball since I was demobbed."

"Maybe not, but look at the success you had when you played in your army teams."

"So did you."

Sam laughed. "You're joking. I played a lot, yes, but I'm not your class, Neil, and from what I've heard of what our local team did last season, they're certainly needing some new blood."

"In other words, they'll sign anyone who knows the shape of a football."

"Neil, be serious. I know they won't pay much, but it'll be something all the year round and it wouldn't interfere with your studies, and you could always take on a summer job too. And besides, Neil, to be honest, you're needing a new interest, something to take you out of this room. You've practically made it your prison."

"Come on, let's have that swim and we can talk it through on our way."

On their way back to The Willows, Neil said "OK, Sam, I'll give it a try, but I'll have to get fit first and you'll have to help me in that. It could be just like old times."

SO NOW NEIL had completed his third season with Levenford and had promised to sign on for another while he was at the Teachers' Training College. During the three years he had corresponded regularly with Georges and sent gifts for him, Brigitte and Mari-ella. He knew that Georges had made a number of decisions which sometimes astonished Neil. He had registered the baby as Mari-ella Munro, giving Neil as the father with his home address. He had informed Neil that his daughter was bi-lingual as while Brigitte spoke to her in German, he always addressed her in English. Snapshots of Mari-ella now adorned Neil's room, but in his heart, he wondered if she would really ever be his. The process of bringing Mari-ella into Britain was proving to be a long and involved one and even if he were to be successful in bringing her home, he would have to rely on others to look after her. The matter wasn't made any easier by the fact that he had never been able to have a full and frank discussion with his mother about the possibility of Mari-ella staying at The Willows. His father would remain a stumbling block even if his mother was willing. And Hazel had her own family to look after.

But now he had obtained his degree, he would go to Germany to see his daughter for the first time.

Hamburg

Dear Sam and Hazel,

It's two weeks since I arrived here and you're probably wondering how I have found things.

Mari-ella is a beautiful little girl and she had taken to me after being somewhat dubious about this man who was her real 'daddy'. But Georges had done a lot of very useful spadework. He really is marvellous. I don't know how I can ever repay him. I only hope that one day he can come to Levenford – that's what he would like to do.

You'll remember what Hamburg was like, Sam, after the bombing. Street upon street in ruins. You've got to hand it to the Germans. What workers they are! Night and day they go at it – rebuilding – recreating their city. Brigitte's house is an apartment, what we would call a flat, in a block which was partially demolished and due to be pulled down entirely. There are two bedrooms, Mari-ella shares with Brigitte – not an ideal arrangement. I'm in with Georges, so we're a bit cramped, but we are all getting on very well. They are hoping, however, to be re-housed in another part of the city, but nothing is definite. It's all a bit worrying, but Brigitte seems confident they'll be all right. I hope so.

This past week I have had Mari-ella to myself during the day. She is an enchanting child and she speaks English very well – you've got to believe me – and German too of course.

Obviously lots of things are still very difficult here and that is why I hope I'll be able to bring Mari-ella home soon, although I know Brigitte and Georges will be sorry to lose her. But after all, she is my daughter, and it would be wonderful if she could grow up with you and your family. I'm not saying that I'm asking you to say you'd look after her, Hazel. You have enough to do as it is. I'll find a way. It's only that I feel that Dad will still be reluctant to accept Mari-ella. But if he could only see her – he'd have her in his arms in no time. I doubt though if there's any chance of that happening for some time. I haven't made any further progress here as yet. I knew it would be difficult and that's how it is. I'll be heartbroken having to leave here at the end of my stay and not take Mari-ella with me. How I regret not coming over sooner, all these wasted years. But what's done is done. This is a terrible letter, but I know you'll both understand how I'm feeling.

Lots of love to everyone, Neil.

SAM FOLDED the letter which he had read several times and looked at Hazel. "I guess Neil has a problem."

Hazel thought for a moment before she said, "Sam, she could stay with us. I mean by the time Neil manages to get everything arranged, I would be able to cope."

"I'm not saying you wouldn't, and you know how I feel about Neil, I'd do anything for him, anything. But if Mari-ella came to live with us, Neil would have to come too. It would be pretty heavy going for you, and you come first, Hazel, you're – oh, I'm hopeless sometimes with words. I love you so much."

"And I love you with all my heart, Sam, you've done so much, you've worked so hard, you've been wonderful. I won't promise anything, but if Neil is stuck, we'll have to help him."

"Yes, I know, we owe it to him. But what if he were to marry. That would mean Mari-ella would have to get used to yet another new person. It is so complicated. Neil always has chosen the hard way. Still," and Sam suddenly smiled, "if he hadn't reformed me, and that was difficult enough, I'd never have married you."

- 27 -

WITH Sam and his family now settled into their new home and the Nursery fairly well established, the work rate of the two men became less frenzied. There was still plenty to do but as autumn drifted slowly into winter, both Sam and Kent found that they were free to relax in the evenings. Kent, however, refused to intrude on Sam and Hazel's privacy, apart from a Sunday, when he joined them for dinner and one evening a week when he kept Sam company while Hazel visited The Willows.

"You know, Kent," Sam said as they sat in front of a roaring log fire, "you've changed. You always struck me as a person who needed company. Now you're quite happy to spend your evenings on your own. Don't you wish you had someone to share them?"

"What do you mean?"

"I mean, Kent, are you going to remain single all your life?"

Kent laughed. "Have you someone in mind for me, then?"

"No, of course not, but you used to be such a one for the girls."

"I like that. You can talk."

"Now, that's not true and you know it."

"Sam, I've told you before I'm perfectly happy. I've my wireless, I read, and I'm still working away on some of the junk furniture that's left, and come the spring I'm going to start converting the stables."

"Well, that's hopeful, you must be thinking of getting married some day."

"We'll see. I've always fancied having a big house of my own," Kent grinned. "Not in your class of course."

"You think I've aimed too high then?"

"Not a bit of it, Sam, you've done just swell."

"To get back to the marriage stakes, maybe you've your eye on one of our customers. You chat them up plenty now you're attending to the shop more or less on your own."

"Just sales talk, Sam."

"I'll have to keep my eyes open from now on."

But Kent only laughed.

THE LAND ROVER drew up just as Kent was finishing his morning tea break. He watched as the woman driver, muffled in a duffle coat, corduroy trousers tucked into gum boots, brightly coloured headsquare showing whisps of blonde hair, stepped down into the court-yard and looked around her.

Kent moved down his stair, opened his door and called, "Good morning, Madam, can I help you?"

"Oh, good morning, are you in charge here?"

"Well, I work here."

"I see. Sorry to seem rude. I've only just arrived in this place. Is this the Nursery?"

"It is."

"Ah, good, so I can buy vegetables here."

"Yes, you can, just tell me what you would like."

When Kent had collected all the items which were on the list which he had been handed he asked, "Put them in the back, shall I?"

"Thank you, if you would be so kind."

"You say you've just arrived here, you mean –?" Kent hesitated.

"My husband and I have just taken the cottage about a mile along the road, Hillside, it's called, perhaps you know it."

"Yes, I do. We heard it was being opened up again as there were workmen in."

"So everyone knows everyone else's business around here?"

"Well, we're that bit out from the town and not many houses about, so, yes, I suppose one does get to know what's going on, but I'm sure there's no harm meant."

"If you say so. Now, you are?"

"Kent Mollison, and I work for Sam Cairns who owns the Nursery and lives in Glenleven House. I have the place at the back of the courtyard."

"It's a large house. I take it he's married with a family."

"Yes, his wife is Hazel and they have two little girls, Sara and Karen."

"And how many children have you?"

"I'm not married."

"Oh."

"And you are?"

"Lilias Gray. My husband is Major Gray and he's just been posted to Germany, but I decided not to go with him on this occasion. I'm an artist and I wanted to get down to some serious work. I find that living in army quarters doesn't give me much chance to follow my chosen career."

"So you'll be on your own at Hillside."

"Yes, but I'm not afraid of that. I welcome the opportunity to have peace and quiet and I shall be very busy. So, now we've each given a run down of who and what we are, I shall bid you good-day."

"Well, she's a cool customer if ever there was one," Kent said to himself, and later when Sam returned from delivering to the shops in Levenford, he recounted his morning adventure with Lilias Gray.

"Good looking, too, in a superior sort of way, typical army officer's wife, maybe she expected me to stand to attention."

Sam laughed. "You'd better watch your step there, Kent, or she'll have you up before the Major on a fizzer."

"I wouldn't put it past her."

WINTER SET IN hard and Sam and Kent's activities were confined mainly to work in the greenhouses. Customers at Glenleven were few and far between. Lilias Gray, however, came regularly every week as she was, Kent discovered, a vegetarian. Her manner had remained formal and rather stiff and Kent had reciprocated by being polite and correct, never attempting to speak in jest in any way.

One snowy morning he was busy working in the shop which Sam had decided to extend to include a proper office, when the telephone rang.

In his usual fashion Kent answered the call, "Good morning, Glenleven Nurseries."

"Oh Kent," said the voice at the other end, "it's Lilias Gray here, I'm sorry to trouble you, but I can't get the Land Rover started, and I was coming over for some vegetables. Could you possibly spare the time and bring them along? I should be so grateful."

"Yes, I'll do that. Tell me what you want, but our stocks are running rather low."

"Oh, I see, well, bring what you can."

Sam raised his eyebrows when Kent related the conversation. "You know, mate, I think she's got you by the short and curlies."

"Rubbish! It's the least I can do. She's practically cut off, probably with hardly any food. You know what these arty types are like – no organisation. Anyway it'll be interesting to see what sort of place she's got."

"I'm telling you, Kent, you've gone soft on her, but you go. We must keep all our customers happy. Are you taking the truck?"

189

"No, I'd never get up her road. If it's OK by you, I'll walk over."

"Sure, go ahead."

"You're laughing at me, Sam."

"Kent, if the boot was on the other foot you'd be taking the mickey, wouldn't you?"

"Yeah, I suppose you're right, but hell, Sam, she sort of fascinates me. I wonder what she paints."

WHEN KENT left the main road he found himself almost knee deep in snow and was glad when he finally reached the door of Hillside Cottage.

"Oh, how splendid of you to come so soon, Kent, thank you very much. Let's get this door shut and keep in the warmth. You'll stay for a coffee. I like this weather, but it does isolate one in a place like this. Even if I had managed to start the Land Rover I don't suppose I could have ploughed my way down to the main road."

As she talked on without a pause she took Kent's army greatcoat and motioned him to a seat beside a roaring fire.

"I haven't seen a soul for days, and apart from you folks at the Nursery, I haven't had time to get to know anyone yet, so I can't even phone a friend for a chat. But I'm not complaining, I'm enjoying it here and I am getting a start made again to my painting. It's amazing how rusty one gets. I've been outside sketching, but the light goes so soon, and even with the picture window I had put in, I've found I can't get the colours right so far, but I'm sure it'll all come back."

At last Kent was able to speak. "Have you been away from it for a while? I mean, painting."

"About four years, that's what comes from travelling about with one's husband. Is your coffee all right?"

"Yes, grand, thank you. You've got this place looking very nice."

"I'm getting to like it now I have it organised with what I call my studio at the far end, and my sitting room here where we are just now. At last it's beginning to warm up. I keep the fire going all the time. This was two rooms of course, so there is now only one rather small bedroom, and the kitchen and bathroom are in what I believe was a garage or workshop."

"I didn't realise so much was being done to the place, but it's off the main road and we tend always to be going the other way into Levenford, or along to The Willows, that's where Hazel's parents live. So you must have planned to come to this place before your husband was posted to Germany."

"Yes, we did, but only to use it in the summer months. My husband was left it by some distant relative whom he hardly knew and he was all for selling it, but when I saw it, I thought, here's the place I've been looking for. Now tell me about yourself, obviously you're not a Scot."

"No, but I'm sure there's not much about me that will interest you."

"Ah, but I like to know something about my subject's background."

"What do you mean?"

"I've been sitting looking at you and I've decided I'm going to use you as a model."

"You're what!"

"Yes, you have good features and wonderful hands. So has your friend Sam, but then he's married and his wife might object."

Kent regarded Lilias for a moment or two and then said slowly, "You're not suggesting I pose for you in the nude?"

"Not right away, that will come in time."

"But –" Kent spluttered.

"Now don't tell me a man of your experience is modest. First I want to make sketches of various parts of you, your hands, the angle of your arm, the bend of your knee, the tilt of your head, when you're doing various things. When you're sitting relaxed as now, or when you're sawing logs as I've seen you doing, or digging, kneeling, reaching up – I've got to practise all these techniques before I start on the real work. Oh, I can do landscapes, but I want to have people in my paintings and you seem to be the ideal person for me to practise on. I told you I was rusty."

"Yes, you did."

"Now, when can we make a start? What about the weekend, could you come along then and sit for me for a couple of hours?"

"Well, I'm not sure. Wouldn't your husband object?"

"My husband? Of course not. Right, Saturday afternoon or Sunday morning, just give me a ring."

"I'll think about it, now, I must be off, thanks for the coffee."

"Oh Kent, are you any good with car engines?"

"Yes, I dare say."

"Well, could you when you come across at the weekend have a look at the Land Rover?"

"Oh, all right."

"SHE COULD talk you into anything, that dame," Kent expostulated when he returned to Glenleven, and found Sam busy in the office.

"I told you, Kent, you'd better watch out there, she'll have you standing starkers yet, my friend."

"Not in this bloody weather, she won't, or even if there's a broiling heat wave."

"Famous last words."

- 28 -

JOHN and Ella Munro were on their weekly Saturday afternoon visit to Glenleven House.

"Sam away somewhere?" John enquired of Hazel when he joined her in the kitchen where she was preparing tea.

"He's working."

"Oh, I thought he usually had this afternoon off."

"Yes, but things are a bit behind because of the weather we've had lately."

"I'll have a walk out and see him before tea."

"HELLO SAM, how's it going?"

"Fine."

"On your own?"

"Yes, Kent's off somewhere."

"Everything all right?"

Sam wiped his hands on his overalls and joined his father-in-law on the path.

"Let's have a seat. I'm needing to have a talk with you."

They moved to the top end of the Nursery where there was a wooden bench set against the garden wall.

"We've been struggling recently," Sam went on, "I suppose in this sort of business you're bound to have your good and bad seasons, and I daresay I'm still short on expertise. I made a mess of the tomato crop last year and it cost us. I've used up most of my capital, you know the money my dad left me, and although I have assets, we're just taking in enough to keep our heads above water. And I'm ashamed of how little I pay Kent."

"Sam," John Munro broke in, "I know my attitude to you when you were first married was pretty harsh. I hope that's all in the past now, so if I can help in any way, just say so. After all, you and Hazel and the girls are our family."

"I know and I appreciate that, but" – Sam gave a wry smile – "it's not money that's the problem as it has turned out. It was, but it's not now."

"Sorry Sam, I'm not with you."

"I've confused you. What I've said is right, the turnover from the Nursery is not enough. But on Wednesday, the day after Mrs Whyte's funeral, I was called to the lawyers who are dealing with her estate. To my great surprise, she left me everything, farm and all. I was taken aback I can tell you. It seems she had no relatives left." Sam shook his head before going on. "It's made me feel bad, for what did I ever do for Ma Whyte? Yes, I grew fond of her and I looked in to see her regularly, but in a way I suppose I deserted her. She had lost her husband and her two sons; I was the only one left …" Sam turned away

John Munro put a reassuring hand round Sam's shoulders. "Sam, you have nothing to reproach yourself with. When you worked on the farm, you worked hard, I know that, and after both Fred and Rob had gone off Mrs Whyte relied on you a lot. Oh yes, she did. And she was very fond of you, more than you perhaps ever realised."

"But that's what I'm trying to say, I gave so little in return for all she did for me."

"Look Sam, when you came back from the forces, you had already made up your mind that the farm was not for you, and you had a wife and child to consider. Of course you could have gone back to the farm but you simply didn't want that. So now we've got that out of the way, what are the problems."

"Well OK, but it'll take some time to forgive myself for not being more attentive to Ma. There's a bit of money and of course the dairy herd is in good shape and brings in a steady income. Then there are some fields apart from the grazing land."

"Quite a lot to consider."

"There is. I've talked it over with Hazel, but, bless her, she feels I'm the one with the business brain," Sam smiled.

"You've done pretty well so far, Sam, even though you say the Nursery isn't as profitable as you'd like it to be."

"Thanks, but remember, you, Neil and Kent have all given me good advice."

"What are you thinking of doing then?"

"I could put the lot up for sale and the money would prop me up, but I want to make a real success of the Nursery. I want to make it pay."

"So?"

"I don't want to be bothered with the milk herd and supplying dairies and the various customers throughout Levenford. I don't need the farmhouse, but I could use some of the land to expand the Nursery. Then I'd like to buy over the two greengrocer's shops I supply with what I grow. I feel they could be run better than they are at present. That would take quite a bit of the money I'd make if I sold the farm. What do you think?"

"It's a bold step, Sam, and maybe I'm the wrong person to ask. You see, my generation has always tended to err on the side of caution, at least most of us have. I daresay I could think of some who have made a name for themselves by taking risks. The war has changed a lot, Sam, we've all gone through a sticky period since peace came again, that was only to be expected, but maybe we're needing lads like you to take a gamble."

"Is a risk different from a gamble?"

"I think we'd have to ask Neil to tell us the answer to that. Have you had a chance to speak to him about this?"

"No, not yet."

"What about Kent?"

"No, Kent – well –"

"This lady at the cottage?"

"You've heard then?" Sam said.

"Oh, not much, but yes, it's been mentioned to me a couple of times."

"At least it hasn't affected his work, give Kent his due, but he spends all his free time over there with her."

"Well, he's old enough to know what he's doing."

"Yes, but as I said earlier, I feel I've had almost slave labour from Kent. I couldn't do it without him, I'd like to make him a partner."

"Are you sure that would be a good idea? As a partner he should put in some capital."

"Yes, you're right, and here's how he could do it. I could work out what I'm due to him since he started work here if I had been paying him a reasonable wage, but instead of giving him the money, ask him to use it to buy a share of the business."

"He'd be a junior partner."

"Granted, and Kent would accept that, I'm sure."

"He has the house, Sam, don't forget, that's worth a bit."

"Yes, but really, Kent has made it what it is himself, with no help from me."

"He's a good lad, Kent. Don't think I'm against him, I'm just trying to put both sides of the argument. Apart from his fascination for Mrs Gray, he's always seemed a steady enough chap."

"So, have we reached any conclusion?"

"Sam, I think Hazel's right, you're the one with the business brain."

"Funny how lucky I've been in adult life. First Hazel, then being able to buy Glenleven House and start the Nursery with the money my father left me, and now this."

"You deserve it, Sam. Now I'm sure tea will be ready."

IN THE EVENING Sam went off on his own to Millside and stood in the yard looking at the milk lorry, the same one in which he had set off with Fred on his first morning as a working lad at the farm. His fondest memory of Fred was of his struggling to ask him to be his best man at his wedding to Rosie, and his delight when he agreed. Fred had been happy then. He crossed to the bothy, climbed the wooden stair to the room where he had his dreams, so long ago now it seemed, and if they had not all come true – well, he certainly wasn't complaining. Then through the dairy into the farmhouse, the kitchen quiet now that Ma had gone. He looked at her old rocking chair still now, and at the clock which alone broke the silence with its steady tick-tock. Somehow he could not picture Dugald Whyte – perhaps he did not want to – or Rob, for he had never been close to him.

The tangle of brambles and wild dog roses still bordered the track to the river where the marsh marigolds spread a golden carpet to the secret hide-out. He looked forward to the day when Sara and Karen would be old enough to share part of his past, or should it just remain that?

He thought of Neil as he sat on the river bank, Neil about to go off again to Germany, to share the joy of holding a daughter close to him, and then too soon the long parting. Yes, he had been the lucky one, he who had nothing as boy, but now seemed to have everything.

And what of Kent, with whom he had faced enemy fire so many times and survived. Kent, who was a lady's man, and yet still hadn't found the partner to share his life. Kent, who was so much at ease with Sara and Karen, with no offspring of his own to love.

Sam retraced his steps back to the farm, pausing momentarily to sense the stillness of an ending; tomorrow morning he would visit the cemetery and say a true farewell to Mrs Whyte, and he'd take some flowers to place on Rosie's grave – from Fred, at rest, somewhere far off in Normandy.

- 29 -

KENT was in thoughtful mood as he made his way to Hillside Cottage and he realised that prior to each visit he was always in a similar frame of mind. If someone had asked him what he thought of Lilias Gray, he would have found it a difficult question to answer. In some ways he resented her, but he somehow felt drawn to her. He resented her in that she expected him to do various chores for her, sawing logs, chopping sticks, checking her Land Rover and almost anything that was requiring attention. Oh yes, while he was slaving away, Lilias was making rough sketches of him, getting the 'angle right', as she kept telling him, and on the last occasion she had taken photographs, having announced that she had set up a dark room in one of the large walk-in cupboards off the kitchen.

Kent had to admit Lilias had talent and that her techniques were improving all the time. And when she felt she had done enough for the day, of course it was pleasant to sit together and chat and enjoy a coffee and later a meal. But what did he really want from her? That was the question that Kent kept turning over in his mind. There had never been any suggestion that their liaison should go beyond mere friendship. The relationship was like that of sister and brother, he thought, but no, it wasn't. Neil and Hazel reacted to each other quite differently. Lilias was an officer's wife and she treated him as if he was her husband's batman. Yes, that was it, even over a meal, damn her eyes, she was condescending – well it seemed that way. He wouldn't come again after today.

But his resolve weakened when he saw Lilias sitting at the front door of the cottage waiting for him. He had to admit she was an attractive woman.

"Hello, Kent, lovely to see you again. I haven't spoken to anyone for a couple of days, so I'm ready for lots of conversation. Isn't it a glorious day – warm enough for you to strip off and sit for me?"

"Sorry, I don't quite follow."

"You know I said some long time ago I wanted to draw you in the nude, well, the day has arrived. I'm ready. I feel I have mastered all the techniques which were requiring to be practised."

"And what if I refuse?"

"Oh Kent, come on, be adult. You were in the army for five years. Surely you lost all your modesty then?"

"That was different. We were all men together, no one thought anything of it."

"Now don't tell me you've never had your clothes off in front of a woman, Kent. You're too man of the world still to be a virgin, or am I mistaken?"

"Of course not, what I mean is – well, yes, I've been to bed with a few women, but I tell you this is not the same thing."

"I didn't think you'd be so childish. I've done this sort of thing often and I can assure you it's always been carried out in a professional manner. However, if you're so timid about stepping out of your pants, then you might as well go. You have disappointed me." Lilias turned and went into the cottage.

Kent stood looking at the closed door, his mind in turmoil. She was a tantalising bitch, and inwardly he despised himself for not turning round immediately and returning to Glenleven. But he was a sucker; he had never been able to say no to any woman whom he really liked. And damn it, he did like Lilias, despite her using him. She wasn't asking him to do very much and he was in good physical shape. He'd nothing to be ashamed of.

He opened the door quietly. "Where do you want me to stand or sit or whatever?"

Lilias turned and in her forthright manner said, "I had thought just outside the door, but perhaps it would be better if we went up into the little wood to the clearing. It would be quite private there."

"All right, what can I carry for you?"

When they reached the clearing, Lilias had Kent move around for some time until she finally decided that the best place was beside a tree stump.

"I'm going to take a photograph of you in various stages of undress so I can refer to them when you're not here. You can have them all when I've finished my painting, and the negatives. That suit you?"

"Well, OK, if you must."

"Right, let's get started."

When finally Kent stood naked, one foot on the tree stump, his chin resting in the palm of one hand, his elbow supported on his bent knee, he had to suppress a smile.

"If Sam were to appear now, he'd laugh his head off, and say that she had me by the short and curlies", he said to himself, "I really am this woman's slave."

When Lilias called, "Right, Kent, that'll do for now," he walked over to her easel.

"I know you don't usually let me see anything until it's completely finished, but I simply must have a peek today."

Kent stood and regarded the drawing and when he passed no comment, Lilias said, "You are quite a handsome man, Kent, with all the physical attributes which appeal to a woman."

Kent looked at Lilias, but she turned away. "Let's get back and have something to eat. I have it all ready and maybe later we could go somewhere out of town for a drink."

"Fine, I'm all for that."

THEY DROVE to Aberfoyle and spent a pleasant hour in the Bailie Nicol Jarvie Hotel before setting off for home again.

"I have enjoyed this evening, Kent. I become so tied up in my work that I completely forget that I should be getting out more. I was so tired of all the Mess parties, making conversation with other officers' wives, some of whom were positively dim, pretending to be interested in all their boring domestic problems, that I finally rebelled. Oh, Charles, my husband, was quite put out, but I'm sure he'll have found some female to console him in his wifeless state."

"Just as you have found me."

"Touché, my dear Kent. Now I'll let you off here, you'll manage to walk the rest of the way." Lilias pulled up at the road which led up to her cottage. "Come over tomorrow afternoon." And before Kent could reply, she was off.

Kent watched the Land Rover disappear from view and then gave vent to his feelings.

"Cool bitch. Lead a man on, then dump him at the side of the road. Bitch! Bitch!" He shouted.

He thought for a moment of following her to the cottage, then he decided he wouldn't give her the opportunity of turfing him out a second time.

He trudged along the road, deep in thought. Was he in love with her? No, he didn't think so. Was she in love with him? If she was, she had a funny way of showing it. Cold fish! Did he simply want to bed her? He couldn't be sure. It would be some sort of conquest, rather than any show of tender affection. She always bested him in everything and he realised that what he wanted was to turn the tables on her. And if he had to take her against her will? No, never, that was not in his book.

KENT SLEPT late on the following Sunday morning and decided, after having some breakfast that work was the best antidote for his depression. He knew Sam and Hazel with Sara and Karen would be going to The Willows, so he would have the place to himself. He was invited by the Munros on the first Sunday of each month to join in the family get-together and he was glad that he would not be expected today. Maybe he was wrong though, being on his own would only allow him to think about Lilias.

He set to work with a vengeance to clear the last area of rough ground which had been reserved for another greenhouse – if they could afford it, Kent thought, as he cast his shirt. He was fully aware that money was tight – Sam and he were still close enough to share all the problems of the business. But Kent was an optimist and he had a gut feeling that they would pull through. Besides, Sam was no quitter, and my goodness he had a good head on him. Oh they'd had their disasters and Sam was always insisting on taking the blame, but they were both learning and they worked in harmony. Sam was a bit huffed about Lilias, but he'd never say anything. Pity he didn't, thought Kent, it might bring me to my senses.

Thus Kent mused as he struggled to move a particularly large boulder from the site. To recover from the physical effort, he paused on his knees and did not hear the footsteps until a voice behind him said,

"Remember me?"

Kent looked round. "Jo! Oh Jo!" he gasped.

"Here, what have you been up to? You're out of breath."

"I'm all right," Kent said, standing up. "Gosh, you look great. Fantastic. And look at me, tousled hair, unshaven, sweaty, Jo, you've caught me out. I'm ashamed of myself. And if I had been decent, I could have given you a great big hug."

Jo smiled. "But are you sure you're all right? Have you lifted all these boulders on your own?"

"Of course I have, it was just that last one, it was a bit of a –. Sorry, language, language. But look, I can stop now. Can you still make coffee?"

"Of course."

"Right, while I clean up, you make the coffee and some sandwiches. Everything's in the same place as before."

When Kent, washed, shaved and dressed in flannels and sports shirt, appeared in the kitchen, Jo looked up and said, "Wow! I'll have that big hug now, you gorgeous man!"

"Why not," and Kent put his arms round Jo and kissed her lightly on the forehead. Then still holding her, said, "My bonnie Jo." They looked at each other steadily for a few moments before Kent released his hold. "Come on, let's eat."

"DID YOU have a rough night?" Jo suddenly asked.

"Gosh, what do you know about rough nights?"

"I'm studying to be a doctor."

"Goodness, did I look that awful?"

"No, not really, I thought you looked like a big film star when he's been on the tiles."

Kent threw back his head and laughed. "Jo, you are priceless, but how I enjoy your company. But to answer your question, Dr Jo Blackwood, yes, I had a rough time last night, but no it wasn't because I drank a lot or was out particularly late. Far from it."

"Cherchez la femme?"

"What? Oh, I get you. Yes, it was a woman."

"Oh."

"Nothing to worry about, I'll get over it. Come on, tell me all you've been doing at St Andrews this past year. Tell me about life at a university, I'd like to know what goes on in such a place."

Some time later Kent said, "Fascinating, Jo, I just wish I'd been blessed with some more brains so that I could have gone to a place like that. But what about the love life? Surely you must have lots of boy friends."

"Oh scores."

"That's to be expected, but is there one particular one?"

Jo was quiet for a moment before she said, "Yes, you could say there is."

"I thought so, that accounts for the twinkle in your eye. He's a lucky fellow, Jo."

"I only wish he –" Jo stopped in mid-sentence.

"You mean he hasn't fallen as hard for you as you have for him?"

"You could say that."

"Well, he wants his head examined, Jo. Never mind, maybe one day he'll wake up."

At that moment the outside telephone bell started ringing. "Dash it, I thought Sam had switched that thing off. Who could that be on a Sunday afternoon?" Kent sounded annoyed.

"Do you still have to answer it from the office?"

"Yes, I've a good mind to ignore it."

"I'll run down and see who it is," and Jo was off before Kent could stop her. She was back in a few moments, calling at the foot of the stairs, "Kent, a lady called Lilias Gray wants to speak to you."

"Oh hell!" Kent exploded. "Did you say I was here?"

"Yes, I did. Shouldn't I have?"

"No, I mean, oh it doesn't matter. I'll have a word with her."

Kent closed the door of the office before he reached for the receiver. "Hi, Lilias, what can I do for you?"

"Why haven't you come over? I've been waiting for hours. The light has been perfect for continuing with my painting and you're not here. I'm furious with you, Kent."

"Look Lilias," Kent began, trying to keep his temper. "I didn't say I'd be over and I'm sorry, but I have other things to do today."

"Such as entertaining young girls." And with that the line went dead very abruptly.

Kent slowly shook his head at the telephone. "Women!" he said fiercely. He rose and found Jo sitting at the foot of his stairs.

"The cause of last night's rough time?"

"Yeah."

"Well, I'd better be going, but are you taking me on again during my holidays?"

"Oh! Yes, but maybe we'd better see Sam first."

"Have you arranged for someone else?"

"No. No, it's just that – well, Sam's the boss. I'm just the labourer."

"Oh Kent, that's not true, you know a great deal about gardening."

"You think so?" Kent sounded glum.

"Kent, she'll make it up, I'm sure of it."

"What? Oh her! I couldn't care less."

"Will I give you a ring in the morning about the job?"

"Yeah, you do that. I'll speak to Sam."

"Bye then and thanks for a lovely time."

"Sure. Bye Jo."

Kent continued sitting on the stair feeling the afternoon had been completely spoiled by the telephone call. Who did she think she was? She seemed to expect him to jump at her command. Well, she'd had it. If he went back to Hillside, it was when it suited him. He would have to go back to get those wretched photographs. He couldn't risk these falling into anyone else's hands – especially her husband's. He should never have agreed to do it. It had been a mistake. Yet that painting was going to be good, really good. There was no doubt she was working up to her peak. Damn her. Maybe he should phone her back.

But just as he was crossing to the office, Sam and Hazel arrived back with Sara. Hazel remarked, "We passed Jo on her way home. I guess she was out to see you."

Kent gave a rueful smile. "I think I'll stick to girls of your age, Sara."

"Oh, trouble? Not with Jo, surely?"

"Jo? No of course not."

Sam looked hard at Kent. "Our friend at Hillside, I take it."

Kent nodded. "But forget it, Sam."

"I'll come over later and have a chat."

"So, you've been busy today," Sam greeted Kent when he joined him in the evening.

"I did a little."

"A little! There was no need, Kent."

"It's done, Sam. Listen, Jo wants her summer job here again. I said I'd have to ask you but Sam, I'll willingly pay her wage, for I know money's tight just now."

"Kent! How could you? You only get a mere pittance."

"I have some money of my own."

"Don't be ridiculous, Kent. Jo Blackwood doesn't need the money."

"I bet you it helps, what she makes here. It's a bit of pocket money. I'll employ her myself."

"Calm down Kent and listen. You've made up my mind for me. Jo will have her job and I'll pay her. Now are you all ears?"

Sam repeated the gist of the conversation he'd had the previous day with John Munro and finished, "I've decided, Kent, we're going to expand, I'm going to make you a partner; we'll put some of the money from the sale of the farm into a reserve fund for emergencies. I'll get Neil to put it all down on paper so I'll have it in front of me when I see a lawyer."

"Sam, I appreciate what you're doing. Thanks."

"Kent, I couldn't have come this far without you."

- 30 -

AMIDST a hive of activity the summer months sped past. Sam felt at last they had turned the corner and although he knew there would be more setbacks, he thought he was ready for any future contingency. He had gone boldly ahead with his plans and had refurbished the two shops which he now owned in the town. He'd been fortunate in being able to engage two reliable and capable managers and already business was improving.

Millside had been sold and the land he retained was ideal for his plans for growing extra fruit and vegetables. It would take time, but he knew it would be successful and it seemed that here too the new staff he employed were proving their worth. Hazel, Sara and Karen gave Sam the incentive to succeed and he revelled in the warmth of their affection.

AFTER A LOT of heart searching Kent had resumed his visits to the cottage at Hillside and he had allowed Lilias to complete her painting of him in the woods.

"But what are you going to do with it?" Kent asked, when she declared she was satisfied with her efforts.

"Sell it."

"Sell it! Not round here you're not."

"Of course not. I'll sell it abroad."

"Who would want to buy it?"

"Are you suggesting it's not worth buying?"

"No, it's good, I'll admit that, but who the hell wants a picture of a bloke standing starkers in a wood?"

"You'd be surprised."

"Must be bloody perverts then."

"Nonsense. It's a work of art. Look at it. You're a woodcutter, you've cut down a tree, it was hard work and you were very hot, so you stripped off your clothes, one by one. See how they are strewn haphazardly around you as you threw them down."

"You cheated, it's fake. You painted the tree I was supposed to have felled and the axe, and make the tree stump jagged. Thank goodness it wasn't or my foot would have suffered."

"But I sketched all these in my earlier work, you know that. I've just incorporated them in the painting."

"It's a fraud."

"You won't say that when I sell it and give you a share of what I can get for it."

"You can keep it. Just give me the photographs you took of me in the buff and the negatives. I'm going to burn the lot."

"Let's have some wine, Kent, and relax."

"That's another thing, you've got me drinking wine instead of sinking pints of beer."

"You're not a drinker, Kent, in that way."

"Maybe not now, but I still enjoy the odd one with Sam."

"Don't you like my wine?"

"It's all right, but it's not me."

"What do you drink, then, when you visit your girl friend?"

"What girl friend?"

"The doctor's daughter."

"If you want to know, it's coffee."

JO WAS LEARNING to drive and she had asked Kent if he was willing to go out with her in her mother's car.

"They say only the good die young, so I should be all right," Kent quipped.

"That's not nice of you, I'm quite competent, I'm only needing more practise."

"Sorry Jo, I couldn't resist. I'm sure like everything else you tackle, you'll do it well."

So on two, sometimes three evenings a week Kent walked along to the Blackwood residence and off they went, and on returning Jo always insisted that Kent had some supper before he set back to Glenleven.

"I could easily run you back," Mrs Blackwood had offered on several occasions, but Kent had always countered that he enjoyed the walk.

And while tramping along the back road, Kent mulled over the events of the day, usually concentrating on his time with Jo. She really was a super kid; she would go far, he'd no doubt about that, and to say he enjoyed her company was an understatement. It was puzzling though; the Blackwoods and Lilias Gray were on the same rung of the social ladder, he reckoned, yet they were poles apart. He himself was from a very average working class home, and yet he felt at ease with Jo and her mother, and with Dr Blackwood too, for that matter, but with Lilias he always seemed to be on edge. But he couldn't throw her off. The Blackwoods were like Ross Clark's parents – absolutely no side. You had to be like that of course in the medical profession. Jo would make a first class GP – unless she specialised, but he knew her father wanted her to join him in his practice. Maybe it was army officers and their wives. Some of them thought they were God's own gift to mankind. Yet Neil wasn't like that, he'd been an officer, he was another great guy.

"I'm surrounded by folk who treat me as an equal, how lucky can I get? If it wasn't for bloody Lilias Gray, I'd be quids in. Damn her," he spoke the words aloud as he undressed and slipped between the sheets.

SOME WEEKS later Kent waited for Jo to return from sitting her driving test, and when she appeared he was surprised when she looked rather subdued.

"Jo, don't say you haven't passed."

"Yes, I have."

"Why so glum then?"

"We won't be able to go out together any more in the evenings," and Jo pressed her face against Kent's chest.

"Now, steady on, Jo," Kent put his hand under her chin and raised her head and saw her eyes had filled with tears.

"Oh Jo, my bonnie Jo, you're a knockout," and he kissed her full on the lips.

When he released her, Kent said, "Now enough of that nonsense. Look, you've only a couple of weeks left before you go back to St Andrews. I tell you what, one evening before that, I'll get Sam's car and we'll have a meal out somewhere to celebrate your passing your driving test."

"Oh Kent, I –" but before she could continue, Kent put his fingers to her lips and said,

"No, Jo, don't say any more, let's just leave it as it has been up till now."

Jo turned away. "All right," she said quietly, but Kent pulled her round to face him again.

"Jo, you must know I think you're a very wonderful person. I've an idea of what you were going to say, and yes, I have feelings about you too, but let's leave it for the moment. Come on, give me a smile. That's better, and all right, just one more kiss, my bonnie Jo."

"YOU'RE VERY smart, Kent. New oufit?" Hazel greeted him as he crossed the courtyard to Sam's car.

"Yes, like it?"

"I've said so. Who's the lucky lady?"

Kent grinned. "It's Jo. I promised I'd take her out if she passed her driving test." And to himself he added, "Well, it's almost the truth."

"Oh."

"Surprised, are you? Thought it might be someone else?"

"No – no, why should I think that?" Hazel turned to Sam who had just appeared. "What do you think of this Romeo?"

"Wow! Kent! Jo certainly made a hit with you. When did you last dress up like this?"

"Here, less of it, you're making out I'm always scruffy, and Sam, Jo's only a kid."

"Is she? She's more than half way to being a doctor."

"Maybe, but it's not like what you're suggesting, Sam."

"I won't argue, best not keep her waiting. Have fun."

"Thanks, I'm sure I will."

When Kent had gone Hazel turned to Sam. "You knew it was Jo he was taking out. Why didn't you tell me?"

"Didn't I? Sorry sweetheart, I must have forgotten."

"Sometimes Kent and you are too close for words."

"Oh Hazel, that's not fair, there's very little I don't tell you."

"All right Sam, you're forgiven, I daresay you men must have some secrets between you."

"It wasn't a secret."

"I thought it was Lilias Gray he was wining and dining."

"Aren't you glad it's not?"

"I don't really know the said lady. I've seen her, but after all Sam, she's married."

"Kent won't ever say very much about her, so I don't know what the score is, but in my opinion he's being a fool going along to Hillside so often. It surprises me, for although Kent has always been one for the ladies, he's usually so level headed about it."

"But do you think there's anything going on between them?"

"No, definitely not, and that's what is maybe bugging Kent in a way. She seems to have some sort of hold on him."

"What about Jo?"

"You heard what he said – as far as Kent is concerned, she's just a kid."

THE FOLLOWING day was Sunday. Sam, knowing Kent would be having a lie-in, decided to pay him a call.

Kent stretched himself and yawned. "Hi Sam, you're on the go early."

"If you had two young daughters you would be too. So how was last night?"

"Great, just great."

"Kent, I know you'll laugh at me to scorn, but it's obvious Jo has fallen for you in a big way."

"Has she told you then, Sam? I wouldn't ever have believed you'd be so discerning."

"Just don't break her heart. I happen to like that girl a hell of a lot."

"And you think I don't?" Kent sat up. "Listen, Sam, I'll be honest with you and I'll say this to you and no one else. Yes, I love Jo, but that's as far as it can go."

"What do you mean?"

"Be sensible, Sam. Jo has a brilliant brain and she'll be a first class doctor. How could she possibly be handicapped by having someone like me? I'm just an odd job man."

"That you are not. You are a nurseryman like me, yes, you can turn your hand to almost anything, but you're certainly not just an odd job man."

"Even so, Sam, it's not on, and as I said last night, Jo's only a kid. She'll get over me. For her it's puppy love."

"Have you ever thought about Hazel and me?"

"That was different. You may not admit it, Sam, but you're a clever sort of guy. You're the one with the ideas. OK, I'm good at helping you to carry them through."

"What's that got to do with it?"

"Sam, I'll say it again, it's just not on. Once Jo's away she'll forget about me. Anyway she has a special bloke at St Andrews, she told me so herself."

"She's having you on. So you admit you've fallen for her."

"Yeah, OK. I tried to tell myself I hadn't but last night I realised that I couldn't kid myself any longer."

"Did you say anything to Jo?"

"No, maybe I didn't need to. Actions speak louder than words sometimes.

Now don't get me wrong. Nothing out of place happened. As far as Jo's concerned, she's too precious to me to take advantage of her."

"I think you've put yourself in an impossible situation."

"Jo understands, she'll be all right. I'll get over her, just as she will me."

WHEN SAM had gone Kent's thoughts returned to the previous evening. Yes, it had been wonderful to be with such a lovely, vivacious girl, and to feel totally relaxed in her company. But he had decided on the way home that it was an impossible dream and he had pulled the car off the road and stopped the engine.

He had turned and taken hold of Jo's hands. "Jo, I want to say our goodbyes here, not at your place. Will you do something for me?"

"Of course."

"When you go back to St Andrews, I want you to work hard at your studies, because that's the whole point of your being there. Then I want you to enjoy your usual social activities and accept the invitations from all the young lads who ask you out – that's if you like them – and particularly that special one you told me about."

"And will you be doing the same – will you be taking someone else out here?"

"Well, I might. It's not something I do regularly, mind you, but what I mean is this Jo, you must go with lads of your own age who share your interests. Promise me."

Jo sat in silence, then said, "All right, I promise. Will you write to me?"

"Jo, I'm no use at letters, so that's not on. I'll be here when you come home at Christmas, I won't run away."

Kent drew Jo to him. "And since you've promised, and been such a wonderful companion, not only tonight, but all these weeks you've helped me at the Nursery, I think you deserve a kiss, a real one."

When he released her, Kent said looking into her eyes, "My bonnie Jo, take care." Then reaching over to the back seat continued, "Mustn't forget your chocolates," and kissed her again.

"You treated her like a child, which she definitely is not, and you know you're her special one," Kent said to himself as he stepped under the shower, "but for me, it'll have to remain a dream, my bonnie Jo."

31

ALTHOUGH the main growing season was over, Sam and Kent were as busy as ever, but the latter found the Nursery strangely quiet without Jo. They had worked together, laughed together, had their coffee and tea breaks together – and now Kent realised how much she meant to him. As he threw himself into his work he had long arguments with his inner self, but he always arrived at the same conclusion – he could not ask Jo to marry him. Despite the fact that there were definite signs that the Nursery was now paying its way, he still had practically nothing behind him. Sam had of course increased his wages and he was a partner now in the business, but it would be some time before his share of the profits amounted to a substantial sum. Yet he was happy enough, enjoyed working with Sam and shared his determination to succeed. He had a home, and he had furnished it to provide him with the basic comforts; his diet he knew was pretty spartan, but he was fit and healthy, oh yes, he certainly was. If Sam and he went into Levenford for a drink, they always walked, and they swam once a week all the year round, mostly in the river, and when that was too cold, at the swimming baths. Not only that, they ran to the river and ran back home. That had been Sam's idea. He had laughed at first, but when Sam threw it down as a challenge, he'd accepted. When Neil was free he went along too, but neither Sam nor he would allow Hazel or Jo to join them.

"It's our link with the past," Kent said, "and it's for men only. Oh I know we wear our trunks now, but it's something we want to keep to ourselves."

"OK, I feel privileged being allowed to join in this ancient ritual."

It was as they returned from an early morning session at the swimming baths that Sam asked, "Have you stopped going to visit at Hillside?"

"I haven't been for some time, certainly, but I was thinking of going along again when I've time to spare. There was nothing doing there and never will be, Sam, but I don't want just to drop Lilias altogether. It's lonely for her at the cottage."

"It's her choice to stay there on her own."

"I know, but she does need help sometimes."

"Doesn't her husband ever come up here when he's on leave?"

"No, Lilias goes south. Apparently they have a place still in Surrey. He thinks it's too cold up here. In fact I wouldn't be surprised if Lilias stayed there over the next few months. She found the last winter pretty hard to take."

"You know, Kent, it puzzles me why you haven't gone back to visit your father."

"We still keep in touch, I manage the occasional letter and I might just go off one of these days and surprise him."

"You do that, Kent."

"I know how you feel on that score, Sam; don't worry, I haven't cast aside my old man, not by any means, but this is my home now. I like it here, I'm settled. I have a job I'm interested in, I have a place of my own, what more could a fellow ask for? Don't say it – I know – a wife. Yeah, you're right, Sam it would be wonderful, but – well – let's leave it. In the meantime, I'll get by."

THE NEXT weekend Kent decided to walk over to Hillside on the Saturday afternoon. It was almost dark when he approached the cottage and did not notice the car parked behind the Land Rover. He had lifted the door knocker when he heard the sound of raised voices and lowered it quietly and listened. Who could be with Lilias? An intruder? Was she in danger?

Kent moved on tiptoe along the front of the cottage to the windows, hoping to catch a glimpse of who was inside with Lilias, but the curtains were all completely closed. As he turned he caught site of the car and it came to him in a flash that Major Gray was the visitor. In that case, he thought, he best beat a dignified retreat.

Kent started down the track leading to the main road but he had only gone a few yards when a piercing scream made him stop dead. He turned and impulsively raced back to the cottage. As he burst through the door he almost crashed into Lilias and her husband who were staggering about the room as they struggled together.

"What the hell's going on here?" he shouted.

Major Gray turned and bellowed. "Ah, here's your precious little lover boy come to rescue you. Well we'll see about that." He made to lunge at Kent, but Lilias somehow managed to hold him firm.

"Look what the bastard did to my painting," she screamed, and Kent, risking taking his eyes off the irate major, looked at the easel bearing the painting of him in the wood, propped drunkenly against the wall and saw that a knife had been used to rip down the canvas, the obvious vicious slashes aimed at disfiguring the vital parts of his body.

"And that's what I aim to do again but this time it'll be for real," Major Gray roared, "you conniving little sneak."

"I think you should calm down and listen," Kent tried to keep his voice steady.

"Listen! To you! A bloody sergeant. Stand to attention when you speak to me."

"Look mate, I'm not in the army now, and if I was, I don't think I'd bother standing to attention to an ignorant slob like you. For your information, I haven't had an affair with your wife, I've never tried anything on with her. If I had I'd have got nowhere because she certainly made it plain that she didn't fancy me in the way you're obviously thinking. Yes, I stripped off and posed for her, but I could have been a statue of stone for all she cared."

"You wanted her, you weren't turned to stone, you're a liar," and Major Gray broke from his wife's grasp and hurtled himself at Kent. But the latter was prepared and side-stepped him neatly.

"It's not worth getting into a scrap about it, but if that's what you're after, all right." Kent slipped off his jacket.

"No! No! Stop it, both of you or I'll fire."

Both Kent and Major Gray jerked their heads round to Lilias and saw she was holding a revolver, which Kent recognized as a deadly German Luger.

"I mean it," Lilias continued, as the two men stared at her in awed silence. "Kent, you'd better go, and you'll go too, Charles. I'm through with you."

"Oh no you're not, you double crossing bitch," then turning to Kent, "you're just one in a long line of men she's seduced; at least all the others were officers, not scum like you."

"That's not true, Charles, and you know it. It was you who had the affairs with other officers' wives."

"And if I did, was it not because I didn't turn you on, that I wasn't hung sufficiently well, not like your friend here. You and your art, your painting, it's all subterfuge to get young men to strip off so you can feast your eyes on their equipment. That's how you get your kicks, you vixen." And he threw himself at Lilias who, taken by surprise, fell back against the wall, but managed to retain her grasp of the revolver even though her husband had seized her firmly by the wrist.

Kent stood for a second undecided as to what to do, then he shouted, "Give me the gun, Lilias," and moved in close to the two struggling bodies.

He saw Lilias weakening and her arm was being forced down by Major Gray as he strove to secure the revolver before Kent could.

Suddenly there was a loud report and Kent felt his whole body go numb. He reached out to a chair for support as his legs gave way under him.

"Oh my God, you've shot him!" Lilias gasped. She pushed her husband aside. "Look, there's blood everywhere. Help him! For goodness sake, help him!"

Major Gray looked at Kent. "It's only his foot, woman, nothing serious, just a scratch."

"Just a scratch! He'll bleed to death. Out of my way." Lilias ran to the bathroom and reappeared with towels. "Quick, get the Land Rover started while I try to stem the flow of blood. We've got to get him to hospital. Wait! Phone them first, tell them there's been a shooting accident and to alert Dr Blackwood, and tell them we're bringing him in. Go on, the directory is by the phone. Hurry!"

Major Gray somewhat reluctantly did her bidding while she attended to Kent, who was struggling to sit upright.

"Lie back, Kent, try not to move just yet, we'll get you to hospital as soon as we can."

When they succeeded in lifting Kent into the Land Rover, Lilias said, "I'll drive, you hold him steady from behind. I'll have to go slowly till we reach the main road."

"What are you going to tell them?" Major Gray demanded as they neared the approach to the hospital.

"That it was an accident, that we were examining the gun when it suddenly went off." She glanced sideways at Kent. "Will you go along with that?"

Kent who had been sitting with his eyes closed mumbled. "If that's how you want it."

HE DIDN'T recall being lifted out of the Land Rover and carried into the hospital, or of being undressed and taken to the operating theatre; of seeing nurses, doctors, policemen hovering round him. His last recollection was of what Lilias had asked him to agree to and when he opened his eyes and saw Dr Blackwood standing at his bedside, looking intently at him, his first words were, "It was an accident."

"Yes, Kent, so it seems."

"What's the damage?"

"I'm afraid you've lost four of your toes on your right foot."

"That's all? Will I be OK? I mean I'll be able to walk again. Is that a dumb question?"

"Yes, it'll take time to adjust and you'll maybe find you limp along for a while, but yes, you'll be all right."

"So when can I get out of this place?"

"Like all healthy people you don't like hospitals."

"No, I don't."

"Well, you have a bit of a temperature so you'll have to stay put in the meantime."

THE SHOCK and the delay in getting Kent to hospital resulted in pneumonia and for several days he was very ill.

Sam, Neil and Hazel took turns in visiting the hospital and sitting quietly by his bedside, listening to the ravings of Kent's delirium, feeling a deep anxiety for the man who was so close to all of them.

When Dr Blackwood returned home after an afternoon visit to the hospital his wife asked, "How is Kent today?"

"Hopefully I think he's reached the turn. He was in very good physical shape which has helped."

"He'll pull through all right?"

"Yes, but we'll keep a close eye on him to guard against any chance of a relapse."

"I'm so glad."

"I know that even to you I should not divulge what Kent has said during this period of delirium, but as it concerns Jo, I feel I must mention it."

"Jo – Joanna?"

"Yes, Jo. He's in love with her and she with him apparently, but from what he's said I gather that he's told her that it's not on."

"Oh dear, that explains why she was so quiet when she went off to St Andrews at the start of the session. Does Joanna know about Kent's accident?"

"No."

"Should we tell her?"

"No, we'll leave it in the meantime."

"What do you feel about Kent?"

Dr Blackwood thought for a moment before he replied. "As a man, I like him very much and I don't think Sam would have got where he is today without him, but as a husband for Jo – I'm inclined to agree with what he says himself, it's just not on."

"Oh dear, these young people do get their love lives all mixed up. It seemed so much easier in our day."

"Do you think so? I wonder."

"I'm sure the war has had something to do with it."

"Well, what's your opinion of Kent?"

"I like him, how can one do otherwise? He's the same type as Sam and I admire him for the stand he's taken with Joanna, if what you say is right."

"Oh it is. I managed to bring the subject up with Sam and he confirmed it."

"Oh Bill, was that really necessary? Was it fair to Kent when he's in the state he's in, poor man?"

"Maybe not. The whole thing has me worried. I only want Jo to be happy."

"And it doesn't matter about Kent?"

"I didn't say that my dear. Let's shelve that problem for the present. My main priority is to get Kent well again."

"Would it be out of place to pay him a visit?"

"I won't stop you."

ALICE BLACKWOOD waited until Kent was on the mend before she went to see him in hospital.

"Hello Kent," she greeted him. "I'm so pleased you're getting better and stronger by the day. Everyone has been so worried about you."

Kent gave a wry smile. "I remember saying to Jo when she asked me to go out with her when she was learning to drive that only the good die young. I guess I was right."

"At least you haven't lost your sense of humour. Now Kent, is there anything I can do for you?"

"If you can persuade Dr Blackwood to let me home soon, I'd be very grateful."

"I'm afraid that's one area where I have no say at all, Kent, but you must realise that you've been seriously ill, and it will take a while to build up your strength again."

"I won't do that lying in a hospital bed."

"Try to be patient. Now, have you written to Jo?"

"Written to Jo? Why – I mean …." Kent closed his eyes and lay back on his pillow. With an effort he started again. "No, we agreed not to write. Jo has her own life to lead. She'll get on fine without me. That's how I want it. She's a great girl, my bonnie Jo."

Kent continued to lie back with his eyes closed and Alice saw a tear trickle slowly down his cheek. She leaned forward, kissed him gently on the forehead and tiptoed away.

A FORTNIGHT later, Kent was allowed home, but at Hazel's insistence, she prepared all his meals and did his household chores.

"When you're ready, I'll allow you to take over again gradually," she told him after he'd been back at Glenleven for a week.

"What can I say to you and Sam and Neil, and to everyone who's been so good to me?"

"That's what friends are for, Kent."

"Hazel," Kent hesitated before going on. "Are things all right here at the Nursery?"

Hazel looked puzzled. "Yes, why shouldn't they be?"

When Kent was silent, Hazel went on. "I'm sorry, perhaps I have misunderstood you."

"Hazel, I'll be frank with you. When I was able to take in what was going on around me in hospital, I started catching bits and pieces of tittle tattle. Then during visiting hours I began to notice the meaningful glances directed towards me, the slight nodding of heads. Oh yes, I saw it all, and I soon came to realise that someone had been spreading it around about me and Lilias."

Hazel took hold of Kent's hand. "Listen, Kent, we know that it's malicious gossip, as Sam puts it."

"So you all know about it."

Hazel bit her lip. "Oh dear, I shouldn't have said that, but no, we must bring it out into the open. In Neil's opinion it was the work of some cub reporter out to catch the headlines."

"Sorry, I'm not with you, Hazel."

"There was a report in the local newspaper about what happened at Hillside the night you were hurt. It said you were a close family friend of the Grays and a frequent visitor to the cottage."

"But that's rubbish. I certainly knew Lilias but that night was the first time I'd ever set eyes on that swine of a husband."

"That's what we all say, it was untrue."

"I'll say it was, just like the story Lilias asked me to tell."

"What story?"

"That it was an accident. Accident be damned. That bloke was out to do murder if I hadn't stopped him."

"Kent, why didn't you say so before?"

"Oh I suppose I took the easy way out. It's the one thing I seemed to remember, Lilias telling me on the way to hospital to say it was an accident. I must have said it over and over again to the doctor and the police. I didn't quite realise just what a state of shock I was in, but I only wanted everyone to go away and leave me alone. What worries me now is that it will have an adverse effect on the business."

"Oh I shouldn't think so. It'll be a nine day wonder, most folk will probably have forgotten about it already, that's Levenford. Believe me, I know."

"Yes, I daresay you do, Hazel, but I think it best I go away."

"Go away? What do you mean, Kent?"

"What I say. Leave here."

"But why?"

"Otherwise Sam and you will suffer."

"Kent, you're not serious. Look, you're still not fully fit, that's why you're thinking this way. Anyway, where would you go?"

"There's only one place I can go – back to York. If I can't fit in with Dad and his new wife, I'll stay somewhere else."

"Kent, I feel quite upset about all this. Why not talk it over with Sam before you decide."

"No, please, Hazel, don't say anything to Sam yet. Give me a week to think it over."

"All right, but Kent, you're part of our family here. What would Sam do without you? What about Sara and Karen, they worship you."

"Yes Hazel, I know all that, and I fully realise what this place means to me, but I feel that the finger of guilt is pointing at me."

"Oh Kent," Hazel's eyes filled with tears, "it's all so unfair, because none of it is true. Don't you think by going away you would be admitting there was something in these wild stories?"

"Perhaps – but – well, I'll think about it. The thing is, I did visit Lilias frequently, as the report said, but it was only as a friend."

"I believe you, Kent."

TWO DAYS LATER Hazel went over in the middle of the morning to visit Kent and found a note lying on his kitchen table.

Dear Hazel, I've decided to go. Please explain to Sam. Much love to all of you, Kent.

SO JO RETURNED to Levenford for her Christmas vacation anticipating finding Kent at home and was stunned when she discovered he had gone and then shattered as the events of the previous weeks were gradually unfolded to her.

"But why didn't you write and tell me?" she demanded of her father and mother.

"That's quite easily answered, my dear. Kent wouldn't allow us to, and we felt we had to respect his wishes."

"But Daddy, I love him, and he loves me, I know he does."

"Has he told you so?"

"Not in so many words, but –"

"I'm sorry, my dear, you'll just have to accept that Kent does not have the same feelings for you."

"But he does, he does."

"Joanna, listen," her mother pleaded, "you can't force a man to love you, a man will always declare his love if he feels it in his heart. You're only hurting yourself by trying to make Kent love you."

32

A S the train slowed to a halt Kent moved into the corridor and glimpsed the first of the station signs bearing the word 'York'.

So he was coming home, or was he? Did he have a feeling of nostalgia as he saw the name of his home town in even larger letters? He couldn't be sure. He had spent the entire journey from Glasgow going over events since the fateful night at Hillside – at least what he could remember of them. What he could not forget, however, were the stories which he knew were circulating in Levenford, and when he had managed to obtain a copy of the paper which carried the report about the 'Incident at Hillside' as it had been headlined, it had finally decided him.

As he made his way from the station Kent glanced at his watch and slowed his pace. He didn't want to arrive home before his father returned from work. He'd still be at the swimming baths where he'd returned to his old job as boilerman. He could go there, have a shower and freshen up after his long train journey.

The path to the rear door of the baths had an old familiar look; there always had been a litter of non-descript items lying about in the days when Kent had paid regular visits to his father. The paint was peeling off the door and it creaked as he pushed it open and immediately his ears were assailed by the noise of the boilers and the scrape of a shovel as it dug into the pile of coal in an effort to assuage their seemingly insatiable appetite. He stood for a moment as he watched his father, stripped to the waist, straighten up and take a breather. He moved nearer him and putting his hands on the sweat laden shoulders said, "Hello Dad."

As his father swung round he saw a look of apprehension and surprise in the bright blue eyes, beaming out from the grime streaked face.

"Kent! What are you doing here?"

"I've come to visit you. Don't you think it's about time I looked you up?"

"Yes, well –"

"Gosh, that's a welcome for your only son."

"I mean, it's such a surprise. I didn't expect you, especially since it's almost Christmas."

"What better time to come back home?"

"Yes, I suppose that's right. Are you having a holiday?"

"Sort of."

"Have you been to the house yet?"

"No. I thought I'd come here first and go home with you. Any chance of a shower? Still got your own private one down here?"

"Yes, nothing has changed. Maybe some day they'll modernise the place, but it won't be in my time."

"You've a bit to go yet, Dad, before you can pack it in. Why did you come back here when the war was over? That's what has always puzzled me."

"I suppose I like the place."

Kent smiled. "OK, I'll believe you. When are you finishing tonight?"

"Six o'clock. I was just about to have a shower myself and clean up before going home."

"You do that. I'll swim a couple of lengths and then pop in after you."

AS HE TOWELLED himself dry Kent looked at his father and said, "I hope I still look as young and fit when I'm your age as you do, Dad. You could be taken for my brother. By the way, how's Jane?"

"Fine, just fine."

The shortness of the reply made Kent look up at his father again. "Everything all right, Dad?"

"Yes, sure."

"Look, I'm sorry landing on you like this. I can find somewhere else to stay if it's not convenient."

"We'll manage. Come on, I always walk home."

"Suits me."

His father went on ahead of him as they entered by the back lane, past the outside lavatory, through the tiny yard, into the kitchen. He heard his father call, "Jane, we've a visitor. Kent's home."

Kent stopped dead in his tracks when Jane came through from the kitchen. He couldn't believe his eyes. She was the largest pregnant woman he thought he'd ever seen.

"Good God!" he exploded, turning to his father, "why didn't you tell me?"

"I wanted to, Kent, but I couldn't get the words out."

"But you never mentioned it when you last wrote."

"I just didn't know how to put it down on paper. I'm sorry, lad."

Then turning to Jane, Kent said, "You look as if you're ready to drop it any day now."

"Yes, it's due tomorrow, Christmas Eve."

Kent re-buttoned his greatcoat. "Well, it's obvious I can't stay here," he began.

"Kent, at least stay and have a meal with us. It'll give you time to think."

"Yes, please stay, Kent," put in Jane. "Come on through to the fire."

Reluctantly Kent did their bidding and sat down opposite his father. He looked round the room and saw that Jane had made a number of changes. In fact, it just didn't look like his home any more. He smiled wryly to himself as his thoughts went back to the end of his train journey. He'd been right. This was no longer his home. But for his father to sire another child! It was unthinkable! He looked across at him again and suddenly felt a wave of pity for him. As he had remarked at the baths, his father was still a relatively young man. What right had he to expect him not to lead a normal married life blessed with a child? Was he jealous? Maybe, a bit, but had he a right to be?

His thoughts were broken into by his father rising from his chair and saying. "I could be doing with a drink. I won a bottle of whisky in a raffle last week. I was going to keep it till the – till Christmas, but well, why not tonight. Join me?"

"Yes, OK."

When his father handed him the glass, Kent raised it and said, "Here's luck then, Dad, to you and Jane."

"Thanks, Kent."

THE MEAL was eaten in comparative silence and when it was over Kent rose and said, "I best be off and try to find a place to kip for a couple of nights or so."

"There's no need, Kent, we can easy manage you here."

"Thanks, but it's out of the question. I hope everything goes well. Thanks for the meal, bye for now."

"I'll see you down to the bottom of the lane, Kent."

They set off in silence and then his father asked anxiously, "Will you find a place? It seems awful you going away like this."

"Dad, be sensible, it's just not on my staying, so forget it. I shouldn't have come without letting you know."

"Kent, listen, this child, it'll make no difference to how I feel about you. Maybe it's been a mistake, I just don't know, but Jane was so keen. At her age it can be difficult, but the doctor says she should be all right."

"I'm sure she will be."

"Kent, don't judge me too hard."

"Dad, I'm not, it's just a bit of a shock."

They had reached the end of the lane. "Kent, you'll keep in touch."

"Yeah, I'll do that. Bye, Dad."

"Bye lad, take care."

KENT WALKED on, not knowing where his steps were leading him. Yes, he was upset, there was no use denying it, whether he had a right to be or not, he could not decide. He stopped to try to take his bearings and realised he was not far from where Dolly lived. He hesitated, trying to decide. He hadn't bothered to write to her since he had left York for Levenford. Should he? At least she'd listen, she'd always been ready to do that.

Kent was surprised when he reached the street where Dolly lived to see that some of the houses were boarded up and as he regarded them rather thoughtfully an old man emerged from the shadows.

"They're knocking them down. Been standing near a hundred years. I'm eighty three and I've lived all my life in them. Now we're all being moved to the new estate."

"Oh, where's that?"

"Away out on the road to Selby, miles from anywhere."

"And has everyone in this street gone there?"

"Mostly, and if they've not there already they'll be soon." The old man shook his head and moved back into the darkness muttering away to himself.

Kent walked on and as he had fully expected the house where he and Dolly had shared some happy hours in and out of bed was like most of the others in the street, quite deserted.

Suddenly he felt tired and his leg was aching. He thought wistfully of his home and pictured his father and Jane sitting beside the roaring fire. He turned and started to limp his way back to the centre of the city. Funny, he mused, that his father had not noticed his limp, although he realised that it would not have been so obvious after the long sit in the train. And he had not remarked on his deformed foot when he had stepped out of the shower. Yes, Kent thought, he really had been worried about telling him about the imminent birth, for he had sat watching as he, Kent, had dried off before dressing.

HE WENT INTO the first hotel he saw and asked for a room.

"A single, sir?" the clerk enquired.

"Yes."

"Will you be staying over Christmas?"

Kent thought for a moment. "Can I, if I want to?"

"Yes, by all means, it's just for meals, we try to give as many of the staff time off over the holiday period."

"Oh yes, I see. Can I let you know tomorrow when I see how I'm fixed?"

The clerk looked dubious, so Kent added, "Look, as long as I have the room, I'll manage without the meals if it's a bother."

"Very good, sir, but if you require meals other than breakfast you can have them if they are available."

"OK."

"Worse than bloody wartime," Kent muttered to himself as he undressed and slipped between the sheets.

- 33 -

AFTER breakfast on the following morning Kent set out walking towards Selby to find the new housing scheme. It certainly was quite a tramp but eventually it came into view. The problem was to find where Dolly lived and Kent realised this was not going to be easy since quite a number of the houses appeared to be occupied. He toyed with the idea of going to the first house and asking the occupant, but looking further ahead he saw a man busy digging his front garden.

"Good morning, that's a fine way to spend Christmas Eve."

The middle aged man looked up and regarded Kent for a moment before he asked, "Do I know you?"

"No, I was only being friendly."

The man grunted and resumed his digging.

Kent cleared his throat and tried again. "What I really wanted to ask you was whether or not you know if a Dolly Lorimer lives round here."

The man's foot held the spade firmly down in the soil. "Come again."

Kent repeated what he had asked.

"And if I do know where she is, what is it to you?"

"I knew her when I used to live in York and as I'm here again on a visit, I thought I'd look her up. I was told she had moved to one of these new houses."

"What did you say your name was?"

"I didn't, but it's Kent Mollison."

"Kent Mollison." The name was repeated slowly. "Well, I've got news for you, Mr Kent Mollison, I'm Mr Daniel Lorimer."

Kent looked puzzled for a moment, then recovering said, "Oh, you must be one of her brothers. She told me she had four."

"Her brother!" The words came out with a roar. "I'm her husband and have been for the last ten years."

"But –" Kent stammered, "Dolly said she was a widow."

"A widow! I bet she did! The conniving bitch. She walked out on me, but she won't do it again, you can be sure of that." And jabbing a finger into Kent's chest, he continued in a tense tone, "You better just get lost, Mr Smart-arse

Mollison. I know all about you, the great bedroom jockey. Now get going, before I bust that pretty face of yours."

Kent stood his ground. "Look mate, don't try any rough stuff with me, you might just come off second best, big as you are. As far as everyone in the factory where we worked knew, Dolly was a widow and it was on that basis that we became friends. If she walked out on you, then I'm not surprised and I'm sorry for Dolly if she's lumbered again with a swine like you, and – I said – don't try anything," Kent finished, while he held the other's wrist in a vice-like grip.

He looked to the door as he heard it open and saw Dolly move towards them.

"Hello Kent," she said, and he saw the chastened look in her eyes. "I think you'd better go before there's any trouble."

Kent hesitated for a moment. "All right, Dolly, I guess it'll be for the best," then turning to her husband, "Listen mate, don't you dare lay a hand on her. You're a lucky man having Dolly for a wife, she's tops, so just you have a think to yourself. OK, we had a bit of fun together, but that's all in the past. If she's your wife, then so be it. Bye Dolly."

KENT RETURNED to his hotel room and flopped on to his bed. The long walk had made his foot ache again and he felt thoroughly despondent. He no longer had a place in his father's home; Dolly belonged to someone else – just who had he in York? He could still find a number of people with whom he had been friendly before he had gone off to Levenford, but he realised they had been drinking pals and he was fully aware that he had changed and enjoyed only the once a week drink with Sam.

Sam, Hazel, Sara, Karen, Neil and Jo. A mental picture of them all flashed through his mind. He rolled over on his face and groaned. What a fool he'd been! Damn that bloody Lilias Gray. And damn himself for being so weak-kneed. He dozed off and on throughout the afternoon, then being assailed by the pangs of hunger, decided to go out and look for a café.

Everyone seemed to be in a hurry, then everyone seemed to have somewhere to go. And he had nowhere. The food in the café failed to revive his spirits and he decided to find a pub where it would be warm and on Christmas Eve there would be plenty of goodwill around. At least, he hoped so. The episode with Dolly's husband had depressed him more than he thought.

The pub was busy, but Kent managed to find a place at the bar and was soon engaged in a series of short term conversations with an assortment of people all of whom appeared to know everyone else and who therefore moved about continually. Kent drank steadily, all the while sinking deeper and deeper into a mood of utter depression. Gradually he ceased to respond to greetings from any of the other customers in the pub and just before ten o'clock he staggered out on to the street.

He could not remember in which direction the hotel lay, or indeed its name. He propped himself up against a wall and tried to obtain some signal from his befuddled head, but none would come. He propelled himself forward, bumping into passers-by, but he did not return their friendly repartee. He stopped again and fumbled for his cigarettes and then somehow recalled from the depth of his mind that he had stopped smoking some considerable time ago.

"That's right, Kent," he muttered to himself, "Sam and Neil, fitness fanatics, throw away the weed, Kent. But hell, I could do with a fag now. Sorry Sam, sorry Neil."

He stumbled across the street to where he saw a light in a shop window, but when he reached it, he found the door closed and locked. He rattled it, then banged on it, until he heard a voice call, "I'm shut."

He continued to belabour the door and the voice, louder now, "Go away, can't a fellow have a rest at Christmas."

Kent was not deterred. "I only want some fags," he slurred. "Please, I'm desperate for a smoke."

"Oh, all right, anything to get rid of you."

As the bolts were being drawn the voice continued. "If it wasn't for Christmas, I'd have phoned the coppers and had you locked up."

When the door was finally opened, Kent fell forward into the shop and lay face down on the floor.

"Oh hell, I'll have to get the police after all. Here let's have a look at you."

Kent was rolled over on his back. "Crikey, you're a dead weight. Hi, wait a minute, I think I know you, yes, you handsome bastard, you're Kent Mollison, although you're not going to be quite so handsome when you've slept this off. Come on, sit up."

Kent's eyelids moved slightly upwards as the shopkeeper turned to close and lock the door, then he fell back again, out to the world.

HE WOKE slowly and realised he was in bed and thought he must have somehow managed to find the hotel. He opened his eyes again. The room was unfamiliar. Where the hell was he? He lifted his head from the pillow but allowed it to fall back immediately as a searing pain shot across his temples. He tried to think, but it was all a blank. He felt himself under the covers. He was completely naked. Christ! Had he picked up some tart? He moved his arm behind his back to see if there was anyone else in the bed, but to his relief he was alone. He tried lifting his head again and had managed to half sit up when the door opened.

"So you're awake at last, Kent. A fine state you were in last night, I must say."

Kent focused with difficulty. "I know you, yes, it's Terry Richards, my bench mate at the factory. I'm not back working there am I? How the hell did I get here?"

"I'm not surprised you don't remember, you were pissed up to the eyeballs. You just about broke down my shop door last night."

"I did?"

"Yeah, demanded cigarettes or you'd die."

"What? I don't smoke now."

"You were well away mate. Anyhow you flaked out on the floor downstairs. I had one hell of a job getting you up here, believe you me. Then I thought for old times sake I might as well make the bastard comfortable, so I stripped you off and heaved you into bed. My bed! The only bed in the place. And I was damned if I was going to sleep in a chair, on the settee, on the floor or even in the bath, not on Christmas Eve I wasn't, not in my own house. No sir! So you had company my friend, but you were completely blotto."

"Terry, what can I say? I'd have done the same for you."

"Like hell you would, Kent Mollison. Sore head or not you still have the smart retort."

"Sore head! You can say that again."

"Wait!"

Terry returned with a tumbler. "Here, drink this, and after you've got it down, get under the shower."

"All mod cons."

"Sure. When you're ready, we'll have something to eat."

"Food. Oh, no thank you."

"Yes you will, you must, and by the way, Merry Christmas!"

Half an hour later Kent felt a lot better and was ready for some sustenance.

"Listen Terry, I thought you were married."

"I was, in fact I still am, but waiting for a divorce."

"Gosh, what happened?"

"Everything. She went off with a damned Yank; my old man passed away, my mother died during the war, and I had to take over the shop."

"You had to?"

"Well, maybe I didn't have to, but I did. Like you, I wasn't keen to return to the factory. I couldn't see there was any future there for me. I thought, to hell with it, I'll try the shop, it's a good going concern and when I've made enough, I can bugger off and do what I'm keen on."

"What's that?"

"Photography. That's why there's only one bedroom now. I turned the other one into a dark room."

"Oh God!" Kent groaned. "Not another bloody photographer."

"Why do you say that?"

"Never mind. I best get back to the hotel. You must have plans seeing it's Christmas. Thanks for what you did."

"Now wait a minute. Not so fast. You're going nowhere."

"Come again."

"Kent, I'd like you to stay and spend Christmas with me, then if you want, you can go. You mentioned a hotel, so obviously you're not staying with your old man. Please Kent, I'd like you to."

Kent looked at Terry and saw the earnest look in his eyes.

"OK."

"You see," Terry went on, "when my wife left me I was completely knocked out. I couldn't believe it, we had been so much in love. I was devastated. In fact, taking over the shop saved me from losing my sanity I think. At the back of my mind I suppose I had the idea that she might come back to me if she thought I was going to make my pile. Vain hope. And gradually I gave up and decided to hell with it. I'll work my fingers to the bone, then sell up and go."

"And are you near to going?"

"No! The shop's a killer. Long hours, hard graft. Ever tried being nice day in day out to every bastard under the sun who blames you for every bloody shortage there is? So I decided I'd be on my very own on Christmas Day, with not a complaining, whining voice in earshot."

"And I've spoiled it for you."

"No, Kent, you haven't. I'd have been miserable all on my own. There's a saying, 'No man is an island,' and I guess it's right. I may have contact with hundreds of folk, but I have tried to cut myself off – I've dropped all my friends. It's a mistake, although I must admit that running a general store is more than a full time job. I'm always so completely knackered that I can't even be bothered going out for a drink."

"We make a fine pair."

"Why do you say that?"

"It's a long story."

"OK, tell me the tale over our Christmas dinner, on which, by the way, I'll have to get cracking."

"Look Terry, I feel like some fresh air, the old head isn't quite clear yet. I'll collect my gear from the hotel while I'm out."

Terry looked quizzically at Kent.

"If it's OK by you, I'll accept your invitation to stay – for a few days, if that's possible and I'll sleep on the settee in the kitchen."

"Crikey, that old thing has springs sticking up all over the place. I've been meaning to get rid of it for ages."

"It'll do me."

"Suit yourself, but I tell you what, if you decide to stay for a spell, I'll get a proper bed for you. There's plenty of room in the bedroom for one."

NEW YEAR passed and Kent found himself still lodging with Terry, helping him now and then with odd jobs, and at other times taking long walks.

Terry had listened quietly while Kent filled him in on how he had spent his life between leaving and returning to York.

"It's up to you, mate, but I reckon you've thrown away a good job, and as for your girl Jo, I never thought that Kent Mollison would be a faint hearted lover."

"It's not that, Terry," Kent protested. "As I said to Sam, I'm not in Jo's class. I couldn't bear to see her lumbered with me, just a coarse swaddie really."

"It's you saying that, Kent. But who am I to give advice?"

"Oh, let's change the subject, let's not be a pair of miseries."

THEY FOUND they could relax in each other's company, but if they had been pressed, each would have admitted that there was a missing ingredient in their lives.

By the middle of January Kent's funds were running low. "If I'm staying on here, Terry, I'll have to find a proper job."

"There's one right here."

"No, that's not for me. I don't mind helping in the back shop and doing the cleaning up after closing time, but serving over the counter – no thank you. I know you can say I do that at Glenleven, but there it's only a small part of the job, and somehow it's different."

"And if you can't find anything?"

"I'll move on."

"Where to?"

Kent shrugged his shoulders. "I don't know. Pass me the local rag and I'll scan the jobs column."

- 34 -

THE bell at the end of the afternoon sounded and Neil dismissed his fifth form class. When he had cleared his desk, he locked his cupboards, hung up his gown and made his way over to the gymnasium where he knew Phil Davidson would be waiting.

As Neil undressed before slipping on a pair of football shorts Phil asked. "You've not had second thoughts?"

"No, tomorrow is my last game for Levenford. I'm definitely hanging up my boots. Time for some of the younger lads to take over."

"You're fitter than most of them, Neil, you'd be good for another couple of seasons."

"No, I want to go out while I'm still playing reasonably well and anyway at thirty it's time I packed it in."

"I'll miss these training sessions we've had since you started here."

"No reason why they should stop. I won't be training twice a week at Bogside, but since I've every intention of continuing to play tennis and badminton, I mean to keep as fit as I am now, as long as I can."

"Won't you miss it, though, Neil? Don't you still get a thrill when you send the ball crashing into the net and hear the roar of the crowd?"

Neil smiled. "Oh, I'll miss it, but I'm sure I'll survive. I owe Levenford FC a very great deal. Playing for them, being part of the set-up, mixing with the lads, sharing the victories and defeats, oh yes, it's been great, and it's compensated for the other things in my life I seem to be missing out on."

"One thing I've admired about you, Neil, is that you've never been bitter, even although things haven't worked out the way you wanted them to."

"I've had my own thoughts, but come on, let's get started, not too strenuous, then a good rub down and hot shower."

YES, HE CERTAINLY had his own thoughts about the events of the years since his first visit to Germany to see his daughter. When he had returned home he was more determined than ever to bring Mari-ella to Scotland so that he could give her a proper home. But these very words, 'a proper home', had been thrown back in his face by his father when Neil had discussed the matter with his parents. All the old bitterness had surfaced again.

"What do you mean, give her a proper home? A proper home in my opinion is what you have had here, where there is a father and a mother. Do you honestly expect your mother to take on the responsibility of bringing up this young girl? Or are you hoping Hazel will offer?" John Munro's voice was firm and calm. "I don't think you have worked out what this would involve, Neil."

"Dad, I know it wouldn't be easy, but after all, Mari-ella is my responsibility."

"From what you say, the girl seems perfectly happy with your friends in Hamburg."

"She is, but that's not the point. I'm her father and I want her to grow up beside me, can't you put yourself in my position?"

"I would have had the good sense not to land myself in your position."

"You've always been the perfect gentleman, of course."

"Neil, that's not how to speak to your father," Ella Munro interrupted, "you'll apologise for what you said."

"All right, I'm sorry, but you'd think I'd committed some crime the way you go on. You won't recognise that Mari-ella is one of your grandchildren just as much as Sara and Karen are. Don't you think that by your refusal to do so hurts me? Yes, it hurts me a lot."

Neil left his parents and retired to his room. It was not long before there was a tap on his door and his mother's head appeared.

"Neil, may I come in?"

"Yes," Neil answered in a choked voice, which brought his mother to his side and as she put her arms around him whispered, "Oh Neil, don't give up hope. There's bound to be a way. Let's talk some more about it."

"Is there any point?"

"Of course. Listen Neil, there's a lot in what Dad says, but when you get permission, could you not bring Mari-ella over just for a holiday, to see how she would fit in here and how you could manage to keep her permanently. You're right in what you said, we haven't thought of Mari-ella as our grandchild, and I'm sorry if you feel hurt about that."

"Forget it, Mum, I think the best thing would be for me to go away from here once I finish college. I don't fit in any longer."

"Oh Neil, don't say that, I'd hate to see you go."

"Mum, there comes a time when the fledglings must leave the nest. You and Dad, I'm sure, would be happier without me."

"Neil, what a thing to say. If you were to marry, that would be different, but as long as you're single, this is your home."

"And as long as I don't bring Mari-ella here to stay."

"Neil, I'm serious about my suggestion about bringing her for a holiday. Never mind what Dad says, I'll talk him round."

WHEN THE team bus reached Glasgow after Levenford's away game at Stenhousemuir, Neil decided to drop off with those of his team mates who lived in the city and make his way to Jordanhill College for the Saturday night hop.

Neil was finding the Training College rather a contrast to the University, where he felt that you were left to stand on your own two feet and if you couldn't, it was just too bad. Jordanhill seemed like going back to school with petty rules and regulations and lecturers bearing schoolmarmish airs without the graces. While the setting of the building was picturesque, the interior reminded Neil of a hospital with its long corridors with white tiled walls. He wondered if it was geared more to students going straight there from school, than for battle hardened ex-servicemen. He admitted he was learning the basics of his trade at the college and enjoyed some of the lectures, but he was impatient to see his time through and start teaching.

Neil had decided, despite his lack of enthusiasm for Jordanhill, there was quite an abundance of talent among the female students, so he had come to have a closer look. Being an athlete, Neil was neat and nimble on the dance floor and he was soon enjoying himself with a number of different partners, but finding making conversation rather difficult. He realised that the girls with whom he had been dancing were all quite a few years younger than he was and that their diffident manner and shyness was probably due to his more mature looks and confident style. He felt that perhaps a Saturday night hop was not really his scene and he was on the point of leaving when he noticed a late arrival.

He watched as the tall, dark haired girl greeted her friends and he felt his pulse quicken. She turned to wave to someone sitting along from Neil, and he got the benefit of her wide smile. He knew why this newcomer was having such an effect on him. She reminded him of Anna Maria. He watched as she was whirled away by a lad whom Neil recognized as one of the Physical Training students and he kept his eyes glued to them both as they moved round the floor, engaged in animated conversation. He was relieved when at the end of the dance they parted, each to their own group of friends, and when the next dance was announced he made a beeline to ask if she would care to dance.

After some brief opening exchanges, Neil, to his dismay, found himself unable to think of what to say, and it wasn't until the band brought the quick step to an end with a flourish, that he managed to find his voice again.

"I take it you're a student here?"

"Yes, I am. Why do you ask?"

Noticing they were now the only couple left on the floor, Neil said, "Shall we leave centre stage and sit down?"

When they had found two empty chairs Neil continued, "It's just that I haven't noticed you before."

"Nor have I, you."

Neil smiled, "I deserved that. By the way, I'm Neil Munro."

"Oh, you're the footballer."

Neil was taken aback. "How did you know that?"

"Ah, that's got you guessing. I saw your photograph in the paper when Partick Thistle tried to sign you. My father is a Jags supporter, so it was he who told me you were to be a student here and you weren't going to leave Levenford until you had finished your studies."

"Fame at last," Neil quipped, "but now you know who I am, what about you?"

"I'm Laura Williams and I'm a final year student, hoping to be a Primary School teacher when I finish."

They danced again and this time the conversation was easy, but Neil found Laura was much in demand and he had to be quick off his mark to make sure of partnering her again on the dance floor.

So began a friendship which seemed soon to be blossoming into a serious romance. Although his footballing activities meant that Neil's free time was limited, he did contrive to spend much of it in Laura's company, and he arranged to stay some weekends in Glasgow with Tommy Smith, one of the Levenford players, which made things a lot easier.

John and Ella Munro were delighted at this turn of events and encouraged Neil to bring Laura to The Willows. And when he did, their approval was very evident.

After Neil had taken Laura to Glenleven House to meet Hazel and Sam, the latter asked, "So, my good friend, do I hear wedding bells in the air?"

Neil looked into space. "I just don't know Sam, I'm not sure. I'm very fond of Laura and I reckon she is of me, but is that enough?"

"Neil, only you can decide that, but tell me, does Laura know about Mari-ella?"

"No."

"Neil, for goodness sake, you'll have to tell her."

"I know, but I never seem able to."

"You're not thinking of abandoning Mari-ella?"

"Of course not, how could I?"

BEING AN ex-serviceman, Neil's time at the College extended over two terms only and he left the beginning of April to take up a post in Levenford Academy after the Easter holiday period. He had been going with Laura for six months, had been a frequent visitor to her home and felt he had been accepted by her parents.

At the end of June, Neil, having completed his first term as a teacher, and Laura having finished at College, they decided to celebrate by having dinner in an hotel in the centre of Glasgow. Later they took a tramcar ride and arrived at Kelvingrove Gardens.

As they sat on the grass among other courting couples, Neil looked at Laura. "Happy?"

"Yes, very."

It was now or never, Neil thought, but it was hardly the place to propose, if that was what he was going to do, but there was something to be got over before that.

"Look Laura, it's a bit public here."

Laura laughed. "I suppose it is. But what had you in mind?"

"I want to say something very private to you."

"Oh Neil!"

"I know. I have the key to Tommy Smith's flat and both he and his mother are away just now. We can go there."

"Would he mind?"

"No, of course not. I often stay with him as you know. The tenement is a bit grotty, but once you're inside the flat you'll find it spotless."

"I don't think I'll be able to take in my surroundings, Neil, I'm so excited."

THEY SAT in silence on the settee for a few moments holding hands before Neil, after swallowing hard, began, "Laura, before I ask you, I've something to tell you."

"Neil, before you ask me what?"

"Laura, please, I'm putting it badly." He tried again. "What I'm trying to say is – I'm going to ask you to marry me after I've told you –" Neil's voice trailed off.

"Told me what? Neil, you're being very mysterious."

"I have a five year old daughter."

"You've what?"

"As I say, I have a little girl."

"You mean you've been married before?"

"No, I haven't."

"She's illegitimate."

Neil looked down at the floor. "I suppose, yes, if you want to put it like that."

"How else can I put it? And does she stay with her mother?"

"No."

"No! Then where?"

"Her mother died when Mari-ella was born."

"Mari-ella? That's a strange name."

"Laura, let me tell you the whole story. Will you listen?"

"Yes, all right."

Neil rose and walked to the window. He did not turn round until he had almost finished.

"You see, Laura, you reminded me so much of Anna Maria the moment I saw you."

"So, I'm a substitute for your German slut," Laura rose, eyes blazing. "I thought you loved me for what I was myself, not because I reminded you of her. If you're looking for someone to look after your darling little daughter, as you've described her, you can look elsewhere. Goodbye."

Laura rushed from the flat, with Neil close behind.

"Laura, please, wait. Can't we discuss it?"

"There's nothing to discuss."

"Please, Laura, at least let me see you home."

"I'm quite capable of seeing myself home. Now please leave me alone. I don't want to see you again – ever."

AND THAT'S how it had been, Neil mused, as he retired to his room after his evening meal to listen to some of his favourite records before having an early night. Tomorrow would see the closing of another chapter in his life when he made his last appearance in a Levenford shirt.

He pulled out 'Eine Kleine Nacht Musik', but hesitated before placing it on the turntable. He hadn't played it for some time. Should he smash it in smithereens and close another chapter of his life? He had to admit that the memory of Anna Maria was fading. He had, after all, known her for a relatively short time and they had been able to share so few activities that Neil was beginning to wonder if their romance had ever happened.

But there was of course Mari-ella to prove it had, but his attempts to bring her to Levenford had not borne fruition, for to Neil's bitter disappointment his little daughter had refused to leave Brigitte and Georges, even to go on holiday to France with him. He had continued to visit Hamburg whenever he was on holiday, but the situation remained unchanged.

Yet Neil knew that part of his life was happy. He enjoyed his work as a teacher at Levenford Academy and had become especially popular with the pupils because of the time he willingly spent coaching them in a variety of sports along with Phil Davidson, the Physical Education teacher. And of course there was Sam and Hazel, Sara and Karen at Glenleven. Things had settled down there again now that Kent was back. Kent, he felt, had his problems too. That was life.

He slipped 'Eine Kleine Nacht Musik' back into its sleeve and went to bed.

- 35 -

FOR March it was a relatively mild Sunday evening and Kent had reached the city centre. He found himself standing on the bridge over the River Ouse and his thoughts went back to Levenford and Sam, and the river there that he loved. He recalled something Sam had once said when they had been sitting on the river bank after a swim.

"Have you ever wondered, Kent, why we survived the war?"

"Not really. I suppose we were just two of the lucky ones."

"Maybe, but I wonder."

"Go on, you wonder what?"

"I sometimes feel that if you survive such a hazard as fighting in a war, it's because you're meant to, that you have a job to do in this life. Oh, it's daft really, but when I think of how things have turned out, yes, perhaps there's something in what I'm saying."

"Sam. We used to say you were quite a philosopher and we were right. But we met, became friends, we saw it through, we parted, and now we're together and making a real go of it."

Damn it, what was he doing here? He had been living a lie for the last fifteen months or so, ever since he had left Terry's.

THE HOUSE reminded him of Sam's home in Glenleven and for a moment he faltered, but no, he decided he was not turning back. He walked smartly up to the massive front door and rang the bell. Several minutes passed before it was opened by a slightly flustered looking young girl in a maid's uniform.

"Good morning," Kent said as the girl looked at him rather blankly. "I've come about this advert for a chauffeur/gardener/handyman."

"Oh!"

"Could you tell me who I should see?"

The girl hesitated, then said, "It'll be Mrs Emmerson, I think –" then a voice from somewhere behind her asked, "Who is it Rita?"

Rita retreated inside and was replaced by an older woman who demanded, "Yes, what to do you want?"

Kent repeated what he had said to Rita.

"Servants don't come to the front entrance."

Kent almost took a step backwards, then recovering said, "I beg your pardon, as far as I'm aware, I'm not a servant – yet, and I don't like rudeness so you can keep your job."

But as he turned to walk away, he heard another voice call, "Mrs Niven, what does that young man want?"

"He came about the job, madam."

"Well for goodness sake show him into the study and send that girl Rita along to Mr Emmerson's room."

Kent hesitated but decided this new voice sounded as if it belonged to a pleasanter person, so he waited and then obeyed the curt motion of the hand which Mrs Niven made for him to enter, before she led the way to the study, and left him with a toss of her head and a disapproving look on her face.

A tall good looking woman, whom Kent guessed to be in her late thirties, came into the study and greeted Kent.

"Good morning, please sit down. Sorry about all that. It's Rita's first morning and I'm afraid she's a bit lost. Never mind. You've come about the job – I was expecting an older man, but tell me about yourself, where you're from, where you've been working, what experience you have, and I expect, war service."

When Kent had given a run down of his career to date, Mrs Emmerson said, "That sounds all right. Have you any references?"

"No, I haven't, but I could send for one to Sam Cairns who owned the Nursery."

"Well, all right. I'm puzzled though why you left such a good job – at least you've given me the impression that it was. But perhaps I'd better put you in the picture first. Mr Emmerson, my husband, had a stroke some months ago which left him paralysed down his right side. He now has regained partial use of his arm, but not his leg, and it's unlikely he ever will. He's confined to a wheelchair."

"I'm sorry about that, it must be hard to take at his age."

"What do you mean? Oh, I see. Let me explain. I'm Mr Emmerson's second wife, he's quite a number of years older than I am."

"I beg your pardon, I just thought, looking at you –"

"It's all right. Let me continue. My husband has now retired from business, much to his disgust. He lived for it, and now he finds time hangs heavily on his hands. He likes being taken out in the car which has been specially adapted for him, and when he's not being driven around, he's in the grounds supervising the work there. We have one gardener but he does need help. That's why I'm looking for someone who can combine the two jobs."

"Do you have anyone just now to drive your husband about?"

"I had, but he's left, Mr – er …"

"Kent Mollison."

"Yes, Mr Mollison, I'll be quite straight with you – my husband can be, and often is, rather difficult."

"I see."

"Look, I'm prepared to take you on a month's trial without references, because I must have someone now. What do you say?"

"I'll give it a try. I'm free to start today if you like."

"Fine. Now, you say you're not married so you could live here – it would be so much more convenient to have you on hand when you're needed."

"You mean, it will be a twenty four hour a day job?"

"Oh, not exactly, only sometimes my husband needs help with dressing and I may not always manage by myself. If I've to call on Mrs Niven, my housekeeper, he doesn't like it much. He prefers a man."

Kent thought inwardly, "I'm not surprised", and as if she had heard, Mrs Emmerson went on,

"Mrs Niven's bark is worse than her bite. She's been here for years and thinks the world of my husband. Now, you'll have a large room on the first floor with a bathroom for your own use. My husband's bedroom is now on the ground floor and I have the room next to his. In fact I seldom go upstairs now – I have concentrated everything here on this floor."

"Sensible arrangement."

"There is a basement flat which Mrs Niven has and Rita's room is there too. So?"

"I said I'd give it a try and, yes, I'll move in."

"Fine, come and meet my husband."

AT THE end of the month, Kent agreed to say on with the Emmersons. There was no doubt that, to put it mildly, Mr Emmerson could be difficult, but Kent found he was able to bear with him and he had a sneaking suspicion that the old man quite liked him despite his gruffness and his habit of never saying thanks. He doubted if Mrs Niven's icy manner would ever melt as far as he was concerned, but she was certainly a good cook and he had to admit that his quarters were very comfortable and Rita, despite having a lot to learn, kept them spic and span.

Kent realised that Levenford and Jo Blackwood were never far from his mind, and that the challenge he had found at the Nursery was now missing from his life. One consolation was that Josh Simmonds, the Emmersons' gardener, was an expert, and Kent, when he had time to spend with him, was increasing his knowledge in that direction.

He had discovered from visiting the local pub that Mr Emmerson had been in the wool trade and was worth a packet; that his present wife had been his secretary and married him for his money, a year after the first Mrs Emmerson had died, and that Mrs Niven had no love for her. Well, he thought, that's what folk would say. As far as he was concerned, Mrs Emmerson seemed to be pretty fond of her husband and looked after him with great care.

KENT WAS allowed off on a Sunday when he usually visited Terry Richards and if the weather was fine they went for long tramps, but never once did Kent go to visit his father.

Terry was intrigued from the start about the Emmerson household and was always eager to know the latest happenings and on one particular Sunday said "You'd better watch your step, mate, or you'll be getting embroiled as you did with that dame up in Levenford, what was her name again, Lilias?"

"No fear, I learned my lesson there."

"But you must admit Mrs E and you are getting along together nicely. You're forever doing things with her or taking her places."

"I am the chauffeur after all and she doesn't drive, and as often as not the old man is there as well."

"You never know. You might be on a good thing there. If Mr E was to snuff it, she'd be left all the brass, and you'd be the man on the spot. You'd be quids in."

"Look Terry, I like Mrs E as you call her, but I have no designs on her at all."

"I still say then, be careful."

KENT HAD thought over what Terry had said and had to admit that he had struck up a good relationship with his employers. He admired Mrs Emmerson for the woman she was, and yes, he felt sorry for her quite often when Mr Emmerson was being particularly awkward, when no one could do anything to please him. There was no doubt that these occasions were becoming more frequent and despite her always pleasant approach to her husband, Kent realised that Mrs Emmerson was beginning to feel the strain and that more and more she was calling on Kent to assist her and relying on him to deal with her husband during his difficult spells. She had made the habit of asking Kent to join her in a drink after Mr Emmerson had been settled in bed for the night and he had to admit that he quite enjoyed relaxing with her in the study and listening to her records of classical music of which she was very fond.

AS HE MOVED away from the river Kent went over again the happenings of the morning. He was about to leave for his weekly visit to Terry when the latter had phoned to say he had a heavy cold and was spending the day in bed.

He had returned to his room and was debating with himself how he would spend his day when the bell, which had been installed to enable Mr Emmerson to summon him, started ringing. For a moment Kent looked at it with annoyance. Dash it all, it was his day off. He went downstairs and was met by Mrs Emmerson who looked near to tears.

"Kent, I'm sorry, could you go to him. I simply can't cope this morning. He insists on getting up."

It took Kent the best part of an hour to dress Mr Emmerson and he realised that the old man's condition was deteriorating and that he really should have remained in bed. When he had settled him in his chair by the window and placed the Sunday newspapers in easy reach, Kent went along to the study where he found Mrs Emmerson. He sat down beside her on the small settee and was somewhat taken by surprise when she almost fell against him and burst into tears. Instinctively he put his arms round her in a gesture of comfort, saying nothing, but as the sobbing continued, was moved to gently stroke the sleek blonde hair, now in some disarray. As he felt her gradually relax in his arms, Kent experienced a surge of contentment as a woman's softness moulded into the firmness of his masculine frame. He closed his eyes and thought of Jo, his bonnie Jo, whom he still loved dearly. Almost unaware of what he was doing, he turned and drew Mrs Emmerson closer to him and their lips met. When they parted, he was startled to hear the words whispered close to his ear. "Not here, Kent, come to my room tonight."

HE HAD broken away, but before he could say anything, Mrs Emmerson was gone. He sat with his head in his hands. Did she really think that he wanted to go to bed with her? Did he? It would be so easy, but it would be meaningless. He had imagined it was Jo he had been holding. There would never be anyone else. And as he had told Terry, he had learned his lesson with Lilias.

But what was he going to do? What would happen if he didn't go to Mrs Emmerson's room? A woman scorned! What was the quotation? Neil would have had it out in a flash. Damn, it was no time for smart sayings. It was decision time. He needed to get out; out into the fresh air; away from the stifling hothouse atmosphere; away from the cantankerous old man, even although he sympathized with him and understood his frustrations; away from the beautiful tempting woman, with whom he was sure he could find an outlet for his sexual desires.

If asked he could not have told where he had gone, or where he had eaten or what. And as he walked on, the muted singing from the church slowed his step and he moved across to stand under one of the stained glass windows, casting its patterned glow on the pavement.

It had been a long time since he had been inside a church – not since his army days – but he thought back to his childhood when he had gone regularly with his mother. He listened again to the singing, and recognized it as one of his mother's favourites, 'The Old Rugged Cross'. He could remember standing beside her as a small boy occasionally looking up to her as she sang with fervour. What a wonderful person she had been. How he missed her still! But had she not passed on any of her qualities to him? People had always said he 'took after his mother'. "He's a credit to you", they would say. There wasn't much evidence of that now, not the way he had been carrying on recently. It was time he pulled himself together and went back to Levenford. That's where he belonged. But first he had to do certain things.

HE KNOCKED and waited for the door to be opened.

"Kent! Come in! What are you standing out there for? Dad, it's Kent!"

Bert Mollison drew his son close to him. "Oh lad, I was thinking you'd never come home again. Where have you been? I don't know how many letters your friends at Levenford have sent you and nothing we could do about them."

"I haven't been far away, I've had a job, but I'm going back to Levenford

243

in a few days. I had to come and have a look first though at my brother, or have I a sister?"

Jane Mollison threw her arms around him. "Oh Kent," was all she could manage.

"We've another boy, Kent," his father guided him through to the bedroom which once had been his. "He reminds me of you when you lay in that same cot. And I hope he'll grow up like you."

"Do you, Dad? No, he'll have to do better than me." And looking down at the small child he whispered, "Yes mate, don't make the same mistakes I have."

He left with a feeling of well-being, in the knowledge that he would always be a part of the home in which he had grown up, and with his father's quiet words still in his ears.

"Some day, Kent, your brother might need you. I hope you'll help him if you can."

"I will, Dad, you can depend on that."

KENT DID not relish the prospect of meeting Mrs Emmerson the following morning, but he knew it had to be done. He found, somewhat to his surprise, that Mrs Emmerson seemed very relaxed when he entered the study and greeted him in a friendly way. Then she paused if unsure how to continue, but pulling herself together, smiled and said,

"I owe you an apology, Kent, for what I suggested yesterday. I was glad you didn't come. You must think I'm a –"

"Don't say another word, Mrs Emmerson. It wasn't that I didn't want to come to your room, but I knew there was no future in it for either of us. I'm not afraid to say that, as a person, I admire you tremendously. I think you're really super and you certainly have been under tremendous strain recently. But having me in your bed is not the solution. What your husband is needing is a full time nurse and that's my advice to you."

"Thank you Kent for what you've said. I needn't deny that I've become very fond of you, and I couldn't have managed without you these last months, but you're right, Mr Emmerson is not fit to go out or even to be out of bed, and it is too much for me, even though you are always on hand to help."

"Now that's what I really came to tell you, I'm leaving. No, it's not because of what happened or didn't happen last night although it has a bearing on it. If you think back when you first interviewed me, you said you found it hard to understand why I left Levenford. I didn't leave, I ran away, because I hadn't the guts to stand up and look some folk straight in the eye, folk who were throwing mud in my direction, mud which I didn't deserve. I've let down a lot of people who are my friends. So now it's time to go back."

"I see," Mrs Emmerson said quietly. "I can't persuade you to stay? No?"

"No, I'd like to leave tomorrow."

"I shall miss you very, very much, and so shall my husband."

"Thank you for saying that. I've enjoyed my time here and I've been glad to help, but it's time to go."

"Kent, is there a girl at Levenford whom you love very much?"

"How did you guess that?"

"Oh, there usually is. I hope you'll both find happiness."

Kent smiled, "I hope so."

KENT LEFT the train at Edinburgh and studied the timetables on the bill boards. It would be four o'clock before he would arrive at St Andrews, so he'd probably find somewhere to spend the night there and set off for Levenford in the morning.

He took a taxi and went straight to the University office and eventually managed to obtain the address of Jo's flat. There was no answer to his knocking so he decided to wait at the mouth of a close on the other side of the street. It would be nice to give Jo a real surprise.

Half past six came and Kent was on the point of leaving to find somewhere to stay the night and then returning later when he saw a young man and girl appear with their arms round each other. He did not need to give a second glance to see the girl was Jo. As they neared, he could see that Jo was looking up into the young man's face and laughing. Laughing with happiness, and it did not surprise Kent that when they reached the door of Jo's flat, they stopped and kissed with a passion that he knew was real. He watched them disappear inside, saw a light go on in the room above the door, and Jo reach up to draw the curtains.

"Well", Kent thought, "that is what I wanted for you Jo, so I can't complain, even though I came here to tell you I do love you with all my heart and to ask you to marry me, my bonnie Jo."

1962

- 36 -

AFTER almost eighteen years there were bound to be changes, Neil thought, as he neared the village of Little Burton, and he almost passed the camp without noticing what was left of it. He drew his car into the grassy edge of the road and walked back to where the main gate had been and stood looking across the derelict site, picking out the tarmac road and the square, now sprouting knee high weeds. All the Nissen huts had gone, but some of the crumbling concrete floors remained and the water tower still stood tall, a lone survivor mourning what once had been.

Neil looked at the board which informed anyone who passed by and might wish to stray that this was Ministry of Defence property and ordered them to 'Keep Out'. He smiled to himself and retraced his steps to the car and moved nearer to the village, noticing the cluster of new houses which had sprung up on the outskirts, and which he saw, when he slowed the car, almost ringed the perimeter of the original village. Here were new shops, and 'The Bull' had certainly been spruced up, no doubt having some competition from the new hotel which he had passed just before he reached the old campsite.

Leaving his car, Neil wandered round the village knowing where his footsteps would eventually lead him. He reached the Rectory and hesitated for a moment before moving slowly down the lane. Here there seemed to be few, if any, changes, but when he came to Rose Cottage, he noticed that two dormer windows had been built out from the roof to provide, he supposed, one or two bedrooms in what had previously been a large loft area used only for storage. The cottage still lived up to its name, for there were masses of roses everywhere in full bloom and the standards growing on either side almost hid from view the polished brass plate, bearing the inscription, 'Dr S T Britton, MB.Ch.B.'

So Susan still lived here with her husband Tom, and Neil's mind went back to the last time he had spoken to Susan all these years ago. It had been foolish to return, a foolish whim, and would only serve to re-awaken memories of a best forgotten past. He moved along up the lane to peer through the trellis, festooned with ramblers, to catch a glimpse of the summer house and hurriedly withdrew when he saw a youth, clad only in shorts, sunbathing on a rug spread out on the grass. Neil was certain he hadn't been spotted and decided to risk another look to see if there was by chance anyone else in the garden. But no, the boy appeared to be alone. Suddenly he sat up and seemed to look directly at Neil, who for a moment felt himself rooted to the spot, until he managed to step back and after a pause, retreated up the lane, willing himself not to look round.

When he reached his car, Neil suddenly felt tired and decided to return to the new hotel and book in for the night and in the morning he'd decide whether or not to drive any further south or start on his homeward journey.

SUSAN RETURNED to Rose Cottage just half an hour after Neil had been and found her son still in the garden.

"Hello Gavin, you're getting quite a tan."

"Hi Mum."

"Gosh it's hot. Thank goodness I'm off now until Tuesday morning."

"Grandad's going to cope?"

"Yes, bless him. I hope there won't be too many calls."

"You wouldn't think people would be ill in this weather."

Susan laughed. "Maybe they shouldn't be, but babies sometimes decide to make their entry into the world on a really fine day. Well I'm going to have some tea."

"I'll do it, Mum, you have a seat."

"Sure? Gavin, you're an angel. Yes, I'm dying to sit down."

When later they sat back to enjoy the sun Gavin said, "Mum, there was a man in the lane this afternoon."

"So, what's unusual about that? We often have people wandering down this way just out of curiosity."

"But he was standing looking in through the trellis."

"People do that too, and although I say it to myself, we have a very attractive garden, thanks to old Bates."

"Yes, I know that happens, Mum, but there was something about this fellow that made me get up and have another look at him as he went back down the lane towards the Rectory."

"Do you think he might have been, as the Yanks say, 'casing the joint'?"

"Mum, you are a scream sometimes. No, he wasn't that type at all. He reminded me of someone but I can't think who."

"Well, I don't think we can do much about your mysterious stranger,

Gavin. Life's full of mysteries, that's what makes it so exciting sometimes. Now tomorrow we'll have our lunch out at the new hotel. I've been told it's very good."

"Oh great!"

SUNDAY DAWNED with the promise of another scorcher and the thought of being cooped up in a car driving north had no appeal for Neil and he had decided if he did set out on his homeward journey, it would not be until the late evening. If he was unable to obtain a room again at the hotel he would surely find one somewhere. After breakfast he took himself into the garden, found a comfortable chair, and settled down to enjoy the sun.

"DO I NEED to dress up to go to this place, Mum?"

"No, of course not, just look smart, your flannels and shirt, no tie, but hurry, we want to get there before the rush. I've heard it is very busy at weekends."

When Susan and Gavin arrived at the Greenfields Hotel they found a table on the veranda. "This is nice," Susan said, as she sank into her chair.

"I hope the food matches the décor and surroundings, I'm starving."

"Gavin you had an enormous breakfast. You're going to eat me out of house and home if you go on at this rate."

"I'm still a growing boy," Gavin grinned.

"At seventeen!"

"I'll get a holiday job, Mum, if you can't support me."

"I don't think that will be necessary, unless you're going to be bored. It's a while until you start University in October."

"As long as this weather continues I just want to be free to do as I please."

The waiter arrived and produced the menus and when they had ordered, they both sat back in silence, content to relax while they watched other diners arrive.

Suddenly Gavin sat up and leaned over the table. "Mum," he whispered, "there he is."

"There's who?"

"The man who was in the lane yesterday."

"Where?"

"He must be staying here. He came round from the back carrying newspapers. I wonder if he's coming to lunch."

"What if he is, you can't go up to him and accuse him of peeping into our garden. I told you, it's a showpiece at the moment."

"It's not that, Mum, there's just something about him. Look, there he is!"

Susan turned to look at the man who stood at the entrance to the veranda looking for a table and then half rose from her seat.

Gavin regarded her in astonishment as he heard her say softly. "It can't be, it can't be, but it is." Then she stood straight up and made as if to move forward but then stopped.

Gavin jumped up. "Mum, what's the matter? You look as if you've seen a ghost. Who is that man?"

As they stood together Neil's eye lighted on Susan and Gavin, and he moved along the veranda to their table.

He held out his hand and simply said, "Hello Susan, remember me?"

"Yes, Neil, I do. How are you?"

"I'm very well, thank you. What about yourself?"

"Fine, just fine. Oh Neil, this is Gavin, my son."

"Hello Gavin," Neil shook hands with Susan's fair haired son.

"Neil, would you like to join us for lunch?"

"Yes, thank you, if Gavin doesn't mind."

"Of course he doesn't mind. Gavin, Neil was stationed at the old camp during the war and we became friends, but he moved away and, well, we haven't seen each other since. How many years would it be, Neil?"

"About eighteen, I reckon, for it was in 1943 if I remember correctly that my regiment was here for a few months."

"Are you on holiday, Neil?"

"Yes, I decided to try to visit all the places where I had been stationed during the war. Silly idea, really, for so many changes have taken place since then and like the camp here, there's practically nothing left to see. But I thought if I didn't do it this year I'd never do it. I'm taking up a new post as head teacher in August – it's my first headship – and I wanted a complete change from the educational world. Normally I holiday with my daughter, but she's gone off with my sister and her family this year."

"How old is your daughter?"

"She'll be fourteen in September. Wait, I have a recent photograph of her."

"Oh, she's a lovely girl. Gavin, what do you think?"

Gavin pursed his lips. "Yes, she's OK."

"Gavin!" His mother reproached him.

Neil laughed. "It's just what I would have said at your age, Gavin, if I had anything to say at all."

Neil held the photograph for a moment before returning it to his wallet. "She's very like Anna Maria."

"Anna Maria?" Susan queried.

"Anna Maria was her mother. She died when Mari-ella was born."

"Oh Neil, I'm sorry."

Neil gave a sad smile. "Time heals the wounds, they say, and I daresay it's right."

Gavin suddenly asked. "Why did you come along the lane yesterday?"

"Oh yes. You must have seen me. I do apologise for being so rude, but I have very happy memories of Rose Cottage and I couldn't resist having a look."

"But why didn't you ring the bell and ask if Mum was at home. Didn't you want to see her again?"

"Of course I did. I just don't know. I wasn't sure that it would be the right thing to do. After all, if your father had been at home – well, I never met him – it might have been a bit awkward."

"My father –" Gavin started to say before Susan interrupted.

"Tom was lost at sea."

"Oh, how sad for you, but the plate on the wall says, Dr S T Britton."

"Yes, that's right, that's me. Tom and I had the same initials."

"So you're a doctor now?"

"Yes, I am."

Their conversation was halted by the arrival of their meal and as the tables were rapidly filling up, Neil felt it best not to pursue finding out more about what Susan had done during the intervening years.

When they had finished coffee, Neil said, "What about coming out to the garden at the back here for a while?"

Susan looked at Gavin, who finally said, "I'd like to go to the tennis club, if that's all right with you, Mum. You two could catch up on old times."

"Are you going to walk to the club?"

"Why not? Aren't you always telling me walking is good for me?"

"Yes, I am; all right Gavin, I'll see you later."

When Gavin had gone Susan said, "Neil, would you mind, if instead, we went for a stroll. There is a little wood near here, if you remember."

"Yes, I do. Fine."

They walked in silence for some time until Susan asked, "What do you think of Gavin?"

Neil didn't reply for a moment. "He seems a very nice lad."

"Is that all?"

"I don't quite know what you mean."

Susan stopped and pulled Neil round to face her. "Neil, you said your daughter is very like her mother; your son is very like his father."

Neil opened his mouth but no words came out. He looked at Susan, then beyond her into the valley stretching down from the end of the wood. His gaze alighted on the shimmering heat and as if from a far distance he heard Susan speak again.

"You knew, Neil, you knew yesterday. You could have gone away, but you didn't. You wanted to meet me again and Gavin too."

"I'm not sure," Neil stammered, "how could it be? Your husband was home on leave soon after that night."

"I was pregnant before he came. I was a nurse then, Neil, I knew."

"Did you tell him? Did he ever know?"

"If you mean what happened between us, no, he didn't. I did write and tell him I was going to have a baby. To my eternal shame I suggested to Tom when he was on that last leave that we tried for a child and he agreed. I knew I was cheating him and when he went down with his ship, I felt it was my punishment. On his last voyage he must have been thinking about me and the child I was carrying, dreaming of coming home to his family, and then curtains."

Susan sat down on a fallen tree, her head bowed. Neil knelt before her and took her hands in his. "I was equally to blame."

Susan shook her head slowly. "No, Neil, it was my decision, remember. You offered to go if your suggestion to make love appalled me, but I wanted you, oh yes, I did. Maybe it was only a short wartime romance for you, but for me it was more. I had grown to love you and I found it so easy to enjoy your company. Yes, I loved Tom, but I always felt he was a much superior being to me, that I had to try to live up to his standards all the time. That doesn't excuse me in any way for what I did."

"But when I telephoned and Tom answered and then you spoke, I got the impression that you wanted to forget me and what had happened that night."

"How else could I have reacted? I'm glad you didn't hear what Tom said when he handed me the phone."

"Not very complimentary, I take it."

"No, it wasn't. He could be very sarcastic. I didn't know what to do. I hoped you would contact me again, but you never did."

"So what made you decide to become a doctor?"

"My grandfather died just after the war ended and left me a considerable sum of money which meant that I would have a very comfortable life, but Gavin was growing more and more like you and I knew it wouldn't be long before somebody in the village put two and two together. You see, Tom was very dark and I am too, so I just had to get away. I had thought of doing medicine when I left school, but I didn't have the confidence in myself to tackle the course and settled for nursing."

"And presumably you went away from here."

"Yes. Again I was very fortunate. I finally told my father the truth, but he had already guessed that Gavin was not Tom's child. It was he who arranged everything for me. He had a sister in Aberdeen and I went there with Gavin and stayed with her while I completed my course at the University, then my year in the Infirmary and my time attached to a practice. In all it was ten years before I returned to Little Burton because my father was getting on and although he had acquired a partner to replace Tom, he wanted to ease himself gradually out of the practice, but in fact he still hasn't quite done that, for he takes over at weekends to give me a break."

"And you had Gavin with you all the time?"

"Until he was nine, then he went to prep school, then to boarding school. My grandfather had left money in his will for that and I followed his wishes."

"It's incredible that you were in Scotland all these years and in Aberdeen, for that's where I'm going to take up my new appointment."

"How strange!"

"Was there any reaction from the villagers when you returned?"

"No, not really. Maybe some had their own private thoughts, but they've kept them to themselves. As you've seen, the village has grown tremendously since you were here during the war, and while there's still a core of older people, even their ranks are thinner. I had rented out the cottage and before I came back I had it modernised and extended."

"Susan, what about Gavin?"

"I'm sure he's guessed, he's very bright."

"What shall we do?"

"We'll have to tell him straight out. I'd like you to do that, Neil."

"Me!"

"Yes, he'd take it better from a man. I've rarely spoken about Tom, I've always tried to avoid the subject of his father. There was a time when he often asked me about him. I was always truthful, but I know I never satisfied him with my answers."

"But I was intending leaving here if not tonight, then certainly tomorrow."

"Oh Neil, please for my sake, stay until it's done. Come and stay in the cottage."

"Stay with you and Gavin!"

"Yes, Neil, please, don't you have any feelings for me at all?" Susan stood up and looked hard at Neil, then added, "Or for your son?"

"My son!"

"Yes, your son. Gavin is your son."

"I know he is, but he'll probably hate me. He didn't look particularly pleased to meet me without being sure of who I was."

"Please Neil, try, then you can go off and forget us."

"Is that what you want?"

"Neil, I can't ask you for anything. I was the guilty party."

"No, as I've already said, Susan, I'm equally to blame. Will you give me a few hours to think this through?"

"All right."

- 37 -

IT was Tuesday morning and although Neil had acceded to Susan's wish to stay at the cottage, so far he had been unable to find the words to tell Gavin that he was his father. He had told Susan about Anna Maria and she had listened quietly and then simply said,

"Neil, you have suffered just as I have."

He rose and crossed to the window to look down into the garden, appreciating its colourful splendour in the early morning sunshine and turned as there was a tap at the door before Gavin entered carrying a tray.

"Sorry, I thought you were still in bed. Mum had an early call and then straight to the surgery so she asked me to bring you breakfast."

"That's good of you Gavin. I'll get back into bed. My apologies for being in a state of undress, but I never wear pyjamas."

Gavin grinned. "That makes two of us. Anyway there's no harm in seeing your father in the nude, is there?"

Neil's mouth fell open. He tried to speak but only a croak came from him.

Gavin placed the tray on the bed and went on, "Are you going to marry Mum?"

Neil found his voice. "Am I going to marry ..." he repeated.

"Yes, you heard what I said. I'm going off in October to the University in Aberdeen, isn't that a coincidence? And I want to be able to say to my fellow students that I have a father as well as a mother."

"So you know?"

"Of course, I'm not stupid. I've suspected for some time that there was something not quite right about who my father was."

"Oh."

"Yes. About a year ago Mum was dashing off to an emergency and she called to me from downstairs to bring a handkerchief from the drawer of her dressing table. I noticed a photograph under the pile of handkerchiefs which I looked at briefly before flying down to see her off. But I returned and studied the photograph. It was you, taken in the garden outside the summerhouse. You had on your officer's uniform, but it could easily have been me."

"So what did you do?"

"Nothing. I was just about to return to boarding school so I didn't have time to decide whether or not to ask about it. Anyway I felt I had been prying and Mum, well, she's always been so super, I couldn't bring myself to upset her. I did want to find out more and I had decided I would ask her one day. Then when I saw you looking into the garden, I knew."

"And what do you feel about me?"

Gavin turned to the window and looked out. "I've waited seventeen years to have a father, I think you've a lot to make up to me."

He turned and faced Neil. "Eat your breakfast, then let's go and have a game of tennis. Mum says you were quite an athlete when you were in the army and I reckon you're not all that old yet. I'll give you half and hour to get ready." And with that he left the room.

Neil ate slowly, deep in thought, and was surprised when he felt a tear roll slowly down his cheek. When he had put aside his tray he rose and looking in the mirror addressed himself. "When last did you feel like this? Your son has more guts than you."

He shaved and showered, looked out his shorts which had remained unworn in his suitcase, found a clean short sleeved shirt and his white gym shoes which he always seemed to pack and had just opened the bedroom door when Gavin called up from the hall.

"Ready?"

"Coming."

"Well, you look the part. I won't be too hard on you."

Neil said nothing for Gavin was not to know that he still played regularly in Levenford, was in fact the captain of his tennis club, and generally was still as fit as he ever had been.

LATER A PERSPIRING and defeated Gavin gasped, "You might have told me you were a star player."

"You didn't ask. Now I think I'd like to go back and have a shower."

"Me too."

They walked back in silence, neither knowing what to say, until reaching the cottage, Gavin spoke. "Mum doesn't seem to be back yet. You go and shower first and I'll make some coffee. She usually pops in for a cup before she starts her rounds."

But Susan phoned to say that she wouldn't be home until lunchtime, so

Neil and Gavin had their coffee together in the summerhouse.

Again silence reigned. Neil was desperately trying to think of how to start a conversation when Gavin suddenly said, "Dad, can you stay on here for another week?"

"What did you call me?"

"Dad. You are my dad aren't you?"

"Yes, but –"

"Look, all my way through school I was the only boy in my year who didn't have a father and I resented it, in fact I sometimes hated some of my best friends because they had something I didn't have. Now you've appeared at last, I'm not going to waste any time about making up my mind about whether I want you around or not. I do want you, and as a matter of fact I like you a lot already."

Neil swallowed hard. "Gavin, I don't know what to say. I expected, well, I don't really know what I expected. I thought perhaps you would resent me suddenly breaking into your life and your mother's."

"But I don't. I don't. I need you. Now will you stay here for another week?"

"I don't quite understand."

"Oh I know you'll have to go back to your job in Aberdeen, but you see, I would like you to partner me in the doubles tennis tournament. I always play in the singles, but living here only during the holidays, I've never found anyone to play with. Everyone gets fixed up before I come home."

"I see, but isn't it too late to enter?"

"No, it's not Wimbledon, you know. There's not a big membership in the village club, so it's simply a case of turning up when the tournament starts and putting your name in for the draw. Now will you? Please Dad."

"All right. I'll have to do a bit of phoning and make some explanations."

"Great. Now there's something else I want to ask you again. You didn't give me an answer the first time I asked. When are you going to marry Mum?"

"When am I … Gavin, for goodness sake, don't rush things. Your mum and I – well, we haven't discussed anything yet."

"Don't you love Mum?"

"Gavin, please, listen to me. It's not a case of whether or not I love your mother. We've come together again after a period of eighteen years. During that time we've each established our own careers and life styles. I have a young daughter, my parents are still alive – I have a sister who married my best friend. They have two daughters and a son – you see I have a family, and I have to think of them."

"But I'm yours, I'm part of your family, I want to belong too," Gavin burst out.

Neil held his head in his hands. "Yes, I know, but please, don't rush things. For your part you must consider your mother and her work here, and your grandparents."

"But surely it's Mum, you and me, we come first."

"I'll tell you again, I have a daughter who is very, very dear to me. Aren't you being rather selfish?"

Gavin stood up and after a moment left the summerhouse. Neil made to go after him then changed his mind and sank back in his chair. He was still lying with his eyes closed, his mind in turmoil when he heard a voice saying, "Neil, are you all right?" and looked up and saw Susan.

"I don't know, it's all been too much for me to take. Sit down and I'll tell you what's happened."

"No need to, Gavin has already done so. I've told him to apologise to you for being so rude."

Neil sat up. "He wasn't, Susan, it was just I couldn't handle the situation. I couldn't seem to explain that it might not work out as easily as he thought."

"He still has no right to force you into making instant decisions. He's like that, always wants things done straight away. Now I'll see to lunch."

As Susan rose Neil caught her hand to detain her. "Susan, Gavin's is probably the ideal solution, but I need time, we both need time. We can't rush into this. After all I've never had a wife, it's only now at this late date that I'm about to take the plunge, that's of course if you would have me."

Susan smiled down at Neil. "You're right, all of us must stop and think. And anyway it's hypothetical. You haven't actually asked me to marry you – and you're not going to start now, for I'm hungry."

"Oh Susan, as Gavin says, you are a super person. I'll go and see him."

GAVIN WAS lying face down on his bed when Neil entered his room after tapping lightly on the door. He sat down on the bed and put his arms round Gavin's shoulders.

"Gavin, it's difficult enough when you become a father in the usual way, I mean when your wife gives birth to a baby, but when you're suddenly presented with a seventeen year old son who's intelligent, articulate, and I daresay as good looking and athletic as his father – well – you're simply bowled over."

Gavin turned to look at Neil and was forced to smile. "I'm sorry for being so rude."

"No, you weren't rude, no need to apologise, it was just I couldn't cope. Willing to give your dad time to think things through?"

Gavin sat up and hugged Neil. "Oh Dad," he whispered, "of course."

"Now, come on, lunch will be ready soon and afterwards it's back to the tennis courts. If we're going to win this doubles tournament, we've got to get working on your backhand."

"WOULD YOU like to tell me more about your daughter?" Susan asked, after they had finished their meal on Neil's last evening before he set off north again.

Neil smiled. "Of course, it's funny really, to do so to my son and his mother."

"But it's great," Gavin broke in, "to find that suddenly I have a father and a sister, even if she's only a stepsister, it's still wonderful."

"As I've already told you Mari-ella is now fourteen and she was ten years old before she first came to Scotland. I had been trying to persuade her to come for some years, but she was so happy where she was and so dubious about coming to live with me that I had despaired of it ever happening."

"Didn't she like you?" Gavin asked.

Susan gave him a reproving glance, but Neil was unperturbed by the question.

"The frustrating thing was that she did, she had taken to me from the start and once she went to school she wrote me a letter almost every week. She is a very bright girl."

"Takes her beauty from her mother and her brains from her father," Susan rested her hand on Neil's.

"Maybe. Then one day I received a letter from Georges."

Neil could remember how it had read.

My dear Neil,

How are you, my good friend? Very well I hope as we are here. I shall not beat about the bush (that is one of the sayings I have learned from you). I am being married next month to my friend, Sophie, and we are going to stay with her parents until we can find a place of our own.

I hope you will be able to come to the wedding; you should be on holiday then. Mari-ella is to be a bridesgirl, I think you call it, and she is very excited. I shall have another surprise for you when you come.

Georges.

"And what was the other surprise?" Susan asked eagerly.

"I should explain that Georges was by this time a local government official and he had managed somehow to obtain a visa for Mari-ella to come to this country for a holiday after his wedding. Georges has always amazed me. When I think back at all the flak he had to take from some of the officers in the Mess, I shake my head. Some of them, mainly the regulars, weren't fit to lace his boots, but they treated him like dirt sometimes if they had to wait for their drinks. And Georges worked like a Trojan. Never mind, that's all in the past."

"And did Mari-ella come willingly?"

"Yes, no problems at all. Georges again. He had talked her round and by this time she had a lot more confidence in herself. Although I am indebted to Brigitte for bringing her up, I think perhaps she was the real stumbling block. But who could blame either Brigitte or Mari-ella?"

"And did she fit in with your family?"

"We both stayed with my sister Hazel and Sam, her husband, and of course their children, Sara, Karen and Mark."

"So that's an uncle, and aunt and three cousins," Gavin grinned again.

"Yes, you're doing very well, Gavin, instant relations while you wait. But to return to Mari-ella, her first visit went extremely well, much better than I had dared hope. My father, of course, was my big worry and he was still very reluctant to accept Mari-ella. My mother, however, did welcome her although I felt she found it difficult to recognise her as a grand-daughter."

"Presumably Mari-ella returned to Germany after that first visit."

"Yes, she did, but having made the trip once, she was ready to come again the following year and then finally she came to stay for good. Brigitte, who is now well over sixty and not very fit, was finding looking after Mari-ella a bit of a strain, so that made the break easier."

"And is Mari-ella going with you to Aberdeen?"

"Yes, to boarding school there, but she'll stay with me at weekends."

"So you have a place of your own in Aberdeen?"

"I've bought quite a large flat; it has in fact four bedrooms, so Gavin, if you feel like spending your weekends with me and Mari-ella, you'll be welcome."

"Thanks Dad, but couldn't I stay with you all the time?"

Neil looked at Susan, but she only smiled, so he added, "All right, I'm willing to have you Gavin, but you must think it through carefully before you decide. We'll sit down and discuss it when you come up to Aberdeen. By the way, Susan, does your father's sister still live there?"

"She does, but in a private nursing home."

"I see, so have you in fact, Gavin, arranged to stay anywhere?"

"I have booked a place at one of the halls of residence, but I'd much rather live at home, having spent most of my life up to now in boarding schools."

"OK, that settles it, you move in with me."

"Dad, I appreciate that. Thanks a lot. I would like to ask you something else, but I won't." Gavin rose from his seat, "I'll just have to be patient."

WHEN THEY were alone Neil and Susan sat in silence for some time before the former finally said, "Susan, I still don't want to rush into things, and to be realistic, I'm going to be very busy settling into my new job and getting my house in order and coping with my son and daughter. I might manage better if you were there of course. I'm not usually so inept at making decisions. Maybe it's because I can't realise how all my dreams have come true. I've got to be fair to you too. You must have time to settle things here, that's only fair to your father and your partner. If I said to you come to Aberdeen and spend Christmas with us, would you think I was being very off-hand?"

"No, of course not, that's a very sensible idea."

Neil took Susan in his arms. "Yes, I do love you and I do want to marry you, and I want the four of us to be a real family."

"And I love you, Neil, and I'm going to marry you, and be part of your family."

~ 38 ~

SAM straightened up from planting out some biennials and called over to Kent. "I'm off for an early lunch. Hazel's going into town and wants me to go with her to see about some of the things she needs for the tearoom."

"OK, Sam, I'll hold the fort." Then looking at Sam, Kent continued, "It's a good idea, the tearoom, it's bound to attract more customers and with the extras we're stocking up with in the shop, sales will take off. I'm sure of it. We'll need to go flat out though to have everything ready for the opening, but I reckon we'll make it."

Sam said nothing.

"What's wrong, Sam?"

Sam hesitated for a moment. "I don't know, it's going to be a lot of work for Hazel and lately she doesn't seem to have been her usual self."

"But the girls will be able to help at weekends as that's when we'll be busiest. We'll all lend a hand, we've always mucked in together. Don't worry, we'll manage."

"I hope you're right, Kent."

AS SAM turned the car into Church Street, Hazel said, "Stop at the doctor's, Sam. I have an appointment to see him."

"You've what! What's wrong with you?"

Hazel was silent, then said, "Just do as I say, Sam, I don't want to be late."

Sam parked the car and said. "Do you think you'll be long?"

"No, but I want you to come with me."

Sam looked surprised. "Hazel, you're not ill are you?"

"No. Come on."

And with that she pushed open to the door of the consulting room.

Dr Blackwood appeared almost immediately. "Hello Hazel, Sam, right on time, come away through. Now have a seat. Well now, how are things at Glenleven these days?"

"Fine, just fine," Sam replied looking rather puzzled. "Sorry, but I'm not quite sure what I'm doing here."

Dr Blackwood sat back in his chair. "Ah Sam, it's not often someone gets the better of you."

"Is Hazel ill?"

"Ill? Oh no, far from it. Now I won't keep you in suspense any longer. Sam, you're going to be a father again."

"I'm what!" Sam half rose from his chair. "Hazel, is it – are you –?"

"Sam, it's true, I am pregnant. Dr Blackwood phoned me this morning to confirm it."

"But – how could it happen? I mean ..." Sam looked confused.

"Sam, listen, these things do happen despite any precautions you take. There's nothing you can do about it now except pay heed to what I have to say to you. Hazel is a fine healthy woman and she had no trouble with either of the girls, so there's no reason to think there might be this time, except that she is older, so I'm going to take special care of her during her pregnancy. Now that's not to say she's to be wrapped in cotton wool, no, Hazel will just carry on as usual, but she'll have regular checks to make sure everything is going along fine."

When they were back in the car Sam sat looking straight ahead for some time, then he said, "Well, that puts the kybosh on the tearoom."

Hazel took Sam's hand. "I'm sorry Sam, I maybe should have told you, but I thought if it was a false alarm there was no point in bothering you."

"I always thought we shared everything, good or bad."

"I know, Sam, but you've been so busy lately with the tearoom and I thought you'd maybe be upset. Sam, you won't resent this child?"

"As long as you're all right I won't."

"Oh Sam, you mustn't be like that, of course I'll be all right."

"It's just that I thought our family was complete, and well, the girls – what are they going to think?"

"Why should they think other than that they're going to have a baby brother or sister, and probably thrilled about it?"

"They're both grown up."

"I know, Sam, but it's not terribly unusual for people to have a late baby. After all we're not old. Promise me Sam, you'll love this child as much as you love the girls."

"All right. I guess you knocked me out of my stride, it's just that I love you so much."

"And I love you too, Sam. Now there's just one thing – the tearoom goes ahead, no, I'm not going to listen to any protests. I'm not an invalid as

Dr Blackwood said, and you're not going to treat me as such. We'll get help when we need it, we can afford it now."

"I'll have to think about it."

"WELL, THERE'S life in the old devil yet," Kent teased, when Sam told him his news. "Great, just great, I bet you it's a boy this time."

"It'll be my luck to have another girl."

"Sam, your two daughters adore you, you know that, and you, them, so if it's a third one, it'll be just the same."

"What do you think about the tearoom now? After all, Hazel was to do all the baking for it, which was fine before all this happened. She felt she had time for it, but now?"

"Sam, we'll manage, we'll be able to employ someone to help out."

"That's what Hazel said."

"There you are then."

SO THE TEAROOM opened on schedule in March and as Kent had predicted attracted more customers. Business was brisk and everyone was hard at it. Hazel was taking her pregnancy in her stride, but at the beginning of June Maggie Watson came to work as the tearoom cook. She was a cheery middle aged woman who fitted into the Glenleven setup with ease, and Hazel found she could leave Maggie to see everything was done as she herself would have wanted it. Sara and Karen on holiday from school were always willing to help out and indeed both seemed to revel in working alongside their father and Kent, even although the latter teased them unmercifully.

It was Kent who insisted that Sam had a week's holiday in July and took Hazel, Sara and Karen off to North Berwick.

"Go and enjoy yourselves, you owe it to Hazel and the girls for they've been great as always. And you, Sam, are needing a break. Forget about this place for a week and it'll set you up for the next arrival in the Cairns family."

Although the weather was a mixture of sunshine and showers Sam and his daughters enjoyed to the full swimming in the sea and in the pool, while Hazel sat back, a contented spectator.

"You know," Sam said as he stretched out beside her on the beach one afternoon, "I can hardly keep up with the girls these days, I must be getting old. After all I'll be forty next year."

"Oh dear, Sam, that's a dreadful age," Hazel teased. "But you still look about thirty, my love, and you better feel that age, because you've to be just as wonderful a father again as you were to Sara and Karen when they were young."

"And am I not wonderful to them now?"

"Of course you are, Sam. I want to ask you to do something for me."

"Oh, what's that?"

"If you don't want to, well, all right."

"This sounds very mysterious, but I usually do what you ask me."

"I know, but this is something special."

"Go on then."

"You know I'm having the baby at home. I'd like you to be present at the birth."

Sam sat in silence for some time, then turned to face Hazel, "All right, why not, I'd like to."

"Oh Sam, I didn't think you'd agree so readily."

"I still love you very much, even more so now. Need I say anything else?"

"Oh Sam, you are a dear man."

THE END OF July brought some really hot weather and Hazel was glad to remain indoors out of the sun. The baby was due in the first week of August, but as both Sara and Karen had made their entry into the world a fortnight later then had been expected, Hazel was prepared to hold her increasing discomfort for another while.

It was Saturday the third of August, and as business in the Nursery was fairly quiet Sam had joined Hazel for an afternoon cup of tea in the cool of their sitting room in Glenleven House.

Hazel had just filled Sam's cup a second time when she said, "Sam, it's starting."

For a moment Sam sat as if frozen, then as he saw Hazel grip the arms of her chair he leapt up. "Come on, then, can you manage the stairs?"

"Yes, but give me a hand, then phone the midwife and the doctor."

Sam was dry-mouthed as he held Hazel's hand while she obeyed the midwife's exhortations to push. He looked in wonderment as first the child's head appeared, then with another great effort, Hazel delivered the complete new being.

"It's a boy," the midwife said as she busied herself with the new born baby.

"Thank goodness," Hazel gasped and she felt Sam's hot tears on her cheek as he buried his face close to hers.

After a few moments he looked up at his son but he could not find words.

"Come on, Mr Cairns, help me to weigh this lovely boy." The midwife was in full charge.

LATER AS Sam sat beside Hazel's bed he looked at her and said, "I wonder what the thirteen year old Sam Cairns would have said if it had been suggested that he would weep tears of joy when his son was born."

Hazel smiled. "We've come a long way since those days, Sam."

"Yes, but this is definitely the last one, that's our family complete. Are you sure you're all right?"

"A bit tired, but I'm fine and I'm thrilled to have given you a son. You know we've never discussed a name."

"There's only one name for him – Mark, after my father."

"Mark Cairns, yes Sam, you're right. Now go and call the girls, they're desperate to see their brother again. They only had a little glimpse of him."

SOON LIFE at Glenleven House resumed its normal routine, except that young Mark was very demanding during the hours when Sam and Hazel had grown accustomed to undisturbed sleep. Sam, however, showed his usual resilience and rose without a grumble to attend to his little son's needs.

"He's going to be spoiled, if we're not careful," Hazel said as she watched Sam nursing the small bundle in his arms. "He has four people dancing attention on him."

"He is someone special, though," Sam protested mildly.

"I suppose he is, and he's growing more like you every day."

"If he is, we'd better make sure he's not going to turn into the little devil I was when I was young."

FROM THE time he could walk, Mark was ready to follow his father wherever he went, and adored as he was by Sara and Karen, he was always able to persuade them to do his bidding.

"That child doesn't really need a mother," Hazel laughingly said to Kent as they watched Sam go off with Mark on his back.

"Oh, don't you believe it, Hazel, that little lad knows who really looks after his needs."

"I'll say this for him, he's been no bother so far. Oh, he likes to be fed on time, but apart from that, he's great. I suppose Sam just wants to make sure he has all the love he was denied when he was a child."

"Yes, he's a lucky lad having such a wonderful family. I only wish he was mine."

"Regrets, Kent? Thinking of what might have been?"

Kent gave a smile which had more than a hint of sadness. "Maybe, Hazel, but being able to share your family, as it were, by living so close to them, has meant a lot to me and made up for what I've missed out on. Of course, I have my brother, although I see him only a couple of times a year."

"It's a pity you live so far apart."

"Can't do anything about that, this is my home now, where I belong." Kent laughed, "I found that out the hard way."

"You'll be going to York again at Christmas?"

"Yes, it won't be long in coming round."

But Kent was to make the journey before Christmas.

"GOOD AFTERNOON, Sam."

"Hello Sergeant Fraser, what can I do for you? Not trouble, I hope."

"No, Sam, not trouble. Is Kent around?"

"Kent?" and seeing the grave look on Sergeant Fraser's face, he added, "Something wrong?"

"Yes, bad news, I'm afraid."

At that moment Kent appeared in the doorway of the office and seeing the policeman said jokingly, "I'll call again."

"Kent," Sam called, "come in and shut the door."

Kent looked from one to the other, "What's going on?"

Sergeant Fraser cleared his throat. "Kent, I think you should sit down, I've something to tell you."

"Me? Well, go on."

"We've had a message from York –"

"My dad!" Kent burst out and leapt from his chair. "Something's happened to him."

"I'm sorry, Kent, your father and your mother –"

"Jane's my stepmother, what is it?"

"They've been involved in a car accident."

"Are they badly hurt?"

Sergeant Fraser hesitated, struggling to find the words. "I'm sorry, Kent, they were both killed, outright, it seems."

"I don't believe it. It's not true, it can't be. Not my dad, not Jane."

"I'm afraid it is."

"What about Grant, my brother?"

"He's all right."

"He's all right! And Dad and Jane are dead! Oh my God, the poor kid! I'll have to go to him. Are you sure Sergeant? There couldn't be some mistake?" Kent looked desperately at the policeman, but the latter shook his head.

Sam moved across and put his arm round Kent's shoulders, "Come on, I'll help you get ready, then I'll run you to Glasgow; you should manage to get a train tonight."

KENT LEANED across and took hold of his brother's hand.

"We're almost at Levenford, Grant, Sam will be at the station to meet us. Sam's my best friend, you'll like him, and Hazel his wife is a super person too. Then their two girls, Sara and Karen are really something. They're looking forward to having you at Glenleven, and of course there's Mark, their little brother, so you'll have plenty of company."

Kent had said the same thing several times over during the train journey from York, but it still evoked no response from the solemn, dark haired boy, who looked surprisingly like Kent. He had spoken very few words since the tragedy which had robbed him at ten years of age of his father and mother.

As the train slowed to a halt, Kent reached up to the rack for his suitcase, then held the door of the carriage open for Grant to step down on to the platform. When they neared the stair leading down to the street, Kent felt his free hand gripped by his brother's and looking down at him saw the appeal in his eyes.

"Don't worry, Grant, I'll look after you – always."

1972

EPILOGUE

WHEN Mark was seven, Sara was married. She had followed in her mother's footsteps and trained as a teacher of Physical Education, and it was when she was taking part in an inter-district swimming competition at the Commonwealth Pool in Edinburgh that she had met Jim Forrester, a young accountant.

As Sam watched from the foot of the stairs as Sara came down in her wedding finery, he felt a lump in his throat.

"You look absolutely beautiful, Sara. Your Uncle Neil will no doubt put it better than that, but you are a picture."

"Thanks, Dad, you're looking very smart yourself."

"Sara, before we go, I'd just like to say – well – maybe since Mark came on the scene I haven't seemed to have so much time for you and Karen, but believe me, my love for you both hasn't lessened in any way."

"I know that, Dad, and anyway, when Jim came into my life, you had to take a back seat. There, I've put that badly. Oh, Daddy …"

"Now you can't appear red-eyed at the church, so come now, we'd better go. I'd just like to say one more thing. I hope you'll be as happy as your mum and I have been."

THUS ONE bird flew from the nest and two years later Karen followed her sister into marriage, and left Levenford to live in London with her husband, Frank Styles, a successful freelance journalist.

"That's the result of having two beautiful daughters, Sam," Kent consoled him as they sat with Neil on the river bank on the morning after Karen's wedding.

"Hmm, I daresay it was inevitable."

"Don't feel so sad, Sam, you still have Mark."

"Yes, I still have Mark, and you have Grant."

"Yes, but not for long now. He'll be off to college in Aberdeen in October."

"You'll miss him."

"I will. I just hope he doesn't miss all of us here too much. It's the first time he'll have been on his own. I'm glad though he'll have you, Neil, and Susan to fall back on."

"I shouldn't worry about Grant. He takes after his big brother and draws the ladies like a magnet, so he'll have plenty of company, I'll bet, but he'll be very welcome at our house. Now that both Gavin and Mari-ella are off on their own, Susan and I find it rather quiet."

"It's funny, thinking back again Sam, to what you once said, that if you survived the war it meant you had a purpose in life, a job to do. For a long time I felt I was going nowhere even though I was very happy at Glenleven. I had my ups and downs, and then it seemed when I came back here after my sojourn in York, I was settling into a nice cosy rut. And then, wham! I got, as it were, an almighty kick up the backside, when I was left to look after Grant."

"Yes, Kent, and if Hazel and I can make as good a job with Mark as you have with Grant, then we'll be smiling. You've been father, mother and big brother to that lad and he is a credit to you. And here he comes to join us."

Kent looked up as Grant appeared at the far end of the track and thought, "Yes, here comes my success story. He could have been my son, in fact sometimes I felt he was. Maybe it was my recompense for missing out on Jo, but I owed it to my dad and Jane. It was a long hard slog, but it was worth it."

He stood up, and cupping his hands round his mouth, shouted, "Come on, Grant, get a move on."

GLOSSARY

ANDERSON SHELTER
Anderson shelters protected against shocks from bomb blasts. They were made of sheets of corrugated steel that were bolted together and put in a pit about one metre (three feet) deep in the back garden. The dug out earth from the pit was put on top of the shelter for added protection.

ATS
Auxiliary Territorial Service

BLIGHTY
British Army slang for England/Britain

CO
Commanding Officer

LCT
Landing Craft Tank

LST
Landing Ship Tank

MO
Medical Officer

NAAFI
Navy, Army and Air Force Institutes

NCO
Non-commissioned Officer

OC
Officer Commanding

RAF
Royal Air Force

RSM
Regimental Sergeant Major

YMCA
Young Men's Christian Association